Tennis Shoes
and the
Feathered Serpent

BOOK TWO: THE CONCLUSION

Tennis Shoes
and the
Feathered Serpent

BOOK TWO: THE CONCLUSION

A Novel

Chris Heimerdinger

Covenant Communications, Inc

Published by Covenant Communications, Inc.
American Fork, Utah

Printed in the United States of America
First Printing: March 1996

01 00 99 98 97 96   10 9 8 7 6 5 4 3

ISBN 1-55503-916-2

*For all my readers,
the patient ones*

(and, okay, the not-so-patient ones, too)

AUTHOR'S NOTE

Although much of this book is based on Book of Mormon characters and events, it is primarily imagination and speculation. I'm most gratified when readers tell me they went to the scriptures to see how much I got right. Better yet if they linger there.

C.H.

PROLOGUE

Recently I started collecting portraits of the Savior. Everybody has one or two. I have hundreds.

And yet none of them quite strikes me the way it should. I think of all the many artists throughout the ages, poised at canvas or clay, their eyes moist with tears, their hearts burning with prayer, seeking just the right line, just the right curve, and in the end having to submit to the limits of their medium. Two, or even three, dimensions are simply not enough.

In spite of this, I find myself gathering up every painting, print, and statuette I can lay my hands on, from medieval wall paintings where his image is crowned by a glowing halo to portraits by modern artists who invariably depict a being with long hair, beard, flowing white robe, warm eyes, and a smile subtle and penetrating like the Mona Lisa.

My father is very patient with my obsession. He understands it and even encourages it. From time to time he'll bring home to me yet another portrait by yet another master artist to add to my collection. Because even if a single painting doesn't quite capture the image, the whole of them together, nourished by the love of so many artists, comes very close.

But more importantly, each picture serves to remind me that there were once people who lived on this earth—people who once stood before his face or brushed his shoulder or took currency from his hand—who hardly noticed him at all. They saw only a man—

just another among hundreds, among thousands. And then there were others who saw in his eyes something so familiar, so overwhelming, that it took no persuasion at all for them to kneel and call him Master.

For the first sixteen years of my life, I think I'd have been part of the first category. I'm sure I'd have looked right past him. It's not that I didn't believe in him. But in my mind I'd decided I already knew what he looked like. I'd squarely defined him according to my own desires and opinions. I left him no opportunity to define himself according to his Holy Spirit.

I'm not really certain how I let this happen. I suppose I wasn't quite satisfied by the place I seemed to have been assigned in his kingdom. The prospect of being only a wife and a mother, the eternal nurturer who stood at the sidelines, always subordinate to the leadership of men, didn't appeal to me very much. Especially when I considered that most men did a pretty poor job at the helm. But whenever I expressed such feelings, I was always informed that my views were at variance with the way of heaven and the will of the Master. So, to an extent, I created my own Master, in my own image—a person whose views of the universe were in harmony with my own.

Don't get me wrong. I'm not saying I was some sort of ultra-feminist. I just preferred to believe that my Savior wanted for me exactly the things that I wanted for myself. Whatever made me happy, made him happy. It never occurred to me that I might have turned the whole thing exactly backwards—that I might, in all humility, approach the Master, and rather than telling him who he was or who I wanted him to be, that I might ask him instead. That I might inquire to know his heart, and then to know who he wanted me to be. Although at that time I doubt I would have been prepared for the answer.

But one look into the Master's eyes, one touch from the flesh of his hand, one breath of his presence, and all the towers of opinion we've built through years of study and labor come crumbling down. Suddenly we find ourselves willing to say, "This time, Master, I'll build whatever you want me to build."

So this is my objective. Now and for the rest of mortality. I'll strive for it until that day when I can look into his eyes and breathe in his presence again and forever.

All my portraits help me to remember this goal. Because each image of the Master, no matter how unequal or imperfect the artist's stroke, takes me back to that one moment, as long ago as eternity and as recent as a single heartbeat, when I—Melody Hawkins—had the honor, the privilege, and the glory to bathe his feet with my tears.

PART THREE: HEART OF THE GADIANTON

CHAPTER 1

Let's see. Now where were we?

Where were *we? Are you serious, Dad? You leave everybody hanging at one of the most critical moments in the story, and you can't remember where we are?*

Was it really so critical? I'm sorry. I tend to see the story as one big *whole*. It's sometimes hard for me to judge what someone else might find important. When the lives of your loved ones are at stake, *all* the moments seem critical.

Well, when you're telling a story, certain moments are definitely more important than others. Otherwise the story doesn't make any sense.

Since you've suddenly become the storytelling expert, why don't you bring us up to speed?

Okay. You started out very gloomy—a bad habit of yours, by the way. It was your fortieth birthday, which is gloomy enough, but then you told us all about Mom's death from ovarian cancer a few years before and how you couldn't stop thinking about her.
On top of that you reported how your boss gave you a big demotion at work. All in all, your fortieth birthday was a pretty horrible

occasion. But the most explosive event may have occurred when you hired a young man named Marcos Alberto Sanchez.

Ah, yes. Marcos Sanchez. Prince of Jacobugath. Son of the man who masterminded your kidnapping and framed me for murder.

Don't get ahead of yourself, Dad.
Before that you explained how right after Mom's funeral, Uncle Garth and Aunt Jenny traveled back to the time of the Nephites. They'd promised to come back a year later, but they never returned. We had no idea what had happened to them. The three of us kids were particularly confused, especially since we'd never been told a thing about underground passages or Rainbow Rooms.
After that you finally told us about the murder of your boss, Doug Bowman, and how you were foolish enough to get caught at the scene with the murder weapon in your hands.

I wasn't foolish. The whole thing was a setup.

Which you fell for hook, line, and sinker. Everything pointed to you as the killer. The police arrested you and tossed you into the Salt Lake County Jail when in reality the killer was a man you hadn't seen for eighteen years—a Gadianton robber named Boaz who now went by the alias of Jacob Moon.

Yes. Jacob of the Moon.
Jacob's hatred for me had burned for eighteen years. He relished his moment of revenge, grinning at me through the grill and mesh of the visitor's booth in the Salt Lake County jail as if an old thorn, prickling and needling his side for decades, had finally been removed.
When he left me alone in the visitor's booth, I felt utterly devastated. My universe had been shattered. My family was at the mercy of a madman. And if matters weren't bleak enough, the police revealed that I was the prime suspect in more murders than one—including the mysterious and perhaps doom-fated disappearance of Garth and Jennifer Plimpton.

But in the midst of all this hopelessness, a miracle occurred. A miracle so unexpected and auspicious that I bask in wonder even now. I escaped with the help of a stranger—a man with platinum-white hair dressed in the uniform of a police officer. Who the man really was or why he had done this was left a mystery to me, except for one detail. He said he was repaying an old debt. I had never seen this man before. I could not have guessed how such a debt had been incurred.

He also gave me his name—Jonas.

In the meantime, as you were escaping from the police, another plot was underway to kidnap me.

And if we want to talk about being foolish . . .

I know I made a horrible mistake. No need to rub it in.

I was abducted and tossed into the trunk of a Lincoln Continental. My kidnappers drove all night until we reached a cave at the top of a mountain. This cave, I came to find out, served as a passageway to the ancient world of the Nephites and Lamanites.

I had no idea what my abductors wanted from me. I was told only that they were taking me to be reunited with my Uncle Garth, who was being held captive in a faraway city called Jacobugath.

It wasn't until later that I was able to piece together Jacob's motives for kidnapping you. As far as I could determine, Jacob wanted to use you as a bargaining chip to blackmail Garth Plimpton into revealing important information. This information involved the secret location of a settlement of wealthy dissenters who'd fled from Zarahemla a few years earlier. These former Christians had taken their wealth with them. With such a treasure, Jacob hoped he could build an army powerful enough to invade the land of Zarahemla.

I thought I was giving this summary, Dad.

But I remember where we left off now. I'll just take us that far.

Shoulda figured.

Anyway, I gathered up my fourteen-year-old daughter, Steffanie, and my ten-year-old son, Harrison, and followed Melody and her abductors to northern Wyoming. At the top of Cedar Mountain, near the town of Cody, we descended into the spiraling tunnels of Frost Cave.

Our first taste of the ancient lands was rather bitter. We were captured by apostate Lamanites and accused of being robbers and sorcerers. While incarcerated we met up with another prisoner—a Nephite missionary named Shemnon. Shemnon revealed to us that we were fast approaching the day and time of the great destruction prior to the Savior's appearance.

With the help of two Lamanite Christians named Mathoni and Mathonihah, we escaped and fled to the encampment of the renowned prophet, Samuel the Lamanite. The next morning, the apostates attacked the encampment. Samuel's followers set out for the land of Bountiful while Samuel himself, now feeble with age, elected to remain behind to delay the attackers. The encampment was set ablaze. I believe my family and I were witnesses to the tragic moment of Samuel's martyrdom.

Shemnon became our guide as we traveled to the Nephite capital of Zarahemla. But along the trail we were ambushed by slave traders and taken the rest of the way to Zarahemla in bonds. The Prophet Nephi himself arranged for our liberation, after which I was reunited with my sister, Jennifer, and her two small children. Prior to the time when Jenny had departed with Garth to return to the land of the Nephites, she had been unable to have children. The Lord had blessed Jenny and Garth with little Joshua and Rebecca during their sojourn among the Nephites.

Shortly after our reunion, we took part in the frantic exodus of all faithful Christians from the now-hostile city of Zarahemla. During this exodus, we saw the prophet's brother, Timothy, stoned to death before our eyes. Then we watched as he was raised from the dead by the power of God under the hands of Nephi.

And all the while, Melody's situation and whereabouts were

entirely unknown to us.

Does that about cover it, my daughter?

You forgot to mention how Marcos, during our journey toward the city of Jacobugath, suddenly blurted out how beautiful he thought I was.

Oh, we mustn't forget to mention that.

I didn't know how to react at the time. Mostly, I was repulsed. I had no idea how significant his feelings would later prove to be. And how dangerous for both of us.

And that brings us up to where I left off.

The morning after our flight from Zarahemla, I watched the sun rise from behind the Falls of Gideon with Harry and Steffanie lying on either of my shoulders. It was the final sunrise we would watch together for a long time. I prayed that it wouldn't be the last.

That morning was one of the most difficult mornings of my life. I was leaving behind my only son and my youngest daughter, as well as my sister and her two small children. Under Nephi's leadership, my family and the rest of the Christian refugees would make a grueling seven- to fourteen-day march to the land of Bountiful. I would embark in a different direction with five Nephite companions on the far-riskier prospect of locating Melody and Garth in a secret city far to the north. I would then have to find a way of delivering us all from the clutches of the most treacherous man I had ever known, King Jacob of the Moon.

As the six of us—myself, Zedekiah the Elder, Gidgiddonihah the warrior, Jonathan the giant, Naaman the tracker, and Lamachi the former Gadianton—separated ourselves that morning from the rest of the refugees, my mind was tormented with guilt. A terrible vision haunted my thoughts. By abandoning my two younger children, might I be sacrificing my entire family? Would it have been better if I had remained with Harry and Steffanie to guide them through the uncertainties of this ancient world until they were safely settled in Bountiful?

My pangs of regret persisted all that morning as we descended into the forest of feathery ferns that swept the pathway under brisk gusts of wind. The wind was steadily building in momentum. Gidgiddonihah, nephew of the celebrated general Gidgiddoni, marched at point. His movements reminded me of a tiger, wary of the most minute disturbance in the brush. Close behind him marched Naaman, the tracker. Naaman had been handpicked by Gidgiddonihah. I guessed that the two men had been together on previous campaigns. Jonathan and Lamachi marched next in line while Zedekiah and I took up the rear.

All in all, we were a pretty motley crew. Timothy had promised that he would choose "strong and righteous men" to attend me on the expedition. From this I'd imagined that I would be surrounded by men akin to Helaman's stripling warriors. And in many ways, I was. But if I thought my companions were teetering at the edge of translation, I was mistaken. They were human, each at various stages of dealing with their own weaknesses and flaws.

This, of course, made me feel right at home. Sometimes I felt I had the corner on the market when it came to weaknesses. I pondered the words of the blessing that Nephi had pronounced upon my head before we left. He promised that I would see my family again upon the rolling plains of Bountiful, but he'd included in this promise a curious condition. I could only assure the blessing's fruition if I "repulsed the arm of flesh."

In my life I'd always had a tendency to make decisions out of rashness or desperation without relying upon the Spirit of the Lord. I'd been so quick to rely upon my own wits and strength that I wasn't certain I understood how to give myself over to the Lord in a crucial moment. Apparently, this was a lesson I would soon have to learn.

I was so entranced with my thoughts that I was slow in registering the precariousness of our circumstances. The weather had worsened even further. When we had departed that morning from the Falls of Gideon, there had only been a light drizzle and distant thunder. Now a northern tempest had arrived with such force that the raindrops were beginning to sting my face.

Elder Zedekiah, the leader of our expedition, shouted over the wind, "We should find shelter!"

Briskly, the six of us veered off the trail. I wasn't certain what we expected to find. To me either side of the pathway looked equally inhospitable. The dense foliage whipped wildly with every gust.

We were soaked to the bone by the time Gidgiddonihah and Naaman found what they considered to be a proper arrangement of trees. Jonathan, the tallest and brawniest of the group, unstrapped his tumpline backpack and brought out a heavy fold of canvas that had been waterproofed by some sort of gum or sap. Within two minutes my comrades had thrown up a makeshift shelter large enough to encompass the six of us. That is, it might have encompassed the six of us. One of us was rather reluctant to climb inside. That person was Lamachi—the one-time Gadianton who had been baptized a Christian only two days before.

Lamachi hadn't offered any assistance in erecting the shelter. While the rest of us worked, he'd stood some distance away, between the trunks of two trees, his arms stretched outward, palms pressed against the velvety barks. Lamachi was only eighteen years old, yet he may have been the most important member of our expedition. He was the only one who claimed to know the secret route to Jacobugath, having learned it during some phase of his initiation into the ranks of the Gadiantons. Therefore it was of some concern when he entirely ignored Gidgiddonihah's shouts for him to get inside the shelter. The wind and rain beat hard against his clothing. Smaller branches were beginning to snap from treetops. One of these might easily hit him and cause a nasty cut or bruise.

Yet Lamachi was smiling, eyes closed, seemingly *enjoying* the storm the way one might enjoy a cooling breeze on a hot day. At first I thought the boy was engaged in some sort of adolescent foolishness—proving to the rest of us that he was "tough" enough to withstand the tempest. Then we noticed that his lips were moving. He was mumbling something. We couldn't hear the words, but each of us felt we knew the intent.

Naaman started to rise. His fists were clenched. He seemed determined to bring Lamachi into the shelter by force if necessary.

Zedekiah put his hand on Naaman's shoulder. "Let him be, Naaman."

Naaman pointed a stern finger toward Lamachi. "That boy is speaking sorceries. If we let him continue, we might *all* be cursed!"

"Remember who he is," said Zedekiah. "Remember what he was. We can't expect his mind to adjust to all of the ways and patterns of a Christian overnight."

"If he doesn't *think* like a Christian, he should have never been baptized," Naaman declared.

"He's an infant in the Spirit," said Zedekiah. "We must set the example. We must teach him—and not by force."

Reluctantly, Naaman sat down again, continuing to eye Lamachi with disdain. I'd begun to wonder if the premature grayness at Naaman's temples was the result of stress and hot-headedness. He was a fierce-looking man with a large hawk-shaped nose that reminded me of pictures I'd seen of the ancient Mayans. Perhaps Naaman was a direct ancestor of that race. But Naaman wasn't the only one who felt uncomfortable with Lamachi's mumblings. Even Zedekiah, who had defended the boy, looked reasonably concerned. Lamachi's expression had grown intense. His fingernails seemed to dig into the bark of the trees.

The rancor felt by the other members of the expedition was understandable. With the exception of Jonathan and Lamachi, each of the Nephites present were veterans of the Gadianton wars, which had ended twelve years before. Gidgiddonihah and Naaman had both been present on the day when Captain Gidgiddoni executed the last Gadianton leader, Zemnarihah, by hanging him from a tree. They watched as the tree was felled to the earth—a symbol to show how all who sought to slay the Lord's people for the sake of power and gain through secret combinations would similarly fall.

Shemnon had explained to me during our journey to

Zarahemla that since Zemnarihah's death, those who continued to practice the secret signs and rituals were very careful not to use the name of Gadianton. This minor forfeiture gave the sorcerers a chance to reorganize and regroup, change the face of their rituals and practices just enough to suit their purposes and, in turn, arouse the suspicions of very few. But most importantly, it granted them many opportunities to proselyte among disaffected Nephites and Lamanites without frightening them away by uttering that universally hated name, Gadianton. Gadianton was a word now used only by those who shunned secret combinations, as a way of lumping all sorcerers, conspirators, and power-seekers into one category. Even the followers of King Jacob more generally referred to themselves as "Men of Jacob," or more formally as "Seekers of the True and Perfect Light of the Divine Jaguar."

Lamachi would have named himself as a member of this sect far more readily than he would have called himself a Gadianton, although the Christians who had converted him at Zarahemla did their best to convince him that Men of Jacob and Gadiantons were fundamentally the same. They had precisely the same objectives—power and gain through sorcery, treachery, and murder.

For war veterans like Naaman, Gidgiddonihah, and Zedekiah, who had seen so much misery and bloodshed at the hands of secret combinations, accepting the presence of someone like Lamachi was a hard pill to swallow, especially since it was now apparent that he had not fully abandoned his old ways. It was particularly hard for a man like Naaman, who, it seemed to me, was not very educated in areas outside his immediate trade as a hunter and tracker.

We continued to watch Lamachi for several more minutes, the rain pelting his face.

"He'll catch his death," commented Jonathan. Our gentle giant of six feet and two inches watched with his neck bent to one side to keep his head from poking up through the canvas. "At the very least, he'll get sick."

"Maybe he has chants to prevent that as well," said Gidgiddonihah.

Naaman and Jonathan laughed, though not with mirth. It sounded rather like the mocking laughter of school boys.

More jokes were exchanged over Lamachi's behavior. I kept to myself. Not that they would have expected me to join in. If I had laughed, it probably would have killed the moment. I still felt very much the outsider. No one knew quite what to think of me. Some of them might have thought I was far more strange and suspicious than Lamachi. Since it was clear that my physical stamina was not yet equal to theirs, some of them may have wondered why I'd been brought along at all, despite the fact that it was me who'd inspired the expedition in the first place.

But it wasn't because I didn't feel included that I kept silent. I couldn't help but wonder how Nephi and my family were faring in this weather. The storm was undoubtedly blasting all six hundred or so of Zarahemla's Christian refugees with equal ferocity. Would they have been as adept as Gidgiddonihah at building shelters? I wondered about the mind of God that he would allow such a storm to torment his people on today of all days when they were so frayed and weary. And then I recalled the fears expressed by Nephi that his enemies in Zarahemla might launch an army to stop him from fleeing. A storm like this might effectively dishearten any such attempt by the angry tribes of Zarahemla. After further consideration, I determined not to question the mind of God.

About that time Lamachi removed his hands from the two trees that had prevented his skinny frame from blowing away. He faced the tent, his hair and clothing drenched in rain, but his face giddy with satisfaction. He requested admittance to the shelter.

As he climbed inside, he reported, "The storm will cease within the hour—at least in our vicinity."

There was an uncomfortable pause. At last Zedekiah inquired, "In whose name did you make this supplication, my boy?"

"No one's name," Lamachi replied. "Unless 'nature' has a name. Nature has its own voice, you know."

Naaman blurted out, "If your words were not to God, they are not *of* God!"

The enthusiasm fled from Lamachi's face. Zedekiah raised his hand to quell Naaman's temper. He spoke mildly to Lamachi.

"Do you remember what you were taught, Lamachi?" said Zedekiah. "A Christian raises his voice only to the Father, and to no other being or force—not even nature."

"But the Father is nature, is he not?"

"No," said Zedekiah. "Nature is his *creation*. It is not an entity that we address in prayer."

"But if the storm abates, what does it matter?" asked Lamachi. "Wouldn't it still have abated by the power of God our Father?"

Zedekiah sighed, determined not to lose his patience. Naaman, however, did not have such discipline.

"It's sorcery, pure and simple!" he shouted. "And I'll not tolerate another—!"

"Naaman!" Zedekiah scolded.

Lamachi was on the verge of tears, angry and defensive. "I only wanted to help our cause. Is there nothing I can contribute? Is all my knowledge of no worth?"

I decided to speak. "Of course your knowledge is of worth. There is much for you to contribute, Lamachi. We're depending on you to take us to Jacobugath. I'm depending on you to help me rescue my daughter."

"Thank you," said Lamachi. Then he gave Naaman a spiteful look. "At least *someone* appreciates my presence."

"No more of this," said Zedekiah. "We are all grateful for Lamachi's presence. And I'm sure Lamachi will direct his prayers to the Father from this time forth." He looked to Lamachi for some sort of confirmation.

Lamachi nodded glumly, uneasily, his eyes toward the ground.

"Good," said Zedekiah. "We should take this opportunity to discuss the provisions that we'll need to purchase in Nimrod."

Nimrod was a modest settlement to the northwest situated along the banks of the River Sidon. If all went well, we expected to reach this village early tomorrow. In Nimrod we hoped to purchase canoes. We would then spend two days on the river until we reached the much larger city of Sidom. Gidgiddonihah estimated that this would cinch the gap between ourselves and King Jacob's army by three days. Jacob was by now four or five days ahead of us. This concerned me gravely. Jacob obviously would not wait for us to catch up before offering Melody's life in exchange for Garth's information. Before we could even get there, Melody and Garth might already have been executed.

Gidgiddonihah assured me that we would close in on Jacob more and more every day—that is, if I managed to keep the pace. Six men could move much faster than an army. He even entertained the hope that we might arrive in Jacobugath *before* King Jacob.

Gidgiddonihah assured us all that in Sidom we could purchase decent weapons: spears and obsidian-edged swords. As of now, we were armed only with rudimentary cutting blades and one small copper hatchet that Gidgiddonihah kept strapped to his waist. Jonathan had also brought a reed pipe about twenty inches long that served as a blowgun, as well as several palm-stem darts, the tips black with poison. He claimed to be quite proficient at the weapon and told us he could provide us with small game and other meat on demand.

"Wouldn't the poison make the meat inedible?" I asked foolishly.

He shook his head. "The juice of the arrow-poison vine does not affect the stomach. You could eat as much as you wanted. But don't cut your finger on the dart's tip. You would stiffen like a canoe. It might take two days for you to recover, if you recovered at all."

Jonathan offered to show me one of the darts, but I declined. Back home I couldn't even sew a button on my shirt without pricking myself at least once.

From Sidom, Gidgiddonihah told us, we would float on the river another half day and then venture westward into the wilderness of Desolation. This region was unknown to all but Naaman, who had served as a tracker in the rugged mountains of Desolation toward the end of the Gadianton wars, flushing out the last robber holdouts. Our course beyond the wilderness of Desolation was unknown. From that point, we would be dependent upon Lamachi's guidance.

About an hour after we climbed inside the shelter, an amazing thing happened. Gidgiddonihah had started a sentence and before he had finished it, the wind had completely died away. The rain had stopped. The only sound was the patter of the last remaining droplets as they fell from the overhanging trees and smacked the top of our canvas.

Lamachi was the only one who didn't look surprised. He smirked to himself as he crawled out of the shelter and began restrapping his pack.

"Time to go," he said casually.

The rest of us emerged from the shelter, looking at the sky for some explanation. The clouds overhead were still gray, but to the north they were breaking up. There were inviting slivers of blue.

Naaman huffed. "It would have blown over anyway."

"It's a blessing," said Zedekiah. "A gift from the *Lord*." And as he emphasized the word "Lord" he glanced at Lamachi, who made no argument.

But as our company refolded the canvas and started back toward the trail, Lamachi mumbled something for my ears only. Because I'd defended him, he decided I might be his most likely confidant on this expedition. Yet the words he spoke sent ice up my spine.

"Sorcery, bah!" he said. "Christians just don't know how to pray."

I made no reply and did my best to mask my agitation. It was clear now that all of us had given ourselves over to a young man whose spiritual convictions were as fragile as a house of cards—a boy who for many years had had it branded onto his mind that any non-initiates of the Divine Jaguar who sought to learn the secret whereabouts of the city Jacobugath deserved one consequence.

They deserved to die.

CHAPTER 2

The spasms in my stomach began the morning after I watched the blue smoke change shapes over the tent of King Jacob and Balam the Diviner. It wasn't the first time that I'd ever had such an attack. Once or twice a year, since I was ten or eleven years old, I would get these terrible, wrenching pains in my stomach that would go on for about eight hours. The pain would become so excruciating that my dad often had to take me to the emergency room. The doctors and nurses performed various tests and took x-rays of my stomach, but they could never figure out what was causing the problem.

The year that my mother died, I had four different attacks. My dad finally ended up taking me to a gastrointestinal expert at the University of Utah Medical Center. This doctor determined that I had a rare condition involving a kink in my intestines. Under normal circumstances the kink would cause me no problems, but if I ate badly or experienced high stress, that kink would close off to where nothing could get through. After all this, the doctor's profound advice to me was that I start eating a high-fiber diet. She also said I should try to avoid high-stress situations—as if such a thing were possible.

I don't think I can describe the pain well enough to do it justice. It's something you simply have to experience. I'm convinced there is no worse pain in this world—childbirth and torture racks included.

This subject might sound rather indelicate, but only by sharing this background can anyone possibly begin to appreciate the intense physical suffering I endured as King Jacob's caravan made its way across this strange and enchanted country toward the city of Jacobugath. •

The first attack began just after sunrise. By the time Marcos discovered me in the bottom of my canopied litter, I was almost incoherent with agony. I think Marcos was convinced I was actually dying. He went and told his father. King Jacob looked in at me while I lay there groaning in the rabbit furs of my carrier, my knees curled into my chest.

"We should inform Balam," said Marcos. "Perhaps he knows of a medicine—"

Suddenly my pain intensified. The mere thought of having that repulsive little man with the holes in his cheeks come near me would have brought on terrible nausea under any circumstances. King Jacob wasn't keen on the idea anyway.

"Balam will not interfere," he declared. "He is a Diviner of the highest order. Above this sort of nonsense."

"Then perhaps we shouldn't travel today," Marcos suggested. "We should wait until she recovers."

Jacob's face reddened with anger. "Fool! Would you risk my life? Would you risk us all? We cannot linger in this land. There are enemies all about us. If she is dying, which I doubt very much, then we must try to reach Jacobugath in time for her to fulfill her purpose."

Meekly, Marcos pointed to the leather collar around my neck— the one attached to the top of the canopy that made me feel like a dog on a clothesline. "Then at least let me remove the collar to make her more comfortable."

"The collar stays!" said Jacob firmly. "I've given Jimhawkins' troublesome daughter the most comfortable transportation that exists in our land. Her suffering, if in fact it is real and not concocted to earn your sympathies, is undoubtedly the will of the Omnipotent One to keep her reticent and tractable. Bother me no more on this matter. Prepare to depart!"

A few minutes later, the caravan commenced traveling. Marcos was never far from me during my anguish. He plodded along with the six porters who carried my litter on their shoulders, ready to provide food or water to me upon request. I never asked for any. I knew that if I ate anything, it would have never stayed down. The bumps and jerks of the moving carrier made this the worst attack I'd ever experienced. I felt certain my insides were about to explode. The spasms were so bad I became drenched in sweat. I rolled and rolled in the furs of my litter, unable to find any position that was comfortable. Around mid-afternoon, right on schedule, the pain began to subside.

I fell into a half-sleeping state of bliss—so grateful to God that it was over and that I had survived. Soon, however, the reality of my situation came flooding back, and the acids in my stomach began churning again.

This pattern continued for the next two days. I would awaken just before sunrise with the pain in my stomach steadily building. By the time we started traveling, I was in unbearable agony. Never in my life had I experienced an attack two days in a row. On the third morning, when the waves of pain began building again, I actually told my Heavenly Father that I would rather die than endure another day like the last. Wasn't my situation bad enough? Wasn't it enough that I had been torn from the only world I knew to become a slave to ancient savages? Why, I asked my Father in Heaven, did I have to endure such excruciating pain on top of everything else?

Later that day, Marcos worked up the nerve to approach his father again. He knew that by doing so he was putting his own life at risk. I'd been told that other men in our company had already been executed for lesser annoyances, including one warrior who lost his life because he'd sprained his ankle on a tree root and could no longer keep up.

But if something wasn't done, Marcos felt certain I would die. After all, nothing I'd consumed for the last three days had stayed down. I was famished and dehydrated. There wasn't enough water in my system now to even sweat properly.

My recollection of what happened that day when Marcos returned to walk alongside my carrier is rather hazy. The pain was so bad that I felt my sanity slipping. Nevertheless, I vaguely remember Marcos' face coming into focus. He leaned down over the rim of

*the litter. Struggling to suppress obvious excitement he announced,
"Lord Jacob has consented to let Balam perform the appropriate
ceremony to relieve you of your suffering."*

*He paused a moment, waiting, I suppose, for me to indicate
some sign of gleeful relief, as if I'd received some great honor. But to
be honest, I was hardly paying attention. My current wave of pain
had reached its apex.*

*Marcos continued, his expression more sober. "But there is one
condition, Melody. When Balam comes over here, you must formally request his help by reciting an oath of obeisance to the
supreme goodness and power of the Divine Jaguar. This will prepare your heart and body so that the spirit of the Omnipotent One
may merge with yours and wrench the disease from your soul. It is
only a few words. Do you feel strong enough to speak?"*

*I had barely registered what he was saying. Without thinking,
I almost replied, "Fine. I don't care. Just stop the pain. Get Balam.
I'll repeat anything you want me to." A strange feeling settled over
my heart—a feeling that was pleasant and yet disturbing. I suddenly knew that the promise Marcos had given me was true. Into
my consciousness crept a firm conviction that if I did exactly as
Marcos had instructed, Balam would in fact bring an end to the
spasms in my stomach now and forever. It was so simple. So sure. I
came so close to consenting that I shudder even now.*

*Somehow I dredged up the presence of mind to comprehend
exactly what Marcos was offering. He was, in essence, inviting me
to abandon my God for his. He'd been listening to my agonized
pleas to my Father in Heaven for three days. It seemed obvious to
him that the being I worshiped wasn't willing to lift a single finger
to relieve me of this distress. It was easy for Marcos to conclude that
the being I worshiped didn't have the* power *to grant a cure. Either
that or my God simply lacked the compassion, preferring instead to
let his subjects wallow in agony. On the other hand, the object of
Marcos' devotions operated on a much simpler formula. Pay the
price, receive the goods. Prove yourself a willing subject, and claim
your immediate prize. Relinquish a paltry snatch of personal freedom, and the world is your oyster.*

The world, but nothing beyond.

"I don't want Balam," I said, my voice screeching for lack of

water. *"Go away."*

Marcos pulled in his chin in surprise. *"Stubborn girl! Don't you realize that you could die?"*

"Go away!" I repeated harshly. *"Leave me alone!"*

Marcos threw up his arms and marched furiously ahead of the litter, mumbling, *"Then die for all I care! Foolish, stubborn, bull-headed . . ."* But he wasn't gone very long. Within a short time he was back at my side, the same look of concern and compassion on his face.

It was during that very hour that my pain began to subside, three full hours before I might have expected. Again I was enveloped in bliss and gratitude—only now my feelings seemed more penetrating than before. The whistles and calls of the forest birds seemed almost like a cheering crowd. Maybe I've exaggerated this description. Whatever I felt—whoever's voices may have been cheering—I felt in my heart that I had won a great victory that day. The peace and assurance that entered my soul was more than enough reward for all that I had endured.

* * *

The following day I awakened with no more spasms, no more pain. Marcos appeared surprised by this. He interrogated me repeatedly about my condition.

"Are you sure you feel all right? No pain at all?"

"My insides feel sore and bruised," I said, *"but there's no pain like there was."*

Marcos nodded uncertainly. *"Great. That's great. It's wonderful."*

His words had the slight edge of a question behind them. My recovery perplexed him. He seemed torn between relief that I was doing better and consternation that I was doing better without Balam's incantations. My recovery seemed to contradict assurances issued the day before by Balam that because I had rejected his services and insulted the Divine Jaguar, my condition would worsen dramatically.

Marcos did not walk alongside my litter that day. I think he walked near the rear of the column to be alone with his thoughts.

This was the first day that I began to appreciate in some small way the beauty and wonder of the land around me. Though I continued to mourn my circumstances, it was hard to ignore all the colors, so bright and brilliant, particularly at midday when the sun was highest. The fiery golds and emerald greens and turquoise blues almost seemed alive and breathing, ready to scatter like birds if we came too close. But of course, the colors never scattered. They blazed in the sun like newly opened chests of treasure. The midday light turned ordinary boulders and rocks and pebbles into precious jewels—diamonds and opals, topaz and amethysts.

We crossed several clearings and meadows, making our way toward a high range of snow-capped mountains to the northwest. All about my carrier fluttered and hovered bright parakeets and gemlike hummingbirds and hundreds of butterflies. Once, as we walked near a tree, a speckled lizard leaped into the carrier and became a hitchhiker, sunning itself on the carrier's rim until it worked up the nerve to leap off into the brush.

Late that afternoon we entered the canopy of a thick forest. The sunlight filtered through the terraces of leaves and dappled the earth with disks and dishes and platters of golden light, causing my porters to unconsciously step with greater care and delicacy so as not to tread upon them. I watched flying squirrels glide from higher branches to lower ones, all the while chittering angrily at us for disturbing their otherwise unruffled tranquillity.

But the time I was given to revel in the beauty and splendor of the land was short-lived. The ugliness of my circumstances was always near, brooding like a thundercloud. Jacob and his men were like a disease moving through an artery of the land. The passage of Jacob's army left an invisible stain. Every region through which we passed seemed stripped of a kind of innocence. It was as if the land itself was committing some unpardonable sin by allowing Jacob to pass through unmolested. I wished the forests and hills had found a way to swallow him up.

At the end of the fifth day, our caravan had reached a bald ridge. In a valley below us we could see a lazy river weaving a northward course. The valley was heavily forested. I could see wisps of smoke rising from a place where the river bent its course. There was some sort of settlement down there.

Jacob's men were stricken with a perceptible anxiousness, greedy and salivating. Our supplies, plundered from villages in the land of Melek, were almost gone. We were running seriously low on food. To a man like Jacob of the Moon, this left only one option.

My litter was placed on the ground with just enough men to guard it while the rest of Jacob's army filled their hands with weapons and stalked into the forest with the object of approaching the village from the west, where the element of surprise would be in their favor. Marcos remained behind to help guard me. I glanced at him as the warriors were slipping into the brush. He must have read the pleading in my eyes—my silent appeal that he do something, somehow prevent what was about to happen. He turned away and kept his distance.

I was not so naive to mistake what was about to happen. Nevertheless, and to my eternal shame, I remained silent, dumbstruck, fooling myself into believing—actually believing—that Jacob would show mercy, that no race of human beings could be completely devoid of compassion. Surely even Jacob of the Moon could not murder innocent, defenseless people in cold blood. He would simply take their property and go. Even Jacob, I thought, must have some shred of humanity in his soul.

But soon I saw the black smoke rising over the river. Even from this distance I could hear the screams. Some of the screams were not men. Some were not adults—

I sank into the rear of my carrier. Monsters! They were monsters! Marcos was no exception. What had become of his conscience? Where was the light of Christ given to him the same as to every man? If I could have stopped Jacob's men—if I could have pressed some switch, punched some button, that would have ended the life of Jacob and every wretched creature under his command, I would have done it. As it was, I could only turn my face into the carrier's rim and weep.

Why, Heavenly Father? *I cried in my mind.* How can you allow anyone to commit such horrors? How can you stand back and watch? Doesn't it affect you? If you truly love your children, do something now! Send down lightning from heaven! Burn Jacob and his men to ashes. What could I have done to stop it, Heavenly Father? Did I miss my chance by staying silent? Oh,

Father, I'm sorry. I'm so sorry.

I was sickened to think I'd wasted so much energy, so much prayer, asking the Lord to relieve me of a stomachache when so many men, women, and children were about to be butchered. I'd have done anything to bring back the pain. I wanted it. I needed it. I deserved it.

In time, the screaming drifted away, carried on the wind. The army of King Jacob returned to our encampment, bloody and boasting, their arms overflowing with plunder. I turned away and dry heaved over the rim of my litter.

Drained of emotion, I remained perfectly still in the bottom of my carrier for almost an hour, tears seeping silently out of my eyes. At last, Marcos' face appeared over me. In his hands was a bowl of fresh food. Fresh plunder from the village. My eyes rested on the bowl, then on him. I didn't move.

He invited me to take the bowl. "Here. You better make up for all those days that you didn't eat."

No remorse. No sign of conscience. No comprehension that dozens of lives had just been snuffed out at his father's command. I felt my teeth clenching. Suddenly, I lunged at Marcos, my finger-nails aiming for his eyes. I missed his eyes and dug my nails into the flesh of his nose and cheek, knocking him off balance and spilling the hot food down the front of his mantle.

Marcos shrieked and dropped the bowl as the food scalded his skin. His neck and upper chest were blister red. His face was bleeding. I settled back into the corner of my litter. I didn't care how Marcos might react. Let him strangle me on the spot if he wished. This would have been anyone's natural reaction.

But instead, Marcos cried out with sincere hurt in his voice, "What did you do that for?"

It struck me as a stupid question. I closed my eyes and turned away. Attacking Marcos may have accomplished nothing, but it was the only outlet I had to vent my hatred and loathing for King Jacob, for Marcos, and for everything they stood for.

"You blame me for the raid on the village?" Marcos inquired innocently.

Still I said nothing.

"I didn't have anything to do with it," he insisted. "I even tried

to talk my father out of it. I suggested that we sell off a few of our porters to purchase provisions. I was afraid if we attacked the village it might incite the wrath of other villages and cause them to come after us."

So noble, *I thought sarcastically.* It wasn't the murder of so many innocent people that had pricked his conscience. It was his fear of reprisal.

"Even now my father wonders if I am a coward because I requested to stay behind and watch over you," he continued. "He wonders if my cushy life in the modern century has made me soft. Lord Jacob sacrifices cowards—whether they're his son or not."

I looked at Marcos again. He dabbed at the blood on his nose with the hem of his mantle. *No, I told myself. I still refused to believe he was any different from the rest of them.* His motives remained selfish to the core. *Maybe Marcos didn't join in the raid because he was a coward.* There was still no hint of remorse over what had happened—no wrenching tears over the slaughter of defenseless people. *No, Marcos was as much a part of the evil as any of them.* I faced the rim of the carrier again.

After several moments, I glanced up. Marcos was gone. After a while he returned. In his arms squirmed a pudgy little dog with hair so sparse it might as well have been considered hairless. I remembered seeing about thirty of these little dogs when the warriors returned from the raid. It was explained to me later that they were "food" dogs. For long-distance travelers such "food" was particularly useful since it transported itself. *How convenient,* I *thought, especially for lazy slobs like the men of Jacob.* The dogs generally foraged for their own food and water. Because they were so shy and timid, they never wandered far from the presence of men. They were totally loyal, despite the fact that they were destined for someone's dinner plate.

For the most part, the breed was not very affectionate. This was likely because they'd never gotten any affection in return. Their masters always treated them like livestock. Marcos, however, had discovered an exception to this. The dog that he brought to me was extremely affectionate, starvingly so. *I wondered if it had been someone's house pet. And then I wondered if its owner had just been cut down before its eyes. Had it been nestling against a silent corpse when Jacob's warrior snatched it up?*

Marcos said nothing as he handed me the dog, but I could have sworn that his eyes moistened slightly when he saw how touched I was. The experience of cuddling something warm and loving in my arms again was overwhelming. That little dog was a breath of life for me. I held it in my arms the way a lonely little girl holds her favorite stuffed animal. And the dog licked away my tears.

I never thanked Marcos for his gift. But I don't think he expected thanks. He lingered there a moment, watching me pat, embrace, and kiss my new pet. Finally he left me to fall asleep with the pudgy little dog inside my arms.

I named my dog Pill, because that's exactly what he was. And because he was just the dose of medicine I needed to go on.

CHAPTER 3

We discovered the track just as we were setting up camp that first night.

"What kind of animal is it?" I inquired.

"Jaguar," Naaman informed me. "Big one. Female."

"You can tell that much from a single track?"

Naaman pointed to another track, less distinguished, about four feet away. "I can tell that much from two."

Naaman informed us that the tracks were less than an hour old. He then sniffed the air and gazed off into the forest in the direction that the tracks indicated.

"We're upwind of her," he concluded. "She probably smelled us and went for those hills. She'll stay there until dark."

"And then what happens?" I asked uneasily.

Naaman looked me in the eye and said gravely, "Then she feeds."

I swallowed. After a moment, Naaman laughed, soaking great pleasure from the expression on my face.

Gidgiddonihah mercifully interrupted, slapping Naaman's shoulder in mild reproach. "*Nothing* happens after dark," he assured me. "We'll keep the fire burning high. A big cat may stalk a campsite's perimeter, but it will never come near a fire."

"I can fashion a convincing cat caller from a hollow stump and a strip of hide," Naaman added. "The sound exactly mimics a jag's low, hungry growl. If we stayed alert, we could slay one before dawn and eat jag meat for breakfast. Tough, but very tasty. Then we could sell the coat in Sidom for—"

"I'll not eat jaguar," said Lamachi self-righteously. "That animal is sacred."

"No animal is sacred," scoffed Naaman. "Every beast was put here by God for—"

"Now, now," cut in Zedekiah before the argument grew heated. "We each need our rest if we are to reach Nimrod tomorrow. There'll be no jaguar hunting tonight."

"Only a fool would hunt jag without a spear anyway," added Jonathan.

"I've killed three with no more than a flint knife," Naaman boasted.

"A flint knife!" laughed Jonathan. "That I would like to see."

"I'll describe it to you . . ."

Naaman regaled us with his exploits of jaguar and cougar hunting while we gathered wood and concocted a meal of beans and corn mush, supplemented by watercress and berries. Naaman showed us a scar on his ribs that he claimed had been inflicted by a jaguar the size of a sea-dragon. (A sea-dragon, I concluded, was a crocodile.) This occurred, he said, while hunting "Reds" (the common vernacular for Gadiantons) in the Mountains of Desolation where jags were as numerous as mosquitoes.

"I thought you told me you got that scar fighting bandits in the East Wilderness," noted Gidgiddonihah, grinning.

"That was a different scar," said Naaman. "Sometimes I get the two confused."

After a while I read through Naaman's bravado and perceived that he had about as much desire to hunt for jaguar tonight as the rest of us. Likely he never would have brought it up unless he was certain that Zedekiah or somebody else would object.

Nevertheless, the danger of a large predator in our vicinity was real and treated with necessary caution.

"I'll take the first watch and keep the fire burning," said Gidgiddonihah.

"There's no need for anyone else to stay awake," said Jonathan. "I sleep as lightly as a waterskipper skips. The slightest sound in the jungle always opens my eyes as wide as coconuts."

I had the distinct impression that the jaguar cats of this day and age were not exactly the animals of the same name that we knew from the latter days. Oh, our modern jaguars may have looked basically the same: shimmering orange coat with black mottling for camouflage. But because of continual encroachment upon the jaguar's territory over the last five hundred years, a certain degree of aggressiveness had disappeared from its nature—an evolution precipitated by its fight for survival. Only the most stealthy and timid cats had managed to survive into the twenty-first century. In other words, the jaguars of this ancient day and time may have been a far more dangerous adversary.

As night descended upon us, every stir in the brush, real or imagined, caused me to sit up straight and gaze off into the darkness. It was a cool night. The fire smelled sweet. The flames felt comforting. Overhead I watched bats and night birds dart this way and that, snatching invisible insects on the wing, and managing almost magically never to collide with one another.

After we finished our meal, Zedekiah came and sat beside me. In his hands was a clay flask containing an herbal brew that he'd concocted during dinner. Our spiritual leader was a small man, even for a Nephite. It was difficult to tell his age. Late fifties, maybe. He was terribly skinny and his face was as pale as cream. I might even compare his skin color to my own, except that in this land and time, such color often indicated frail health. When I was first introduced to Zedekiah and told that he would accompany me on my quest, I was concerned that such a fragile-looking man would never endure the journey. He looked as out of place as an accountant in the wild West. At least Gidgiddonihah and Jonathan, with their size and brawn, had offered a comforting balance. Today I'd been embarrassed to have ever had such thoughts. Zedekiah had kept the pace much better than I did. But now that the day's journey was through, he looked tired and worn.

He put the flask to his lips and drank. His face puckered at the flavor. He caught me staring and smiled. His face was kind and trusting—the kind of face that puts one at ease when confessing sins or secrets.

"Medicine," he answered before I had asked. "It aids me with my various 'sensitivities.'"

I interpreted this to mean allergies. One of these sensitivities seemed to be bug bites. The welts on his arms where he'd been nipped by mosquitoes were unusually large.

I nodded to acknowledge his statement, then gazed back at the fire, thinking about the son and daughter I'd left back at the Falls of Gideon. A part of me still believed we should not have separated.

Zedekiah patted my knee. "They are in good hands," he said, reading my thoughts.

"I know," I said, only half-convinced.

"I would not have left my own wife and children if I was not certain they would be safe in the Prophet's keeping."

I looked up. "I didn't realize you had a family, Zedekiah. Somehow I figured that only men who were unattached would be sent on an expedition like this."

"That is the case with the others," he confirmed. "I don't believe Jonathan has ever married. He is a Christian from the land of Gideon. Naaman, on the other hand, lost his wife to fevers many years ago, during the Gadianton wars. Gidgiddonihah lost his wife only four summers ago while she was giving birth. The unnamed son was taken by the Lord before it reached a year."

"Unnamed?" I repeated.

It took Zedekiah a moment to perceive why I found this so strange. "Most children in our land are not given a name until they are eight years old, when it may be reasonably assumed that they will reach adulthood. Hopeful parents may choose a name in the child's first years, but until they are eight they are usually called by a pet name, like Flower Petal or Rabbit Foot. They are not given their *honored* name until they are baptized."

"Do so many fail to live until they are eight years old?" I asked.

"Heaven knows that I never would have reached that year," said Zedekiah, "if not by the mercy of God. Until I was eight years old I nearly perished from some illness or accident every month of my life. But these are equally vulnerable years for anyone. Is it so different in your land?"

"Yes," I replied. I sounded almost ashamed as I said, "Most newborns in my land live to be adults."

Zedekiah's statement reminded me just how precarious life was in this day. In my own twentieth-century experience, I hadn't known death in any close degree until I was fifteen years old, when my Grandma Tucker passed away. Except for Renae—and with the exception of my adventure in Mexico with Coriantumr's sword—every other death I had seen in my life had been expected, anticipated. It was the person's "time," more or less. What would it have been like to be born in a world where death was so perennial, and "old" was a label given to anyone over thirty-five?

Zedekiah nodded thoughtfully at my statement, waiting perhaps for me to reveal more about my land. The subject had also caught the interest of the other men. They broke off their own conversations to listen.

Gidgiddonihah was the first to inquire, haltingly, "Where . . . is your land, Jimhawkins?"

I was about to offer my standard reply to new inquirers: "to the north." Somehow the intensity of everyone's gaze told me this would not be enough. But I was spared for the time being. Something snapped in the forest darkness.

The attuned reflexes of Naaman and Gidgiddonihah caused them to stand upright in two to three seconds. The rest of us followed their example. Instinctively, we stepped behind the fire so we could peer protectively over the flames into the region of the darkness that had emitted the crack. We became breathlessly silent, waiting for the noise to betray itself one more time.

None of us doubted that it was the female jaguar whose tracks we had found earlier. By the looks on everyone's faces, I don't believe anyone had great faith in Gidgiddonihah's assurance that a jaguar would hold off an attack in the vicinity of a fire. My heart pounded violently. I felt exposed. It was so *dark* out there. My latent childhood fears of darkness resurfaced. To a charging jaguar, we were all as helpless as lambs.

At last we perceived a second sound, less distinct than before. My breath snagged in my throat as I perceived a darker piece of darkness creeping along the perimeter of the camp.

"This is your chance," Jonathan whispered to Naaman. "Show us how a jaguar is killed with a flint knife."

Naaman shook his head vigorously. "Only a fool would use a knife against a jag."

In the next instant Gidgiddonihah rattled my eardrum with a deafening scream. I think the sound was intended to startle the animal and set it bounding away, but its only effect was to cause the darker piece of darkness to stop moving.

Gidgiddonihah screamed again. Like a pack of monkeys we all joined in. But the shadow didn't flinch. Instead, it started creeping *forward!* As the others began backing away, ready to scatter like antelope, I perceived that the shadow was considerably smaller than I might have expected for a man-eating cat. I observed that the shape had risen from its crouched position to stand erect. I heard myself call out to the others, "Wait!"

"Don't hurt me!" cried the shadow. "I'm only a boy! I'm only—" And then the shadow stepped into the firelight, its eyes fixed on me. "Dad? Is that you, Dad?"

"Harry? What on earth—!"

"Dad!"

My son threw his arms about my waist. I yanked him back so I could see his face. I was hyperventilating.

"What in—! How in—! What in blazes are you *doing* here? What happened? Where are Jenny and Steffanie?"

"Still with Nephi, I guess. Dad, you wouldn't believe what I've just been through. I thought I'd never find you. I thought you'd taken a different trail."

The blood was rising so quickly to my face that it must have glowed in the dark. Gritting my teeth, gripping his shoulders, I shouted, "You followed me? After I told you—after I *ordered* you—! Harry, what—? *How could you do something so stupid?!*"

"But what if something had happened to you, Dad? What if I never saw you again?"

I let go of him and began stomping around the campsite in a fluster. The others assembled around us, their hearts still pulsing wildly. If I'd allowed it, I think they would have strangled the kid for stripping ten years from their lives.

I faced Harry again. "Do you know what you've done, Harry? Do you realize? You might have cost Melody her life! We'll lose two full days returning you into the hands of the Prophet Nephi!"

"Five days," corrected Gidgiddonihah. "The only place to cross the river is back at the Falls of Gideon. It'll take us a day to return to those falls, another day to reach Nephi, and then two days to get back here. Today's efforts will have been wasted as well."

I drilled it home as Harry shrank before us, his relief at having found me fading. "Five days! Did you think about that? Did that even cross your mind?"

Harry couldn't look me in the eye. A tear trickled down his cheek. "I wanted to help you."

"What about Jenny and Steffanie? Do they know where you are?"

"I told Joshua to tell them."

"Joshua?" I tousled my hair at my son's lunacy. "Joshua is *four years old!*"

"I told him to say I was going to look for you. That I was going to help you rescue his father and Melody. I made him repeat the message."

I sat back down by the fire and put my head between my knees, drawing deep breaths. Harry too sat down—a good ten feet out of reach.

Everyone's heartbeats started returning to normal. Jonathan had relaxed enough to start laughing. He teased Naaman, "What about a boy, Naaman? Would only a fool have the courage to use a knife against a *boy?*"

My emotions exhausted, I slowly raised my head to look at Harry. My son's frown sunk down to his toes.

I struggled to steady my breathing, then I asked, "What did you do during the storm?"

"I sat under a tree."

I raised my eyebrows. "You stayed out in the open?"

He nodded and said limply, "I'm sorry, Dad."

I might have expected words that showed greater remorse. But I knew this was the best I could expect. Up to now, I'd completely ignored Harry's own emotional state. As the darkness had descended, the kid had probably become scared out of his wits. Harry had already been caged by Lamanites, kidnapped by Pochteca traders, and accosted by stone-throwing apostates. At least on all those occasions his father had been near. Tonight he'd been alone. I recalled the look on his face as he had recognized me at the fire.

I sighed, "Come here, Harry."

Abjectly, he arose and drew close. I gathered him into my arms. "Thank God you're all right." I looked him over again. "*Are* you all right?"

"Yes."

Lamachi volunteered his own appraisal of my son. "You showed a lot of courage, Harry. You're a very brave boy. I was just like you when I was your age. Just like you. I'd have done exactly the same thing. Of course, my father would have killed me. Not that I knew my father. But my *mother* would have killed me—"

"Thank you, Lamachi," I interrupted.

"I'll take him back," Lamachi persisted. "I'll start back right now if you want. I'm a good runner. I could even carry the boy on my back if he got tired. The rest of you could go on without us. I'd catch up to you in Sidom. I'd be gone only four days. Maybe only three."

The thought of leaving Harry in Lamachi's hands made me cringe. I opened my mouth to politely decline when Zedekiah said, "There may be another solution, Jimhawkins. In Sidom there is a branch of Christians. Their spiritual leader is a man named Jeremiah. He is a good man. We will tell him about Nephi's charge that all Christians should gather to the land of Bountiful. Jeremiah may be willing to take your son with him."

Harry objected. "But I want to go with *you*, Dad."

"Harry—!" I said sternly. Then I softened my tone. "I know . . . I know that you're scared for me, Harry. But . . . don't you see how much more dangerous things are if you're with me?"

"No," said Harry. "I could help you, Dad. I'm not just a kid anymore. Please let me help you."

I looked at the ground. "How can I make you understand?"

"I won't bother you, if that's what you're worried about. Most of the time you won't even know I'm here."

"*No!*" I said with finality. "Now I don't want to argue about it anymore."

Harry's countenance fell. But this time I didn't care. I was his father, for crying out loud! When did I lose the ability to convince him that I knew what was best?

I caught queer looks from Jonathan and Naaman. They didn't seem to understand why I wouldn't administer harsher discipline to such a back-talking adolescent.

"If it were me," Naaman mumbled to Jonathan, "my father would have held my face in the yellow smoke of roasting red chili peppers. Eeeooow! Makes my throat burn and my eyes water just thinking about it."

Perhaps they were right. Maybe the situation did call for harsher punishment. Harry had placed his life and the success of our expedition at risk. I had to do something to insure that Harry wouldn't try this again. But tonight I just didn't have the heart. Or the energy. I knew the emotions that were driving him. He was afraid he might lose both a mother and a father. As he fell asleep beside me on my sleeping mat of thatched palm, I couldn't deny that a part of me was grateful to have him near. It would take us three days to reach Sidom. If by then I couldn't make Harry understand by gentle persuasion that he *must* go to Bountiful, I'd be forced to consider other options. One thing I knew for sure: my son was *not* going with me to Jacobugath.

CHAPTER 4

We awakened the next day with every expectation that we would arrive in the village of Nimrod that afternoon. Zedekiah offered the camp prayer that morning. In it he emphasized his hope that we might avoid contention and bickering for the remainder of our journey. He implied that if we failed to do so, we could not succeed. It turned out to be a futile petition. Even before we set out, Lamachi and Naaman got into it again over Lamachi's unwillingness to lift a finger to help break camp.

"Either pull your weight, boy, or I'll give you a licking that you'll never forget!" Naaman promised.

Lamachi's eyes pressed thin and his jaw jutted forward. "You have no power over me, dirt tracker. If you ever lay a hand on me, you'll curse that day for the rest of eternity."

Naaman raised his fists. "Bring it on, you little Red cockroach."

As Naaman bolted forward, I jumped between them.

Gidgiddonihah grabbed Naaman's shoulders. "Back off, Naaman. Leave him be!"

"I'm *no one's* servant!" Lamachi proclaimed. "I was asked to take us to Jacobugath, and that's what I will do."

Zedekiah pulled Naaman aside. "Control your temper, Naaman, or it will be the end of us all. If the boy doesn't wish to work, we can't force him."

Naaman shrugged off Zedekiah, "All right. All right. I'll get off his back."

Despite the reluctant truce, I could tell that Naaman wasn't ready to forget Lamachi's threat. The two had become fast enemies.

By the time we got underway, I'd completely forgotten all the anger I'd felt toward Harry the night before. I might have even become a bit too *fatherly*, encouraging him to clean his teeth according to Zedekiah's example using a soft patch of leather, a tiny wood pick, and a mixture of bee's honey and white ashes. I also convinced him to discard the sweat socks he'd worn under the laces of his sandals for the past four days. The socks were now so tattered and soiled that they created more friction against his skin than the leather laces.

During the journey Harry received a lot of attention from Lamachi. The former Gadianton walked beside my son most of the day, trying, I think, to earn his friendship. Unfortunately, Lamachi had a peculiar way of going about it. I'd never met someone so socially retarded. At one point he said to Harry, "I can read your thoughts. Did you know that?"

"I don't think so," said Harry. "My thoughts are pretty complicated."

"Try me. Go ahead. Think about something. Anything. And I'll tell you what it is."

"All right," said Harry. "What am I thinking about?"

Lamachi didn't even skip a beat. "A bird!" he blurted out. "A bird with a very sweet song."

"Wrong," said Harry. "I was thinking about Dusty Davis, lead singer for the Slashers."

"You see," said Lamachi. "I was right. A bird sings. And so does this Dusty Davis."

"Dusty's not a bird," said Harry. "It might be argued that he doesn't sing either."

"But I was still right," Lamachi insisted. "Think of something else."

"Okay. Got it."

"A deer. You're thinking of a deer that runs and darts very fast."

"Nope. I was thinking of Angel Orbison. He's a soccer player.

His team took the World Cup last—"

"A player! You see? A player! And he runs and darts like a deer. Am I right?"

"Give it up, Lamachi."

"Go on. Think of something else."

"I don't want to play anymore."

Lamachi's face reddened with anger. "I told you to think of something else, boy. Do it! *Now!*"

The sudden turn in Lamachi's mood took Harry by surprise. His eyes flashed at me to indicate that he might need protection.

"Lamachi," I said sternly. "What's come over you?"

Fortunately, Lamachi had enough respect for me to back down. He smiled meekly and said, "I'm sorry. I was just trying to show him a trick."

"He's not interested right now."

"You're right. I'm sorry. I'll show him later. Would that be all right, Harry? Can we play this game again later?"

"Sure," said Harry unconvincingly.

Later Lamachi tried to persuade Harry that raw meat was better than cooked meat. It was more nutritious and a wellspring of hidden powers. Toward the end of the day's journey, Harry made little effort to hide his dislike for Lamachi, literally telling him he didn't want to hear anymore. Finally Harry avoided him altogether by changing his place in the line to anywhere that Lamachi wasn't. I was grateful when snatches of the flowing gray water of the Sidon River reappeared through the trees, and shortly thereafter, the first buildings of the village of Nimrod.

In some respects Nimrod resembled an old farm community where half the buildings are abandoned and decayed while the other half are occupied, but in disrepair. In the center of the town stood an odd shrine constructed of huge black chunks of basalt carved into a flowing shape that reminded me of a geyser—the fountain frozen in stone. There were other geometric patterns at the base of the shrine and a large relief of a face with a solemn expression, eyes closed.

Zedekiah told us that Nimrod had once been a thriving

community along the Sidon River, but in recent decades its status had declined. Many years ago, he said, this village had been called by a different name, although no one remembered what it was. It was said to have been a stopover for Nephi and Lehi—the father and uncle of the current prophet—on their return journey from an unsuccessful missionary expedition to the land northward. As the story went, some sort of miracle occurred and one man was converted. His name, of course, was Nimrod.

But Nimrod did not remain faithful for very long. Soon after Nephi and Lehi left, Nimrod convinced most of the villagers that *he* was the great Messiah that had been prophesied by the missionaries. When Nimrod died some years later—martyred by the hand of an assassin, or so it was rumored—the village built a shrine to his memory. His followers assured each other that Nimrod the Messiah would be resurrected at the end of the world and save all those who believed in him.

"The village enjoyed a brief season of prosperity," said Zedekiah. "But many residents abandoned the religion of Nimrod when the prophecy of Samuel was fulfilled—the day and the night and the day without darkness. Those who stayed with the sect were among the largest group of people who refused to assemble into one place to defend against the robbers of Gadianton. Eventually, Nimrod was occupied by the Gadianton leader, Giddianhi. Most of the inhabitants were enslaved or killed."

Zedekiah explained that General Gidgiddoni liberated the village toward the end of the wars. The followers of Nimrod who survived didn't understand why their promised "messiah" hadn't returned to save them. As a result, they became bitter against *all* religion. Very few of them were receptive to the gospel.

This continued to be the case today. The inhabitants of Nimrod were now a tribe unto themselves numbering less than two hundred souls. They eked a meager existence from the forest and the river, lacking the zeal for much else. While the shrine of Nimrod was choking with weeds, the people were choking with despondency—too disillusioned even to consider the message of hope found in the gospel of Jesus Christ. After all, disappointment at the hands of one "messiah" was enough.

"Here is evidence," said Zedekiah, "of the damage that can be inflicted by one misguided man."

We soon found ourselves down by the river. The bank was littered with garbage and debris that the Sidon had regurgitated back onto the shore rather than carrying it downstream. We found a woodcarver whose yard was a heap of tools in disrepair, as well as a graveyard of rotten and splintered canoes. Near the water, however, we noticed a few dugouts that appeared to be seaworthy. Children in their "birthday suits" darted about the premises. The woodcarver's wife remained out back cooking something that smelled sour and horrid. I hoped it was some kind of cleaning or tanning solution and not dinner. Gidgiddonihah offered the woodcarver a fair price for three of the dugouts. The man agreed without haggling, which was surprising. Honesty in business dealings was not all too common these days.

The woodcarver looked us up and down, and remarked, "You people are *Jesus* Christians, aren't you?"

"Yes, we are," I confessed.

The man smiled at his own sagacity and added, "Your kind seem to come through here regular. Missionaries, are you?"

"Always," Zedekiah replied.

"Well," said the man in a half-interested tone, "I've heard your message. It's the same old thing. Tell me something, Jesus Christian: how can you have faith in a man who is said to be living his whole life in an imaginary land across the oceans? At least my parents had faith in a man who loved the Nephites enough to be born among them and teach them personally."

It was an objection every Christian had heard a thousand times. Zedekiah gave the standard response, spoken with remarkable freshness and sincerity.

"Jesus the Messiah *will* come to this land," he proclaimed. "He *will* teach this people personally. This is the promise of Nephi, and also Samuel, and many other prophets throughout the ages. It will happen very soon."

"I'm familiar with the prophecies of Samuel," said the woodcarver. "I haven't spent all my days in this backwater. But

I'm afraid by all calculations, the time is long expired for the fulfillment of Samuel's prophecy of the three days of darkness. And I have heard it said that his prophecy of the day and the night and the day without darkness was added to Samuel's original words some years after it occurred. I'm sorry, Jesus Christian. Your hope is as vain as that of my parents. As they waited for *their* messiah, the Gadiantons drove them to starvation."

Zedekiah reached out and took the man's shoulder. Such familiarity might have made the stranger uncomfortable, and indeed I thought he would try to pull away, but the instant Zedekiah touched him, something penetrated his heart.

"There is only one Messiah," said Zedekiah, "from the beginning of time until the end of the world. And he is not the Messiah of some. He is the Messiah of all. When our Lord Jesus Christ comes, I promise that I will return here, and I will bring you the joy of his salvation."

The woodcarver huffed once and raised a corner of his mouth, on the verge of uttering some mocking phrase like, "You do that." But he held his tongue, and the corner of his mouth drooped down again. To shake himself from the strange feeling, he abruptly changed the subject, "You'll find good lodging downriver. There's an inn about an hour downstream. If you set out now, you might reach it before dark. Good traveling, Jesus Christian."

The woodcarver made as if to join his wife at the back of the hut, but I caught sight of him watching us as we shoved off from shore and let the village of Nimrod drift behind us.

We soon arrived at the riverside inn described by the woodcarver. Like most of the structures in this district, it was a house of vine-tied saplings with a straw-thatched roof. The innkeeper was a connoisseur of chocolate and demanded that we pay all our fees with cacao beans, of which Gidgiddonihah had brought a plenteous supply. We paid not only for our room, which consisted of the first beds Harry and I had slept in since arriving in this land (a raised wooden platform covered in a real cotton quilt with feather down woven into the layers), but we also paid an extra fee for the use of an outdoor bath hut and steam hut. We declined the innkeeper's proposition concerning the numerous girls and women kept on the premises for the purpose of entertaining travelers.

The bath and steam facilities consisted of two modest round buildings constructed of baked clay bricks. The steam hut worked much like many of the saunas I'd seen in modern health clubs. Volcanic rocks in a center brazier were heated and then doused with water to create the steam. The seven of us wasted no time taking advantage of the steam hut. Gidgiddonihah warned us that beyond the city of Sidom, we might not have another opportunity to take advantage of such facilities and, as he put it, "rid our bodies of all their foul odors." There was just enough room for everyone to fit inside. It was our first moment together as an expedition wherein good feelings prevailed, although Naaman and Lamachi did not exchange a single word.

Naaman tried to gloss over his apparent cowardice in failing to attack the jaguar that turned out to be my son.

"I knew it wasn't a jaguar," he declared through the mists of steam. "The scent of its urine was not in the air. That scent is always dominant when a big cat is near."

"Oh," said Jonathan teasingly, "then that explains why you didn't attack it. You must have thought it was something even *more* dangerous." He laughed, I assumed, because it was common knowledge that there was nothing more dangerous in the wilderness than a jaguar.

But Naaman was eager to correct this assumption. "Don't laugh so casually, young Gideonite. There are indeed beasts more dangerous than jaguars, although I confess that such animals are not to be found around here. But we may well meet up with them in the Mountains of Desolation. In Desolation there are still cureloms. No beast is more dangerous and ruthless."

My ears perked up. "Curelom? Did you say curelom?"

Ever since I was a boy that single verse in the Book of Mormon which mentions this mysterious animal had tickled my imagination. The verse was in Ether. As I recalled, an animal called a curelom, and another one called a cummom, were named with elephants and horses as being especially useful to man. This was in the days of a Jaredite king named Emer. It had been nearly a thousand years since Emer had walked the earth. Still, I found it hard to believe that an animal once domesticated enough to be considered particularly useful to man could transform into something as dangerous and ruthless as the beast Naaman was describing. He must have been exaggerating, as usual.

"Yes," Naaman replied. "Curelom. A creature as big as a temple with great curved teeth the size of cypress trunks, eyes that glow red in the darkness, and a stench so foul it wilts all the mountain flowers."

"There is no such beast," said Gidgiddonihah, munching from a complimentary block of coconut. But although he disbelieved, he was greatly entertained.

"Ah, but I have seen one with my own eyes," Naaman declared, "and I would give all my worldly wealth to tear that black day from my memory."

I doubted this very much since Naaman took such pleasure in telling the tale. Not that Naaman had any worldly wealth to begin with.

"There we were," Naaman began, swirling the steam with his hand gestures, "on a bleak and barren plateau, preparing to march the last of the Gadianton prisoners who'd been holding out in the mountains back to the land of Zarahemla. I thank my God in Heaven that we were awakened that morning by the sound of its blood-chilling roar. I shudder even now to think of it. The earth shook. The other Nephite soldiers and I managed to get out of its path, but every last one of the Reds was crushed and gored where they stood."

"Is that true?" Harry asked me skeptically. "Is there really an animal that would do that?"

"Mark my words, boy," said Naaman. "There *is* such an animal."

"What about cummoms?" I asked Naaman. "Are there still cummoms?"

"Cummoms!" Naaman repeated the name in a declaratory way. I think he desperately wanted to make up an animal to keep the story going, but he sighed and confessed, "No, I can't say as I've ever heard of such a beast. Is this a great predator from your land, Jimhawkins?"

"No," I said. "I'm not sure *what* it is. We have writings that mention them. Cureloms, too. But until now, I'd never heard one described."

Naaman grinned, ecstatic that someone had given evidence to support his tale. But he added, "My description could never do it justice. But you wait. When we reach those mountains— and I suspect we will—" He glanced at Lamachi for some hint of confirmation that we were indeed going in that direction, but Lamachi hinted nothing and Naaman turned back to me "—you may, Jimhawkins, receive an opportunity to create your own description. Although if such an opportunity arises, there is a high probability that none of us will live to tell about it."

* * *

It was a marvelously restful night. So restful that when I awakened, I'd have given anything to have stayed in bed. My muscles were like cement. I wasn't sure I could go on another day without giving them some time to rest. Fortunately providence had given us just such an opportunity. As I rolled out from under my quilt I was struck with elation that today we would not walk. For the next two days we would travel by canoe and my sore muscles would finally have a chance to heal.

The only drawback to our prospects for a pleasant day was Lamachi's choice to ride in the third canoe with Harry and me. True to expectations, he refused to raise the other paddle to offer any assistance. Fortunately, the current did most of the work. The river flowed rather swiftly through this section of land. There were many undercurrents and whirlpools. I now understood what Gidgiddonihah had meant when he said that the last place to cross the river unaided was back at the Falls of Gideon.

Lamachi sat at the head of the dugout. He reminded me of George Washington crossing the Delaware, his eyes scanning the banks, leery of Redcoats and spies. Lamachi was paranoid by nature. I suspected that this was an inherent characteristic found in anyone associated with secret combinations. To me it was further evidence of the fact that Lamachi's basic devotions had not changed. Once as we floated down the river he shocked both Harry and me by confiding that someone in our expedition was trying to kill him. I didn't want to give credibility to his paranoia by feeding it, but I had to ask, "Why would you think something like that?"

"I think it because I *know* it," he replied. "This person feels that I am a threat to everything he believes in."

I might have raised my hand at that moment and confessed, *That would be me*—at least the part about believing he was a threat to our mission. I suspected that every other person in our expedition harbored the same misgivings. But to believe that someone also harbored contemplations of murdering him—

"I think, Lamachi, this is all in your mind," I told him.

"No!" he said defensively. "I have to watch my back every minute. You are both my friends, am I right?"

Harry gave me a sideways glance before he acknowledged, "Sure, Lamachi."

"Of course we're your friends," I added.

"Then we must stick together. We must bind ourselves together—like blood brothers. It's for our own protection. Are we agreed?"

"No, we're *not* agreed," I said firmly. "I'll stand by you, Lamachi. I'll defend you if you're wronged. But I won't make any pact with you that doesn't include the others. Is that understood?"

The finality of my tone caused Lamachi to stick out his lower lip in a pout. "Then I'll watch my *own* back," he said, "*as always*. I can take care of myself. Because . . . I know who my enemy is."

"Who?" asked Harry.

I considered breaking in to tell my son not to encourage his delusions. But Lamachi refused to answer the question directly anyway.

He shook his head. "I won't reveal it until I can prove it." His voice lowered. "But then . . . *I* will strike first."

"Enough of this!" I declared. "Lamachi, if you really have these kinds of fears, we should bring them up before the group."

"That would be unwise," he replied darkly. "I don't wish this person to know that I know. At least not yet."

This was crazy! Lamachi was like a bomb waiting to detonate. Tonight I had to find a moment alone with the others to discuss our alternatives in case Lamachi snapped and went out of control. I couldn't help but wonder who Lamachi had decided was trying to kill him. Anyone's first guess would have been Naaman since the two had nearly come to blows the day before. But what if Lamachi had set his paranoid sights on someone else? What if it was me? What if he had said these things simply to see how I might react? Had it become necessary for me to watch my *own* back? Paranoia was like a disease. If one person had it, the symptoms could become contagious.

The landscape broadened as the day progressed. The forest thinned and gave way to thick and tangled scrub, with yellow and purple blossoms. The banks were more swampy now. Harry reported that he saw an alligator slip into the water. The coconut palms stood more isolated from one another. From their fronds would occasionally burst forth flocks of gold-colored birds.

Toward evening we hoisted our canoes onto a promontory along the riverbank. It was thick with a stiff reddish grass that crunched and crackled when we stepped on it, but it appeared to keep other noxious weeds at bay, making it a common campsite for river travelers. We watched several other canoes pass us by as we struck a fire. They looked disappointed that we had taken the best spot for miles. They did not join us. Trust and camaraderie among strangers in this land remained at an all-time low.

Jonathan made good on his boast that he was highly proficient at the blowgun. In less than an hour he carried into camp three rabbits. Naaman and Gidgiddonihah skinned them and threaded the meat onto green sticks. We discovered a vine with heaps of wild grapes about a hundred yards inland. Harry was eager to harvest as many as he could and take some along in the morning. I managed to talk him into inviting Lamachi to join him. I thought it was probable that Lamachi would reject the offer, but to my surprise, he agreed. For the first time since we'd embarked, he would actually assist in a chore. I promptly used this opportunity to share with the others my concerns about Lamachi's mental stability.

"He believes at least one of us is his mortal enemy," I said, keeping an eye on Lamachi and my son as they picked grapes. "But I think that number could grow if anybody else gave him cause."

"We shouldn't have brought him," snapped Naaman. "Didn't I say this back in Zarahemla?"

"We all knew the risk," sighed Gidgiddonihah.

"But he's the only one who knows the way," reminded Jonathan.

"But is it worth our lives to take him any further?" Naaman challenged. "I say we leave him in Sidom. I don't need him to find Jacobugath. I'm sure it's just beyond the Mountains of Desolation."

"But can we afford to take the chance of going in the wrong direction and losing valuable time?" asked Zedekiah. "The lives of Jonas, Garplimpton, and Jimhawkins' daughter may depend upon our expediency."

"He is a *Gadianton*!" Naaman gruffed. "In all my years I've never seen a Red truly change his heart. The boy should be bound hand and foot while he is among us!"

Gidgiddonihah whispered sharply, "He's coming."

Lamachi and my son returned with several pouches full of grapes. The matter of Lamachi's instability was not discussed again that evening. But all of us were more wary of him, and he in turn seemed more wary of us. Zedekiah called upon Lamachi that evening to offer the prayer. Lamachi outright refused, saying he was not yet ready to offer group prayers.

After everyone had fallen asleep, I heard him muttering to himself, "Help me O Father of Nature. Help me to be stronger than my enemies. Help me to overcome. Help me to uncover the evil among us. Help me to root out the demon. Yes. I must root out the demon among us . . ."

He continued in this vein for some time, until at last I heard only a faint whimpering. I almost felt sorry for him. The demon he was trying to "root out" seemed to be the one that tormented him. I fell asleep before the whimpering ceased. If only somehow I had stayed awake.

In the morning when I opened my eyes, Lamachi was already up. He had started the fire and was busy preparing a breakfast of warm cornmeal and honey. As the others began to stir, I think they were all equally surprised to see Lamachi so eager to serve.

"Arise everyone!" Lamachi called out loud, rousing anyone who might still be lingering in dreamland. "Eat it while it's hot!"

As I was tying my sandals around my feet, I caught the scene out of the corner of my eye as Gidgiddonihah attempted to awaken that last dozer, Naaman. Neither the smell of food nor Lamachi's calls had stirred him. Finally Gidgiddonihah nudged him with his foot. Still Naaman did not move.

"Naaman?"

The concern in Gidgiddonihah's voice caused us all to turn and look. Gidgiddonihah crouched down and peered into Naaman's face. Even from where I stood Naaman's skin looked sallow. Gidgiddonihah touched the flesh.

He recoiled and shouted in anguish, "He's dead! Naaman is dead!"

The electricity of Gidgiddonihah's announcement jolted us all to our feet. Gidgiddonihah dropped again to Naaman's side and cried the name of his friend, as if the sheer determination in his voice might compel him to answer. "Naaman! Naaman!"

We gathered around Naaman's corpse, already stiffened, already cold. There were no visible wounds, no signs of a struggle, no tenseness or stress in his features. It appeared as if the tracker had simply died in his sleep. But no one believed it. Neither did anyone believe the look of innocence and surprise that crossed the features of Lamachi the Gadianton. As everyone's eyes settled heavily upon the teenager, he began to realize by degrees that we all had definite suspicions of who was responsible.

"You're mistaken!" he pleaded. "If anyone took the dirt tracker's life, it was the Father of Nature!"

Unexpectedly, Jonathan dropped to the ground and buried his face in his hands. "This is all my fault! Heaven curse me! I could have prevented it!"

Zedekiah gripped Jonathan's shoulders. "What are you talking about, Jonathan?"

"My darts! The ones for my blowpipe. Two nights ago I counted them. I had fourteen. Yet when I went hunting yesterday I counted only eleven. Three were missing. I thought of saying something. But I decided I must have misplaced them among my supplies or dropped them along the trail."

Gidgiddonihah wasted no time examining Naaman's body. His hands froze as he discovered three minute pricks on Naaman's right shoulder. Now it was irrefutable. Naaman had been murdered.

"One dart is not strong enough to kill a man," Jonathan explained. "But three . . . three would have done the job quite nicely."

My mind was whirling with confusion and grief. It didn't make sense.

"Why wouldn't Naaman have resisted after he felt the first prick?" I asked.

Gidgiddonihah had the answer. "To a sleeping man in the dark, the first prick might have easily been mistaken for an insect. After that, he wouldn't have had the strength to resist, if he awakened at all."

Gidgiddonihah trembled with indignation as he rose to his feet. His gaze centered squarely upon Lamachi, who cowered and shuddered before us. Lamachi's expression seemed exactly that of a criminal caught in the act, stripped of his disguise.

Lamachi bolted. He ran toward the river to try to escape in one of the canoes. But Gidgiddonihah and Jonathan were quickly on top of him. They tackled him in the water before he could push the dugout far enough out from shore. I grabbed the canoe to keep it from floating away. Lamachi fought like a lion, but finally they pinned him face down in the mud at the water's edge. Greased in lime-colored mud from head to foot, he cried out, "Noooo! Noooo!" exactly like a wild animal heaving its final death throe. But Lamachi did not die. He was bound hand and foot, as had been Naaman's final appeal concerning him the night before.

Rage and panic rippled up and down my spine. I tried to come to grips with our new reality. Naaman was gone. Our tracker—the man who knew the best routes through the wilderness of Desolation—would not be there to guide us. Lamachi—the only one who could have taken us beyond Desolation—had finally succumbed to the demon that tormented him. My grief over Naaman's death was overwhelmed by my sense of panic. What would we do? Without Lamachi and Naaman how would we ever reach Jacobugath? How would I ever find Melody?

I knew that bringing Lamachi had been a gamble from the beginning. We had *all* known it and dreaded it. But now that it was clear that the gamble had failed, what was our next step? Only one choice loomed clear. Reach Sidom. Reach Sidom above all else and worry about the rest from there.

Needless to say, none of us ate a single bite of Lamachi's breakfast.

CHAPTER 5

A few days after the men of Jacob raided the village and heaped its meager trappings upon their backs, we started ascending the slopes of the first mountain in the cloud-covered range that had been beckoning us forward since Melek. The trail we had chosen was unfamiliar to all but one or two of the men. Jacob did not wish to cross the wilderness using the same trail he'd used in coming. I guessed this was because somewhere along its course lay the smoldering ruins of another village—one that he'd pillaged a few weeks earlier. He may have feared that its neighbors were ready and waiting for him to return.

My porters spent most of the afternoon hunched forward as they toiled up the slope with my fur-lined litter on their backs. I hadn't heard any of them speak so much as two words in my presence for the past six days. Speaking to me would have been dealt with very harshly. Because of this, I'd almost come to regard them as nondescript pieces of machinery. But as I watched their muscles strain and the sweat stream off their bodies, I couldn't help but sympathize. The water carriers did not come to ease their thirst nearly often enough. Sometimes they had to bend down on their knees, taxing every whit of strength to keep my carrier upright and level so that I, or my dog, did not spill out. By the end of the day all of them had blood and dirt grimed onto their kneecaps. And tomorrow's journey looked twice as difficult.

The trail that went up and over the mountain pass looked like a foaming cascade turned hard and black by the curse of some sorcerer. Actually it was a dried flow of lava from the summit of the snowy volcanic cone that loomed down on us like a magician's castle. Even as the sun descended behind the volcano I could look up the trail and see vapors rising from the lava rock. The surface temperature along that climb would be blistering hot. I feared it would burn right through the leather of my porters' sandals and cook their feet.

And yet as darkness fell, I was surprised at how quickly the temperature plummeted. Before long Pill and I were dependent upon each other for warmth. We shivered together until Marcos showed up late in the evening with an additional blanket.

"Gonna be a cold one," he informed me, as if I hadn't figured this out for myself. The blanket was rough and itchy. "Look at it this way," he continued. "We should enjoy this chill while we can. Tomorrow it's gonna be an oven up there crossing that pass."

"Marcos," I said, "I wonder . . . if it might be possible . . . what I mean is . . . do you think I could walk by myself tomorrow? I'm going crazy sitting in this carrier day after day. I'd give anything to stand up, use my feet, get some exercise."

Marcos sighed. "If we let you walk, we would have to remove the collar from your neck."

I grabbed the line that was attached to it. "What if you just held it?"

Marcos shook his head. "Lord Jacob fears you would try to escape."

"Escape?" I glanced around at the vastness of the peaks and valleys. "Where would I go?"

"That's what I told him," said Marcos. "'Where would you go?'"

So Marcos had already argued this cause for me. This convinced me that my request was futile. I was stuck in this stupid thing for the duration.

Marcos added, "Lord Jacob also fears you might try to commit suicide by hurling yourself over some ledge."

"Over some ledge?" I was appalled that someone would actually consider me capable of taking my own life. Not that the idea seemed wholly unwelcome under the circumstances. Nevertheless, I said, *"I wouldn't have the nerve to do something like that. What does your father care anyway?"*

"He can't afford to take the chance of losing you before we reach Jacobugath. You're very important to his plans."

Since Marcos had brought it up, I decided to see if I could leech a little more information. As of yet, no one had even vaguely hinted why I'd been abducted. *"Why am I so important to him, Marcos? Why has he gone to such lengths to bring me here?"*

"I'll tell you what I know, which isn't very much," said Marcos, leaning against one of the canopy's posts for support. *"Lord Jacob wants you to convince your uncle to help him."*

"Help him what? How could Uncle Garth help someone like Jacob?"

"I am told that somewhere in this land lies a great treasure. Lord Jacob is certain that your uncle knows exactly where it is. But all of Lord Jacob's persuasions have failed to make him tell us. If your efforts fail to convince him, then . . ."

Marcos hesitated. This surprised me. Two days ago I don't think he would have paused to take a breath as he declared, *"then we will have to kill you both."* Now he looked down, almost ashamed. He did not complete the statement. He figured I'd be able to finish it on my own.

"Treasure?" I said abrasively. *"You mean this is all for something as undramatic as money?"*

"The treasure in and of itself means nothing," Marcos retorted. *"It's how the money is used. That's where the glory lies."*

"And how's that?" I inquired.

Marcos sobered. *"I've told you enough. Maybe too much. But I've told you in hopes that you might ponder the best way to persuade your uncle to help us. By now you must know it's pointless to fight us. If you help us, Melody, I promise you . . ."* He hesitated.

"Promise me what?"

Marcos shuffled his feet. *"I promise that you won't be harmed. I promise that I'll do everything in my power to insure that your life is a happy one."*

"You mean you'll help me to get back home? You'll take me and Uncle Garth back to the cavern that brought us here?"

His countenance fell. *"No, Melody. That won't ever be possible.*

You have to put such ideas out of your head. But I hope that, somehow, you'll find a way to be happy among us."

I laughed derisively. "Don't count on it. How could I ever be happy among bandits and murderers and . . . ?" My face twisted with disgust. "I could never be happy with you!"

The statement was not meant to refer specifically to Marcos. That's just how it came out. But in replying the way I did, I think I interpreted the subtle intent behind all his promises. This was further evidenced by the redness that inflamed his face. I couldn't believe it. Marcos in his childish and demented arrogance had actually hoped I might find a way to be happy with him!

My bluntness hurt him deeply. But what did he expect? That I could fall in love with a barbarian like him simply because he willed it? The mere thought made me retch. I'd die before I became so desperate.

Yet Marcos mustered up the self-assurance to say, "In time, I hope you will feel differently."

He turned away before I had a chance to dismiss the notion with another look of ultimate disgust. He left me alone. Pill curled up under the itchy blanket and dropped off to sleep almost immediately. I drifted off thinking of silly things that would never be again: Friday nights watching old movies with my father, Saturday mornings yelling at Steffanie for playing sunrise basketball, summers riding the Colossus at Lagoon and challenging Harry to see who could scream the loudest. As I faded into slumber I imagined my father watching over me from a distance, his arms folded, a look of fatherly concern creasing his brow. The image comforted me. It made me feel as if he was always near. Neither prison bars nor centuries could keep him away. Of course when I awoke the next morning, the fantasy vanished.

We set out early to climb the barren, black and gray trail of the lava flow. As I had anticipated, the pock-marked plain of volcanic rock sucked in the sun's heat and exhaled it doubly and triply hot. The morning that had promised to be so cool and pleasant became unbearable well before noon. Not so much as a thirsty weed grew along that path. No birds chirped. No breeze blew. The only sound was our footsteps, echoing under us as if we walked across the great empty water jars of departed giants.

Then at the top of the pass came the most disheartening view of all, especially for my porters who were already so exhausted that two of them were wheezing for lack of oxygen on these airy heights. I had hoped for their sake to see a welcome easy-going plateau. Instead we were faced by another pair of mountains, cut down the middle by a deep gorge. At the bottom of the gorge flowed the angry white water of another northbound river.

We had no choice but to climb along the cliffs above the river. A meager trail marked the way, but because every mountain in this region was fast crumbling to dust, much of the trail consisted of rubble that shifted ominously beneath my porters' sandals and threatened at any moment to avalanche entirely out from under them. For every three steps forward, they slipped two steps back. I did my best to keep myself and my dog in the center of the litter, but in spite of this, we were tossed about like rag dolls.

I breathed a sigh of relief when we reached a cramped spiral staircase of rock. The physical exertion wouldn't be any easier, but at least the loose ankle-twisting debris that had kept my adrenaline pumping for the last several hours was behind us. However, the adrenaline returned as it registered that some of the passages were so thin it was a challenge to find a wide enough toe-grip. Our progress was understandably slow for the rest of the afternoon. Jacob would often stand atop some overlook and glower down impatiently at us, frazzling the nerves of my porters even more.

As the day progressed, I found myself taking special interest in one particular porter who marched at the rear. He was one of the largest and brawniest of the group, but today he seemed half-awake as he journeyed. His eyes looked glazed and his face and shoulders, already peeling with sunburn, showed a deeper red than usual. Despite the redness, he did not seem to be sweating like the others, as if his body heat was being drawn inward. If I could have felt his forehead, I'm certain it would have told me he was burning with fever, likely from something he'd contracted as a result of the drastic changes in temperature. I thought of asking him if he felt all right, but it was pointless. Even if he had been allowed to acknowledge his misery with a heavy frown or a grimace of pain, he would have been expected to pull his weight just the same.

And yet it was not with this porter that the disaster originated.

It was with the rear porter on the opposite side. Perhaps the reason he stumbled was because of the extra weight he was carrying on account of the porter who was ill. I remember feeling an abrupt jerk as someone's foot slipped out from under them and a large stone tumbled down the slope. Because the porter on the opposite side was so sick, he was unable to exert his full effort to try and halt the backward slippage of the carrier. In fact, to save their own lives, both of the rear porters grabbed onto the litter in a feeble attempt to keep from falling. Perhaps if they had just let go, the other four porters might have saved the day. But gravity and momentum were against them. The carrier tore from their grips.

I think the porter who originally lost his footing was killed or knocked unconscious immediately as the litter came down on top of him, grinding him underneath its base for a dozen yards as it slid down the mountain like a sled on a sheet of ice. The other porter tumbled down the cliff face somewhere to my right, his body sometimes appearing as it bounced. The instant that my carrier had started slipping, I had started to scream. This scream persisted until the carrier hit some sort of obstacle. I fell forward, the wind expelling from my lungs. Until that impact I'd managed to keep ahold of little Pill, half-protecting him, half-pretending he was some sort of life preserver, but as the carrier began flipping end over end, he bounced out of my arms. The overhead canopy collapsed. And then the grinding of rock and wood suddenly ceased. The face of the cliff became perfectly sheer. The carrier had started to free-fall.

As I awaited the impact—the moment of my death—I remember inwardly praying that God would release my spirit before I would have to experience that crushing moment of muscle and bone. Time seemed to dilate. I thought I was falling forever. The cliff and the sky were a swirl of colors and lights. I began to wonder if my spirit had been released. I almost believed I was falling upward instead of downward—falling up into heaven.

But then came the splash—an icy explosion of water. The impact stung my flesh. I might have thought I'd crashed through the frozen surface of a lake, but the water was tumbling and churning. I'd fallen into the river. The current was sweeping swiftly through the gorge. I gasped for breath and tried to swim. But I couldn't go anywhere! The collar was still around my neck! The line was tangled in the collapsed poles of the canopy. Every time I tried to push myself to the surface to gulp some air, the line attached to my collar dragged me back under. Something floated beside me. I tried to grab onto it. It was the body of one of my porters, broken and lifeless. The current carried it out of reach. I tried to surge upward again, gulping more water than air. During one of those upward surges I glimpsed something else splash into the water behind me. I assumed it was the body of the other porter.

I searched for a grip on any part of the battered carrier that was still above water. But suddenly we hit a pocket of rapids and the remains of the litter rolled over, dragging me beneath it. One of the poles shifted against my neck. I was pinned underwater, the collar strangling me. I could no longer surge upward. I had sucked my last breath of air.

As my body began convulsing with panic, I sensed movement to my right—another living thing. It drew close enough that I perceived arms and legs flailing, struggling against the current, but there were too many bubbles—too much churning water to sense much else. And then I felt someone's hand grip my arm. I think I may remember another hand grasping the leather around my neck. I also may have sensed the moment when a knife severed the cord that pinned me under the water, setting me free. But somewhere in the scheme of things, I lost consciousness. It was almost as if I fell asleep. The icy water that surrounded me and filled my lungs became like a blanket enveloping my body, providing me with a kind of blissful and transcendent security. I awoke with a grunt as someone pressed against my stomach and chest, forcing the water to spill from both sides of my mouth. I began choking and coughing. When my vision cleared, Marcos was hunched over me, dripping and shivering.

"Oh, thank God," he said. "Thank God."

Strange words from someone who didn't particularly believe in God. My senses returned to me slowly. I focused on the glow of the sun. I could still hear the roar of the river. I realized I was lying on a thin, rocky bank that was snuggled against the side of the cliff. My body was only inches out of the water. I coughed again and spit up more fluid.

"Where are you hurt?" Marcos asked. "What feels broken?"

He sounded so certain that something would be broken that I had to think about it. Maybe my body was still in shock. Maybe my nerve endings were still frozen from the water and I was unable to perceive bruises and broken bones—

No. I could feel the bruises. There was a big one on my hip and another one on my knee. But I'd never had a broken bone before. Maybe everything was broken and I didn't know it.

"I'm not sure," I answered. "I can't tell."

"Don't move until you're sure," said Marcos.

From somewhere up above, a voice shouted down at us. "Is she alive?"

I recognized on a ledge far up the cliff the face of King Jacob of the Moon. His hands were cupped around his mouth to amplify his shouts. There were dozens more faces peering down all along the cliff. Jacob's question echoed three or four times. He waited for Marcos to reply, making no inquiries whatsoever as to the condition of his son.

"Yes!" Marcos shouted back.

Jacob waited for the echoes to die and then asked, "Can she walk?"

"Don't know yet!" Marcos replied.

I made a move to try and sit up.

"Careful," said Marcos. He leaned forward to support my back.

"It's all right," I said. "I don't think anything is broken."

"Nothing?" said Marcos incredulously. "I don't believe it. Your two porters probably died before they hit the water. They floated past us like a couple of logs."

I caught my breath. "Pill?" I cried. "Where's Pill?"

"The dog?" Marcos shook his head, baffled that I would inquire after such a silly thing. "Dead for sure. Likely drowned. We're lucky that we both didn't drown with it."

I remained still for a moment to let this sink in. At last my heart constricted. I began to sob. Perplexed, Marcos watched me. How could he have understood what that dog had come to mean to me? The only living thing in this ancient world that I had really cared for. The only living thing that had really cared for me. The only—

Suddenly I stopped sobbing and looked into Marcos' eyes. A realization of what he'd just done struck me like a revelation.

"You . . . you saved my life," *I said feebly. My voice carried a thread of bewilderment—and astonishment.*

Marcos brushed it away with a look that seemed to say, I only did what anybody would have done. *But I didn't buy this at all. Marcos had jumped from a ledge several hundred feet high and plunged into the churning rapids of an icy river. Only the most optimistic gambler would have given him a fifty-fifty chance of surviving himself—and Marcos had done it all with the unthinkable expectation that he could reach my carrier, free me from the leather collar, and swim me over to shore. To me the question was not* how *he had managed to do it, but* why?

"Why?" *I asked.*

"Because," *he replied,* "you're very important—to my father, Lord Jacob."

I felt my tears turn hot. For a split second I actually believed him. I'd already seen him condone and contribute to atrocities that only maniacs and psychopaths would be involved with. Was it really so extraordinary to believe this same fanatic would risk his life to save me only because I was important to his fanatical cause?

But then I perceived that Marcos was struggling to suppress a grin. Suppressing it, however, only caused it to come forth with a spurt of laughter. I was tempted to smile with him, but I was too overwhelmed with consternation. The laughter seemed to be saying, And if you believe I did that for my father, you'll believe anything. *But the alternative was even more disturbing. Up until now I'd been comfortable believing that Marcos was incapable of any feelings that were truly human. I'd considered any efforts he might have made to show compassion as veiled efforts at manipulation. As my eyes scrutinized him, he lowered his head shyly. He looked vulnerable. For the first time, I began to wonder if somewhere under there a human heart was beating. Perhaps even a human conscience.*

Jacob's voice boomed overhead again. "I'm sending some men to climb down and help!"

Marcos glanced up at his father. When he turned back to me, he looked disappointed. The fantasy was over. Back to reality. I was a prisoner with a defined and specific purpose. Whether he had saved me out of love or duty or temporary insanity, it would have made no difference to his father. Only that I had been saved to fulfill the destiny that the Divine Jaguar had ordained me to fulfill.

But Marcos did not switch back to reality easily. In his eyes I could still see a yearning to linger in the realm of how things could be, or how they might have been, if the circumstances had been different. I hoped no one would interfere if he chose to nourish those feelings. Because I knew if those perspectives ever became pure—if the feelings in his heart were anything like real love—he'd never feel at home in the web of his father again.

CHAPTER 6

Because of the impromptu funeral, we were late getting started on the last leg of our journey to the city of Sidom. Naaman's body was wrapped in his own palm-woven sleeping mat and laid to rest in a grave about four feet deep. We dug it in the softest ground we could find—the lime-colored soil along the banks of the river. Zedekiah pronounced a short eulogy, praising Naaman's life of service to Christ—a cause he had fought for during a time of much war and upheaval, when only the most valiant had remained true to the faith. He then commended the tracker's soul to his Father in Heaven. It was almost noon by the time we started breaking camp and loading the canoes.

Once I spied Harry wander over to the place where Lamachi had been left to lie in the grass with his hands and feet tightly bound. He hadn't spoken a word since Gidgiddonihah and Jonathan had subdued him. And yet he was not silent. All throughout the digging of the grave and the pronouncement of Zedekiah's eulogy and dedication, we could hear him wailing. He sounded like a tormented hound. Because of Lamachi's wails, none of us could bring ourselves to weep for Naaman. The Gadianton's obnoxious laments made grieving seem almost hypocritical.

I should correct that—no one wept for Naaman except Harry. My son hadn't seen an actual corpse since the open-casket funeral of his mother. What he'd seen this morning was, of course, far more shocking. I think the morning's events had left him quite shaken. We were all shaken. Who wouldn't have been shaken to discover a murderer in their midst? But the rest of us were a little better at veiling our emotions.

Nevertheless, it touched me when I saw Harry approach Lamachi and offer him a drink of water. Until now it hadn't even crossed our minds that the prisoner might be thirsty. During the last half hour as we broke camp, Lamachi had been quiet, staring straight ahead. His face and arms remained covered in mud from his struggle on the riverbank. The coating was now cracked and flaking, giving him the appearance of a scaly reptile. He made no effort to accept the drink that Harry offered him. Nor did he acknowledge Harry's presence in any manner.

Harry made two or three attempts to give him water. I tried to guess what was going through my son's mind. If anything, I'd have thought he'd be afraid of Lamachi. He'd feared him plenty just the day before, when Lamachi was still innocent of any serious crime.

"It's very hot," said Harry. "You have to drink."

At that instant Lamachi sprang to life. Like a dog that looks innocent enough until you put forth your hand to pet it, Lamachi glared his teeth and shouted in Harry's face, "LEAVE ME!"

My son fell back on his tailbone and scrambled away. He was still shaking several minutes later.

All our provisions were arranged inside the canoes. The only item that remained to be loaded was Lamachi. We held counsel to decide what was to be done with him.

"We should end it here," said Gidgiddonihah unflinchingly. He turned to Zedekiah. "You have the authority to sentence and execute him right here if you choose to exercise it. I say we finish it now in the eyes of God and be done with it."

Naaman had been Gidgiddonihah's friend. His need for closure to the day's tragic events was understandable. And after all, capital punishment was standard procedure among the Nephites. This would surely become Lamachi's fate sooner or later. Jonathan, however, suggested postponing a death sentence.

"There is always the chance that he will still reveal crucial information about the location of Jacobugath," he said.

Gidgiddonihah scoffed at this. "If he ever reveals anything, it will be at the very last moment, just before the sword drops."

Zedekiah furrowed his brow and paced the riverbank. He appeared torn between reason and emotion. At last he looked up at Gidgiddonihah and heaved a sigh. "I'm sorry. I'm just not comfortable with the idea of executing him here. I feel strongly that we should take him with us to Sidom. However dark Lamachi's crimes—however doomed his soul—I feel compelled to believe that he may yet fulfill a relevant purpose. That is my decision. Perhaps we will understand more when we reach Sidom."

Sullenly, Gidgiddonihah nodded his assent. Lamachi had lapsed back into catatonia. Gidgiddonihah and Jonathan carried him to one of the dugouts and placed him inside. Gidgiddonihah bluntly refused to ride in the same canoe with him, which may have been safer for Lamachi. The lot fell upon Jonathan. Harry and I would ride in one canoe by ourselves.

For the first part of the journey, Harry was absorbed in thought. I tried to start a conversation by mentioning how worried Jenny and Steffanie probably were about him, but this may not have been the best subject to stir his interest in talking.

Finally, he declared to me, "I don't understand, Dad."

"I know it's hard," I acknowledged. "But we should remember, son, Lamachi had dedicated his soul to evil long before he met us. He was raised in a world that we can't even begin to comprehend."

"No," said Harry. "That's not what I don't understand. I don't understand how it could have happened—how it could have been *allowed* to happen."

"What do you mean?"

"I don't understand why we didn't have any warning. I don't understand why the Holy Ghost didn't warn Zedekiah or Nephi or even *you* way back in Zarahemla that this was going to happen. Why did the Lord allow you to bring Lamachi in the first place?"

As a father, it was hard to confess that I had no succinct answer for him. I replied, "We all have our free agency, Harry. Allowing evil to occur is part of the gospel plan."

That didn't sound so bad, I thought. But Harry wasn't satisfied.

"Every morning and noon and night we've been praying that we would be protected. We've been praying that nothing like what happened this morning would ever happen." Tears welled in my son's eyes. "Now Naaman is dead. What went wrong, Dad? How come God didn't hear us? And don't tell me we weren't righteous enough—"

"I wouldn't have said—"

"—because I know that isn't true. Zedekiah is righteous enough all by himself. Maybe God *never* hears prayers. Not really. Maybe we're just on our own down here. Survival of the fittest."

"Harry, your memory is way too short. Think of all the ways that God has helped us so far. Think of—"

"So is that it? God just kinda picks and chooses the times when he's gonna help and the times when he's not? We really don't have any control over it at all, do we?"

"You're right," I confirmed. "We *don't* control it. God is at the reins. We only control our own actions. And one of those actions, as commanded by God, is to pray. It *does* make a difference, Harry. I can't name all the times that it's made a difference in my life. But prayers aren't answered just because we take the trouble to ask. We don't command God. We *trust* God. We trust that when evil is allowed to occur, there's a reason why God doesn't put forth his hand to stop it. Even if that reason is known only to God. Even if it's only so that the judgments that he makes at the last day will be just."

"But *Naaman,*" mourned Harry. "Naaman wasn't . . . Naaman couldn't . . . Why didn't God tell us in time so that we could at least save Naaman?"

"I don't know," I finally confessed. "Maybe it was Naaman's time. Maybe it was necessary that one of us be sacrificed in order to unmask the killer now instead of later, when the situation might have been far more grim."

"But what if Lamachi isn't the killer?"

My eyes widened. The statement had come so far out of left field that I chuckled a little as I replied, "Of course Lamachi is the killer."

"Nobody saw him. He never confessed."

"Don't be ridiculous, Harry. His reaction when he was confronted with the crime was confession enough. What's the matter with you? Yesterday you couldn't stand him. Why all of a sudden do you feel so inclined to defend him? There's no reason to feel sorry for him, Harry. He's a *murderer*. Maybe God will judge him differently because of the way he was brought up, but that doesn't make him innocent."

"I guess—" Harry shifted in his place. "I guess I just think everybody deserves a fair trial."

I couldn't help but smile at my son's naivete. "This is 33 A.D., Harry. It's not our place to question Nephite justice. Maybe that's why Zedekiah didn't have him executed today—in the interest of some sort of fairness.

"I'm sorry," said Harry. "I was being stupid."

I put forth my hand and stroked the back of his head. "I love you, Harry. You have a good heart. And I hope you never lose that."

Harry nodded and picked up the oar, giving the water several easy strokes on either side of the canoe. I sat back and smiled to myself one more time, shaking my head. I looked over at the dugout that carried Lamachi and Jonathan, about ten boat lengths ahead and to our right. Lamachi still sat with his head bowed, expression blank. Jonathan steered.

Not the killer, I thought scoffingly. I sat back and closed my eyes, letting my imagination drift. I found myself drawn back to that stuffy gray room at the police station as I was interviewed by those two hard-nosed police detectives, Riley and Walpole. *Not the killer*. Those words sounded so familiar. A little over a week ago I had used them to describe myself—but nobody was listening. I was almost offended to hear those same words used in connection with a murderer like . . . a murderer like . . .

Suddenly I felt uncomfortable and sat forward.

Casually, I glanced over at Gidgiddonihah and Zedekiah about twelve boat lengths to our left. Zedekiah noticed me. He nodded and sent a melancholy smile. Gidgiddonihah wore a scowl and focused on the river. An uneasy feeling crept over me. I tried to shake it off. The feeling perplexed me. There was no earthly reason for it. Was it my son's offhand remark? I reminded myself that he was a ten-year-old kid. Sure, *I* was innocent. I hadn't killed Doug Bowman. That didn't mean Lamachi was innocent. That didn't mean all murderers caught red-handed were innocent. Sometimes—*most* of the time—accusers were dead right. I drew a deep breath, and at last, thankfully, my feelings of uneasiness passed.

I had to concede, I was becoming legitimately paranoid.

* * *

The colors of night folded over the land long before we reached the city of Sidom. If we had embarked at the hour we'd originally intended, we'd certainly have arrived in daylight. But the sky turned red and then purple. The shy twinkles of stars became bold sparks. Finally, the first clusters of lamplight began to appear along either bank of the river. Over the next hour the number of lights steadily multiplied. It actually sent a glow up into the night sky. The denizens of Sidom seemed obsessed with lanterns and candles and torches, as if they had a neurotic fear of darkness.

Never in all my experience in the ancient world had I ever seen so many lights. It was spectacular. I might have considered it the ancient equivalent of Las Vegas. Points of light shone in windows, on terraces, cornices, and rooftops, along city avenues, and from the bow and stern of every canoe and raft in the river. And of course each of these lights was displayed twice in brilliant reflection on the surface of the water. The brightest beacons were the torch fires that glowed along the riverfront. The poles were as high as modern streetlights and stretched along both banks in perfect symmetry, like a double necklace of iridescent pearls across the throat of night. Maintaining such lights must have been quite a chore. Because of them, my Nephite companions easily identified the feathered flag over a building's doorway that identified it as a traveler's inn.

Gidgiddonihah was the only one among us who'd been to the city previously. As we tethered our canoes to moorings along the shore, I asked him, "What kind of people live here?"

"Traders," he replied. "Sidom is wall-to-wall with traders."

I shuddered as I recalled Kumarcaah, the Pochteca trader. He hadn't left me with a high opinion of the profession. I determined that I had better guard my son closely.

"Are they Nephites?" I asked.

"Some," said Gidgiddonihah. "Not many. Descendants of Mulek mostly, though I doubt they would care to know it."

This matched a description I'd been given of the city when I was thirteen years old. Not much seemed to have changed.

Before we entered the inn, I took in the city skyline and perceived no visible outline of a city wall. Unlike Zarahemla, Sidom had never erected the defensive bulwarks that characterized so many Nephite cities since the days of Captain Moroni. The reason, I came to learn, was that Sidom did not fear invasion. It prided itself on being magnanimously cosmopolitan—the crossroads of the world. All of humankind were equally welcome and had equal rights as citizens. Who would want to invade a city that already belonged to them?

For the last several centuries the land of Sidom had been the most important trade center in the region. Its placement on the River Sidon and its proximity to the borders of the lands of Desolation, Bountiful, and the narrow pass that led into the land northward made it a convenient stopover for all long-distance travelers. Its population was said to be greater than Zarahemla's, although a census might have been misleading since half of its residents at any given moment were traders and pilgrims.

Local leaders had enacted the most liberal laws in all the ancient world. Sidomians believed in all religions and no religions. Tolerance was the most noble of all human attributes. Thus, they tolerated anything and everything. It was said that in the days of Alma the Younger the city had been converted to the gospel. But that was over a century ago.

Because of its transience, most buildings were small and unobtrusive. Few walls had been splashed with paint. One had to search to find the least ornamentation. Contrary to my initial impression because of all the lights, Sidom's appearance in every other way was remarkably dull.

The inn had only the most rudimentary accommodations—a pounded-earth floor with five well-worn sleeping mats in case we hadn't brought our own. There were no bath or steam huts, although we were assured that such facilities existed a short walk inland. The spartan conditions matched our mood, still markedly depressed from the day's events. The innkeeper, a ruddy-cheeked man with a knobby chin, did not even bat an eye at the sight of our bound prisoner. No doubt the sight of human beings shackled and bound was a common sight in this town. Slaves were transported from Sidom to all corners of ancient America.

"Your slave can sleep in the box," said the innkeeper.

The "box" was a wooden cage of sorts at the back of the inn, which could be barricaded on the outside. It looked almost like a dog house. The innkeeper told us it could accommodate up to three prisoners, although to me it looked as if it would be claustrophobically cramped with one.

"There are larger facilities toward the marketplace," said the innkeeper, "but you'll pay double. We'll even guard him, if you like. You can all rest soundly tonight."

Zedekiah suggested removing Lamachi's bonds, but Gidgiddonihah and Jonathan objected. The more security, the better. Gidgiddonihah could only be persuaded to retie the straps and thereby prevent cutting off his circulation.

For dinner we ate fish. The innkeeper boasted that he and his two teenage sons had caught them right off the moorings. I wondered how long ago they had been caught. The odor of fish had been gaggingly potent ever since we'd arrived. As I might have expected, the pinkish flesh tasted exactly like it smelled. As we picked at our food, we discussed our seemingly grim prospects for the future.

"If we let Lamachi live," said Jonathan, "perhaps he will still lead us to Jacobugath. We will keep him in bonds. His destiny will be decided after we get there."

Gidgiddonihah shook his head. "We could never trust him. He would turn on us at the first opportunity." He looked at Zedekiah. "We need to decide his fate *here*, in Sidom, and go on without him."

"But where will we go?" I asked. "Which direction?"

"Northeast," said Gidgiddonihah, "into the land of Desolation. We will make inquiries in every village from here to the mountains."

Zedekiah nodded absently. "This may be our only choice." And then one eye narrowed and his jaw stiffened, as if he winced from some subtle pain deep in his soul.

"What's wrong?" I asked.

He sighed wearily. "I cannot say for certain. I have felt uneasy for many hours."

"We have all felt uneasy," said Jonathan.

"Yes," said Zedekiah. "Perhaps that's all it is." He relaxed for a few seconds, then the pain in his soul seemed to return. "Tomorrow," he continued, "we will try to find Jeremiah. He is a man of keen insight. Perhaps he can shed further light . . ." Zedekiah's voice trailed off as he drifted into other thoughts.

Harry fidgeted when he heard mention of the local Christian leader, Jeremiah. It reminded him that we would soon be separated again. To put it out of his mind, he made up an extra pallet of food.

"Can I give it to Lamachi?" he asked.

Zedekiah nodded. Harry went outside. The rest of us made ready for bed. My son was gone a long time. I finally called him back. When he returned, he looked nervous. He hesitated before entering the room.

"What's wrong?" I asked him.

My son's gaze moved carefully across each person in the room. "Nothing. I'm fine."

"Did Lamachi say something upsetting?"

"Yes," said Harry. "I mean *no*. Nothing upsetting. Just . . . nothing."

"Don't talk to him," said Gidgiddonihah stiffly. "He'll play with your mind, boy. Don't underestimate him."

"Gidgiddonihah's right," said Jonathan. "He can be very clever. Very cunning."

Harry nodded but made no reply. Jonathan and Gidgiddonihah's comments only seemed to vex him further. Zedekiah called us to prayer. I offered it, but my words sounded hollow. It was hard to get into the spirit. My faith was starting to feel the strain. The day had been so black. Melody was still so far away. Despite all our efforts over the past week and a half, our prospects for reaching her now seemed bleaker than ever. My personal prayers started out equally rote, but I persisted and soon I found myself quietly weeping. *What am I doing wrong?* I pleaded. *Please Father, teach me what to do.*

When I had finished, I looked over at Harry. He lay on his sleeping mat, eyes closed. I lay beside him and fell asleep almost as quickly.

I might have slept three or four hours. Something awakened me, and I sat up. Torches still burned outside. Shadows outside the range of the torchlights were thick. I remained still for a moment, trying to figure out what had roused me. Had it been my nightmare? I'd been dreaming that I was back at Doug Bowman's home in Salt Lake City. I saw Doug's body on the floor, but when I turned him over, it was the face of my son. No, it wasn't the nightmare that had roused me. There had been a noise. A disturbance. But I couldn't have said whether it came from outside or inside. My son was still asleep beside me. All the other members of the expedition appeared to be asleep as well.

I went to the doorway and found one of the water skins that we had hung there. I took a long drink. As I wiped my mouth, something compelled me to go outside. There was a slight breeze. The torch flames flickered and smoked. I wandered behind the inn where Lamachi was imprisoned. As the outline of the box came into view, I became indignant. The innkeeper had not kept his promise. No guard had been posted.

As I drew closer, I realized that the barricades on the cage had been removed. The box lay open—empty! The tethers that had bound Lamachi's hands and feet lay in the dirt. My heart-beat took off like a boat motor. I gripped the nape of the water skin as if in the dark it might resemble a weapon. I searched the shadows for movement.

Someone's footstep crunched behind me. I spun around. Three feet away stood a large man, his face dark in silhouette.

"Jonathan!" I shouted.

Jonathan stepped forward. "What's going on?" he asked, his tone accusing.

"Lamachi's gone!" I reported.

Jonathan pushed me out of his way and took three strides toward the open box. He peered inside, then abruptly turned back to me.

"Where is he? Where did he go?"

Jonathan's tone made me feel defensive, as if he thought I had something to do with Lamachi's escape.

"I don't know," I replied. "I heard a noise and came outside. I found it exactly as you see it."

Jonathan scanned the area. He marched past me and stomped back into the inn. He entered the innkeeper's room and yanked the poor man out of his bed.

"Our prisoner's gone!" he screamed into the innkeeper's face. "Where is the guard? You promised there would be a guard!" He carried the innkeeper outside by the scruff of the neck.

"There was no need," the startled innkeeper defended. "He was bound. I did not think—I did not see any danger of—"

"Well look for yourself!" cried Jonathan. "He's gone!"

The innkeeper's sons followed their father outside. Gidgiddonihah, Zedekiah, and Harry arrived as well.

"I assure you, we will accept full responsibility," promised the innkeeper. "Your slave will be replaced."

"He's not a slave!" gruffed Jonathan. "He was a prisoner—a criminal!"

"Oh, dear," muttered the innkeeper. He turned and scolded his sons. "Who's fault is this? Who was supposed to watch the box?"

The sons looked at each other, bewildered. Obviously neither of them had been assigned this responsibility. The innkeeper was feebly trying to pass the buck.

Gidgiddonihah knelt and picked up one of the tethers that had bound Lamachi's limbs. "This cord has been severed," he said. "Lamachi had help."

Jonathan glowered at the innkeeper and his sons. "Which one of you helped him escape?" Then he looked at me and snapped, *"Which one?"*

I couldn't believe he was including me in the list of suspects. "Are you serious?" I asked. "I was only investigating a noise. Why would *I* have released him?"

Jonathan sighed. "I'm sorry."

Gidgiddonihah stood again. "He can't have gotten far. We'll spread out."

Jonathan and Zedekiah took off in one direction. Gidgiddonihah, the innkeeper, and his sons took off in another. I was about to follow after Jonathan when Harry grabbed the hem of my cloak.

"Stop, Dad," Harry said.

"Harry, there's no time!"

"Dad, listen . . . It was me."

"Huh?"

"I let him go."

"YOU DID WHAT?"

"I came out here while everyone was sleeping. You woke up just as I was laying back down. Lamachi didn't do it, Dad. He didn't kill Naaman."

"How can you say that, Harry? What have you *done?*" It was all I could do to keep from shaking him senseless.

"I believe him, Dad."

"Weren't you listening to Gidgiddonihah and Jonathan last night? Didn't you hear them tell you that Lamachi would play games with your head? He *used* you, Harry! Why didn't you come to me?"

"Because you would have acted just like you're acting now. You wouldn't have believed me. You wouldn't have listened to Lamachi. He knows who the killer really is."

"Why would he tell just you? Why wouldn't he tell everyone?"

"Actually, he wouldn't even tell me."

"He wouldn't *tell* you? Harry this is so—"

"But he said he would tell *you*. He's really scared, Dad. I think he believes the minute he tells, he'll die. Almost like a curse. But he said he's willing to die if it's you that he tells."

"Where is he, Harry?"

"Hiding. Over there."

Harry pointed toward a group of buildings somewhat apart from any others down the river. They looked older and unused. Unlike the rest of the city, there were very few lanterns burning in that district.

I grabbed Harry's arm. "Let's find the others."

"No, Dad! *Just you!* He said if we didn't come alone, he wouldn't talk."

"Harry, has it crossed your mind that this might be a trap? That Lamachi will try to murder us both the way he murdered Naaman?"

"He didn't murder Naaman."

"How do you *know* that, Harry?"

"Think about it, Dad. Just think. Who slept closest to Naaman that night?"

I tried to recall. "Jonathan. And Gidgiddonihah. So?"

"Lamachi slept over by the brush, away from everyone else. You remember that reddish grass?"

"What does this have to do with—?"

"Dad, you remember how it crackled?"

"Yeah. Sure. The grass. It crackled."

"Do you really think Lamachi could have gone all the way across that grass and poked Naaman with those poison things without waking up Gidgiddonihah or Jonathan?"

I almost replied with utmost impatience, *Lamachi is a sorcerer! He could have done anything he wanted!* But I stopped myself and tried to consider the matter logically. Gidgiddonihah was a trained warrior. Jonathan had once professed that he slept as lightly as a waterskipper skips. It was hard to believe that Lamachi's movements would not have roused one or both.

"Are you saying that Jonathan or Gidgiddonihah is the killer?"

"I don't know, Dad. But Lamachi knows."

What my ten-year-old son was suggesting made sense. Why hadn't I seen it myself? All of us were so focused on Lamachi! He'd already shown so much evidence of his instability. Our prejudice had been so ingrained that all Gadianton initiates would kill anyone who sought Jacobugath. And yet it would have been so easy for either Gidgiddonihah or Jonathan to reach over and prick Naaman's shoulder with a poison dart. It would have disturbed no one. Gidgiddonihah claimed to be Naaman's friend. Was it all a ruse to keep suspicions at bay? The darts had belonged to Jonathan in the first place. Had he made up the story about them having been stolen?

"All right, Harry," I said. "We'll go to Lamachi. But stay close to me. If anything happens, I want you to run. At least he won't be armed."

"He is armed, Dad. With a knife."

"What?"

"I stole Gidgiddonihah's knife to cut Lamachi free. He took it with him."

"You stole Gid—!" I stopped and started counting to ten. When I regained my composure, I took Harry's arm again. "Let's go."

It occurred to me that Lamachi's possession of a knife might be further evidence of his innocence. If he was a murderer, he could have easily slit my son's throat then and there. Then again, maybe he'd thought out the whole thing far more carefully than I could have expected. As Harry and I moved through the darkened streets of Sidom, it struck me that Lamachi might have avoided killing my son in order set his bait for a bigger prize—to get Harry and me alone and away from the others, where he could kill us both with relative ease. Was Lamachi really that clever? I had to concede that he might be.

If I'd learned one thing in all my experience, past and present, it was never to underestimate the cunning of a Gadianton.

CHAPTER 7

There were spaces in the sapling walls and in the thatched roofs of the abandoned buildings that gave off a mournful whistle as the night breeze hit them just right. Harry and I treaded lightly down the middle of the avenue, expecting that Lamachi would reveal himself without forcing us to call his name. By walking in the middle of the street there was also less chance that he could ambush us from some dark corner if it turned out that his motives were as murderous as I'd first suspected.

Harry and I soon realized that from the inn, our view toward these buildings had been deceiving. The buildings were not an isolated cluster as we'd first thought, or as Lamachi had thought when he'd selected them as a rendezvous point. The structures crawled along the shore of the Sidon farther than we could have judged. The area reeked of sour smells: urine, defecation, and rotting fish. I surmised that many of these buildings sat abandoned only during certain times of the year. At other seasons they were active ports for hauling in fish from the river—a breed that was probably more appetizing than the one we had been served for dinner. At certain places near the water the ground glistened with old, dried fish scales like a beach covered with gems.

Once my son and I chanced upon a brood of nine or ten sleeping bodies. Beggars, I assumed. If it hadn't been the weariest time of the night, the lot of them would have likely tried to rob us of whatever we were carrying and stomp us as flat as tortillas. As it was, they barely stirred. We passed among them without incident.

We'd gone almost the equivalent of two city blocks when Harry turned to me and said, "We must have missed him."

"All right," I sighed. "We'll backtrack."

"This time," said Harry, "I think we should call his name—softly."

We made our way back toward the inn, but by a slightly varied route set in farther from the river—a route that was better lit and would avoid the sleeping beggars. We walked alongside a smelly gutter constructed of flat chunks of sandstone laid together like a mosaic and sloping from either side to create a depression in the middle. Unlike the sewage canals of Zarahemla (when they were in good repair), these ditches did not have regular flowing water to carry off the refuse. I judged that the gutter may not have run at all except when it rained, leaving the waste material to stagnate and decay. We saw plenty of rats and other vermin scurry back into the shadows at our approach.

When we had backtracked about a block, our spines went rigid at the cry of a human voice. Someone was yelling—a gasping kind of yell, as if the person were warding off blows.

"It's Lamachi!" Harry cried.

We veered toward the sound of the struggle. As we emerged from between two buildings, we saw Gidgiddonihah leaning over Lamachi. The Gadianton teenager was face down on the ground. The knife that Harry had given to him lay in the dirt about four yards away. Apparently, the powerful Gidgiddonihah had tackled him. I had the impression that he may have knocked Lamachi's head once against the ground to insure that he caused no more trouble. Lamachi was not moving. Whether he was unconscious or dead, I couldn't tell.

The instant that Harry and I appeared, Gidgiddonihah shot erect, as if we had startled him. As we came into the light, he looked visibly relieved.

"Oh, it's you," he said. "Never know who you'll meet in these streets."

Harry and I remained still and watched Gidgiddonihah very carefully. I grasped Harry's shoulder to draw him closer. My primal instincts warned me to take my son and run while I could. Standing before us was a Nephite warrior capable of killing us instantly in a dozen different ways if we let him get close enough. Harry's eyes were drawn to Lamachi on the ground.

"Did you . . . kill him?" he asked.

"I don't know," said Gidgiddonihah. He turned Lamachi onto his back. Lamachi was bleeding from a gash in his forehead. Gidgiddonihah put his ear close to Lamachi's mouth and nose to feel if he was breathing. "Yeah, he's alive." Gidgiddonihah sounded almost disappointed. "I bashed his head a good one, but I expect he'll recover soon enough. Not that it matters. In the morning, I'll see him executed whether Zedekiah approves it or not. I'll not tolerate any more trouble from this one."

Harry and I exchanged a surreptitious glance. We knew we had found our killer. It had been Gidgiddonihah all along. Now he'd rendered the only witness who might have proven his guilt incapable of testifying. But if this was true, why couldn't I bring myself to run? As Gidgiddonihah arose and started toward us, my legs wouldn't move. Were they frozen with fear? Had I become like the petrified prey, consigned to my fate?

No.

I didn't run because somewhere inside I still felt a twinge of uncertainty. I wanted Gidgiddonihah to say something more—divulge one more shred of evidence to cast away that last spark of doubt that he was indeed a cold-hearted murderer.

At that instant more people arrived, also alerted by Lamachi's yells. One path brought Jonathan. Another brought the innkeeper and his sons.

Jonathan approached the unconscious Lamachi. "You got him!" he said to Gidgiddonihah excitedly. "Well done!"

"Yes," said Gidgiddonihah. "You better help me carry him back to the inn before he wakes."

"Before he wakes?" Jonathan sounded surprised. "Is he still alive?"

Lamachi stirred and released a groan.

"Why did you let him live?" Jonathan complained.

"We'll execute him properly," said Gidgiddonihah, "in the eyes of God. All condemned men should have a chance to confess their guilt and prepare their souls as much as it may be possible to meet their Maker. It's only civilized."

"*Civilized?*" scoffed Jonathan. "I feel no need to hear his confessions. Let's get it over with."

Jonathan drew his knife and moved toward Lamachi. Gidgiddonihah grabbed Jonathan's arm. He found a pressure point on Jonathan's wrist and disarmed him so cleanly that an observer might have thought that Jonathan had simply dropped the weapon into Gidgiddonihah's palm.

"It can wait until morning," he said to Jonathan firmly. "What's come over you? Are you so eager to see blood spilled, Jonathan? A few hours ago you pleaded to let him live and guide us the rest of the way to Jacobugath."

"That was before his rebellion. Before he tried to escape."

Gidgiddonihah's ears perked up. "Rebellion? What do you mean?"

Jonathan struggled to modify his unusual word choice. "What I mean is, that was before I realized how much difficulty he could cause."

Gidgiddonihah hesitated before he released Jonathan's shoulder. He studied the eyes of the man I'd once called a gentle giant. Jonathan found it difficult to return the gaze. He reached out his hand for Gidgiddonihah to give back the knife. Gidgiddonihah retained his grip on the weapon as he inquired, "Where is Zedekiah?"

"We, uh—we separated," said Jonathan. "He went into a neighborhood north of here."

"Separated?" said Gidgiddonihah dubiously. "Why would he separate from you, Jonathan? Is Elder Zedekiah a fighter all of a sudden? Did he think he could apprehend Lamachi by himself?"

"Actually," said Jonathan, laughing uneasily, "I lost him. I'm afraid his old legs do not move very swiftly." He withdrew his hand, abandoning his hope that Gidgiddonihah would return the knife. "By now he's probably back at the inn. Come. We'd better join him."

Jonathan turned his back and started walking in the direction of the inn. I watched Gidgiddonihah unstrap the sheath on his belt that carried the small copper hatchet. Jonathan had only made it six steps by the time Gidgiddonihah filled his hand with the weapon.

"Jonathan, stop!" warned Gidgiddonihah. "Or I'll split you in two. You know I could do it from here without aiming."

Jonathan stopped, but he did not turn around.

"Now tell me again," Gidgiddonihah demanded. "Where is Zedekiah?"

Jonathan made no reply. Nor did he move. Instinctively, I maneuvered Harry behind me, wary that violence was about to erupt.

When Jonathan turned, he did so slowly, carefully. He kept his hands hidden in front. As he turned, I realized why they'd been hidden. From his tunic, Jonathan had produced his 20-inch reed blowpipe. The end was already set to his lips.

He raised the blowgun and with a puff of his cheeks, expelled a poison-tipped dart. It stuck in the flesh of Gidgiddonihah's neck just as he raised the hatchet overhead. Gidgiddonihah was so startled by the sudden sting in his throat that it impaired his aim. Either that or Jonathan's attempt to dodge it by dropping low succeeded. The hatchet struck the wall of one of the buildings and fell harmlessly to the dirt.

Jonathan did not hesitate. With lightning dexterity he slipped another dart into the blowgun and expelled it into the belly of the innkeeper. Before I even had a chance to register what was happening, another tiny missile came rocketing at me. I threw myself backwards. I felt what I thought was the dart hitting my arm. But I felt no pain—no sting. Had the poison numbed the nerve? I looked at my mantle. I saw the dart embedded in the weavings of my sleeve. It had not pierced my skin.

Harry did not forget my warning to run at the first sign of danger. He fled back between the buildings. The innkeeper's two teenage sons also tried to escape, but they were not so lucky. As they ran, darts hit both of them in the back.

The innkeeper staggered and lost consciousness almost immediately. His sons virtually dropped where they stood. Not so with the powerful Gidgiddonihah. Although he initially fell to one knee, he found one last surge of strength and lunged at Jonathan. He wrapped his fingers around the giant man's throat. The two men rolled, but after a few seconds, Gidgiddonihah lost his battle with the poison. His eyes began to blink rapidly. Finally, he sank onto Jonathan's chest, unmoving.

Jonathan took a moment to recover. At last, he angrily heaved the unconscious Gidgiddonihah off to the side. Panting, he found his feet and brushed off some of the dust. He straightened up and took in the silent bodies that surrounded him. Incredibly, Jonathan had gotten off five darts in less than fifteen seconds. Only Harry had escaped.

I didn't dare move from the precise spot where I had fallen. I thinned my eyes to slits and lay perfectly still to give the impression that I was unconscious and breathing as shallowly as the others. Jonathan placed his hands on his hips in triumph. He laughed once and smirked to himself.

It had all been too easy.

He retrieved the blowgun and his knife from the ground. Then he walked over to where Lamachi was stretched out. After studying him for a moment, he kicked the teenager's hip.

"Get up," he told him.

Lamachi didn't move. Jonathan reached down with both hands and grasped his shoulder and a tuft of hair. He hoisted the boy to his feet.

"I said get up, you wretched little coward!"

It was clear that Lamachi was perfectly conscious. He'd probably been awake for some time. Jonathan held Lamachi's forehead close to his own. The gash above Lamachi's eyebrow continued to bleed. With trembling hands, he attempted to wipe the blood from his eye.

Jonathan maintained a grip on Lamachi's hair and slapped him back and forth. "Who helped you?" he demanded. "Who let you escape?"

"It was the boy!" Lamachi confessed. "It was Harry!"

"Harry!" Jonathan raised his eyebrows in surprise. Then he shook Lamachi, as if trying to dislodge information the way a mugger might dislodge loose change. "What did you tell him?"

"Nothing!" Lamachi sobbed. "I didn't tell him anything!"

Jonathan slapped him again. "But you *wanted* to tell, didn't you? You were *planning* to tell, weren't you? Don't try to lie to me, you miserable cur!"

"Yes," Lamachi peeped. "Yes."

"Why, Lamachi? Why would you betray your people twice? Didn't I promise you in the canoe? Didn't I promise that I would protect you? That I would give you a chance to redeem your sorry soul? And this is the gratitude you show me?" Jonathan delivered his hardest blow yet, this time releasing Lamachi's hair so that he could crumple to the ground. Immediately, Lamachi crawled back to Jonathan's feet and groveled.

"I'm sorry, my master. I'm sorry."

"Don't you call me master. You're not worthy to be my servant. If you were any kind of worthy servant you would have already known me. You would have met me over a year ago. I have personally received all new initiates from the land of Zarahemla into the order of the Third Tier for the last two years. You should have reached the Third Tier when you were sixteen. Are you even of the *Second* Tier, Lamachi, descendant of Kishkumen?"

"Yes," said Lamachi, his face still in the dirt. "I am of the Second Tier."

"Then the Christians were right. You *do* know the way to Jacobugath. Did you actually plan to take these snivelers all the way to the throne of King Jacob, or did you intend to be obedient to your oath and slay them in the wilderness? Again, don't try to lie to me!"

Lamachi answered nothing.

Jonathan sighed like a disappointed parent. "I thank the Divine Jaguar that your father, Jephunni, did not live to see your disgrace. I want you to know something, Lamachi. When I arrived in Nephi's compound the morning before the

Christians departed, my intentions were to assassinate you before the sun had set. I volunteered for this bumbling expedition only because I saw you in the gathering. I was tempted to slit your throat the instant you agreed to help them. Don't you realize what you could have done? How futile it was to even try? If these fools had succeeded in liberating those prisoners it might have threatened everything Lord Jacob of the Moon is trying to accomplish. Did you forget the dream so soon, Lamachi? The very core of our existence? *One land, one king!*"

"But Christians seek the same thing, Master Jonathan," Lamachi whimpered. "Only they seek to do it without war and blood. The one king will be Jesus."

Jonathan's face wrenched with outrage. He kicked Lamachi in the stomach and sent him tumbling.

"I recite the sacred watchwords, and you insult me with this Christian feculence? Stand up, Lamachi. Let's go. On your feet."

Lamachi was very reluctant, fearing he'd only be knocked down again. Nevertheless, there was no disobeying the Master of the Third Tier. Clutching at his ribs, he pushed himself up on one knee. Shakily, he arose the rest of the way.

Jonathan suddenly grew remarkably calm. "Well, Lamachi, I understand now why your clan wanted you eliminated. You have sought to divorce your soul from the Omnipotent One— as if this were possible. From your infancy you have been taught the penalty for attempting a blasphemy so severe. Can you pronounce it?"

Lamachi mumbled something under his breath.

"Say it louder!" Jonathan barked.

"Death," Lamachi repeated.

"And what will be the state of your soul in the underworld?"

Lamachi's spirit was utterly broken. "Torture and torment for all eternity."

"Correct," said Jonathan. "Your death is a penalty that I cannot repeal."

"Yes, Master Jonathan," he whispered, his eyes downcast.

"But I *can* grant you an opportunity for your soul's eventual deliverance from the tortures of Akmul. Fetch the knife."

Jonathan indicated the stone blade that my son had swiped from Gidgiddonihah—the one Lamachi had dropped when Gidgiddonihah tackled him.

Lamachi picked it up.

"Find the boy," Jonathan directed. "Redeem yourself by making of the child's flesh an offering to the Divine Jaguar. I assume you still know how?"

"I do, Master Jonathan."

"Afterwards, I will grant you the dignity to take your own life. And I promise that your suffering in the underworld will have an eventual end."

Lamachi actually looked relieved at this. "Thank you, Master Jonathan."

"I expect you to finish with the boy by the time I finish with the others."

"Will you kill them all, Master Jonathan?"

"No," said Jonathan sarcastically. "I plan to revive them and throw a festival! Of *course* I will kill them. I'd have preferred to have waited until we reached the borders of Jacobugath where I could present their hearts at the Heart of the World, but this will do."

"You will use a blade?" Lamachi inquired. "Not set their souls to sleeping, like Naaman?"

"I've only two darts left," said Jonathan. "To stop their hearts I would need three apiece. What does it matter to you how they die? Get out of here before I revoke my offer. When you've finished the ritual, bring the boy's heart to me. I'll either be here or down that street, where I left the body of their illustrious spiritual leader."

Lamachi turned to depart.

"Oh, and Lamachi—"

Lamachi turned back.

Jonathan eyed the teenager menacingly. "You know better than to try to escape from me, don't you?"

Lamachi cast his eyes down again. "Yes, Master Jonathan."

"Then go!"

Lamachi was off like a shot to prosecute the final act of his life—to find and murder my son. I realized if he found him,

Harry would probably come out of the shadows in perfect trust. I continued to lie as flaccid as a corpse. However, if Jonathan moved any closer he'd easily hear how my breathing had grown quite heavy and erratic. As I'd feared, he did exactly that. He began to move closer, knife in hand.

Jonathan mumbled to himself, "In the meantime, I'll start with this impostor from the world beyond Jacob's cavern."

I knew what I had to do. The dart! I had to retrieve the dart from my sleeve. I could jab it into Jonathan's leg as he came near. But first I had to get it. Precious seconds. I could just as easily prick myself in the process. But I had to try.

My hand jumped to my sleeve. I extracted the dart from the weavings. But I was too slow! How could I have moved any faster? My movement startled Jonathan. He stopped. He was still too far away. I couldn't reach him!

Jonathan's hand slipped into his tunic. In this position I was no match for his blowgun. My plan had failed! In a panic, I scrambled to my feet and flung myself between the same pair of buildings through which my son had escaped. Still off-balance, I rammed my shoulder against a corner post. The impact jarred me upright, and the poison-tipped dart dropped from my fingers. I left it behind. My legs picked up momentum. I could hear Jonathan's footsteps taking up the pursuit.

I leaped the sewage ditch and zigzagged into another alleyway to try to avoid making myself a target. I did not know Jonathan's range of accuracy, but I wasn't about to find out by running in a straight line. I crossed another street and nearly garroted myself on a clothesline. Pushing aside someone's damp laundry, I veered again and ran full force down a long avenue away from the river. Choking for breath, I called out, "Harry! Harry!"

I hadn't seen Lamachi. Perhaps he'd already found my son. Perhaps he'd already begun his ritual. I looked back. Jonathan was not following. Had he given up the pursuit? Had he returned to finish off the others before he came after me? I couldn't take that chance. He could easily be stalking me along a parallel street. So I continued running and calling Harry's name.

I must have gone the equivalent distance of three or four

modern city blocks before exhaustion forced me to stop and bend over, resting my hands on my knees. But I didn't pause long. I veered again, this time to the left. Somehow I had to find a way to circle back. If there was still a chance, I had to try to find my son before Lamachi.

A short distance further, the street turned into mud. I was back near the river, or at least near one of its swampy tributaries. Many of the buildings in this district were elevated on stilts, much like Samuel's house in the land of Melek. Each of my steps was accompanied by a splash and suck as I pulled my heel from the muck. I continued to call out Harry's name, keeping my voice low, for whatever purpose that might have served. At this time of night every sound, no matter how slight, seemed to carry across the entire breadth of the city. Jonathan could have followed my voice as easily as my son.

Once when I whispered Harry's name, I glimpsed a shape moving behind the stilts of one of the buildings. At first there was no way of telling whether it was a beggar, a mugger, Lamachi, or Jonathan. But then the shape replied to my whisper.

"Dad?"

Tears of relief sprang from my eyes. I ran toward my son, my sandals heavy with clods of mud. The water was nearly to my knees when Harry and I embraced. But we didn't linger. I had to get my son to a safe place. And then I had to find a way to reach Zedekiah and Gidgiddonihah. Was it too late to save them? My gut feeling said yes. They were already dead. Harry and I were alone now. There was nothing left. But I couldn't think about this. I couldn't give up. I would *never* give up.

"Come on!" I said to Harry.

No sooner had I set him back on his feet than I heard the puff of Jonathan's blowgun. I saw the black-tipped needle suddenly appear between Harry's shoulder blades. My son gave a short gasp. He looked up into my eyes and uttered, "Dad, Dad," with only the subtlest hint of panic, as if everything remained in my control. As if the mere fact that I was still holding him meant that he would be perfectly safe. But then my son's eyes rolled back into his head. His chin dropped onto his chest.

I raised my eyes and saw Jonathan, a black wraith against the torchlight. The glow illuminated his face just enough to perceive a grin climbing his cheeks. His final dart was already loaded in the blowgun. He raised the pipe to his lips.

I hoisted Harry into my arms. Each of my trudging steps created an explosive splash that splattered us with water and mud. And then I felt the prick in the small of my back. This time it stung. But the pain didn't endure. It spread out from the point of impact until it filtered into every limb and became warm . . . almost soothing . . . almost blissful.

I dropped my son into the muddy water and collapsed onto my knees. It was over. I had lost. Here in the dank streets of Sidom, our expedition had met its end. A rushing sound filled my ears, like a waterfall, or perhaps applause. Yes, applause. The forces of hell were applauding their champion. I turned my head and looked at Jonathan. He was walking toward us. His movements appeared as if they digressed into slow motion . . . slower . . . and slower.

My eyelids blinked. It seemed the longest time before they reopened. When they did, Jonathan was much closer. He was now horizontal instead of vertical. That is, I was horizontal. The side of my face was cushioned in mud. Still in slow motion, I watched as Jonathan suddenly turned. His mouth was agape in surprise. Something was rushing at him, but my vision had grown blurry. I couldn't perceive who or what it was. But I remember a single note of music, long and drawn out, like the pluck of a piano key with the sustain pedal depressed. It drowned out every other sound in my ears. In retrospect I think it might have been a human scream. Jonathan and the rushing shape merged. I might have seen the light reflect off an obsidian blade, but the brightness of that reflection soon filled my entire frame of vision. And then the brightness turned gray, and then it darkened.

And finally, it went black.

* * *

I believe I was awake long before I had the strength to open my eyes. When I finally convinced my muscles to pry them open, the world was a much lighter place. The daylight was subdued, like at sunrise. Overhead a pale canopy gently flapped in a light breeze. I managed to turn my head. Beside me lay two other bodies. One was my son. The other was Zedekiah. Both remained perfectly unconscious.

I rolled my head back to look in the other direction and found myself staring up into the rapt face of Gidgiddonihah. Beyond him sat a dark-complexioned girl, about Melody's age. Her attention was focused on three more bodies stretched out at her feet—the innkeeper and his sons. Only the oldest of the sons was beginning to stir. I tried to raise my head.

"Easy," Gidgiddonihah said. "It's no use to try and do too much at once. You'll just fall asleep again. I've been awake almost three hours and my muscles still feel like I've been wrestling all day with a jaguar."

I opened my mouth to speak, but Gidgiddonihah saved me the trouble.

"Jonathan is dead," he reported. "Lamachi killed him. Thrust him through with my own blade." Gidgiddonihah showed me the knife. Blood stains were still visible in the grooves. "And then Lamachi carried us here. But don't ask me any more than that. I've told you all I know."

Gidgiddonihah pressed his forehead to relieve a headache. I could feel a headache coming on as well. I rolled my head back again and looked at Zedekiah and my son.

"How . . . ?"

Gidgiddonihah finished for me. "How are they? Well, they're breathing, if that's what you want to know. How long they'll remain unconscious is anybody's guess. But they have the rest of the night ahead of them. Hopefully they'll be fine by morning."

"Morning?" I said, puzzled. "But I thought . . . it *was* morning."

Gidgiddonihah chuckled. "I'm afraid you're off by about twelve hours. The sun is sinking, not rising. We've all been unconscious at least sixteen hours. At least I *hope* that's all it's been. For all I know, we might have been lying here for two or three days. That arrow-poison is nasty stuff."

"Yes," I agreed sleepily.

My state of grogginess reminded me of how it felt when I woke up after having my tonsils removed. As a matter of fact, that moment when I fell unconscious was not unlike the sensations I experienced as the anesthesiologist put me under, telling me to count backwards from one hundred. I think I only made it to ninety-seven. Maybe the anesthesia and the poison were made up of the same stuff.

"Where are we?" I asked.

"Back at the inn. That girl—the innkeeper's daughter—put up the canopy so we could be outside where it's cool."

"Where's Lamachi?"

"Getting us some food. I must say, I was pretty shaken a few hours ago when I woke up to see his face leaning over me. Fortunately, I was too weak or I'd have broken his neck then and there. This gave him time to explain. He showed me Jonathan's body down by the moorings to prove it. I don't know how he did it. I don't even know why. Not that it matters. The boy did a remarkable thing. Remarkable."

Lamachi soon returned with a large plate of the awful-smelling fish that we'd eaten the night before. This time I wouldn't be so finicky. I felt famished. Lamachi was so pleased to see me awake that his eyes welled up with tears. He embraced me with the same childlike exuberance I'd seen him exhibit on the day of his baptism. With as much strength as I could muster, I embraced him back. Not many human beings in his life had ever embraced him in sincere friendship, and fewer still with the love of a father, so he held on as long as he could. I didn't resist. Tears pricked at my eyes as well.

Lamachi's whole countenance looked markedly different, as if it had been lightened by a thousand pounds. I couldn't help but think back on Naaman's words when he said that a Gadianton could never truly change his heart. Or even Shemnon's conviction that no oath-bound Gadianton could ever escape the chains of the Evil One. Never again would I doubt the range of the Savior's grasp when reaching out to any human soul who could still cry out for help and healing.

Undoubtedly Lamachi still had many spiritual struggles ahead, many misconceptions to be corrected, and many sleepless nights to come as he struggled to root out the last of the demons who fought to repossess his soul, but I was determined that I would be there for him whenever I could to remind him in whose name all such battles should be waged. The name of Christ.

For the remainder of the evening, I stayed at my son's bedside. During this time Gidgiddonihah made inquiries concerning the Christian leader, Jeremiah. Local merchants told him that every Christian in Sidom had departed about five days previously. It was rumored that they were traveling to Bountiful. Apparently Jeremiah had had the same spiritual promptings as Nephi and Samuel.

When Gidgiddonihah reported to me that Jeremiah was already gone, I received the information with mixed emotions. Harry still hadn't recovered. I'd begun to fear the poison would affect him more severely than an adult, even to point of brain damage. In light of this, it was difficult for me to feel remorseful when I was informed that I would not have the opportunity to leave my son in the hands of perfect strangers. After all we'd been through together, I don't know if I could have left him. When Harry finally recovered sometime in the middle of the night—groggy, but perfectly sound and healthy—I feared for his welfare again. Our expedition was no place for a ten-year-old. But the fact was, I had run out of options. Harry had no place else to go. I would keep him at my side all the way to the borders of Jacobugath. From there, I hoped a better option would reveal itself.

Zedekiah did not awaken that night. Nor did he awaken the following morning. I don't know if his dose of poison was more potent or if his frail constitution had magnified its effects. He did not finally awaken until two or three hours after we had already set out on the last leg of our journey down the Sidon River, our canoes bristling with freshly purchased swords and spears from the markets of Sidom. By the time we reached the landing where we abandoned our canoes for good and started on foot toward a range of jagged, snow-capped peaks to the northwest, we all felt fully recovered and strong.

Because of the evils inflicted by Jonathan of Gideon we had lost nearly two precious days of travel time. I tried not to mourn the point, but in my heart I now conceded that it was unlikely that we would ever reach Melody before she arrived in King Jacob's dark city. But could we arrive in time to save her life? It would take a miracle. Miracles were the fruits of faith and determination.

These were about the only two commodities I had left.

PART FOUR:
TRIALS OF
DESOLATION

CHAPTER 8

The warriors of Jacob arrived. They helped Marcos and me climb out of the river gorge. The bruise on my hip hurt badly. I was afraid to put my full weight on that leg, so at certain junctures Marcos practically carried me.

Even though there were two or three hours of daylight left, the men of Jacob were busily setting up camp. I'm sure if King Jacob had believed that Marcos and I could still travel despite our trauma and injuries, we'd have continued on until darkness. As it was, the company found a place in the cliffs wide enough to hoist the tents and build fires from the scrub brush that grew out of the crags and cracks in the rock.

Marcos received one or two pats on the back for his efforts at saving my life, but overall they fussed over us very little. Balam the Diviner came forward to examine our injuries, but one icy look from me told him that if he tried to touch me, I'd tear his eyes out.

My clothes were damp from the river and filthy from the climb. Earlier in the day our company had come across the hovel of a mountain hermit. In exchange for his life, the hermit had given one of the warriors his thick, shaggy coat. The warrior had doubtless hoped to use the coat against the cold that night, but to his disappointment, Marcos requisitioned it and offered it to me.

Before removing my damp clothes, I draped the coat around me like a blanket. Marcos looked in the opposite direction as I handed him my grungy wrap-around skirt and pullover. It really wasn't necessary for him to look away. Inside that coat I must have looked like a tiny Indian squaw in a gargantuan buffalo hide. I don't even think my toes showed. Still, I appreciated the show of respect.

Only in size did the coat resemble a buffalo hide. It was remarkably comfortable. The texture was like wool, but far more silky. I couldn't have guessed what kind of animal it had come from. Marcos took my clothes to be washed and dried near one of the fires. He also went to find himself a fresh mantle and breechcloth.

I sat near the wall of the cliff, where I was partially protected from the wind. I ran the events of the day through my mind and thanked my Heavenly Father that I had survived. But at the same time, I mourned the loss of my little dog, Pill.

I tried to forget about him, but it was impossible considering the scene taking place before my eyes. Jacob's men were rounding up the remainder of the pudgy little dogs that had crossed the mountains with us. Their numbers had dwindled from thirty to about twelve. The majority had already been eaten, although I guessed that some had died along the trail for lack of food and water at the higher altitudes. Since tomorrow's journey looked equally desolate, several of Jacob's men had decided it would be best to finish them off tonight rather than waste perfectly good food.

Most of the dogs gave the warriors very little trouble, indifferently allowing themselves to be snatched up. But I found myself rooting for one particular little dog who seemed to inspire genuine frustration. Two of the men, while trying to knock it senseless with a club, had knocked themselves senseless instead as they tripped onto their faces. I found the last stumble particularly comical and allowed myself the satisfaction of laughing out loud.

At the sound of my laughter, the little dog halted in its tracks and turned its nose toward me. Encouraged by its hesitation, the fallen warrior scuffled to his feet and resumed the chase. The dog bounded in my direction, the warrior close on its tail. As it drew near, it began to bark. Well, I don't know if you could call it a bark. These little dogs didn't really have voices. It might be more accurate to say it began coughing at me. It was clear that the animal was pleading for protection. It leaped into my lap just as the warrior raised his club to strike. I leaned over to shield it.

"Leave it alone!" I cried.

Marcos arrived at this moment with my dried clothing in hand. He came to my defense and directed the warrior to back off.

"But I was ordered *to catch it," griped the warrior. "We were promised that we would eat meat tonight to ward off the cold."*

"The Shabba lost her pet today," Marcos told him. "She desires another one. Will you risk her curse as well as the curse of my father if you displease her?"

I'd heard the name "Shabba" used to describe me once before. It was just after we had emerged from the cavern. Marcos had remarked that my pale skin had led some of Jacob's men to think I was supernatural, like Shabba, a demon seductress. The man may not have feared repercussions from Jacob. It was likely the king who'd ordered the dogs rounded up in the first place. But calling me "Shabba" seemed to produce the desired effect. The warrior shrank away and went in search of another helpless canine.

"Superstitious, aren't they?" said Marcos.

I was too busy examining and comforting the dog to respond to him. Never in my life have I seen a breed of dog where every individual looked as uniformly similar to all the others. And yet there was something about the look in its eyes. Something about the silly way it sat back on its haunches that made me utter with mild puzzlement, "Pill?"

The dog immediately set to licking my face.

"It is Pill!"

When the dog had leaped into my lap, I'd had no expectation that it could possibly be mine. Pill was dead. He'd bounced out of my arms as we went over the cliff. In a million years I wouldn't have believed he could survive such a fall. And yet here he was!

Marcos sat down beside me. "How would you ever know if it's the same dog? They all look like clones."

"Isn't it obvious?" I declared. "He knows his name."

Marcos made a teasing grimace. "Knows his name? How could he know his name? You've only had him for three days to begin with."

"How many dogs of this kind have you seen that were so affectionate?"

Marcos pursed his lips. "You got me there." He reached over to pet the dog himself.

I tried to formulate a theory that would explain how the dog had survived. Pill must have bounced out of the carrier before it toppled over the edge. As I touched his lower back, he yelped in pain. As he'd fallen out of the carrier, he'd injured himself on the rocks. Somehow he'd managed to scramble back up to the trail and rejoin the other dogs.

Marcos watched intently as I groomed and caressed my little Pill. I raised my eyes and smiled back at him. Behind our smiles we could both perceive each other's stress. What would happen now? What did the future hold for us? As a comforting gesture, Marcos placed his hand over my hand.

I glanced down at his hand cupped over mine, and then back at his face. Marcos' dark brown irises were almost luminescent. I'd never seen such clear, redless eyes. But there was a new quality in those eyes now. Caring and tenderness—qualities I never would have guessed could abide in a person with such a dark legacy. I wondered how long his conscience could endure seeing me treated like a slave and an animal. What would he do if his father decided to harm me because things weren't going as planned? Marcos had put his life on the line for me once. Would he do it again if it meant alienating him from the only existence he had ever known? I watched his face muscles tense. I felt certain that these were the very questions he was asking himself.

As if the answer settled unexpectedly and forcefully over his heart, I saw his expression change. The turmoil seemed to disappear, replaced by another emotion, calm and determined. I became nervous as his eyes lingered on mine. I must have encouraged him not to look away; my own gaze was locked just as surely. I'd seen that look in a boy's eyes before. I knew exactly what it meant. Gradually, almost imperceptibly, Marcos leaned forward.

I don't know why I didn't turn away. Was it attraction? I suppose so. Was it gratitude? Probably. Marcos had saved my life in a feat more heroic than anything I'd ever seen—anything I'd ever heard of! Even if he'd had the face of a frog—which he definitely did not—to have refused his kiss would have made me the heel of the century. And yet if I'd been thinking clearly, if I'd let it register in my mind how much I really cared for him, I would have done everything in my power to refuse that kiss. I would have hurled myself backwards or raised up the dog to give him a mouthful of fuzz. Here we were, in open view of the entire camp—perhaps in perfect view of Jacob or Balam or someone else who would have cut Marcos to ribbons for such a display. Marcos had allowed his emotions to block out reason and discretion, and I was too slow on the draw to snap him out of it.

Was it an act of heaven that just before our lips touched someone in the center of camp started hollering? The shout made us leap out of our skins. Instantly, the spell was broken.

"Gather around!" shouted the voice of Balam the Diviner. "Witness for yourselves the consequences of weakness and incompetence in the kingdom of Lord Jacob of the Moon!"

"It's an execution," Marcos surmised.

"Who?" I asked. "Why?"

As my hands worked quickly under the coat to tie the skirt around my waist, the answer to those questions no longer seemed to matter. Death and cruelty were a daily occurrence in the vicinity of King Jacob. Everyone around him had become spiritually and emotionally numb. I would not let this happen to me. I'd witnessed enough blood and carnage. If I lived to see another day, I would not witness any more. Then I saw the faces of the individuals Jacob was planning to execute. I realized that if I failed to take action it would burn in my conscience forever. On their knees in the center of the camp, arms bound and spirits broken, were the four surviving porters who'd carried my litter.

"It is the blood of men like these for whom the Omnipotent One is most thirsty," Balam continued. "Let their deaths be a lesson for all of us who seek the light of the Divine Jaguar, but dishonor him through carelessness and negligence!" His knife raised high.

"NO!" I lunged forward and draped myself over the body of the first porter. "It wasn't their fault! It wasn't anyone's fault! It was an accident!"

The porter whose death I had just forestalled gaped at me with his eyes as wide as everyone else's. Balam had most likely just given him a speech about how his death was the only way to redeem his soul. In his heart, he'd already resigned himself to his fate. I was only delaying the inevitable, and he looked mildly annoyed.

Balam flew into a rage. Spittle actually sprayed out of his

mouth like a cobra as he cried, "Why is this girl out of bonds? Remove her immediately!"

I locked my arms more firmly around the porter's neck and under his shoulder. Standing in the background I saw King Jacob. He looked nearly as perturbed as Balam. He started forward, prepared to remove me himself if no one else took the cue. But Balam had signaled two warriors.

The men stepped forward, arms wide to seize me.

I was like a bug to these Neanderthals. They could brush me aside as easily as a fly. But I couldn't let them. Four innocent people were about to die. What could I do?

As they leaned down to grasp me, I considered gouging them in the eyes, biting, flailing—anything to fight them off. But it would have been pointless. I was no match for them. Without a weapon I wasn't even—

A weapon!

The instant that this notion glanced off my mind, I grabbed the knife on one of the men's belts. His arms were presently occupied trying to get a handle on my shoulders, so the opportunity to snatch it was perfect.

"She has a blade!" someone cried.

Both warriors leaped back. The one whose knife I'd stolen bared his teeth. The second one drew his own blade.

"Stop, you idiots!" Jacob clamored as more men reached for their sheaths. He stepped in front of Balam. "If anyone harms the girl, I'll skin him like an iguana."

Everyone, including Balam, backed away from me. But they stopped suddenly when they realized that I was not thrusting the blade at them. Instead, I had turned it on myself. I knew I was playing a dangerous game, but I pressed the copper tip against my own abdomen.

Marcos tried to reach out to me. "Melody, what are you trying to—?"

I moved behind the porter to keep out of reach of Marcos or anyone else. "If anybody comes closer," I threatened, "if anybody tries to harm these men . . . I'll do it."

Balam grinned and cackled. "She's bluffing. Take the knife."

I pressed the knife harder. The tip actually pierced my skin. But *my body was so pumped with adrenaline that I barely realized it.*

"All right," Jacob acquiesced. "Everyone keep back!"

The warriors who had been edging closer turned aside. Only Jacob of the Moon stepped closer.

"One more step," I snapped, "and it's over."

"Haven't you carried this charade far enough, Melody?" said Jacob calmly.

His tone did not affect me. Every muscle in my body vibrated with tension. My grip on the knife was like iron. My teeth were clenched so hard that my eyes were tearing.

Jacob sighed in mock defeat. "Very well. You win. Their lives will be spared. Give me the knife."

I shook my head. It was too easy. Jacob was lying.

"I don't believe you," I said. "So I'll make you a promise. Right here and now I swear to you that if you kill these men, I will never reach Jacobugath alive. I don't care how I do it. Over a cliff. Starvation. Slashing my wrists on a stone. It doesn't matter. I'll find a way. I will not live with these men on my conscience. I will not live knowing that they died because of an accident that brought me no harm."

Jacob chewed on this for a moment. From the beginning he might have suspected that my threat was empty. And if the moment of truth had arrived, he would have realized that he was right. He would have gloated at his victory as I let the blade fall from my hand. But he did not call my bluff. Just a few days ago he'd told Marcos that he feared I might commit suicide if I were allowed to walk freely. Considering how bleak my future was anyway, my threat may have seemed totally plausible. Jacob of the Moon had known—and created—many men who would have killed themselves for a cause. He had to consider that I might also be capable of such action.

I'm sure it crossed his mind that all he had to do was agree to my terms, take the knife away, bind me hand and foot, and then proceed with the execution as planned. If I refused to eat . . . well, we were close enough to our destination now that I'd most likely survive long enough. But sometime in the course of his musings it must have also occurred to him that we no longer possessed a carrier. To stop and build one now—even a crude one—might cost an entire day. And that was with the proper wood and tools, which were not available up here in the mountains. It had already taken him several days longer to cross these mountains than he had planned.

Jacob realized he couldn't *bind me. I needed my arms and legs. I had to walk. This meant I would likely have many opportunities to take my own life. As these realizations swept across his mind, his face reddened with ire. Jacob of the Moon did not like it when someone else was in control.*

"These men have elected to die willingly!" he clamored. "If you deny them this, their souls will be forever chained in the darkness and nothingness of Akmul! The nothingness of hell!*"*

Jacob said these words for the sake of the men. I didn't buy for one minute that he actually believed it. These porters were dying because he wanted to make an example of them—no other reason. Saving their souls was the farthest thought from his mind.

Marcos dropped to his knees at Jacob's feet, lowering his eyes. "Lord, my great Lord Jacob. What she says is true. These men were not responsible for the accident. The Divine Jaguar has already claimed the souls of the guilty. They were washed away in the river. These men are strong and loyal warriors. They will yet serve valiantly in your kingdom. You have the authority to absolve them, my great Lord Jacob. You have the power."

Slowly, Marcos raised his eyes to see how his entreaty had been received. At first Jacob didn't recognize that his son had given him an opening to back out of this affair with some semblance of grace. Jacob's chest pumped in and out. How could Marcos be siding with the prisoner? His eyes darted around as if he were looking for a knife to slit Marcos' throat. Let his son *be the example! But the rage subsided. Reason and logic bubbled to the surface. Why* not *play the part of the merciful dictator just once? If it served his ultimate ends, he might even chalk it up to his own ingenuity.*

He formed a tight smile. His eyes scanned the gathering, settling finally on the four porters who found the courage to lift their eyes.

"Absolved!" he declared, almost snidely, with a petty wave of the hand. "Untie them." And with that Jacob of the Moon went back into his tent, paying me only a casual glance as he turned around.

Marcos came to his feet. Cautiously, he took my arm and

encouraged me to pull the knife away from my abdomen. My hand was still shaking as he pried open my fingers and relieved me of the weapon. He ordered one of the men to dampen a cloth so that he could set it against the small puncture that I'd inflicted.

I caught the eyes of the four porters looking up at me as Balam cut the tethers that bound their hands. Half entranced, half bewildered, they didn't seem to know what to make of me. What I'd done for them was so foreign to their life experience that they didn't know how to feel. Some of them actually looked sad. I started to think I might have underestimated the devotion they felt toward their religion. They might have believed I'd denied them their only opportunity for salvation. I hoped in time they would see it differently. But this didn't matter to me. I'd done what I had to do. I'd followed my conscience.

The company of warriors mumbled among themselves, convincing each other that Jacob's decision was an act of strength and not weakness. The only one who looked truly incensed was Balam. As he cut the tethers he gave Marcos a look that would have melted steel. Something wasn't right and he knew it. Marcos was different. He had changed. As Balam's baleful gaze moved slowly from Marcos to me, I wondered if he also thought he might know the reason.

* * *

That night the cold didn't seep into my bones like the night before, nor was the day as ruthlessly hot. The trail, however, was bent and twisted and jagged. The bruise on my hip bothered me some. The fact that it had been a week and a half since I'd regularly used my legs didn't help either. I huffed and puffed all morning and snatched every chance I could to rest and pamper my scrapes and bruises. Yet, overall, I think the trail was tapering off. Now and then as we rounded a hilltop I sighted a break in the clouds, like a tunnel through a misty dream, that revealed below us a fertile valley pocked with cool blue lakes.

Pill scampered at my feet, or else he ran just ahead, turning back on occasion to encourage me to catch up. He was the only one of the pudgy little dogs remaining, the last of his tribe. I felt an obligation to watch him closely in case one of the warriors got the wrong idea about what to serve for dinner.

Marcos had grown very shy and pensive. Quite often I would catch him looking at me. When he realized he'd been caught he would grin and look away, almost mischievously, as if he was glad he'd been caught. He babied me almost every step of the journey, letting me hang on his arm, making sure I never misplaced my foot and insisting that I finish off the last of his waterskin even though we were told we wouldn't have a chance to refill it until night. It must have been embarrassingly obvious to any observer that the son of Jacob Moon had developed feelings for me that were far less than professional.

I found myself flirting and teasing almost unconsciously. Thank goodness we didn't have a mirror. I might have dropped dead at my own appearance. I groomed myself as best I could and worked hard to make my hair look a little less like a rat's nest.

Marcos accepted each flirtation like kisses on the wind. I felt guilty inside. I knew that I was leading him on to believe something totally, completely, and utterly impossible. The only thing that Marcos and I had in common was our mutual membership in the human race—and even that was debatable. In a way, I was just like my dog, Pill—having only one friend and advocate among a horde of creatures who would have just as soon eaten me for dinner. So maybe I flirted with him because I thought it was important that he fall in love with me. Maybe I felt it was crucial to my survival.

But were my motives totally self-centered? Could I honestly say that I felt nothing for him? No, I couldn't, and I scolded myself inwardly for it. Marcos had been my enemy. His manner had been as cold and cruel as any Nazi. And yet today I trusted him more than any other living soul to protect and watch over me. And that's what made our situation so dangerous. If Jacob found out that his son would rally to my cause and fight for my honor in every circumstance, how long would it take him to decide that Marcos was no longer an asset, but a serious liability?

But before I would let my feelings get the better of me—before I opened the floodgates of my heart and confessed to myself that I was falling in love—there was one question that I needed to have *answered. It was a horrible, strangling question. I'd have given anything not to have asked, but I couldn't ignore it any longer. I put the question to him the very next night, our last night in the mountains.*

"Marcos," I said, "what part did you play in my dad's arrest and the murder of his boss, Doug Bowman?"

I watched for the reaction in his eyes. I was afraid the question might reawaken a sleeping demon. A shadow passed over his countenance. The question was like a blow to his stomach. It wrenched him back into the world that he'd fooled himself into believing he might escape. He came to his feet, unable to look in my eyes.

"I didn't . . . kill him. I-I didn't pull the trigger, but . . ."

I waited for him to finish. "But . . . ?"

He sat down again and wiped the sweat from his brow. "Melody, I . . . God help me. You don't understand. Please . . . please don't ask me what I've done."

In a quiet voice that was no less firm with resolve, I said, "I have to ask you, Marcos. I have to know. Did you help frame my father for murder?"

The air seeped from his lungs like a moan of wind from a hollow place. "Yes," he replied. "I did what my father, Lord Jacob, requested. I went to work at your father's company. My instructions were to find someone with whom your father was estranged. Someone who people would believe your father was capable of . . ."

"Murdering?"

The life in his brown eyes seemed to blow out. He stared blankly ahead. He swallowed, and his Adam's apple rolled painfully down his throat. He closed his eyes and minutely nodded to confirm what I had said.

I tried to exhale, but the air wouldn't release. I don't know what I had expected to hear. I guess I'd harbored a secret hope that Marcos might lay all the blame at the feet of his father, the true villain, the only villain. In my imagination I had heard Marcos say, I didn't know what my father was doing. By the time I realized what was happening, it was too late for me to stop him. Too late to save poor Doug Bowman. Too late to save your father.

He might have said it. There was nothing to stop him. I might have conned myself into believing every word. But Marcos did not lie. The weight of his crime crashed down on me. The floodgates of my heart slammed shut. The emotion that I might have called love evaporated into steam.

Marcos was an accessory to the blackest act a man could commit. He had openly, willingly, and brutally participated in the premeditated murder of another human being. How could I view him as any less guilty than the person who had pulled the trigger? Surely his crimes did not end there. How many more unpardonable sins seared his soul? How many more murders and brutalities and deceits?

When the air finally released from my lungs, it came out like a shattered squeal. I felt terrible loathing and embarrassment that I'd almost given my devotions to a creature of the night. That I had almost touched my lips to a person whose soul was cankered and rotting. Marcos Alberto Sanchez had knowingly destroyed my family. Did it matter that he'd saved my life? He'd crushed everything that I had lived for—my family, my security—like dry leaves. My fingers tightened into fists. I wanted badly to lay into him with all the fury I could bring to bear, pounding and scratching until his flesh was raw and bleeding. I caught him glance at me and it seemed as if he secretly wanted me to attack. He would have welcomed it, offering no ounce of resistance even if I had delivered a stroke to end his life.

But all at once my hatred drained away. My fists could no longer remain clenched. I began to sob.

"No," I heard Marcos whisper. *He spoke it with tortured anguish, as if his spirit was crying,* No, Melody. Do anything. Hurt me, kill me. I can take any punishment you can inflict—but not your tears. Not the realization that I've broken your heart beyond repair.

And yet who could deny that this was precisely what he'd done? I felt him move closer. I'm certain he wanted to hold me like before, provide me with some human comfort, but the act would have reeked with such hypocrisy that even Marcos recognized that it was best to hold back. There was nothing he could do. This may have been the hardest truth for him to bear.

Instead it was me, beyond all fidelity and reason, who reached out to touch my destroyer. Before I realized it, I had buried my face in his chest and begun to soak his cloak with my tears. He held me firmly, yet gently, like something fragile and cracked, something he'd broken himself.

"I'm sorry, Melody," I heard him say. "I don't know what to do. Tell me what I should do. If you say it, I promise you, on my life, that I will do it. I promise it, Melody."

I looked into his eyes, but I never had the chance to reply. At that instant, the mutilated face of Balam the Diviner swooped down on top of us. His cold fingers gripped the backs of our necks. He pulled us apart. After he'd hoisted us to our feet, he positioned himself eye-to-eye with Marcos.

"By the order of your father, Lord Jacob of the Moon, you have been relieved of any and all duties with respect to the girl. She is now assigned exclusively to my *keeping. You are commanded to keep your distance at all times. From this time henceforth, if you speak a single word to her, your tongue will be cut out, skewered on a stick, and fed back to you again. If you touch her, Marcos, I am granted the authority to kill you without trial, without warning, without even the obligation of telling Lord Jacob that you are dead. I hope I have made myself clear."*

He strapped a new leather collar around my neck, cinching it much tighter than the first one. It was difficult to breathe. My fingers groped to relieve the pressure and allow air into my windpipe. Balam started dragging me away.

Marcos stood there watching, his eyes blazing with indignation as I was torn out of his life. I could feel him straining to suppress the urge to lunge at Balam, but this would have been fatal. Three other warriors had accompanied Balam in case of just such an outburst.

So the emotional attachment between Marcos and me had not escaped the attention of Jacob's Diviner. It had likely taken Balam very little persuasion to convince Jacob that his son was no longer trustworthy in matters pertaining to me. I fought to keep Marcos in my vision as long as I could before Balam forced me to turn away. Pill tried to follow us, but Balam kicked the dog in the face. Pill yelped and fled.

Of all the moments I'd yet faced in this cyclone that had become my life, this was the most devastating moment of all. I no longer had the courage to believe I would ever again enjoy the companionship of friends.

CHAPTER 9

Until now I had avoided Balam like the plague. One of my reasons for this was because I was literally afraid that he carried the plague. In contrast with the elaborate jewelry that dangled from the holes in his face, I wondered if in the course of his entire life he'd ever taken a bath. The combination of dirt mixed with human perspiration had, over the years, dyed his skin to a hue that was almost purple and left the surface coarse and scaly. Ever since that night in the Harmon's parking lot when he'd rendered me helpless with the stun gun, I'd come to know his unmistakable odor. It was nauseating enough to stand within a few yards. But until tonight I hadn't had the intolerable experience of sleeping in an enclosed tent with it. The night was one long, uninterrupted nightmare.

Balam lay on the ground across from me, snoring obnoxiously in spite of the fact that his mouth was closed. The snores came through the holes in his cheeks, sounding exactly like the growl of a pit bull. Even in his sleep he kept the rope connected to my collar firmly in his grip. He'd loosened the collar slightly so that I could breathe a little easier, but I'm not sure if this was a blessing. All that night I tried to filter the odor through the fabric of my sleeve. To recreate such a smell one would have to concoct a recipe of many different dead and rotting things, spice it with the juices of whatever naturally excretes from human pores, seal the whole thing in a bottle, let it ferment for a period of years, and then release it with a hiss into unpolluted air.

But the smell was only part of my horror. How can I describe the crawling torment of having to sleep in close proximity to such a reptile? It was like cuddling up close to a dog with rabies. Needless to say, I did not sleep. I'd have sobbed through the night, but this would have forced me to draw deeper breaths, which I was not willing to do.

The following day we left the slopes of the mountains and entered a forested valley. Balam led me like a mule, rarely glancing back to see how I was doing and never allowing me to stop or rest unless he himself felt inclined to do so. I'd have lost it entirely—I'd have gone completely insane—if I hadn't been able to pour out my soul to my Father in Heaven. My life was a hurricane, but through prayer I discovered that the hurricane had an eye. As the hours dragged by, my silent prayers continued. After a while I didn't feel the exhaustion in my legs. I think of that poem "Footprints" back home on our refrigerator door. I understand that poem now. Because that day, I was truly carried.

As instructed, Marcos kept his distance. In fact, I only saw him once. That evening he stood at the top of a rocky knoll overlooking the place where Balam had raised his tent. In his arms he held my little dog. Marcos was close enough that I could read the misery in his eyes. A lump froze in my throat. Marcos didn't wave or make it obvious that he was watching me. Balam, gnawing on a rabbit leg, had his back to Marcos. The instant it appeared that he might change his position and look up the knoll, Marcos faded back.

Because most of the time Balam remained in close proximity to King Jacob, I had the unenviable privilege of observing this miserable ferret of a man up close. Jacob of the Moon was obsessed with cleanliness. I suspected he'd once known great poverty. He wouldn't have tolerated its trappings now if his life had depended on it. In this manner he was exactly the opposite of his odious advisor and diviner, Balam. Like "Felix and Oscar," they seemed the most mismatched pair in history. I marveled that they could stand each other's presence at all. Mutual respect, coupled with mutual fear, seemed to hold the relationship together.

Every morning, noon, and night Jacob's servants gave him a towel bath, groomed and perfumed his skin and hair, changed his garments, and even cleaned his teeth. He expected no less than per-

fection from his servants, and for the most part, he got it. They groveled to meet his every need. He must have screened servants for years to find ones who could live up to his rigorous demands. The losers, I assumed, were not around to help train the replacements.

Never did I see Jacob falter in his efforts to project an image of ultimate power. He therefore associated with his men as little as possible, usually only to bark a command. No one looked directly into his eyes and no one spoke to Jacob unless Jacob spoke to them first. Though it might have seemed to me that such an existence would drive a person crazy with loneliness, Jacob seemed to thrive on it. Every time I had the opportunity to observe him by himself, he appeared disconnected, absorbed in thought, perfectly content with his own companionship as his mind hatched his elaborate schemes to divide and conquer the universe.

His objective while traveling with our little army of three hundred or so warriors had been to travel incognito and draw very little attention to himself. He feared that some enemy might recognize him. So he made it a point to dress exactly like the rest of his warriors. Still, if an enemy had come upon us, Jacob would have stuck out like a sore thumb. He was the only one who didn't smell like a horse or have dirt under his fingernails.

Jacob's charade ended after we reached the first settlement in his kingdom. Appropriately, it was called Kishkumen, after the old scumbag who had first established secret combinations among the Nephites. Local citizens turned out to watch as we made our way along the main thoroughfare. To my surprise, the place was meticulously neat and clean. I might have expected a Gadianton town to be the epitome of filth. Instead, the buildings were freshly painted. The streets were free of garbage. All of the citizens appeared well-fed and healthy—even the slaves. If filth or corruption were to be found in Kishkumen, it thrived in the secret recesses of the people's hearts.

It was in Kishkumen's market square that Jacob tossed off his common rags and demanded of the local leaders garments more fitting to his office—a loincloth of rich, red leather, a cape of glossy white cotton with green and blue parrot feathers down the sides, and alligator-skin sandals that laced all the way up to his knees.

He left his paunched stomach bare to boldly display his blood-red tattoo. It circled around the navel and extended up across his chest to form a pattern that reminded me of the markings on a black widow spider. It was the sight of this tattoo—somehow a symbol of Jacob's kingly rank—that caused every resident of Kishkumen who saw it to fall forward and kiss the dirt. Several of them slithered even closer to claim the honor of kissing his feet.

King Jacob's arrival in the city of Kishkumen had been anticipated. Awaiting him was a newly fashioned and glittering litter with no less than twelve porters to carry it. It looked more like a portable house, complete with a roof of heavy clay shingles and red-and-black striped curtains over its two open sides. Since there were still five or six hours of daylight, we prepared to set out for a nearby city called Gadiandi—another appropriately named town in a kingdom born of secret combinations. I guessed that we would arrive in the capital city of Jacobugath sometime tomorrow.

A servant got down on his hands and knees so that Jacob might use his back as a step stool. But before Jacob climbed inside the carrier and slipped behind the thick curtain, he signaled Balam to step forward. Balam approached, dragging me, of course, behind him.

The king glanced me over from head to foot. The attention made me squirm. I looked away. My body was caked with dirt and grit. I was badly sunburned. My lips were cracked. Not a soul on earth had shown me the least compassion for the past three days, and I certainly expected none from this creep. So it took me by surprise when Jacob said to Balam, "Tie off the line above the curtain. She will ride with me."

Was it selfish to confess that for a second I felt elated? I'd started to believe I would never again enjoy simple human comforts. I was sure that Balam's stench would permeate my lungs for the rest of my life. Jacob saw my eyes brighten and it seemed to please him. But my elation was short-lived. It burst the instant I entered the shadowy interior of Jacob's lair. I found myself sitting across from him on a bench of quilted white fur as soft as chinchilla.

Suddenly I would have given anything to be back with Balam. I was gripped by a sensation of excruciating coldness, as if slivers of ice flowed in my blood. I hugged my arms around my chest and shrank as far away from Jacob as I could. I did my best to avoid looking directly at him. For the first few minutes, as the porters lift-

ed the carrier and our journey to the next town began, Jacob ignored me. He pulled back the curtain and called for a pipe. Someone handed him a ten-inch tube carved of jadestone. A crimson ash burned at one end. At the other end was a mouthpiece from which Jacob sucked a long, satisfying draw.

He held the smoke in his lungs as long as he could. When he finally released it, the interior of the carrier was filled with a thick cloud that smelled like pipe tobacco mingled with strong spices that I couldn't have named. I coughed several times the way someone would when enclosed in a car and wished a window to be opened. But Jacob didn't act concerned. I drew back the curtain just enough to inhale the fresh, open air.

I still refused to look at him, but I could feel his eyes on me. He watched me like a predator. Why had he brought me here? For what reason would he desire my company? I tried not to think about the darkest motives a man might have for making such arrangements. I comforted myself that my appearance would have discouraged such feelings even in the most lecherous male, particularly someone as fastidious as Jacob of the Moon. Yet he continued leering gratuitously as he sucked on his jadestone pipe.

Finally, I heard his voice utter somewhere through the smoke, "You think I am cruel and contemptible, don't you, Melody?"

I might have replied something like, Is the Pope Catholic? *But I doubted he would have understood the reference so I contented myself with a snide grunt.*

After a moment, Jacob continued, "I can understand why you would feel that way. From your perspective, how could you be expected to feel any other way?"

At last I replied, though it was barely audible, "From anyone's *perspective."*

"What was that?" said Jacob, and he leaned forward to see if I might repeat the phrase. I didn't. He laughed to himself and took another draw on his pipe.

For the life of me I couldn't figure out what he thought he was doing. Was he trying to make friends with me? Frighten me? Manipulate me?

"You're a spirited girl, Melody. You've caused me a great deal of trouble. I partially blame you that it's taken us four days longer to

make this trip than I had expected. But now we are here, in the borders of my kingdom. Tell me, what do you think of it so far?"

I sent him the coldest look I could manage. I was not interested in offering an opinion or even in carrying on any kind of conversation whatsoever. The mere thought of conversing with him made my flesh crawl. Yet Jacob took the look on my face as a kind of compliment, an admission that I had found his kingdom to be far greater than I had anticipated.

"Just wait, Melody. Before the day is through, you'll see grander sights than you can see in all the lands of Nephi and Laman. Tomorrow you shall set your eyes on Jacobugath—the pearl of my empire. And to think I built it all from the foundations of an aboriginal ruin in a little over two years. Yet this is just the beginning. Think how the world will look in two more years. The possibilities stagger the common mind—but not mine. I see it all as sharply as the rising sun. In your religion there is a saying: 'By their fruits ye shall know them.' Tomorrow you shall apply a definition to that phrase that you never dreamed possible."

I held my tongue no longer. "I've already seen your fruits. Murder and terror and destruction."

I choked on the last word and spoiled the delivery. Jacob's gaze seemed to drain the energy right out of me. I couldn't generate the tone of righteous indignation that I wanted. My hands were trembling. I grasped them together to steady them.

"Those are not fruits," Jacob replied. "Those are methods employed in nourishing the orchard. What grove is not best served by burning and cutting and pruning? Violent devices to be sure, but in the end every tree that survives is much better for it, far more invincible, and its fruit is superior to all the others."

My mouth was dry. I swallowed and said sneeringly, "So the ends justify the means?"

Jacob scoffed. "Your culture has given that slogan an unseemly image. Yet if you open up your mind, you'll perceive that such a philosophy identifies the forces behind all creation. Every planet in the galaxy is formed by fire and violence and destruction. To build greatness, inferiority must be smashed, broken up, reshaped. The process usually requires great pain. This would not be necessary if inferior forces did not resist, but they do and they will. It is the nature of ignorance to resist. Nevertheless, to believe that perfection can be achieved any other way is foolish and vain."

My heart was booming. I barely heard my own words as I replied, "I believe it can—through Jesus Christ."

Jacob waved this off with his hand. "You recite the epigrams of your religion like a parrot."

My voice became almost pleading, as if some corner of my mind believed I might actually convince Jacob of the error of his ways. "You must know," I said, "that your ideas don't come from God. They come from Satan."

"Of course I know it," said Jacob. He took another draw on his pipe.

I was floored by his frankness. "You know *it?"*

"Satan, the Devil, the Dragon. These are just a few of the derogatory little nicknames that your people have tagged onto him. His true name is Lucifer, and he is the glorified Son of the Morning."

"Then what—" I was trembling so badly now that no grip in the world could have steadied my hands "—what's all that stuff about a Divine Jaguar?"

"Packaging," said Jacob. "To use the language of your world, all products must be packaged to meet the needs of the consumer. Lucifer may take any shape he chooses. It is by his power that all things are created and made."

"H-how can you believe that?" I stuttered. "That's exactly . . . it's exactly . . . the opposite! It's through Jesus Christ that all things—"

"Yes, yes," said Jacob impatiently. "I'm perfectly acquainted with all of the precepts of your misguided cult. I was even baptized into your ludicrous religion the day after they hung that fool Zemnarihah. Strictly for self-preservation, you understand. Nevertheless, I came to learn the seductiveness of the Christian lie. I don't expect you so quickly to abandon all the deceits that have brainwashed you since birth. Remember what I told you? Ignorance always resists."

I was in way over my head, yet I heard myself say, "There is no deception in Christ. Only love and trust. Freedom. Even you *believed in our Heavenly Father's Plan once, or else you wouldn't have been born. You would have been cast out for rebellion—"*

"Did it ever occur to you that some of us may have feigned

acceptance so that we might receive a body?" asked Jacob.

Again the wind was knocked out of me. "That's . . . that's impossible. You can't fool God."

Jacob laughed again. "Don't underestimate who can and can't be fooled. I understand the intricacies of the War in Heaven far better than you do, little girl. I have seen myself in vision standing with Lucifer in the grand council, pleading for the welfare of all humanity. Your Gods presented a plan that favored the few, and abandoned the rest. Think about it, Melody. For the first time in your life, listen to your voice of conscience. Lucifer's plan would have glorified every soul ever born under the stars of eternity. Every last vestibule of intelligence would have inherited an estate of celestial glory. If only you could perceive some small portion of the selfishness that rages in the hearts of the beings you worship. Are you not taught that the majority of souls born into this world will receive an inheritance in the lowest kingdom of glory?"

"Well . . . yes, but that's because—"

"Are you not taught that 'wide is the gate that leads to destruction and narrow is the way that leads to eternal life'? Why doesn't this enrage you, Melody? Why are you not consumed with indignation every moment to think that a plan of salvation was ultimately adopted that limited the hopes of so many billions and billions of souls? Yes, Melody. I know the Father of my spirit. And I reject His plan. I spit upon every piece, portion, and particle of it."

I was shaking so badly now that I could actually hear the rushing in my ears. Every cell in my body screamed to get out of this man's presence. Tears burned a smoldering trail down my cheeks. The words I spoke next came out in choking gasps. "You're a . . . a s-son of . . . perdition."

I don't pretend that I knew the full meaning of what I'd said. I spoke it in knee-jerk reaction to the stinging blasphemies that had cut me to the heart. Jacob did not know the Father of his spirit. He did not know his elder brother, Jesus Christ. It was impossible to become a son of perdition without such knowledge. But how, I wondered, how could such a twisted, perverted concept of the universe actually find sanctuary in a human heart? And then I realized his sly objective. Jacob was using all the images and icons that I held most sacred to try and crush and manipulate me.

He acted further amused by my indictment. "We are all sons of perdition, Melody. Your Gods have made us so. Consider for a moment—one brief moment—that it is you who have been hoodwinked. Not me. Consider for a moment that the weight of power is in reality possessed by the being I worship. Lucifer's rivals have launched a brilliant scheme to fool some, but your numbers are so minuscule as to barely merit mention. I have basked in the glory of the Omnipotent One. I have seen the power of the endless legions at his command. If only you could touch and taste that image for one minute, Melody, you would doubt the final destiny of this universe no longer."

Somewhere in the midst of this last harangue, I made a conscious decision that I would not, could not, be afraid any longer. I had no reason to be afraid. On my side were the powers of God and the gift of the Holy Spirit. The instant that I made this decision, the rushing in my ears went silent. My tears stopped flowing and my hands ceased to tremble. The crushing weight I felt became as light as a feather.

I turned toward Jacob and said as calmly and placidly as I could, "You're going to lose, Jacob of the Moon. The Divine Jaguar won't win. He can't win."

Jacob tried to pretend he was unmoved by my restoration of confidence. He mimicked my calmness. With all the empathy of a caring parent, he replied, "Oh, my dear child. He's already won. The prosperity of my kingdom proves it. Soon the victory trumpet will sound."

"Jacob," I said mildly, as if to awaken him to a point that he had conveniently overlooked, "your kingdom will be destroyed."

He leaned forward in an attempt to revive his powers of intimidation. "Why?" he snapped. "Because your precious Book of Mormon says it will? Don't count on it. That book is one of the most brilliant collections of lies that your Gods have ever conceived. Not the most brilliant. Frankly, they might have done much better. But Melody, please sit back, close your eyes, and revel in the possibilities. My kingdom is upheld by powers you can't begin to comprehend."

I shook my head casually. Then I smiled slightly and replied, "If you really believed that, why would you need me? Why would you need my Uncle Garth? Why can't these so-called powers simply tell you what you wish to know?"

Jacob sat back again, his jaw stiff. He was boiling inside. I could sense it. I could feel it. And yet he would not allow himself to lose control. Patiently, he let his composure return. Then he said, "You've missed the obvious, dear girl. You see, I have you. I have your Uncle Garth. And soon I will learn what I need to know."

"So is that why you've brought me inside here? To make sure I didn't miss the obvious?"

"Yes," Jacob gruffed. "To paint it as vividly as I can. I carried you from your world through the dark caverns of Akmul and across the mountains of Desolation for one purpose and one purpose only. And that was to die, dear girl. To die as surely as you have ever lived. And this will still be your destiny—I promise it—if you fail to convince your uncle to tell me where in the land of Gilgal is hidden the treasure of Haberekiah."

I pretended to examine the weavings on the curtain. "Why can't you get my uncle to help you without me? Surely you're not above torturing another human being."

Jacob became more vexed than ever. "Your insipid uncle is—!" He calmed himself again. "Let's just say he . . . has some remarkable powers of resistance. Of course we would never attempt something that would drive the poor idiot out of his mind. That wouldn't be helpful to anyone. And we couldn't risk actually killing the fellow. That's where you come in, Melody. I won't lie to you. If you cannot convince Garplimpton to help us, I will be forced to torture you slowly and systematically until you are dead. Your uncle will be forced to witness every procedure, listen to every scream. I will give you one day, Melody. One day to decide whether or not you're going to help me."

"How considerate," I said smugly, though I could feel my fears returning and the weight of dread pressing down. "Why even give me one day?"

"Because of the waste, sweet girl. The horrendous waste." He sighed like a weary parent, frustrated because the child didn't seem to get the point. "I know you think everything I represent is brutal and violent. Soon, Melody, you will see that this is not true. I am also a patron of great beauty and order. In the realms of the

Omnipotent One, chaos is only a temporary state. Perfection and beauty are the inevitable ends. Every person in my kingdom has a purpose, a place. If you succeed in this tiny act of persuasion, there is also a place awaiting you. A place above and beyond any position that a common girl like you might obtain. I offer you the loftiest position of all. To stand at my side as one of my queens."

My eyebrows shot up. "Excuse me?"

"All the riches of Jacobugath would be yours, Melody. In time, all of the riches of the world. As my queen you would realize powers and pleasures that few women have ever known. Ever will know."

The image of me standing at the side of this sixty-year-old lecher sent my stomach acids into overdrive. No wonder he'd been so anxious to separate me from his son. No wonder he'd commanded Marcos to keep his distance. Somewhere in the course of our journey, he'd set his sights on having me for himself. I tasted bile in my throat.

"But don't worry yourself," Jacob continued. "As I said, I will give you one day to ponder my request and my reward. Tomorrow I will expect your answer. I encourage you to remember, Melody, your only other option is death." He leaned forward and reached out his hand as if to take mine. "Surely, you don't find me so unattractive . . ."

That did it.

I retched once, and then it came up. The contents of my lunch spilled all over the soft white fur of Jacob's litter, all over Jacob's hand, and all over his new alligator-skin sandals.

* * *

Needless to say, I walked the rest of the way to Gadiandi.

Jacob ordered the caravan to halt. His servants were ordered to fetch him new footwear, clean the mess in his litter, and soak both the fur and his feet in perfumes. His face was beet-red with fury. My response to his marriage proposal had insulted and revolted him. Nevertheless, he did not withdraw his offer.

"Tomorrow, Melody," he repeated harshly, "I will have your answer."

When I was turned back over to Balam, I felt so relieved. Who'd have thought that anyone's presence could be worse than Balam's. Oh, how wrong I was! Balam was a rabid dog. But Jacob was the knowing, willing, eager advocate of the purest kind of darkness. Compared to Jacob of the Moon, Balam's presence was like a breath of fresh air.

Our journey recommenced. I found myself plodding upon my blistered feet again, but the courage I'd received inside Jacob's litter did not abandon me entirely. If it had, my heart might have literally burst inside me. Before today, I'd never understood the corrosiveness of that emotion called fear. I hadn't realized that this emotion, in and of itself, was an enemy that could easily become as lethal as the thing that inspires it. Keeping it at bay was a discipline that I desperately needed to master if I expected to survive the next several days.

But my immediate dilemma remained. What would I say to Jacob tomorrow? Would I agree to try and convince my uncle to help him? It was only a treasure. A silly treasure. What did it matter if Jacob got his hands on it? His empire would still fail eventually. Wouldn't it? But then there was the matter of Jacob's reward. I became dizzy with nausea every time I thought of it.

I looked around to see if I might spot Marcos. I needed to see him. Just to know that he was there. But I never found him, nor did I see any sign of my little dog. I began to wonder if Marcos was still part of our company. Had his father sent him off in another direction? This might have been too much for my soul to bear, so I convinced myself that Marcos was hidden somewhere in the ranks, keeping his distance as ordered.

Beyond the neatly cobbled road that connected Kishkumen and Gadiandi, the farm fields were flowing with grain and produce. Jacob's boasting of the beauty and orderliness of his kingdom was no exaggeration. It didn't make sense. Everything I'd ever read about Gadiantons portrayed them as lazy slobs, glutting themselves on the labor of others. Their behavior during the march seemed to confirm this. But everything I was seeing now contradicted it.

Just as the sun touched the edge of the hills that burgeoned with corn and pineapple and cacao beans, we entered the community of Gadiandi. Like Kishkumen, Gadiandi was not at all what I might have expected from a community founded upon wickedness. New buildings were under construction everywhere. Flower gardens blossomed along the streets. The people were festooned in fabrics so bright and neatly woven that they looked almost modern. Children laughed and played on rooftops and in the market square. Hordes of citizens lined both sides of the avenues, kissing the ground in solemn reverence as Jacob's litter approached, then rising to an energetic cheer as it passed.

Was it all a show? Did they do this for fear of their lives? Or did the people literally worship Jacob as a god? I couldn't put my finger on it. But I had every impression that they really and truly adored him.

The pride of Gadiandi was a natural hot spring that erupted in the town square. Most of the spring was enclosed by roofless walls. Limestone tiling around the edges of the pools along with other cement work gave it the appearance of a resort, almost like an ancient Greek spa. With hearty approval from the proprietors, Jacob and his warriors took over the entire premises. For the first time since Marcos had saved me from drowning in the icy river, I was given the opportunity to bathe. A private chamber was provided for me that had an actual shower built into the wall. From a clay pipe jutting out of the ceiling flowed a continuous cascade of warm water that emptied into another hole in the floor. Balam removed my leather collar. Even with it off, it must have looked like I was still wearing it. Chafing and sunburning had left a distinct ring around my neck.

Balam and several other guards waited outside as I tore off my scummy clothing and immersed myself in the cascade. The floor was slick with algae, so I slunk down and made myself as tight as I could with my arms wrapped around my knees so the liquid wouldn't miss a single inch. I wished I could have washed away more than the dirt. I wished I could have washed away the memory—the stain—of everything that had happened that day, everything I'd heard from the lips of King Jacob. Unfortunately, water can only do so much.

That evening our company was treated to an immense buffet in the city's central court. The ghastly image of the Divine Jaguar glared at us from a hundred different places—repeated in the stone friezes along the top of the buildings, muraled on walls, painted on cups and platters, and molded into virtually every ornament and piece of jewelry. Despite my recent shower and the softness of my new sunflower-colored garments, this image served to remind me of the filthiness that continued to permeate my surroundings. The larger the Jaguar's image, the more attention was paid to macabre details like a fleshless jaw with bloody teeth or eyes that glowed with the jeweled redness of hate. No one in Jacob's kingdom could ever doubt that "big brother" was watching.

The air was saturated with sweet and musky smells from burning incense urns. I'd attended countless potlucks and family reunions in my life, yet I'd never seen a spread of food comparable to this. Dozens of bonfires broiled the carcasses of meat and birds. Basins and barrels overflowed with a yellow-colored wine and other drinks. Our army of three hundred warriors, city nobles, and well-to-do guests couldn't possibly have consumed even a fourth of all the food if they had continued eating and disgorging throughout the night. I think it was a matter of local pride to present the king with every mound of sustenance that could be scraped together. I was appalled to think how much would be spoiled and wasted.

I sampled a few of the batter-fried vegetables, but otherwise I ate very little. This was because Jacob kept me close by during dinner. I was afraid if he tried to approach me or touch me, I'd throw it up. Fortunately, the king paid me no attention. After all, I was a slave. Fraternizing with my kind in public would not have been dignified.

My leather collar was tied off at the nearest post, like a horse at a saloon. I felt utterly humiliated and dreadfully lonely. Who'd have thought this was possible in a crowded city square? As a multitude of torches and artificially colored urn fires were ignited to meet the coming darkness, I made one final effort to glimpse Marcos among the throngs, but he never made even the briefest appearance. Later I heard one of Jacob's henchmen make a comment about having successfully dispatched a small contingent of warriors to make sure everything was in order at the capital. I suspected that Marcos was part of this contingent. I felt a stab in my heart as I considered that I might never set my eyes on him again.

Long before the festivities had concluded, my line was untied *and I was taken to a sleeping chamber in the nearby government complex. I counted forty guards in the hall outside my room and in the courtyard below my window. My "leash" was retied to a cross-beam overhead and out of reach.*

A rather more abstract rendition of the Divine Jaguar with red flourishes projecting off the head like the points of a star glowered down on me from the ceiling. I settled into bed and tried to pretend it wasn't there. An awning of gossamer threads had been hung over my bedding to ward off mosquitoes and gnats.

Before falling asleep, I knelt on top of my mattress and tried to pray. To my distress, the prayer didn't come easy. For some reason, it was only now, in the quiet privacy of the darkness that the full horror of the day's events stirred up inside me. Phrases that Jacob had recited while I was inside his carrier screamed from every corner of my mind: My kingdom is upheld by powers you can't even begin to comprehend! Soon the victory trumpet will sound! We are *all* sons of perdition! I reject His plan! I spit upon every piece, portion, and particle of it!

These blasphemies pulsed and resounded—an endless barrage of missiles determined to blast to oblivion every thought I might send to my Father in Heaven. I recalled the commitment that I had made just before we reached Gadiandi. Gritting my teeth, I struggled to push all the fears out of my mind. But Jacob's words were relentless. They boomed and shouted until they became one massive jumble reverberating over the distant echo of my own sobs.

But at last one thought broke through—Give me peace, Father. I repeated this over and over until, all at once, my mind was filled with light—not a visible light nor a fiery kind of light—but a kind of tangible brightness that seemed to define the very reason my mind was able to function in the first place. As this light broke onto the scene, the cacophony of Jacob's words amplified for one brief millisecond into a terrible shriek, like a million voices wrenching backwards to scramble free from the inferno of an exploding star. But the light and heat of this star did not repulse me. Instead, it weaved itself into every fiber of my being. It did not wrench my spirit backwards. Rather I was drawn toward it, cleansed by it, healed through it.

The cacophony went silent. No hint of it interfered with my thoughts any longer. The same warmth that had overwhelmed me also beckoned me to continue my prayer. I did so, and the Comforter listened. My sobs were now perfectly audible in my own ears. For a time I felt as though the Spirit actually wept with me. It wept for the wickedness of the world, wept for the offspring of God who had been given every opportunity under the sun to turn their hearts back to the Father, but they would not. After a while I found myself weeping for the exact same reason. I tasted the fleetingness of my own trials and pain, and I realized that the only source of true sorrow in the universe rested with this reality. And no one, not God, not Christ, nor the angels of heaven, was immune from the unquenchable pangs of it.

I fell asleep with my head nestled in the lap of the Comforter, my hopes sparkling inside me like the coals of a fire fanned by a warm wind. I found the peace of mind to set aside the anxieties of the coming day and concentrate only on positive things. For one, our long and arduous journey was near an end. For another, and this one far and wide outweighed the first, before the next setting of the sun, I would lay my eyes on a loved one I hadn't seen in almost two and a half years.

My indomitable Uncle Garth.

CHAPTER 10

The peaks and ridges of the mountains of Desolation had been casting shadows over us for the last two days. The more intimidating elevations were seen to the southwest, while to the northeast, somewhat softer and greener mountains nibbled at the sky.

"This is the highway of the Smoke Eater," Lamachi informed us. "It's the main trail into the valley of Jacobugath. This is the route we were told to take during the rites of our initiation into the Second Tier. If dissenters among the Nephites want to unite with the people of the Divine Jaguar, this is the road they have to travel."

"Are you saying that any travelers we meet will more than likely be Reds?" asked Gidgiddonihah.

"More than likely, they are of the order of the Stalking Wind—assassins who are appointed to patrol the borders of the valley," said Lamachi. "Their job is to eliminate any intruders who are non-initiates of the Divine Jaguar. To get you to identify yourself they'll use subtle hand signals—they'll touch their fingers to their lips like this and slide it to here, as if they have an itch. Then they'll expect you to reply by placing your fingers here on your cheek and slide them back in the opposite direction. After that you have to mix blood with them and recite the oaths of obeisance."

"Mix blood?" asked Harry.

"It's a ritual," Lamachi replied. "Every Seeker has to comply. I can teach you all the various hand signals with the appropriate reply. As for the rest, perhaps they'll be happy enough if just I participate—"

"*No,*" said Zedekiah firmly. "We will not, cannot, and *shall not* put forth the pretense that we are servants of evil—not even for one instant! Not even for a single *gesture!* Such a lie would compound itself. The Adversary would put a stranglehold on all of us!"

"You're overreacting," Lamachi argued. "The things I know can save us. They can. I guarantee it. Then we can all go on to accomplish a far greater good—"

Zedekiah shook his head vigorously. He put his hands on the teenager's shoulders. "Listen to me, Lamachi. To contend that one might commit some meager sin to accomplish some greater feat of righteousness is a justification as old as evil itself. Such logic is always contrary to the laws of heaven. Righteousness begets righteousness. Sin begets sin. We will proclaim ourselves servants of Christ, or proclaim nothing at all."

Lamachi's lips drooped into a pout. He let Zedekiah's words sink in for a moment.

"All right, all right," he said with an edge of resentment. "I won't do any rituals."

Zedekiah pushed it further, "Or gestures."

Lamachi rolled his eyes. "Or gestures."

I wondered if Lamachi could keep such a promise. Many of these Gadianton formalities were second nature to him. Most of them were so simple. They could be executed swiftly. One wisp of the hand and our lives might be spared. Lamachi would have to work hard to catch himself.

His presentiments about the dangers we might face on the road caused Gidgiddonihah to march far out ahead of the rest of us. We only sighted him intermittently as a distant dot while we crossed some wide or flat place where the brush and trees were sparse. As the day progressed our lead scout shouted back no warnings. The road had become far less distinct than it had been in the land of Zarahemla. Much of the trail was covered with a fine, light dust. Our feet kicked it up, and the wind carried it high in the air. We tugged our mantles up over our mouths, but our eyes still watered and grit collected in our nostrils.

At last the trail carried us up a steep knoll covered with bushes that resembled sagebrush and large plants with spiked leaves. We were startled to find Gidgiddonihah crouched about halfway to the top. His spear and obsidian-edged sword, purchased in the markets of Sidom, were laid neatly side by side, as if ready for use.

"Stop," he said quietly. "There are six men just over that rise. Of Lamanite descent, as far as I can tell. Rough types, resting right in the middle of the road where it passes through a grove of trees. Preparing for a midday bite to eat from the looks of it."

"Assassins?" asked Harry.

"Possibly," said Gidgiddonihah.

"Definitely," said Lamachi. "I'd wager we're within three days of Jacobugath. That is said to be the most distant perimeter of the Stalking Wind patrols."

Adrenaline seeped into my veins. My eyes began scanning the surrounding hills. My fingers found the hilt of my sword. "Are there others watching us?"

"I've been studying the hills for some time," said Gidgiddonihah. "I've seen no sign."

"Then they don't know we're here," I said confidently.

Gidgiddonihah shattered that confidence. "Oh, they know we're here. Who needs long-range lookouts with all this dust we've been kicking up? I'm quite certain they already know we're coming."

"Is there a way we can avoid these men—just go around them?" asked Zedekiah.

Gidgiddonihah shook his head. "If we fail to make an appearance, they'll only come looking for us. No, I'm afraid this is a confrontation we cannot avoid."

"Do they know our numbers?" asked Zedekiah.

"Doubtful," said Gidgiddonihah. "But by the amount of dust we've raised, they'll know that we are not many."

"So what will be their first move?" I asked soberly. "How

can we prepare?"

"Wait here," said Gidgiddonihah. He climbed back toward the top of the knoll. Then he laid on his belly and crawled out of sight.

"What's he doing?" asked Harry.

I shook my head. After a minute, Gidgiddonihah reappeared, crawling backwards. When he felt he'd slunk far enough down the slope, he stood and rejoined us.

He snorted knowingly. "Now there are only three to be seen. It's the oldest robber trick in existence. As soon as we descend into their camp, they will courteously invite us to join them in their meal. The instant we reveal that we are not of their fellowship, they will signal the others to close in."

"I will recognize that signal," said Lamachi.

"Not that it will matter right away," said Gidgiddonihah. "If all goes according to their desires, they will wait until you are lulled into a friendly sense of security—until you can be convinced to lay your weapons far off to the side."

"*Our* weapons?" I said alarmingly. "Where are *you* going to be?"

"I will be doing precisely what they're doing," he replied. "I'll imitate their method of ambush, but from a more distant position. This will allow me to determine the location of the other three men. In the meantime, the rest of you will march right into the trap as if you haven't been forewarned. Accept their invitation to stop and rest and eat. But do not appear too stupid and trusting or they'll immediately become suspicious. The situation will become far more grave."

"You'll need help," said Lamachi. "I'll go with you."

"No," said Gidgiddonihah firmly. "I work better alone. The others will need you with them."

Gidgiddonihah hesitated a moment. His eyes scanned us from top to bottom—myself, my ten-year-old son, Zedekiah, and the teenager, Lamachi. He glanced at the ground in what I perceived to be slight disappointment, then he uttered, "God be with us." He picked up his weapons and disappeared stealthily around one side of the knoll.

I understood Gidgiddonihah's apprehensions. The two

members of our expedition whom he had been counting on as comrades in battle were both dead. Now he stood alone—the only man among us with any formal training as a fighter. In essence, it was up to him to protect us all, and he undoubtedly felt the weight of it. There was something to be said for the character of someone who refused to shrink in the face of such depressing odds.

Despite our lack of training, we were nevertheless armed to the teeth, with the sole exception of Zedekiah, who wore only a long stone knife. He felt it was pointless to carry anything else since an enemy would have known at a glance that he was entirely incapable of wielding it.

Even Harry carried a bow. Gidgiddonihah had purchased one just his size in Sidom, as well as three arrows. From time to time during the past few days he'd paused to take aim at a pheasant or an armadillo or some other type of small game, but as yet he hadn't succeeded in hitting one.

Lamachi looked the most ludicrous of all. He carried two spears—one long and one short—an obsidian-edged sword, a shield which hung behind his neck as well as a club and a knife hooked to his belt. He'd also purchased protective padding for his legs and arms as well as a war helmet that probably hadn't seen battle since the days of Captain Moroni. The helmet's crown was overlaid with eagle feathers, now worn and scraggly. Since Lamachi remained reluctant to carry any other supplies besides his meager travel-pack filled with corn and jerky, he might not have been any more weighted down than the rest of us, but he certainly looked more awkward.

The flint knife he wore was the same one he'd used to kill Jonathan. Gidgiddonihah had given it to him as a gesture of thanks. It still revealed the stain of Jonathan's blood. None of us had yet worked up the nerve to tell him that wearing a bloody weapon was uncouth at best. I think events in Sidom had led him to believe he was some kind of one-man liberation force. That morning he'd informed my son that if it wasn't for him, we'd all be "meat for the maggots." He was absolutely right, so it was hard to be offended. But a speech extolling the dangers of unrighteous pride was certainly due.

As for myself, I carried only an obsidian-edged sword. As a boy I'd enjoyed the benefit of some expert training with this weapon under the tutelage of Hagoth and another Nephite named Benjamin. But that was almost thirty years ago. Soon after we had purchased the weapon in Sidom, Gidgiddonihah had to reteach me how to strap it onto my back. This confirmed for me how little I remembered.

We made our way to the top of the knoll at a casual stride. Just before we stepped into full view of the assassin's camp, I felt compelled to pull Harry to a halt.

"You will wait here," I said to him.

Harry frowned as if he might argue the point. But he held his tongue and gave a reluctant nod.

"Stay low," I ordered him. "Don't make your presence known for any reason. Approach only after you feel certain that things are safe."

Harry got down on the ground. He tried to send me a reassuring smile, but it appeared mechanical. He was terrified. So was I.

We continued our progress over the knoll. The campsite fell into view. The three Lamanite men were nonchalantly feeding sticks to a newly kindled fire. We continued toward them in single file. They acted only mildly concerned at our approach, focusing most of their attention on propping a pair of spits over the fire to cook some fresh game. Zedekiah raised his arm in greeting. One of the Lamanites rose to his feet. He, like his companions, wore only a shoulder mantle with a scanty loincloth and leather leggings.

"Welcome, fellow travelers!" he called out, grinning amiably. "We haven't enjoyed anyone's companionship but our own for the past four days. Come! Will you share our patch of shade? Perhaps even a bite of our humble fare?"

He indicated two skinny birds that his comrades were threading onto the spits. Only about eighty percent of the feathers had been removed. The head and the feet were still attached, but this seemed good enough for them.

"Thank you," I replied. "We'd be delighted. Been living on corn mush since we left Sidom."

"Sidom, you say?" one of the other men replied. "Oh, how I miss Sidom. The food. The wine . . ."

"The women!" added the third man, earning a jovial slap on the arm from his friend.

"Here," the first man continued. "Take off your packs. Rest with us. They say the next signs of civilization are in the city of Gilgal, two days north. Might this be your destination, friends?"

We hesitated a second. "Yes," Lamachi finally replied.

"I see," said the Lamanite. "Well, my name is Korihah. This is Mithgil and Agash."

We gave them our names and settled around the fire. But we did not set aside our weapons—a point that didn't seem to concern them very much for now. I only gave them my first name. As always, my nationality inspired conversation.

"You have a unique appearance, Jim," Korihah told me. "Where is your clan?"

"North," I replied.

"Beyond the great deserts?"

"That's right."

"How interesting. I've never met a man from that region."

"Now you have," I said. I glanced at the two birds roasting over the flames. "You know, those scrawny birds will scarcely feed the three of you. We have a dozen of our porters out hunting at this very moment. They should be back any time. Perhaps they will add to our meal."

Korihah's grin changed into a hurtful look. He said reproachfully, "So quickly you refer to your unseen numbers. That's not very congenial. Do you take us for bandits, friends?"

And there it was. He touched his face in exactly the manner that Lamachi had described. The dark sign had been given. Lamachi brought his own hand to his face. I thought for certain he would ignore all the counsel Zedekiah had given him and return the sign. But at the last instant, he bit down on his fingernail and looked away.

"Of course not," Zedekiah replied. "As you can see, we have nothing of value for you to steal."

Korihah hesitated, his eyes still on Lamachi. He sensed that

Lamachi had recognized the sign. But if this was so, why had no countersign been offered?

"We are traveling light ourselves," said Korihah. "It's shameful that so little trust exists on the roads these days. I offer a proposal. Let us set aside all of our weapons and enjoy a warm meal."

To set the example, he snatched up his own spear and prepared to place it ostensibly out of reach. But before he leaned it against a nearby tree, he raised it in the air and gave it a twirl. Lamachi looked at me to indicate that the sign for the others to close in had just been issued. Where was Gidgiddonihah?

"There," said Korihah, plopping back down at the fire. "Now if you will just show us the same courtesy, I will have Mithgil and Agash do the same, and we can enjoy a fine lunch together."

The three men watched us and waited. I glanced over at Lamachi and then at Zedekiah. I could tell by the looks on their faces that they were not about to comply.

I turned back to Korihah and said. "Your good will is commendable, but I think we feel more comfortable with our property close at hand."

Several tense seconds ticked by. I feared violence was close at hand. At last Korihah smiled and turned up his wrists in acquiescence. "As you wish." Fortunately, he did not retrieve his spear. This would have been an obvious act of aggression and he wasn't quite ready to play this card.

The one called Mithgil said to Lamachi, "That's a very interesting helmet. Quite the relic." I perceived that he was being sarcastic. "May I see it?"

Lamachi shook his head. "I never let anyone else touch it."

"As well you shouldn't," Mithgil patronized. "It's terribly fearsome-looking."

"So tell us," I continued nervously, "how is the road to Gilgal this time of year? Is there anything we should be wary of?"

"Oh, yes," said Korihah. "It's a miserable road. Robbers do abound. I might better recommend the road to . . . Jacobugath." He studied us for a reaction.

"Jacobugath?" I said, feigning ignorance. "I've never heard of such a place."

"Haven't you?" said Korihah. "Then you might wish to know"—his eyes narrowed—"you missed the road to Gilgal by a day."

My heart pounded. My reflexes became as taut as catapults. No more games. We knew each other now as enemies.

All at once, Korihah sprang to his feet, at the same time releasing a guttural cry—the signal for his comrades to attack. Agash reached for his sword. He lunged toward Lamachi who reached for his own sword. I raised my own blade. And Zedekiah—yes, frail Zedekiah—leaped to tackle Korihah before he could retrieve his spear against the tree.

Mithgil armed himself as well, but as he poised himself to fight, his eyes darted around in confusion. Where were the others? Why hadn't they emerged from the undergrowth to join in the slaughter?

Korihah managed easily to throw Zedekiah off to the side. He began scrambling again for the spear. Mithgil raised his sword and began charging at me. Out of the corner of my eye, I noticed that as Korihah grasped for the spear, another blade came swinging around from the other side of the trunk. Gidgiddonihah's sword struck beneath his ribs.

I raised my sword to ward off Mithgil's blow. As our two weapons collided, chips of obsidian shattered. I felt one of the slivers hit near my eye, which distracted me for half a second. My opponent might have used this opportunity to finish me, but instead I saw him arch his spine and throw back his head. Gidgiddonihah's spear had been hurled into his back.

Lamachi and Agash continued their struggle. Lamachi was down. His sword had been knocked free. The weight of all his other weapons made it difficult for him to rise. Agash might have slain him without expending much effort, but he didn't appear all too eager. There was an arrow protruding from the flesh under his armpit. *An arrow?* I thought. The only one with a bow was—

"Yes!" Harry cried, clenching his fist in victory.

My son stood within a dozen yards of the clearing.

Pheasants and foxes had escaped his aim, but Agash had not. Harry's arrow had not penetrated deeply. The wound was just obnoxious enough that it had caused the assassin to look about. He saw that his companions were dead. The others had not appeared. Agash abandoned his objective to slit Lamachi's throat and fled into the foliage.

Armed now with only his sword, Gidgiddonihah crashed into the underbrush after him. The rest of us gathered around Lamachi, who appeared to be in some pain. Zedekiah knelt at his side.

"Are you all right, my boy?" asked Zedekiah.

"Yes," said Lamachi. "His knife scraped me, but I'll be all right."

There was a hefty tear in his mantle over the stomach, and evidence of blood.

"Let me take a look," said Zedekiah, leaning forward.

Lamachi flailed his arms. "I'm *fine!*" he insisted. "You think I can't handle a scrape? I'm perfectly fine."

"At least let us dress it for you," said Zedekiah.

"I'll dress it myself." And to prove his machismo, he came to his feet without a wince and went to make himself a bandage.

I turned to my son, my temper ready to explode for having been disobeyed—*again.*

Harry threw up his hands. "Before you lose it, Dad, I want you to know, I didn't come down off that hill until I saw Gidgiddonihah sneaking toward you. If he was closing in, I figured the other three guys were taken care of. You said to wait until I was sure it was safe."

It was on the tip of my tongue to start ranting, *Safe? Have you lost your mind? What if the man had attacked you instead of running?* I'm glad I didn't say it. I swallowed my anger and cupped my hand around the back of Harry's head. "You did fine, son. Just fine."

Harry tried to steal a look at the bodies of the other two assassins. I attempted to spare him the sight by blocking his view. Then I noticed that Korihah was still alive. I approached him with Zedekiah. Korihah's torso was cut open. He'd lost more blood than I thought a man could lose and still be lucid; nevertheless he dredged up the energy to spit a curse.

"May you rot—all of you!—rot in the nothingness of Akmul! Spies! Vermin! You think you can reach it? The sacred city? You think you will ever live to report to your people? I will die in glory! You will die in disgrace! My name will be remembered. Yours will be a hiss on the night wind."

"It won't be long now," said Zedekiah calmly, "and you will know for certain how wrong you have been."

Korihah seethed, "It won't be long for you either, Christian!"

"How did you know that we were Christians?" Zedekiah inquired.

The expression on Korihah's face softened. It became quizzical, as if he was seriously trying to figure out how he knew this.

"May God be merciful to you, Korihah," said Zedekiah.

Suddenly Korihah's expression transformed again—this time into one of breathless terror. The sight of it was chilling. Right before our eyes his face turned ashen white. It was with that expression locked in place that the final gasp seeped out of his lungs.

He never answered Zedekiah's question. I might easily suppose that he had deduced our religion by some mannerism. Or perhaps it was possible that in those final seconds of life something of his preexistent awareness returned. I don't want to make more out of this than it merits, but I'll never forget that expression. I'd give anything if I could reproduce it at will for the benefit of anyone still procrastinating repentance.

"So we're even, right?" Harry said to Lamachi. "You saved my life. I saved yours."

"Right," said Lamachi, wincing as he pressed a dampened cloth against his wound. "Even."

Harry hadn't expected Lamachi to agree so readily. My son beamed.

A few moments later Gidgiddonihah returned to the clearing, sweating and panting. He made an exasperated groan. If he'd been a profane man, I'm sure he'd have spouted off more than a few.

"I lost him! I can't believe it! He slipped away from me! Just slipped away! No sign at all. If only Naaman had been here—"

"He'll warn others," I said.

"*Of course* he'll warn others!" said Gidgiddonihah. "In less than two days this valley will be *boiling* with Reds. The road to Jacobugath will be shoulder to shoulder with assassins! Each of them will have an eyewitness description. *They'll know us on sight!*"

"Let's be calm," said Zedekiah, "and consider our options."

"What options?" gruffed Gidgiddonihah. "At least before today we had the luxury of anonymity! Now we have *nothing!*" He faced the underbrush again. "I have to find that man!"

I stopped him. "It's pointless. It was bound to happen. Lamachi warned us that there would be patrols. We couldn't have avoided them."

Zedekiah turned to Lamachi, "Is there another road to Jacobugath?"

Lamachi continued to press the rag against his wound. "They say there is another. Somewhere over there." He pointed feebly to the southwest. "But I think it's very distant. I don't know the way. I never learned it."

"Then we must travel in that direction," said Zedekiah. "It's our only option."

We turned toward the southwest. Less than a mile away arose a steep slope smothered in vines and undergrowth. Beyond it was a line of peaks even higher and more foreboding. The sight was disheartening. It would have been a comparable situation if the Mormon pioneers had tried to enter the Salt Lake Valley by climbing over every summit in the Wasatch Front instead of arriving through one of the canyons.

"Going that way might take weeks," I contended. "My daughter can't wait that long! I need to reach her *now!*"

Zedekiah offered some words of encouragement. "How can we know what's beyond those peaks? We might lose a day, we might even gain a day. Since we don't seem to have any other choice, we would do best to trust in the Lord's opportunities."

"If we go in that direction," said Lamachi, "I can't help you. I only know the highway of the Smoke Eater."

Gidgiddonihah continued gazing off toward the slopes, ruminating on the possibilities. "If we entered the valley of Jacobugath by such an impractical route, we might find ourselves beyond the patrols. No one would inquire after our affiliations. Our anonymity would be restored. It might work. It just might work."

I couldn't deny the logic. But it was tearing at my heart—it was driving me out of my mind—to consider that I could possibly lose any more time. I saw that we had no other choice. I hoisted my pack.

"If we're going," I said, "then let's get going."

CHAPTER 11

During the fight with Jacob's assassins, a piece of obsidian had made a nasty cut at the corner of my eye. It didn't bleed very much. In fact I didn't think it was going to bother me at all until shortly after we started climbing. Sweat started oozing into it, mingled with dirt. It stung like the dickens.

After a few hours we conquered the first summit. Then, to our dismay, we found that it was only a brief interlude before our next ascent. As the sun began to settle behind the mountains, we were still in the process of climbing the second slope, striving hard to keep from knocking loose any debris that might send the person to the rear tumbling to his death. We made our camp on a very thin ledge. One wouldn't think that insects would be so pesky at such an unlikely spot, but the little varmints nearly ate us alive. At least there was plenty of brush, so we had a warm fire to reheat our dinner, which consisted of the two birds left by our assassin friends. However, just before the final advent of darkness, Gidgiddonihah snuffed the flames completely out.

"At this height," he proclaimed, "a fire would be like a beacon, drawing our enemies to us as surely as it draws these blasted mosquitoes." He slapped one on his chin.

Throughout the evening, Lamachi was uncharacteristically quiet, apparently favoring his wound. We had all expressed concern for him throughout the day, but any inquiry about his condition was rudely repulsed with, "I'm fine! Worry about yourself!"

Since he seemed to be keeping up well enough, even with all his weapons dangling about him, we had not allowed ourselves to become overly concerned. But now that the day was over, it was clear that he was *not* fine. All of us were exhausted, but Lamachi looked like death warmed over. And he was the teenager. He should have been in the prime of fitness. All of us suspected that the wound was much worse than he'd first let on, but he staunchly refused to let us examine it, keeping it hidden beneath his shield.

At sunup, we started climbing again. Before noon we had scaled the next summit. At first our spirits were buoyed by the sight of a level plateau, but as we entered it, we found it utterly choked by the nastiest sorts of thorns and briars. It took us the rest of the morning just to find a way through it. To our good fortune, however, we found a freshwater spring and eagerly began refilling our leather canteens.

I put my face into the stream and drank blissfully. Lamachi staggered up behind me. I was so entranced by the taste of the cool water that I didn't notice right away that he just stood there, staring into the stream, desperate for a drink, but lacking the strength even to kneel down and take it. I finally turned to look at him. His eyes appeared listless, hypnotized.

"Lamachi?" I asked.

As he continued staring at the water, the shield he'd used to cover the wound finally dropped to his side. For the first time, I noticed that his lap was drenched in blood.

"Lamachi!" I exclaimed. "You're bleeding!"

"It's nothing," he said dreamily. "I tore it a little . . . that's all."

Zedekiah came forward and said severely, "You will show me that wound, boy. You will show it to me this instant."

Before Zedekiah had even finished speaking, Lamachi's eyelids fluttered. He started to collapse. I caught him in my arms.

Zedekiah removed the blood-soaked bandages from Lamachi's stomach. We all got our first look at the wound that Lamachi had tried to convince us was little more than a scratch. It cut all the way from his navel halfway to his right hip. Maybe it hadn't looked quite so ghastly when the assassin had first inflicted it, but with all our marching and climbing, it was now nearly two inches deep and seething with infection. I feared that behind the film of infection the internal organs themselves might be exposed. I felt Lamachi's head. He was burning with fever. I was astonished that he had made it as far as he had. I think each of us felt guilt-stricken that we had not forced him to show us the wound earlier.

Having lost consciousness for only a few seconds, Lamachi continued to be defiant of our attentions. "Why make such a fuss?" he said. "Just wash it. Wash it and let's get going."

"It needs more than a washing," said Gidgiddonihah. "It needs to be cauterized."

"I've never seen such a deep wound in such a vital place cauterized," said Zedekiah.

"Are there plants around here we could use to make medicine?" I asked.

Gidgiddonihah shook his head. "I know little of the healing arts."

Zedekiah looked around. "I'm familiar with the herbs of Zarahemla. But these plants . . . these are unfamiliar to me."

"A blessing," said Harry. "You can give him a blessing, Dad."

I clasped my son in gratitude. Leave it to a child to be the voice of inspiration in a time of panic. I said to Zedekiah, "If ever we needed the healing power of God, it's now."

Zedekiah agreed. We laid our hands upon Lamachi's head. I think it would have been more appropriate to allow Zedekiah to pronounce the blessing, but at the time I was not thinking about appropriateness. I was eager to invoke the power of God and continue our journey with as little delay as possible.

I called Lamachi by name and declared, "By the power and authority of the Holy Melchizedek priesthood, I lay my hands upon your head and pronounce a blessing upon you—that you may be healed, that you may recover fully and completely, that you may . . . be healed . . . recover . . ." My train of thought escaped me. I shook myself and tried to continue. "I bless you that you may be restored to perfect . . . perfect . . ." I shook myself again. For the life of me I could not concentrate! This had never happened to me before—not even during the multiple blessings that I had given my sweet Renae. But she had ended up dying anyway!

At last I drew what I thought was a reasonable conclusion. I had usurped Zedekiah's authority. I opened my eyes. Everyone was gaping at me with great curiosity. Everyone except Lamachi, whose eyes remained closed as he drew short breaths.

I turned to Zedekiah. "Forgive me. You should pronounce it."

Zedekiah hesitated a moment, then he nodded, lowered his chin, and closed his eyes. The rest of us did the same.

"By the authority of the Holy Priesthood," he began, "I declare by the voice of the Holy Spirit which is in me . . ." He paused as he truly sought to be in tune with that Voice. ". . . I declare that you, Lamachi, shall know of a certainty the goodness and glory of God, your Eternal Father . . . You, Lamachi, having renounced the wickedness of your upbringing, and the corruption of your youth, having embraced the joy and salvation of your Lord, Jesus Christ . . . shall be comforted in your trials and in your pain from this time henceforth and forever . . . Your Father in Heaven loves you . . . He knows your heart in a way that no other living creature knows it . . . Let his Holy Spirit embrace you now and administer unto your soul that great and final healing . . . found only through the peace, and the power, and the perfection of God. In the sacred and holy name of Jesus Christ. Amen."

I opened my eyes. The first thought that came to me was, *What kind of a blessing was that?* I ran the contents of the blessing through my mind and tried to decide if Lamachi had been promised to live or die. I gave Zedekiah a quizzical look, hoping he might offer enlightenment, but I sensed that he considered himself only the messenger, having spoken only the words dictated to him by the power of the Spirit.

I looked down at Lamachi. He seemed to be asleep, but his breathing was much easier, and there was a distinct solemnity to his face.

A gray sky was moving over us. For Lamachi's sake, we

decided to find shelter. The landscape did not look promising for this. Mostly it was a flat plateau blanketed with briars and pale grasses as well as the occasional cluster of cedar trees and another tree whose species I could not name. But in the far distance we could just make out what appeared to be some outcroppings of rock. We each made an effort to unstrap, unbuckle, and untie all the weapons and gear that Lamachi had weighted around his body. We left the bulk of it by the spring. Gidgiddonihah lifted the sleeping Lamachi into his arms. I thought for sure he would cry out as he was lifted, but he was so weak that he didn't even awaken.

After half an hour we reached the rocks. Rain had started to drizzle. The weather was surprisingly chilly. All of us could have done with another layer of clothing. It was not a comforting thought to imagine what the temperature might be like after sundown.

Gidgiddonihah was starting to strain with the weight of the injured teenager. Lamachi's blood had soaked his chest. I came forward and relieved him of his burden. Lamachi remained asleep as he was transferred to my arms. I looked into his face, so helpless and so *young*. He was only eighteen years old—just a kid. Never had I missed my own century more than now. A modern physician probably could have healed him in a heartbeat. Even an ancient physician might have saved him. But here we were in the middle of nowhere. He was entirely in the hands of God.

Lamachi was heavier than I'd anticipated. My forearms weren't quite as developed as the husky Gidgiddonihah. Fortunately, Harry pointed out to us what looked like the mouth of a cave.

After a few minutes, we reached the entrance. The tunnel went in for quite some distance, although none of us were eager to explore it. I set Lamachi down on a sleeping mat that Zedekiah had laid out. Gidgiddonihah broke out the flint and tinder to build a fire just inside the mouth while my son and I set out to gather wood.

Soon we'd built a blaze from the branches of those sagebrush-looking plants that I'd noted at the lower altitude. It was a smoky fire, but quite warm, and we huddled around it. Lamachi awakened, but he was still delirious with fever. Zedekiah undressed the wound. He placed the blade of Gidgiddonihah's copper hatchet in the fire to heat it for cauterizing.

"I'll be fine in just a little while," Lamachi mumbled. "You'll see. Just a little while . . . and I'll be fine."

I glanced at my son. His fingers were white and knotted together like a cauliflower. He watched Lamachi's every move, a desperate prayer beating in his heart. Lamachi's condition had disturbed him more than I'd realized. I tried to imagine myself as a ten-year-old boy again. I tried to comprehend the emotional roller coaster that Harry had been riding nonstop since the night of my arrest. If Lamachi died, I feared he would not handle it well. It might be the last straw that would finally break his flagging spirit. He stood and began wringing his hands. I could tell the pressure was becoming too much. He had to get out of here.

"He should have meat," Harry decided. "I'll go hunting, see if I can bring something back for him."

Zedekiah smiled approvingly. We still had four or five hours of daylight. "Good idea," he said. "I'm sure he would enjoy that very much."

"Careful," Gidgiddonihah interjected. "I saw jaguar dung a ways back. They aren't known to hunt at this time of day, but there's always the exception."

This announcement helped me decide to accompany Harry on his hunting expedition. At the same time, I couldn't resist asking, "What do jaguars *normally* do at this time of day?"

"Sleep," said Gidgiddonihah.

"Sleep where?"

Everyone's eyes turned toward the darkened tunnel of the cave.

"Don't worry," said Gidgiddonihah. "If there was a jaguar about, it would have made its presence known the moment it heard our voices."

Rain continued drizzling outside, but this didn't discourage us. If we'd insisted on staying inside whenever there was a little rain, we'd still be in Zarahemla. Harry and I wandered toward the west, away from the cave, where the plateau dropped into a ravine before sloping upward to a somewhat higher shelf.

"We might see something up there, don't you think?" I said. "Maybe some deer?"

Harry had an arrow in his bow, but he looked distracted. I sensed that he wasn't all too anxious to shoot anything.

"Dad," he said, "how long before Lamachi gets better?"

"I don't know," I replied. I touched my son's shoulder. "Harry, you should be prepared. Lamachi, he . . . he may not get better."

"Yes, he will," said Harry. "Zedekiah promised that he would be healed."

"That's . . . not exactly what he promised." I tried to recall the words so I could repeat them, but I couldn't remember.

"I thought I'd made us even," said Harry.

"Even?"

"I thought when I'd shot that assassin . . . I thought I'd saved his life. But I didn't. I was too slow."

"It wasn't your fault," I consoled. "Don't blame yourself. You can't always take such things so personally."

He may have surmised that I was also referring to the blame he took upon himself for the death of his mother. Still, my amateur psychology had little effect on the ten-year-old. Harry continued to look downcast as we started climbing the other side of the ravine. I was about to change the subject, suggest some strategies for brushing out game, when my foot sank into something quite foul. I turned my eyes downward and pulled my sandal from a pile of manure that was larger than any pile I'd ever seen. It was five times the size of anything I'd noticed in my Uncle Spencer's cow pasture. My foot had broken through a dried outer crust to reveal a mushy, green interior. But whereas I'd have normally sought some patch of grass on which I could wipe my shoe, I just stood there, flabbergasted.

"What in blazes—?"

"Wow," said Harry, his voice subdued. "What do you think made *that*?"

I shook my head and examined the manure pile a little more

closely to be sure it wasn't some bizarre kind of mushroom or fungus. Its odor eliminated all other possibilities. "I know this much," I said. "It's not something we're gonna bring down with one of your arrows."

"Curelom," said Harry. The word made us feel very uneasy as we recalled Naaman's eerie tales.

Harry started up the hill again, only now with considerably more caution. I almost suggested that we go back to the cave. But I couldn't deny that I was driven by an insatiable curiosity—the same curiosity that had beset me ever since the very day I had read that unusual word in the Book of Ether. What in the world *was* a curelom?

Toward the top of the ravine, Harry and I knelt and climbed the rest of the way on our hands and knees. At the top, we peered over the rim. It was just another grassy shelf that went on for about a hundred yards before it sloped up another hill, this time dropping off the other side, keeping the landscape beyond a total mystery. Harry and I stood.

"Do you want to go back?" I asked.

"Do you?" he replied.

I stared ahead. "Let's just see what's on the other side of that hill. Then we'll go back."

"Agreed," said Harry.

I wondered, however, what we might do if we simply saw *another* hill beyond it. Would either of us have the willpower to turn back rather than climb just one more hill? Sooner or later we would surely find a vantage point that would allow us to take in the breadth of the entire plateau.

Harry and I had barely gone another ten steps when we found a second pile of manure. Only this one did not have a dried outer crust. It looked and smelled as fresh as if it had been dropped there that morning.

"Wow," said Harry, again in his subdued, understated tone.

"Let me have your bow and arrow," I said.

"Why?" asked Harry.

"Just give it to me!" I said impatiently.

After I had added meagerly to my own security with Harry's loaded bow, my son and I continued trudging toward the next gentle slope. We saw two more piles of manure before we started to climb. One was so fresh that I'd have sworn the drizzling rain was causing it to give off steam. As we started up the hill, Harry suddenly grabbed my arm.

"Did you hear that?" he asked.

"Hear what?"

"The ground," he said. "It rumbled. I felt a vibration."

We paused and listened. I felt and heard nothing.

"It's your imagination," I said.

"Let's go back," said Harry.

"Are you sure?" I asked. Then I felt ashamed. Who was the father here anyway? It was time to heed the warning signal in my gut. "All right. We'll go back."

We'd barely turned back around when I heard the sound. Was it a growl? A snort? I spun back and looked toward the top of the ridge. Something was up there. I knew it. It was just over the other side. Whatever it was, my instincts told me that it was headed this way.

"Should we run?" Harry whispered.

I shook my head. I feared that this would be a serious mistake. When I was a kid I'd watched some documentary on grizzly bears that had advised that when confronted by a predator, the best thing to do was stand your ground. *Stand your ground???* Maybe I was remembering it wrong. Anyway, I decided to meet this advice halfway.

"Over here," I said to my son.

To our left grew three of those large prickly-leaf plants that had dominated much of the mountain landscape. The fronds were woven tightly together, and might hide us fairly well. We took cover behind the plants and peeled our eyes toward the top of the ridge. I felt another rumble in the earth. There was definitely something up there.

I drew my son close to me. Neither of us breathed. Our hearts pounded in stereo. When would it appear? Would my son and I become the first twentieth-century humans to lay our eyes on an actual, real-life curelom?

All at once, something brown came into view beyond the grasses at the top of the ridge—two humps, bobbing up and down, as if the animal that owned the humps was uncertain of the direction it had chosen. Perhaps it had smelled us. Perhaps it was stalking us.

As more of the humps came into view, I determined that the animal was not stalking anything. It bobbed as it fed. The animal was eating grasses at the top of the ridge. Maybe this should have comforted me. Cureloms were harmless herbivores. Then I remembered several examples of predators that ate both plants *and* meat—grizzlies for one.

Harry gave a jerk, as if the urge to run had become overwhelming. I tightened my hold on him. I would not let my son flee across the plateau only to watch him be run down like a rabbit and swallowed whole by a creature as a large as a house.

And then, to our breathless wonderment, the entire creature lumbered into view. For several seconds, Harry and I were stunned. Our hearts stopped. In all of my life I'd never seen anything as terrible and magnificent. It stood against the shrill gray sky, not an inch less than fifteen feet in height. It had at least ten tons of girth, a sloping back, a high, dome-shaped head, and fur as brown as chocolate except for a patch of silver on its chest. Its yellowish "teeth" as Naaman had called them, were actually tusks, ten feet long, jutting out from either side of its mouth and then curving and twisting inward like the rakes of some great piece of farm machinery. Its trunk curled around large swatches of grass and plants, yanking them out of the earth and stuffing them into its mouth.

Harry could barely find his breath as he muttered, "That's a . . . that's a m-mam-mam—"

I completed the word for him, but with no less consternation in my voice. "Mammoth. It's a woolly mammoth."

I couldn't believe what I was seeing! Standing on the hillside less than a hundred yards above us was a creature that inhabited our modern-day world only in fantasies and nightmares. How was this possible? It was like stepping through the movie screen of *Jurassic Park*. Every book I'd ever read claimed that woolly mammoths had been extinct by this date—extinct for thousands of years! Maybe it *wasn't* a woolly mammoth. To be honest, it looked far less "woolly" than pictures I'd seen. There was hair all right, but not the kind of shaggy coat that would have withstood an Arctic winter. It must have been some sort of subspecies. One that had evolved in this warmer climate.

But who cared what subspecies it was? My goodness! The thing was as big as a two-story house! Comparing a modern elephant to it was like comparing a pickup to a semi. Wouldn't some scientist have known that a few isolated mammoths still roamed the earth as late as 33 A.D.?

The mammoth stopped feeding. It raised its head and tusks, as if my pronunciation of its twentieth-century name had been carried on the wind. Once again, Harry and I held our breaths. Its long trunk raised up as well, testing the air. And then the animal did something that I would have never thought possible. It stood on two legs. It actually transferred its massive weight onto its back feet and reared up for a better view of the surrounding terrain. Its front legs, about a third longer than its rear legs, looked considerably more dexterous than the legs of an elephant, as if it might even produce applause with the bottoms of its feet if it felt so inclined.

However, at the moment it did not look in the mood to applaud. It had heard us. It had smelled us. And it didn't seem pleased with the information. The beast dropped back down on all fours. The earth shook as it landed. It began tilting its head from side to side as it produced a half-snort, half-squeal that echoed off the surrounding peaks. I interpreted the sound immediately as a warning or a threat.

"What's it doing?" Harry whispered.

That whisper, so slight by any human perception, was the final piece of information it needed to triangulate our location. Its head turned squarely in our direction. Its massive feet began marching cautiously toward us. Who'd have guessed it could have such keen hearing, especially since its ears were so much smaller than any elephant's? As far as shape, they looked almost human. Maybe that explained it—no floppy "Dumbo-like" appendages to impair hearing.

It didn't take Harry and me long to decide that if we remained where we were, it would march right over the top of us.

"Run!" I cried.

I took Harry's hand and the two of us burst out of our place of hiding, kicking our legs like roadrunners. The mammoth roared—a dizzying sound!—and began to pursue us. We could hear its crashing steps as it accelerated to a full run. This was futile! It was only about seventy-five yards behind us. To believe we might outrun it was insane! The cave was still a quarter-mile away. There was no sanctuary—*nothing* between here and there wherein, -on, or -under we might take refuge. So it would end here, I thought. All our struggles and pains. And of all things, our lives would end as we were trampled into the ground by a ten-ton woolly mammoth.

We scurried toward the lip of the first hill that sloped down into the ravine. I'd have sworn I could actually hear the snorts of its breathing, like the chug of a locomotive. It was gaining on us at three to four times our own speed. And yet Harry and I dared not look back. What else could we do except make a bee-line toward the cave and hope for a miracle? A second roar erupted from its throat as we took our final step toward the lip of the hill. Any second those massive tusks would impale us like shish kebabs.

Unexpectedly, our feet fell out from under us. Harry and I went tumbling down the hillside. We hadn't noticed that erosion had created a three-foot ledge along this part of the hill. As Harry and I tumbled, we dropped off another ledge, this one about five-feet high. We landed with a grunt, but the dirt was quite soft. No sooner had I thrown myself over the top of my son than the sky was darkened by a monstrous shadow as the mammoth leaped right over the top of us and came down with all the force of an earthquake. The ledge above us collapsed under its weight, burying three-fourths of our bodies in dirt and mud. Harry began spitting and started to shake the dirt from his hair, but I pressed my palm against his forehead to keep him from moving.

The mammoth kept right on going down the hillside. It was several seconds before it stopped in confusion and swung its tusks to the left and to the right, trying to figure out where we'd gone. Finally, it turned around. Its fiery eye seemed to be looking right at us, but then it looked beyond us, and then to the right and left again. For the moment, our camouflage of dirt was just enough to deflect its senses.

The beast roared several more times in exasperation. It started galloping back up the hill. Since the climb was easier twenty feet to our left, it chose that path and soon went out of sight. Harry started to say something. I slapped my hand over his mouth, and it's a good thing that I did, because ten seconds later the mammoth returned, more frustrated than ever, tearing up the plants and brush with its tusks, trying to stir us out of our place of hiding. It began moving southward along the hillside where there was a dense bank of brush and shrubs.

I found the courage to turn my head and look down into the ravine, toward the outcropping of rock where the cave was situated. The mouth of the cave itself was just out of view around the other side. I spotted Gidgiddonihah making his way along the rocky shelf on the opposite side of the ravine. He must have heard the mammoth's roars. In his hands he carried a spear. I'd never for a moment considered Gidgiddonihah a fool, but what else could I think as I realized he was moving in the general direction of the mammoth? Even if he managed to sneak up on it, utilizing the same skills he'd used when he'd slayed the assassins, how could he possibly think a single spear could kill such a monster?

As the slope of the hill stretched southward, it made a slight bend. The mammoth had followed the hillside around far enough now that we could no longer see it. Still, we didn't dare make a move. That is, not until I glanced again at Gidgiddonihah and noticed that he was signaling us to make a dash toward the cave. I wondered how Gidgiddonihah had spotted us considering that the mammoth had not. I realized that from his vantage point, figuring out our hiding place would not have been difficult.

As Harry and I began pulling ourselves out of the dirt, I sighted a second mammoth. It was approaching Gidgiddonihah from the southeast. Some distance behind it I could see a *third* mammoth. The roars of the first one had apparently alerted the herd. I was about to warn

Gidgiddonihah, but I realized that the additional mammoths had not escaped his attention. Again, he waved us toward the cave.

"Are you injured?" I asked Harry.

He shook his head. I helped him up, and the two of us tore off down the ravine and then up toward the outcropping of rock. Behind us we could hear the roars of the mammoths, but they did not seem to be roaring at us—they were roaring at Gidgiddonihah.

When we reached the mouth of the cave, we found Zedekiah waiting.

"Where is Gidgiddonihah?" he asked anxiously.

We could all hear the mammoths now. From the echoes, it was impossible to tell where they were. What had made these animals so aggressive? African elephants may have been considered dangerous, but from what I'd heard, unless a person drew too close, particularly to a nursing mother, most of them were generally tolerant of humans. I'd never seen a creature that was so territorial.

Suddenly Gidgiddonihah appeared, running along the ravine, moving full-throttle toward the mouth of the cave. Not twenty-five yards behind him barreled the same steaming mammoth that had nearly killed Harry and me.

He'll never make it, I thought. But it's amazing what a little adrenaline can do. Gidgiddonihah vaulted the various shrubs and other obstructions like an Olympic athlete. There was no longer a spear in his hands to impede his progress. I looked at the mammoth to see if Gidgiddonihah's spear was sticking in its side, but there was no sign of this.

Man and mammoth continued their desperate race. With the beast a mere three steps from crushing him like an ant, Gidgiddonihah came flying into the mouth of the cave. The tusks of the angry curelom thrust themselves inside the cave's mouth. The tip of the right tusk grazed Gidgiddonihah's shoulder as we made a net of our arms to catch him. The massive body of the mammoth impacted the surrounding rock, showering us all with dirt and shale jarred loose from the roof. Hastily, its tusks retracted. Afterwards, it stomped and stammered around outside, tossing its head from side to side, seemingly cussing up a storm.

"Did you hit it with the spear?" I asked Gidgiddonihah.

"Are you serious?" he panted. "I dropped it and ran. Did you think I wanted to make it *really* angry?"

We soon realized that the mammoth had no intention of leaving the area in front of the cave. Shortly, it was joined by the other two mammoths, and then a fourth, and then a fifth. Within an hour we counted six cureloms within a half-mile radius of the cave. By all appearances they were determined to wait us out. Only after they were certain that we were destroyed did it look as though they would return to a normal existence of grazing on the plateau.

"Apparently Naaman's description of the curelom was no exaggeration," noted Zedekiah.

"Apparently not," Gidgiddonihah agreed.

* * *

We'd scarcely caught our breaths from our chase with the mammoths when we found ourselves facing another grim situation. In spite of the fact that his wound had been cauterized, Lamachi had shown no signs of improvement. In fact, his condition had worsened.

Throughout the evening he remained in his state of delirium, too weak to care about the presence of our woolly "guard dogs" outside. It wasn't long before we burned through all of the wood that Harry and I had collected for the fire. Even with his high fever, Lamachi began shivering uncontrollably. It was time to face the truth—none of us expected him to make it through the night. Our concerns over being trapped by a herd of mammoths took a back seat for the time being. As a pale sunset shone in the overcast sky, each of us kept a heartwrenching vigil at Lamachi's side.

The only moment when he showed any sign of lucidity was when he opened his eyes to request a drink of water. Fortunately our replenishment at the spring had allowed us to have plenty on hand. Zedekiah put the waterskin to the boy's lips. After he'd taken no more than what might have been required to moisten a dried mouth, he smiled, first at Zedekiah, and then at each of us in turn. Afterwards, he closed his eyes and drifted back into oblivion.

Zedekiah prayed. Harry wept. I felt guilty that I had ever let Lamachi's social awkwardness offend me. Such petty flaws seemed inconsequential now. We thought only of the fact that he had saved our lives. We testified to each other, and to him as well, though I doubt he heard, that without his guidance, none of us would have made it as far as we had.

In my lengthy prayers that night I asked my Heavenly Father the age-old question. I asked him *why*. Why couldn't he have healed an eighteen-year-old boy with his whole life ahead of him—a life that I felt certain would have been spent as a faithful servant of Christ? Was it because we didn't have enough faith between us? Why had my blessing been rejected? How was it that even Zedekiah had been unable to offer him a straight-forward, healing promise?

I felt myself growing angry inside. For the longest time I couldn't figure out why my feelings were so bitter. The emotions stirring inside me seemed to transcend our current circumstances. At last I realized that as I asked "why?" I was not only asking about Lamachi, I was asking about Renae. Despite the separation of centuries and other obvious differences, there were many things about these two tragedies that seemed remarkably similar. Both were pointless, unnecessary, and untimely. In both cases, the power of the priesthood had been invoked, but to no apparent avail. I'd always had a firm testimony of priesthood power. I'd seen it work in countless cases.

What was so different here? Why hadn't Lamachi—or Renae—qualified to reap the benefits of faith? In Renae's case, there had been no shortage of consolers who spoke of "a greater mission" that she'd been called to perform beyond the veil. Once I had proposed a similar explanation to a family whose daughter had died of leukemia. But in the cold fire of grief, this explanation is not always so consoling. For me it only inspired further questions. What possible mission could she have had that would have been greater than that of a wife and mother in mortality? Having no answer was like being trapped in a fog. Inside that fog, nothing about God's plan makes sense anymore. The temptation is strong to believe precisely what my son had suggested a few days earlier—that there is actually no plan at all. Just cold, random, heartless fate.

Was I destined to never learn the reasons why until I passed beyond the veil? It was only a few days ago that I had sagaciously told my son that some answers may not be forthcoming in this life. Latter-day Saints tell this to each other all the time, and for the most part we hear it with reverence and gratitude.

Why tonight, like that same night two and a half years before, did it sound so hollow?

About an hour past midnight, the announcement came.

"His heart has stopped," said Zedekiah in the darkness. "He's gone."

My son stirred from his half-sleep. Immediately, he sought me out for comfort. I shielded him in my arms. The hurt pierced him to the center of his heart. I wondered if he, too, had drawn parallels between Lamachi's death and the death of his mother.

"Why?" I whispered again.

And then an answer came.

It stirred in my mind like a warm wind from the deepest recesses of the earth: *Be still, and know that I am God.*

I caught my breath and let these words echo through my soul. It was so dark now that I couldn't see my hand in front of my face, and yet I'd rarely felt as surrounded by light as I did at that instant. Just as my arms encircled my son, I could feel myself encircled about by the love of God.

And so I was reminded of the great sustaining secret. Knowing the precise answers is not as crucial as the certainty that the answers do, in fact, exist. All we really want to know is that the helm is not unmanned. That the advocates of goodness and glory are still in control. That righteousness reigns. That perfection awaits. That the Atonement is real and available.

As I contemplated this, I found myself recounting the journey. Not our journey to Jacobugath, but the long, lonely road that I had traveled since Renae's passing, the journey that had brought me to this place and time. I thought about the depth of love that I felt for my children, the renewed strength and conviction that welled in my soul, the sharpening of my powers of discernment, the expansion of my capacity for empathy, the blossoming of my potential to know real, selfless joy, and the confidence I was gaining in my own spiritual wisdom.

As these realizations planted themselves in my heart, I considered the life of Lamachi, the Christian. I pondered his own contribution to my continued understanding of the principles of eternal progression and I realized that his contribution had not been insignificant. Once more the plan of salvation made sense.

I let my tears mingle with those of my son. And later that night, in a whisper as soft as a kiss, I spoke words to the darkness that might have sounded curious to some, but not to the one who most certainly heard, my Father in Heaven. I hoped he would convey the message.

"Thank you, Lamachi. Thank you, my sweet Renae."

CHAPTER 12

The sound awakened me from my sleep. It was a hollow and mournful sound, like a foghorn on a misty ocean. Gidgiddonihah and Zedekiah bolted awake as well. Harry finally stirred the second time it moaned.

It was barely light outside. There was only a slight difference between the darkness inside the cave and the darkness beyond the entrance. None of us eager to move. We were bundled closely together for warmth. Nevertheless, I followed Gidgiddonihah and Zedekiah to the mouth of the tunnel. Morning was rising fast on the landscape. In the pale light we could see the ghostly shapes of the mammoths on the plain before us. The foghorn had stirred them as well. They were rising to their feet, gazing in concern toward the north, where the sound had originated. For the third time, the mournful sound rankled the silence of the early hour.

"Conch-shell trumpet," declared Gidgiddonihah. "Someone is approaching."

They're in for quite a surprise, I thought. Obviously they didn't know that they were about to face the wrath of nearly a hundred tons of fuming mammoths. Maybe the distraction would give us a chance to escape.

To my astonishment, I realized that the mammoths were actually *frightened* by the noise. Frightened enough that all six of them began thundering off in the *opposite* direction. If a town had been in their path, several city blocks would have been leveled.

"This is our chance," I announced. "Let's grab the packs and get out of here."

This meant that we would leave Lamachi's body in the cave. In the dark of night Zedekiah had managed to bundle him inside his sleeping mat. Even so, abandoning him like this seemed an uncharitable way to treat the final remains of our friend. But as I thought about it, who could ask for a more private and secluded tomb? A tomb with a herd of menacing cureloms to guard it?

Just as we started to emerge with all of our gear in tow, we heard the conch-shell trumpet again—much closer. We froze as we realized that all of the mammoths were not gone. One was fast approaching from the north. Though not quite as large as the silver-chested bull who'd chased us into the cave, it was still a formidable thirteen feet high with magnificent tusks that curled almost entirely in front of its face, making it appear from our angle like the pincers of a terrible insect.

We were about to scramble again for the safety of the cave when we realized that the mammoth was wearing a wide leather harness that went under its chest and all the way around its body. There was a basket on its back, held in place by another strap that cinched under its belly. A man rode on the crest of its shoulder hump. In his hands he held the conch-shell trumpet. Just when we'd thought we'd witnessed all of the amazing sights that this world had to offer! A *domesticated* curelom! After our ferocious confrontation yesterday, I wouldn't have believed such a thing was possible. And yet I remembered distinctly that the Book of Ether had stated that these creatures had been employed in the building of the Jaredite civilization.

The man's skin appeared jet black. A Negro? His head and face were shrouded in cloth, almost like an Arabian turban. We remained positioned just outside the cave's mouth, ready to retreat at the first sign of aggression from man or beast. But the man was alone. It hardly seemed likely that he meant us harm.

About fifteen yards from where we stood, he brought his curelom to a halt: "Whoa, Rachel!"

Rachel, I thought. A Hebrew name. Might this man be a Nephite? A Nephite with very dark skin?

"Down!" he commanded.

We found ourselves backing off another few steps as the massive beast slumped to the ground, first onto its foreknees, then onto its back knees, then onto its belly. This method of crouching down seemed rather awkward for a mammoth. I'd have thought that slumping down onto its back legs first would be more natural. But this would have thrown the rider right out of the basket. Teaching it to lower itself in this manner would have been a trainer's first order of business.

But even with the beast slumped onto its stomach, the rider was still a good eight feet above the ground. Climbing *off* might not have been a problem, but getting back on . . .

Just as I thought this, the man tossed a rope ladder with sturdy wooden rungs out of the basket. The ladder dropped down across the mammoth's ribs. As he began to descend, I perceived that his skin was not naturally black. Some substance had been slathered all over his body and left to dry. Only the palms of his hands revealed his natural skin color. I wondered if he'd done this for warmth. Harry and I, as well as Gidgiddonihah and Zedekiah, were bundled in every stitch of clothing we carried. Our sandals had been tied over swaddlings of rags all the way up to our hips to ward off the obsidian-cold winds that had been blowing since late last night. If this person had found a more efficient method of keeping warm, I envied him.

As the man drew closer, he kept his face shrouded. The only thing visible was his mouth and a slat for his eyes. Suddenly he halted. For a split second I thought he was a Gadianton assassin. I feared he'd recognized us from Agash's description. My hand moved toward my sword. But his eyes were riveted on our expedition leader.

"Zedekiah?" the man inquired guardedly.

Zedekiah crinkled his brow. All at once the man began desperately unwinding and tearing away the cloth that shrouded his face. When he had finished, he stood there for our inspection. He looked at Gidgiddonihah and beamed with equal pleasure and surprise.

"Gidgiddonihah! It's *me!*"

Zedekiah burst into tears. Gidgiddonihah lunged forward to embrace him.

As for myself, I stood in numb amazement. I *knew* that face. I knew it almost as surely as I would have known my own face in a mirror. He did not appear to recognize me, but this was perfectly understandable. Missing was the platinum white hair. Missing were the deep, chiseled lines at his eyes and on his forehead. After all, he was *young*. Twenty-five or twenty-six at the most. Still, I knew him. It was the eyes. In a million years I would have still recognized those piercing amber eyes.

It was not necessary to hear his name. I already knew it. Nevertheless, it was exclaimed by Zedekiah.

"Jonas!" he cried with tearful jubilation.

The youngest son of the Prophet Nephi was alive and well.

* * *

Through all the introductions and embraces, my mind swirled with the memory of that night so long ago. That night in the rear parking lot of the police station on 2nd South and 3rd East. The night when Jonas—a much older, more distinguished Jonas—had set me free.

Jonas asked about his wife and children in Zarahemla. Zedekiah and Gidgiddonihah assured him that they were well and then proceeded to fill him in on all that had transpired, including the exodus of all of the Christians of Zarahemla to the land of Bountiful. They also filled him in on the reason for our presence in the mountains of Desolation and the details of our quest to rescue Garth and my daughter.

"We'd anticipated that we might have to rescue you as well," said Zedekiah. "I thank our Eternal Father that we will be spared, at least, of that task."

I couldn't take my eyes off Jonas. I gaped at his face the way a child might gape at Barney the purple dinosaur. Did this young man know his destiny the way that I knew it? Did he know that he would wander the earth until the end of time, bringing souls unto Christ? In all of my fantastic episodes rubbing shoulders with some of the greatest persons who had ever lived, I'd never found myself in a position of knowing so much about the future of a single human being. The realization was almost frightening. And yet so deeply comforting that . . .

Suddenly I found myself mulling over the words of our last conversation—that is, a conversation that would not take place for two thousand years:

"You're setting me free?" I asked.

"Yes," he replied.

"Why are you doing this?"

"Because . . . I owe you. I've owed you for a very, very long time, Jim Hawkins."

The words rippled through me. In the proper scale of events, this moment was the first time we'd ever met. As it stood, he owed me nothing. It was certain that I had not yet accomplished the thing that he felt had indebted him to me. *It was an event in the future!*

It struck me again how precious little I understood the true nature of the circumstances I was in. All the unanswered questions of time and space, reality and dreams, swirled inside me. How did it all fit? What exactly would be my role in the fate of this man—in the fate of *history?*

Was I destined to save his life? Had I been decreed to forestall some major catastrophe?

And then the most alarming question of all: What if I *failed?*

What if something caused me to exercise poor judgment, make a wrong decision? What if I found myself in the wrong place at the wrong time? Would it mean that Jonas would die? Would it mean that history would be altered? Could it mean that no one would arrive on that fateful night to remove the handcuffs from my wrists? What if the microns of reality suddenly shifted and hauled me back to my prison cell in Salt Lake City? My mind reeled. I had no clue of what the future might hold—no hint of what to expect.

Jonas described the black substance caked on his face and arms.

"It's pine sap," he said. "I boiled it down to a paste and then applied it to my skin."

It reminded me of a diver's wet suit. Jonas explained that it was the best way he knew to repel both cold and wetness at this altitude. His eyes gave me a double-take. I could tell he was feeling uncomfortable with my constant gaping.

He approached me. "I've heard a lot about you, Jim Hawkins." Like his father, he did not slur my name together. "Your name came up often in my many long travels with your brother-in-law, Garth Plimpton." He included Zedekiah and Gidgiddonihah in the question as he asked, "Are you certain that he is still alive?"

"No," I confessed. "I knew he was alive three weeks ago, but now . . . I can't be sure. This much I *do* know. If Garth is dead, so is my daughter. And that I will *never* accept."

"You have a lot of courage," said Jonas, "like your brother-in-law. For several months now I have suspected that Garth might be dead. The possibility that he is alive fills me with great joy."

"When did you last see him?" asked Zedekiah.

"Four months ago," said Jonas. "At that time Garth and I had been wholly unsuccessful in our efforts to discover the settlement of Haberekiah."

"Settlement of *who*?" I asked.

Zedekiah clarified, "Haberekiah was the leader of those wealthy Christians who fled from Zarahemla."

"Garth and I searched primarily in the land of Gilgal," Jonas continued. "This was where they were rumored to have gone. In time, Garth and I began to conclude that the people of Haberekiah had leaked this rumor to cover their tracks. For a long time, the city of Gilgal was our supply base. We often made inquiries to discover if anyone had heard tell of a group of Christians from Zarahemla who had settled in the region. Then we would venture into the mountains to search. Some of our inquiries may have been too bold. Gilgal is a godless place. The eyes and ears of Jacob of the Moon are everywhere.

"Somehow a false story was circulated that we had found Haberekiah's settlement. One day Garth set out for the city of Gilgal to purchase supplies. He never returned. I suspected that the spies of King Jacob had abducted him, but I never dared to hope that they would let him live. Surely they would have soon discovered that he didn't possess the information they sought."

"Didn't possess? Are you saying that Garth doesn't know the location of this treasure?"

"I'm quite certain he does not," said Jonas.

I leaned back against the rocks. "So it was all for nothing. Kidnapping my daughter. All of the trouble and pain that Jacob has caused. For nothing."

"By coincidence," said Jonas, "it was during Garth's absence that I learned the truth. I met up with some jaguar hunters who had just returned from the mountains of Desolation with many skins. They spoke of a people who dwelt in the midst of the great cureloms. But the hunters never saw the settlers of whom they spoke. Anyone who knows this wilderness knows to avoid this plateau. The cureloms can be quite dangerous."

"We figured that out," said Gidgiddonihah, massaging his shoulder where the mammoth's tusk had grazed him.

"Except for Rachel here, of course," said Jonas, indicating his own mammoth. "But she's the exception. The rest of the mammoths are the sworn adversaries of any creature that trespasses on these plains. But this danger alone wouldn't have kept the hunters away. The tusk of a curelom is a great prize in these parts. Many hunters might have taken their chances. This particular party avoided the area because it was also said that these settlers were cursed."

"Cursed *how?*" my son asked.

Jonas shook his head. "No one ventured to find out. But the inference was clear. When it is said that a people are cursed, it usually means that they are stricken with disease."

"What made you believe these were the people of Haberekiah?" asked Gidgiddonihah.

"I'd run out of alternatives," said Jonas simply. "I felt strongly it *must* be them. First I returned to the city of Gilgal to search for my companion, but no one could tell me anything. The spies of King Jacob tried to lay their hands on me as well, but by God's grace I escaped and set out for these mountains."

"So are they here?" asked Zedekiah. "Did you find them?"

"I did," said Jonas. "Their settlement is just over that rise. We can see it from over there. I will show you."

Before Jonas led us to a spot where we could overlook the settlement, he unwound a ten-foot chain from his mammoth's leg and staked one end of it into the ground. It wouldn't have taken much for the eight-ton beast to dislodge it. Nevertheless, Rachel showed every sign that she would stay precisely where Jonas had prescribed.

We walked about two hundred yards to another outcropping of rock. I gave my son a boost and we all gathered at the top. Jonas directed our eyes down into a mile-wide depression to the north. At the far end of this depression we perceived a crater with steep cliff walls, almost like the crater of a volcano, except that it was not situated inside the cone of a mountain peak.

There appeared to be only one place around the perimeter that allowed easy access to the crater floor. At this place a kind of fence had been erected. It had a curiously pale hue, as if it had been white-washed.

"What's the fence made of?" I inquired.

"Bones mostly," said Jonas. "The skeletons of cureloms. This is the principal material that they used in all of their dwellings. Bones, hides, tusks, and pine branches for support—"

"They made houses out of dead mammoths?" Harry asked reproachfully.

Jonas drew his brows together quizzically. "I do not know the word 'mammoth.'"

"Never mind," I said to Jonas. "Just tell us, can we get supplies down there? Is it safe?"

"Safe enough," said Jonas. "But you won't find many supplies. Neither will you find people. Only a row of tombs stretching all the way around those canyon walls."

Zedekiah looked dismayed. "The people of Haberekiah . . . are dead?"

Jonas nodded solemnly. "When I arrived here three months ago there were only about sixty left. The last woman—a wife to Haberekiah himself—died only two days ago. I would have interred her body beside that of her husband, but Haberekiah was one of the first to be stricken. His remains were burned in the days when his people still made an effort to stop the spread of the disease. Toward the end they were dying in such numbers that it did not seem to matter."

Jonas proceeded to describe the horrible scene that had transpired. "First their skin would show great bluish blotches. Then would come the fevers. The disease would eat their insides. It took the children first. Then the old. Then it played no favorites. The lives of more than five hundred men, women, and children were taken. I did all I could for them. I cared for them day and night. Washing them. Comforting them. Interring the dead. But in the end, my services made no difference. Not a single soul was spared."

"But *you* were spared?" said Zedekiah. "That, in and of itself, is a miracle."

"I was forewarned," said Jonas. "God forewarned me in a dream. I was commanded not to partake of any of their meals. I was told to prepare my own food, and to avoid the flesh of the curelom."

"Was it the meat then?" I asked. "Is that how the disease was spread?"

"I don't know," said Jonas. "But I did as I was commanded."

I concluded that there must have been something about the flesh of the mammoths, or the way it was prepared, that had given rise to the plague. Perhaps it was because mammoth meat had become the mainstay of their diet. On these high, desolate plains, there weren't many other sources of sustenance. I saw no plowed fields. No unharvested crops. If they had tried their hand at farming, there was no evidence of any success. But then, as Jonas described the spiritual condition of the people, another theory for what had given rise to the plague presented itself.

"Did the people attempt to remain faithful to the gospel of Christ?" Zedekiah inquired.

The question caused Jonas to shudder. He struggled to decide the best way to answer. Finally he said, "If any attempt was made, Elder Zedekiah, it did not succeed. From the beginning, Haberekiah proclaimed himself their spiritual leader. He corrupted many of the laws of heaven, asserting that he was following the command of the Lord. He began to claim for himself all of the unmarried daughters of the people. And then he began to claim even the married women. The institution of marriage itself was declared to be a 'lesser law.' It was more or less dissolved. And there were other unspeakable crimes, the details of which it is not necessary to elaborate."

"So it *was* a curse," said Gidgiddonihah.

"I cannot second-guess the Lord," Jonas sighed. "I only know what my father the prophet told them three years ago. He promised the people of Haberekiah that if they would remain in Zarahemla, their reward would far exceed any benefits they might receive from the fortunes they sought so diligently to protect. Their greed compelled them to come to this dangerous place. They were willing to tolerate these desolate conditions, all in hopes that their gold and their silver and their fine things would not fall into the hands of the tribes of Zarahemla. I suppose now they have reaped their reward. And their material fortune remains."

"Remains *where?*" asked Harry.

I might have scolded him for asking, but it was precisely the question on my mind as well.

"You practically slept right on top of it," Jonas declared.

"In the cave?" said Harry.

Jonas nodded. "They felt it was the safest place. They didn't think they could keep it in the settlement. This would have been the first place an invader would look. The curelom herds were considered natural sentries. But there are hardly enough cureloms left now. When Haberekiah first settled here, there were said to be many hundreds of cureloms roving these plains. Now I can account for only seven."

"The people of Haberekiah slaughtered them all?" asked Gidgiddonihah.

"All but these seven," said Jonas. "The finest tusks—the ones they did not use in their constructions—have been stashed in the cave. They were gathered in the hopes that one day they would return to Zarahemla and use the ivory to double and triple their current fortunes. They became experts at killing the cureloms. Sometimes the killing parties would surround several beasts at once. The various groups would signal each other using the conch-shell trumpets."

"So that's why they ran away this morning," I surmised.

Jonas nodded. "They know the sound of that trumpet very well."

"How did you know we were here?" asked Gidgiddonihah.

"Yesterday, as I was interring the last of the bodies, I heard the roars," said Jonas. "First I thought nothing of it. I often hear those sounds when there is a jaguar on the plateau. Then I saw the smoke from your fire. But by then the sun was sinking fast. I decided to wait until morning."

We climbed down from the rocks and walked back toward the cave. Rachel had not moved from the spot where Jonas had staked her, but she'd consumed nearly every blade of grass within the radius of the chain.

Gidgiddonihah set out to kindle another fire and construct a pair of torches to take into the cave. The rest of us helped Jonas gather limbs from the scrub trees at the edge of the ravine. Following Jonas' lead, we piled our leafy offerings within reach of Rachel. Her trunk curled around the branches and hoisted them to her mouth. Jonas, who stood closest to the animal, might have easily been swept aside and crushed by the tusks, but she was very mindful of him. She moved her head carefully. As Rachel fed, Jonas reached up and patted her cheek.

This gesture ignited Harry's curiosity. "Can I touch it?" he inquired.

"Of course," said Jonas, and waved him forward.

Harry approached. The beast ignored him for the most part and raised her head to stuff more leaves into her mouth. Harry contented himself with feeling the fur on her leg. At that instant she raised her enormous five-toed foot and set it down again. As a father, I became very nervous. One wrong move and my son would be as flat as a pancake.

"That's enough, Harry," I said.

"It's all right, Dad," he protested, reaching up to slap his hand against the animal's hairy knee.

Jonas tried to reassure me. "Rachel is very gentle. She's been around people all of her life."

Harry sniffed the fur on her leg and made a sour face.

"Man! She smells like that old elk hide in the bishop's shed!"

"What's Rachel's story?" I inquired. "Are there more cureloms that have been domesticated?"

"None that I know of," said Jonas. "They say that in the days of the Jaredites, they were all domesticated. Rachel is very old. I was told that King Coriantumr himself rode her into Zarahemla after his people were destroyed at the Hill Ramah. But I'm sure that's an exaggeration. However, she may be close to seventy or eighty."

"Then who trained her?" asked Harry.

"I suspect she was trained by the Sharedites," said Jonas. "The Sharedites are wanderers who once lived in these mountains. Most of them moved into the cities of the lower valleys when the robbers of Gadianton began to take refuge here. The Sharedites were said to have practiced the old arts of raising the cureloms. I was told that the people of Haberekiah purchased Rachel from a nomad soon after they arrived, but her history before that is unknown. A month ago the people wanted desperately to slay Rachel for the meat. It wasn't my place to stop them. She didn't belong to me. But I couldn't bear it. I saved her by releasing her into the hills for a time."

Harry started to hand-feed Rachel by allowing her to take the leafy branches directly from his arms with her trunk. I could no longer resist. I stepped forward and touched the beast's coarse reddish-brown hair. Harry was right. The odor was quite obnoxious, and now I could smell it on my hands. But I ignored it. How many human beings could boast that they had run their fingers along the wrinkled folds of skin on a living woolly mammoth? She even gave me the opportunity of touching the cold, yellowish ivory of one of her enormous tusks. The surface of the tusk was riddled with cracks and fissures. It was the only hint of the animal's great age.

Zedekiah stepped up to Jonas. "You must now journey to Bountiful, Jonas. Your family has been quite worried. You must report to your father of our progress and condition."

Jonas sighed and shook his head. "I can't, Zedekiah. First I will go with you to Jacobugath to free Garth Plimpton and the daughter of Jim Hawkins. Garth is my friend. I know that he would do no less for me."

Zedekiah smiled, and I could tell that he had secretly hoped that Jonas might give just this reply. Our numbers had dwindled so severely that our quest seemed more hopeless than ever before. The addition of Nephi's son to our trouble-plagued expedition boosted our spirits. Jonas' decision to accompany us came as no surprise to me. I might have predicted it. Based on what I already knew, it was destined to be.

Gidgiddonihah succeeded in igniting a new fire at the mouth of the cave. He also constructed a pair of torches. Afterwards, he and I lifted the body of Lamachi, still bundled inside his sleeping mat, and carried it deeper down the corridor of the tunnel. Zedekiah and Jonas carried the torches until we found a secluded corner. We did our best to cover the body with large stones to prevent it from being ravaged by wild beasts.

Next, Jonas led us to the very end of the tunnel. Here the corridor opened up into a wide room, nearly sixty feet in circumference. As Jonas had described, the floor of this room was stacked with the dusty tusks of several dozen mammoths. The sight of them made me achingly depressed, realizing that each pair represented the life of one of the rarest creatures on earth.

Along each of the walls, neat shelves had been cut. In some places the shelves climbed as high as the twelve-foot ceiling. The shelves were adorned with the priceless treasures of the people who had once been Zarahemla's ultra-elite. Thousands of feather quills filled with gold dust had been stacked upright in hundreds of elaborately carved wooden boxes, not unlike the wooden box that Nephi's servants had brought forward when he had purchased my family from Kumarcaah. The room glittered with the reflections of countless jade ornaments, gold and silver sculptures, mosaics, pottery, and jewelry. Many of the finest pieces of art ever produced by the Nephite nation were here, in this lonely hole within the mountains of Desolation. The treasures of King Tut had nothing on this place. In all, I would have guessed that there were four or five tons of crafted gold artifacts alone. I marveled that the people of Haberekiah had been resourceful enough to carry each of these pieces all the way from Zarahemla and then lug them up the rugged slopes of these mountains. Each shelf was carefully partitioned, I assumed so that one family's property might be kept distinct from another's.

As I took in the height and breadth of that room, I found myself fighting back feelings of resentment. It was because of this room that my daughter had been kidnapped. Because of this room, Garth had been imprisoned. So much turmoil, so many lives lost. And all because a man named Haberekiah had refused to heed the words of a prophet.

I had never met Haberekiah. It was clear now that I never would. In fact I would never meet a single member of his community. And yet these people had adversely affected my life in a way that I would never forget. How could Haberekiah have known the far-reaching devastation that would emerge because of the decision he had made so long ago to reject Nephi's words? It caused me to reflect upon the potentially far-reaching effects of my own sins. I realized that there is no such thing as a small sin. If left to canker without repentance, such minor infractions could become the raw material of the most cataclysmic consequences.

If I had been granted the power to crush into dust every chunk of ivory, jade, silver, and gold in that room and scatter it all to the four winds, I would have done it. Even a single statue from here would have supported my family for years in the modern world, and yet the very thought of fetching a souvenir made my stomach turn. If for some reason my daughter's life, or the lives of any member of my family, or the lives of any more of my friends were lost in the course of our plight, I vowed that I would return here one day with a crate of dynamite and blow this place to smithereens, burying forever the treasure it contained.

We made our way back through the tunnel and returned to the outside world. The morning was bright. Most of the overcast sky had moved on.

Gidgiddonihah pointed toward the northwest. "What is beyond this plateau?"

"I'm not sure," said Jonas. "More mountains, I suspect. And

then more valleys. And then probably more mountains."

"We've been told that the valley of Jacobugath is in that direction," said Zedekiah. "Do you know anything about it?"

"It seems reasonable," said Jonas, "but I have no idea what kind of terrain we will encounter. If it's not too rocky or too steep for Rachel, we will make very good time."

"We can ride the mammoth?" asked Harry excitedly, "Er, that is, the curelom?"

"Absolutely," said Jonas. "That basket was designed for ten to fifteen men, although I prefer to ride on the hump."

"I'll ride on the hump too!" announced Harry.

Thrilled by the prospect that we would once again ride rather than walk, we hauled all of our packs and gear up the rope ladder to the mammoth's back. We tied our provisions securely behind the basket. Afterwards, each of us in turn scaled the ladder and found a comfortable place to ride. To Harry's disappointment, I made him sit with me in the basket. Gidgiddonihah took the position opposite Jonas on the mammoth's hump. Gently nudging the mammoth's neck with a long cane, Jonas directed her to turn toward the desired direction and commence the march.

As Rachel climbed toward the top of the plateau, she released an unanticipated roar, almost as if she were bidding farewell. I looked out across the plain. From where we were, I spotted three of the other mammoths, including the mighty silver-chested bull that had given us the chase. In reply to Rachel's roar, the other mammoths raised their heads from grazing and released a roar of their own. It was a language entirely beyond human comprehension. Whatever they had communicated to one another, the message seemed longing, almost sad, as if the mammoths were acknowledging to one another something of their dismal future.

"Are there other cureloms?" asked Harry. "Maybe in another valley?"

"No one has mentioned it," said Jonas. "But perhaps."

"What will happen to these?" I wondered.

"It's not very promising, I'm afraid," said Jonas. "There are only two females. One is Rachel here, but she is far beyond her years for bearing calves. There is another female in the herd. When I first arrived, I remember seeing her with a young calf, but I haven't seen the calf since. It was probably killed by cougars or jaguars. When their numbers were greater, the herd was better able to protect its young. Unfortunately, those days are gone. Even if another calf is born, I fear it would never survive the predators."

I turned back for one final view of the great mammoths and froze the image in my mind. I felt as if I was witnessing the end of an era. The time of the great behemoths that had once roamed the earth was approaching its final curtain. And perhaps this was as it was meant to be. After all, the world was fast approaching the dawn of its brightest age, when the gift of the resurrection would be given to the world. Everything would become new and full of hope.

"According to your reckoning," I asked Zedekiah, "what day is it?"

Zedekiah had to think a moment. Days and weeks had drifted by us so steadily that it was hard to keep it straight. "I believe the five 'hollow days' expired yesterday. Today is the first day of the thirty and fourth year." He turned to Jonas. "Is it not?"

"You've lost track a bit, my friend," said Jonas. "The five 'hollow days' ended the day before yesterday. Today is the *second day* of the thirty and fourth year."

I sat back and balanced myself against the rocking motions of the mammoth, straining to put future events into their proper perspective. For the life of me I could not remember exactly what day had been decreed for the great storms to finally commence. Nor could I recall if the Book of Mormon had mentioned a specific date. If only I had retained the copy we'd brought with us.

I was entirely on my own. I might have chided myself for not studying the book a little more closely, but I decided there was no cause for complaint. It was only fair. I was now in the same nail-biting predicament as every other Christian in this land.

PART FIVE: JACOBUGATH

CHAPTER 13

"Behold!" boomed the voice of Jacob of the Moon, "The Heart of the World!"

The triangular summit with its twin towers stood out against the skyline from several miles outside the capital. It was easily the highest structure in the valley, competing only with the volcanic mountains to the north, south, and east. I'd never seen an ancient temple before history had declared it "ancient." All the ones I'd seen in modern photographs were already time-worn and crumbling, showing no color at all except for the natural shades of stone and earth.

The temple of Jacobugath looked as fresh as the day was new. Its sloping walls gleamed with a whiteness that was almost silver. Its landings and staircases were painted in various reptilian shades of red, yellow, black, and green. To be honest, I'd never seen a more gaudy monstrosity in all my life.

"Two hundred feet high, by your measurements," proclaimed Jacob arrogantly. "The tallest structure in all the known world—my world, that is. And there it stands—in my capital."

I only gave the pyramid a fleeting glance. When I was awakened that morning and reminded that I would be riding again in Jacob's regal litter, I fought down another urge to vomit. I didn't think I could make it. I was sure I would shrivel up and die. But I said a prayer and asked my Father in Heaven to strengthen me. So far so good. I was starting to believe I might actually keep my *sanity intact. But I wasn't about to pretend I was entertained as Jacob pointed out the various tourist attractions of his kingdom.*

My stomach growled. Jacob hadn't allowed me to eat any breakfast, probably because of what had happened the last time we rode together. I glanced down at the place where I'd thrown up and gloated to see that his servants had not been entirely successful at removing the stain from the fur.

Jacob noted my lack of interest. "What's the matter, my dear? Aren't you impressed by the handiwork of my people?"

"I guess I just don't have much of an appreciation for your so-called ancient ingenuity," I replied snidely.

I should have asked him who he thought he was fooling. I doubted if he'd had much, if anything, to do with the construction of that pyramid. He'd only lived in this valley for three years. I'd read somewhere that certain Egyptian pyramids had taken entire generations to build. Just the fact that Jacob was so eager to get his hands on someone else's treasure was evidence enough that he did not have the resources to create such a thing from the ground up. He'd said yesterday that Jacobugath was built on the foundations of an already existing city. Most likely that pyramid had been standing for centuries. Jacob had done little more than give it a face-lift. I couldn't help but wonder if somewhere beneath the gaudy exterior lay the foundations of a building that had once been a holy temple of the Lord, long since desecrated and forgotten.

In a last-ditch effort to regain a posture of intimidation, Jacob grabbed the curtains on either side of the carrier and threw them all the way open. "You will come to appreciate our ancient ingenuity, my girl. It is this ingenuity that will prove the defeat of every inferior kingdom in the universe—including yours."

I tossed a thumb at his precious pyramid. "Then maybe you ought to think about inventing some indoor toilets before you build any more eyesores like that."

Jacob smiled. "As a matter of fact, it's the next thing on my agenda. After I retake Zarahemla, of course."

"Oh, of course. Plunder before plumbing. Always."

Jacob laughed more loudly than the joke deserved. "Plunder before plumbing! Very good." His laughs died suddenly to show that he really hadn't found it funny at all. "You have a sharp wit. But is it sharp enough to distinguish truth from error? Yes, Melody. Conquest must always come first. First we build empires, then civilizations. But these lines need not be drawn so rigidly. Even as it stands, Jacobugath is the most perfect civilization that has ever existed. And that edifice that you so casually call an 'eyesore' is an integral part of how that perfection is maintained. As the Heart of the World, my temple must beat with the blood of both the vanquishers and the vanquished. Look out into those fields, Melody. Tell me what you see. "

I wouldn't have complied, but it was hard to avoid the view. I saw farm workers, busily harvesting the corn and grain. Many, upon seeing the royal caravan, rushed forward to kiss the road.

"Fools, " I replied.

Jacob ignored that. "Do you see any subjects who manifest the least imperfection? Wouldn't you agree that my people are the diamonds and pearls of humanity? Think of it, Melody! A perfect people to co-exist in a perfect world. "

At first I thought Jacob was expressing some sort of warped fatherly pride. Then I observed things more closely. I couldn't explain it, but Jacob was right. There was not a single man or woman, boy or girl in sight who was not in the prime of health and fitness. This may have seemed normal for hard-working farmers, but as I thought back on all the villagers I'd encountered in Kishkumen and Gadiandi, I realized that the quality of Jacob's subjects across the valley was basically the same. Strong and beautiful. Impeccably neat and comely. I saw no cripples, no beggars, no blind or deaf. I couldn't even remember seeing anyone older than Jacob himself.

I'd never seen such an abundance of produce. I'd never seen roads swept so clean or buildings so well maintained. The more I thought about the beauty and orderliness of Jacob's kingdom, the more angry and frustrated I became. Evil begets ugliness, right? Why wasn't this true in Jacobugath?

Our caravan continued its march through the countryside. The great temple loomed larger and larger. All at once we came to a halt. The litter started vibrating. I might have thought that all of our porters had been gripped by some sort of seizure. But as they set us down on the road, I realized that it was the ground itself that was rumbling. An earthquake! In all my sixteen years of life, I'd never felt an earthquake before. My hands gripped the sides of the litter. But then the rumbling ended.

"All right!" Jacob barked at the porters. "Up! Up! Let's get on with it!"

I was still breathless.

"A tremor," said Jacob to relieve my anxiety. "Pay it no mind. We experience many in these mountains. They mean nothing."

"Nothing?"

"If you were hoping to be rescued by an earthquake, you'll be very disappointed. This is the safest spot of ground on the planet, dedicated and sanctified by the Omnipotent One. My city will stand until the end of the world."

"Famous last words," I said.

Jacob smiled. "Thank you." He hadn't understood my intent. I think he thought I'd paid him a compliment.

At last we entered the capital city. Our caravan marched through a great wooden gate. Jacobugath's outer wall was about eight feet high. Built of stone and smoothed with white plaster, its upper edge undulated like the curves of a snake. Its facing was studded with projecting stones, arranged and painted in the pattern of the Divine Jaguar. This pattern was repeated on the inside of the wall, as if to convince every inhabitant that this was the Divine Jaguar's primary domain.

A massive crowd awaited us along the central avenue. At the king's appearance the people sent up a riotous cheer and tossed hundreds of fresh flower petals. A double-line of Jacob's troops forced the people back to allow us room to pass. The troops beat upon drums and blew on trumpets and pounded their spears against their shields.

Within a few city blocks the cheering grew less tumultuous. Not because there were any less people, but because the onlookers had transformed into an endless array of prisoners. Nearly a thousand of them were shackled and bound for the king's inspection. It appeared as if some kind of military campaign had been accomplished in Jacob's absence. But who were these prisoners? Their eyes were narrow, like Orientals, but not Chinese or Japanese. More like Mongolians. It's an inadequate comparison, but it's the best one I can make. Whoever they were, they were not Nephites or Lamanites.

The prisoners looked only slightly outnumbered by the soldiers. I doubted very much if this represented Jacob's entire army. The bulk of his troops must have been stationed elsewhere. Several commanders stood upon platforms in the midst of the prisoners and saluted their king by raising both fists to the air. But if they were looking for acknowledgment or praise for a job well done in their king's absence, they would get none from Jacob. At least not now. Their illustrious leader remained stoic and immovable, his eyes fixed forward. Yet I was sitting close enough to see that he was drinking in this display with the utmost satisfaction.

The only time he broke his imperial posture was to point out more tourist attractions. He acted especially proud of a certain round building that stood out conspicuously along the right side of the road. It was supported by pillars and looked sort of like the tabernacle on Temple Square, but smaller. Enough sunlight shone through the pillars that I could make out some sort of square monument inside. The monument shined of gold, but whether it was real gold or just gold paint, I couldn't say.

"Look there!" said Jacob, "the shrine of our honored First Seer—the great and noble Gadianton."

So if I'd ever wondered what had become of the infamous Gadianton, I now had my answer. Not that I'd ever wondered. Actually, I was more intrigued that somebody would have gone to the trouble to preserve the greasy bones of such a worthless scumbag. Was there really nothing better they could think of to do?

"Gadianton could only dream of this day," said Jacob. "He spent his life a wanderer and an outcast. It will be my honor to finally avenge his name in the land of our forefathers. One day there will be shrines to his memory dotting every hillside and hamlet in Zarahemla. His name will be second only to my own. And, of course, that of the Divine Jaguar."

"Oh, we mustn't forget him," I said sarcastically.

Jacob frowned. "Your impudence is beginning to bore me, my girl." He slapped his hands on his knees. "It's time. I will now have your answer. Will you become my queen and convince your uncle to help us? Or would you prefer to have your blood mingled with *my other prisoners at the Heart of the World? Not an unworthy end, but certainly untimely."*

"Gee," I said, "you make both offers sound so equally appealing."

He leaned forward. "You don't fool me, Melody. A girl as bright and beautiful as you. No doubt you have lusted many times to know what it's like to possess real power. I can give it to you, Melody. With the snap of my fingers, I can hand it to you on a golden platter. In no time at all you will find yourself eternally satiated and satisfied."

"Well, then," I said. "I suppose I should make my choice."

I let an excruciating moment tick by. Jacob glared at me, waiting in what seemed for him a painful suspense.

"I choose . . . not to choose," I said. "At least, not yet."

Jacob's face turned as red as a Washington apple. He stood in the carrier and shouted, "I said you will choose now! This instant! No more games, Melody! Choose or die!" His hand went to the dagger at his waist.

I didn't even flinch. "I'll decide after I've seen my uncle."

Jacob became still, his eyes bulging. I watched the veins throbbing in his neck. I thought the poor wretch might self-destruct. But Jacob of the Moon had an uncanny capacity for finding his composure shortly after it was lost. He removed his fingers from the dagger and seated himself slowly back on the bench. A serene smile crossed his face. He even chuckled once. But he couldn't hide the weariness in his eyes.

"You are an indomitably troublesome girl," he sighed. "Always, you know exactly which cards are in your hand and when to play them. All right, Melody. You win. I will accede to your wishes one final time. You have until sunrise. Not a moment longer. When I see you again, I will be accompanied by my Jaguar priests. You should know, these men have very hearty appetites. One look at you will surely make their mouths water. If you and your uncle are still obstinate tomorrow morning, I will provide them with a very gratifying breakfast."

The carrier had reached a central juncture of the city's two main streets. The king motioned for his porters to set us down. He then called for Balam who had been marching at the head of the procession. I wondered if he'd taken this position so that his odor would cause the crowd to back away and give the caravan more room.

"I will not have her accompany me to the palace," he informed Balam. "Take her to the Island. Let her spend tonight in the 'hole' with her uncle. Tell the jailer to expect my arrival promptly at the first light of dawn."

Balam grinned, relishing the thought of what awaited me. "Yes, my Lord, my great Lord Jacob."

Balam instructed several of his servants to untie the line to my collar. As I climbed out of the carrier, a very nervous man approached the king. His eyes were properly averted as he begged permission to speak. I'd seen this man before. He was one of Jacob's advisors. He'd been with us for the entire journey, but I didn't remember seeing him when we left Kishkumen. I assumed he was part of the detachment sent to forewarn the capital.

They were already starting to lead me away as Jacob gave his consent for the man to speak. His message was for the king's ears only, so I didn't hear a single word. But I heard Jacob's reaction, as I'm sure did everyone else within a full city block.

"Find that miserable cockroach!" he blustered. "Engage the entire city garrison if you have to! I'll have his head—and yours!—if he is not in my palace chambers by nightfall!"

Those were the last words I heard as Balam herded me through the crowd. I had no way to confirm who Jacob was referring to. But I had my suspicions. I couldn't help but wonder if the cockroach who had disappeared was none other than the king's own son, Marcos.

* * *

The street down which Balam and two dozen accompanying warriors led me took us directly through Jacobugath's central market square and beneath the shadow of its monstrous temple-pyramid. The market was virtually empty. Stalls were left unguarded. Everyone who was anyone had gone to witness the procession of their returning king. I found it curious that no one had feared leaving their goods unattended. Were there no thieves in Jacobugath? No poor people who couldn't have resisted such an opportunity?

And then I noticed that the market was not unwatched. Perched upon the various thresholds and platforms of the pyramid were dozens of men, enwrapped in robes of piercing blackness. From here they looked exactly like vultures, scanning the valley floor for signs of something dead or dying. At first I thought they were waiting to pay homage to Jacob. But the king's palace was at the other end of the city. He would not pass this way.

I realized it was not Jacob to whom the vultures paid homage. It was Balam. These men were priests—men who had devoted their lives to the rituals performed at the Heart of the World. As servants of this order, their immediate superior was Balam.

Even from their high perches they would have recognized Balam's dark red pullover with the black designs on the trim. Or they might have spotted the reflection off the ornaments that hung from his lips, cheeks, and ears. Undoubtedly these were the emblems of his rank and station. Although Balam did no more than pass beneath the silver-white pyramid walls, these men did not shirk in their obligation to show him the proper respect. One of the hovering priests began to make a sort of warbling sound. The other priests joined in. I couldn't decide if it more closely resembled a flock of seagulls or a pack of wild Indians. Either way, the sound was unnerving.

The pyramid gave off a peculiar scent that wafted over the market square, in fact over the entire city. It was vaguely antiseptic, like ammonia, but it was not a clean smell. Like dirty mop water, it left hovering an essence of moldy decay.

We left the market square and the squawking of the priests faded behind us. Shortly we reached the western end of the city and the edge of a large, greenish lake, four or five miles wide. The water was quite shallow, more like a marsh. Reeds and other vegetation poked out of much of its surface area. I could see several islands, but the most prominent one arose several hundred yards from shore, encircled by a sheer wall. It was on this island that Jacob had established his prison—a facility nearly one-fourth the size of Jacobugath itself. It was morbid looking—the only place in the valley that had been kept deliberately dismal. Three soot-blackened towers stood out against the sky. The wall was nearly forty feet high—easily four times the height of the walls surrounding Jacobugath, as if Jacob wanted his prison to be more impregnable than his city.

We reached the prison by crossing upon a twelve-foot-wide causeway, constructed of large chunks of rock and leveled off with gravel and soil. The causeway did not rise much higher than the surface of the lake. Short waves licked against the right edge, sometimes spilling over and forcing us to trudge through a sticky, yellowish mud.

As Balam shouted to the sentries to open the gate, I thought of my Uncle Garth. Tears came to my eyes as I envisioned him languishing in such a wretched place. I wondered about Aunt Jenny. What had become of her? Was she dead? Would Garth confirm my worst fears? Had he been grieving alone all these months? At that instant the prospect of seeing my beloved uncle, of embracing him, of holding his hand, made my heart leap and blocked out every other terrible thought that harassed my mind.

It had been two and a half years. What would he look like? Would I find a man as gaunt and haggard as a survivor from Auschwitz? Would he have kept enough of his sanity to know who I was?

As we were led inside, it seemed to me that the guards who worked here had taken on much the same character as the prison. They were hungry looking, like animals that thrived on human flesh. They seemed to stare at us like butchers sizing up a cut of meat.

"How is Lord Jacob's prisoner?" asked Balam.

The ranking guard, a muscle-bound man with an arrowhead-shaped face, recognized instantly who Balam was referring to. "Still in the hole, somewhere. He's alive, I think, if that's what you're asking."

Several of his other guards chuckled indecently. Balam reached up and swiped the ranking guard across the neck and cheek, creating five distinct gashes. That's got to be unsanitary, *I thought. I think I'd have rather been stabbed by a dirty knife than scratched by those bacteria-infested fingernails.*

"If he is not alive and *rational, Urriah," growled Balam, "your blood will run with the prisoners of Cuma-ramah tomorrow at the king's feast—you and all your men!"*

The guards straightened up. During Balam's absence, their manners in the presence of the master Diviner appeared to have slackened.

Urriah became meekly defensive. "But Master Balam, we were ordered to give him no special treatment so as to encourage him to be more submissive to the king's entreaties—"

"Idiots!" *shrieked Balam.* "You were also threatened that if he dies your lives would not be worth a spit in the flames of Akmul!"

"He-he lives, Master Balam," *interrupted a second guard.* "I saw him just yesterday—no! It was this morning. He was helping to tie off corpses. He is alive and well, I promise. The other prisoners in the hole—they protect him."

"This girl," *Balam continued, and he yanked on the line attached to my collar,* "She is the 'Designated One' of Lord Jacob. Reunite her with him. His majesty Lord Jacob of the Moon will be arriving here at the first light of dawn to question them both."

Urriah looked confused. "You're saying she is the 'Designated One,' and you wish to have her thrust into the hole?"

Balam raised his claw, as if to strike again. Urriah covered his first wound and promptly changed his tune. "She will be placed in the hole. His Majesty Lord Jacob of the Moon will be here at the first light of dawn."

The guards began forming a half-circle around me, their eyes crawling over me in a way that made me feel like I was infested with parasites. Each of them seemed anxious to be chosen as the one who might escort me to my uncle.

Balam raised a grimy finger in warning. "If there is any evidence that she has been touched or maltreated in any way, your entire garrison will become food for the king's menagerie."

The half circle disbanded a bit, as if the preference was now to claim no association with me whatsoever.

"B-but she will be in the hole," *Urriah reminded Balam, as if he had forgotten what this meant.* "How can we guarantee that she will not be—?"

Balam had no interest in hearing any further whining. "You have been warned. She is in your keeping." *He and his warrior escort departed through the prison gate.*

The lot fell upon Urriah, as ranking guard, to take me to my uncle. I looked about and saw dozens of guards poised on rooftops and platforms, roving the prison grounds, or playing dice games of various sorts in vacant corners. There might have been several thousand prisoners in this sprawling concentration camp. This includ-ed all of the Oriental-looking prisoners that I'd seen along the parade route. Undoubtedly these prisoners were still inside the city and would be returned here shortly. These fresh war captives were apparently kept in the main courtyard. There were hundreds of unoccupied make-shift shelters.

Assisted by two lesser guards, Urriah steered me across the stony courtyard through a high archway and into a musty corridor that sloped downward and became more narrow. We passed by several other corridors. From them I could hear the despairing cries of both men and women. Now and then I would catch a glimpse of some inmate being led from one place to another.

Prisoners wore little more than a tattered, diaper-like loincloth, or a thread-worn pullover. I made eye contact with a woman pris-oner who had sunken eyes and hair so thin she was almost bald. Malnutrition, I supposed. There was a slight deformity to her lip—a cleft palate, I think. Maybe it was from an injury. She was in and out of my presence in less than three seconds, but in that instant when our eyes met, the pain sank so deep into my heart it might as well have been from a real wound. Oh, how I loathed Jacob's unholy empire! Despite the spotless streets and cheering crowds, I sensed that there was something so dark and so pernicious festering under the surface of this kingdom that it surpassed every evil I'd ever known.

At last we reached an opening in the prison floor about six feet wide. It dropped down into an underground chamber that smelled of human feces and decomposition. The guards produced a long, wooden ladder and began to lower it into the pit. I shook my head. I was not going down there. I'd die for sure if I went down there. It smelled as if many of the prisoners who had descended that lad-der already had.

When Urriah, his face still bleeding from Balam's gashes, per-ceived that I might put up some resistance, he forcefully yanked on my leash, as if to say, "If you won't climb down willingly, I'd just as soon push you over the edge."

Garth is down there, I told myself. This is what gave me the final shred of courage to step onto the ladder. It was murky black inside that hole. I could see no bottom at all. I was descending the *very ladder that would take me into the bowels of hell.*

As I began my descent, I heard splashing sounds. I imagined that a slavering sea creature of some kind awaited me at the bottom. The circle of light overhead became smaller. Toward the bottom, a legion of hands reached up to help me down.

"It's a woman!*" someone declared.*

I was certain that I was about to be torn apart. I looked back up at the guards, but their faces had disappeared from over the hole. What about their promise to Balam? Had they forgotten so soon that they'd be killed if I was harmed?

The announcement that I was a woman caused the prisoners to leap back, as if females were rumored to carry some dread disease. I stepped off the ladder into six inches of slimy water and faced the bewildered gathering. Bodies remained thick in shadow, but I heard several comments: "I'd forgotten how they smelled," said one. "A special gift from Lord Jacob!" declared another.

Suddenly another squall of men broke into the middle of the others. "Get back! Leave her alone!"

The other men scurried off like frightened rats, splashing through the water to some indeterminable corner of the darkness. The man who had spoken approached and scrutinized me severely.

"They don't put many women down here. You must have offended someone awfully important."

The speaker was a large man. There was something wrong with his face, but in the darkness I couldn't exactly tell.

"I've committed no crime," I said. "I'm here to see my uncle. Please. His name is Garth. Garth Plimpton. Is he here? Can you take me to him?"

My uncle's name inspired silence in every listener. Even the random splashing of feet died away.

After a moment someone whispered, "The Designated One?"

"The Designated One!" someone declared more assuredly.

"Impossible!" cried the large man who stood in front of me. "She is a girl. The Designated One will be a man. That is how the prophet has always described it."

"But she knows his name. His true *name!"*

"And she is a relative! That is a requirement!"

"And look! She is pale! She is the Designated One!"

My eyes were adjusting now. I could tell that the face of the large man was brutally scarred, especially on the right side, as if it had been burned. This man addressed me again. "If you are kin to the Pale Prophet, then tell us your name."

"Melody," I replied.

He turned to his companions. "You see? Only one name! The Pale Prophet told us that the Designated One would have two names, like himself."

"M-my full name is Melody Hawkins," I added hastily, omitting my middle name, Constance, to avoid confusion.

I heard a hushed gasp. Mouths fell open in wonder. For a moment, I thought they might kneel in the sludge and worship me. But the large man with the scars simply took my hand. Before I could object, he began leading me quickly through the water. The others followed.

Thin bands of sunlight seeped through gaps in the long wall that stood to our left. Through these gaps I could make out the marshy surface of the lake. The "hole" appeared to be an abandoned cell block. Parts of it were caving in. Other parts were sealed off, as if it hadn't been in general use for centuries. I wondered if it had been part of an earlier prison, one that had existed before this "newer" prison had been built on top of it. The lake had seeped in though some of the gaps. Since much of the chamber was covered in a foot of cold, greasy water, I wondered how long human beings could be expected to survive in here.

I noticed at certain places that the earth had been pushed up to create small dry islands. It was on these islands that the inmates—nearly twenty as far as I could tell—congregated and huddled for warmth. It was on the largest of these islands, situated on the far side of a crumbling partition wall, that I was shown a sleeping figure. He was covered by a thin, mud-encrusted blanket that wasn't even long enough to cover his bare feet.

His ankles showed many red, scabby sores. So did the backs of his hands. I stopped where I stood, wondering if I was emotionally strong enough to take in the full sight of him. The man with the scarred face wasted no time nudging the sleeping man to awaken him.

"Prophet," he said. "The day has come. The Designated One has arrived."

The sleeping man stirred. He looked into the scarred man's face. When the words finally registered, his body jolted.

"Jim is here?" he asked excitedly. He turned abruptly toward me. "Ji—!"

His face became perplexed as he realized I was not Jim—I was not my father. But I knew immediately who he was. Several months of unkempt beard grew down his neck, but even so, it wasn't very thick. Uncle Garth had never had to worry much about facial hair. He did look gaunt and haggard, but not as severely as I'd feared.

I was wearing one of those tight-lipped smiles that one wears when fighting back tears as he rose to his feet. He drew closer, squinting as he struggled to recall my identity. After all, I had been only fourteen years old when he'd last laid eyes on me. My own features had changed far more than his. He came nearly nose to nose with me.

"Renae?" he inquired in a tone that was sincerely mystified. "Can it be?"

I shook my head and took his ice-cold hands in mine. "No, Garth. It's me, Melody. Your niece. Melody."

Garth repeated the name dazedly. "Melody." And then his face filled with awful dread. "Melody!" he cried. "No! Oh, please, no! Jacob would never—! Oh, Father in Heaven! No!"

He nearly collapsed. I caught him and held his head against my neck. He pulled away and took me by the shoulders.

"What have they done to you?"

"It's all right," I said. "I'm all right. I'm with you now. I'm fine. We'll both be fine now."

Perhaps nothing could have been further from the truth, but as I said it, I believed it. It seemed like a lifetime had passed since I'd beheld a familiar face. My uncle's presence, his touch, and even the sound of his voice were like vital nourishment to a starving soul. My heart was reborn.

No doubt some of my energy was drawn from the ragtag gang of inmates who surrounded us. Our reunion caused them to rejoice with infectious enthusiasm. All of these men had been living in this hell-on-earth for who knows how long. Yet somehow my appearance represented something very positive and powerful.

Garth finally calmed himself enough to accept my embrace and embrace me in return. I'd forgotten how much I loved him. How much I had missed him. It went to show that even in hell, there was room for a few miracles.

CHAPTER 14

They hovered around us, their eyes expectant, like puppies awaiting a morsel of food, like a child waiting to hear news that might be good or bad, but hoping secretly that it was good. I soaked up the happiness I felt in reuniting with my uncle, but it was hard to ignore all the pressing strangers.

There was a gap in the wall near the place where Garth had been sleeping. Enough light filtered in that I could see the other inmates fairly well. They were a shocking sight. Not only because they had been living in this despicable place, but because many of them had severe physical handicaps. There were the obvious defects, like the scarred face of the man who had brought me to Garth, or the blind man who hung on the arm of a person missing his right hand. Then there were the defects that I only realized later, like the man who was mute or the man with webbed fingers, or the fifteen-year-old boy who appeared to be mildly retarded.

I'd never spent much time in my life around people with handicaps, so I'm ashamed to confess that I felt a little awkward and uncomfortable. But not my Uncle Garth. He treated them all as equals and friends. Many of them crowded around him and inquired excitedly, "The Beast on the Waters! The Designated One is here! When will we see the Beast on the Waters?"

"Soon," Garth assured them lovingly. "Very soon. But now you must let me speak with my niece."

Reluctantly, the inmates withdrew a little.

Beast on the waters? What a peculiar statement. But at the moment I let it slide. I had so many other questions that seemed more pressing. As Garth and I settled onto the dry island where he'd been sleeping, I decided to first ask the question that might have had the most devastating answer.

"Aunt Jenny?" I asked meekly.

"She is well, I think," Garth replied.

I allowed myself to exhale. "Where is she?"

"She is in good hands," said Garth. "She and our children are with the Christian community of Zarahemla."

My eyes widened. "Your children?*"*

Garth beamed a broad smile. "We have two. A boy and a girl. You've never seen anything so beautiful."

I began crying again. Who'd have thought I would shed tears of joy in such an awful place?

"They call you 'the Pale Prophet'?" I said inquiringly.

"Don't read more into it than it deserves," said Garth. "Ten months ago the Prophet Nephi set me apart as a missionary. My gifts are the same as any missionary."

"But you knew I was coming."

"I knew *someone* was *coming," he clarified. "However, this wasn't a prophecy. 'Designated One' is a title coined by Jacob Moon. He said he would bring someone. I assumed it would be your father. It appears I was wrong."*

"My father is in jail," I reported.

Garth listened in dismay as I told him about the murder, about Dad's arrest, and about the kidnapping.

When I was finished, he looked drained. "It shouldn't surprise me, I suppose, to learn that Jacob would stoop to commit the unthinkable. No man is guilty of more abominable crimes."

"How long have you been down here?" I asked.

"Not long," said Garth. "A few months."

"Months!" I exclaimed. "How have you survived?"

"By not losing hope," said Garth. "By not allowing myself—or anyone else—to give up. The Spirit is strong here, Melody. It may not seem so, but I have witnessed miracles in this dungeon that surpass anything I've ever seen. If you think it's bad now, you should have seen it three months ago. Back then the survival rate for any-

one who remained down here was only five or six days. The water depth throughout the chamber was almost four feet. There were no dry islands. The place was teeming with rats. The rats thrived on the flesh of the dead, and sometimes the living. I found ways to block the inflow of new water from the lake. We heaped up piles of mud to make the islands. And we got rid of the rats. That's how I first earned the devotions of most of these men. If I am nothing else to them, I am the man who killed the rats."

"How did you do it?"

"I didn't," said Garth humbly. "This is perhaps the greatest of the miracles I have witnessed in this place. I solicited the faith of every inmate who would follow me. But the faith was not placed in me. It was placed in the Messiah who will come. Every night the rats would enter the chamber from crevasses in the stone ceiling overhead. By morning they would swim out through the gaps in the outer wall. We built a dam of deep water beneath the place where they entered with a rim high enough to prevent them from escaping. Then we huddled together and prayed throughout the night. By morning not just a few, but all of the rats had drowned in the dam. We tossed the carcasses out into the lake where they were devoured by birds and lake fish. Not a single rat has entered this chamber since."

"What do you eat?"

"Once a day our keepers pour down the entrails of animals and other garbage that the prisoners above us have left behind. But we rarely resort to eating that slop anymore. Instead we put it to a much more useful purpose. And subsequently, we receive an unlimited store of fresh food."

"Fresh food? Down here?"

"Come and I'll show you."

My uncle took me by the hand. He led me toward the far right end of the chamber. The large man with the scars noticed us moving and splashed alongside us. Several others followed as well.

"Going fishing, Prophet?" the large man asked.

"As a matter of fact, Kib, we are."

At the far right end of the chamber, earth and stones had been heaped up to create a pool about the size of a double-car garage. It was nearly four feet deep. The pool was fed by water that came in *though the gaps in the outer wall. To my astonishment, the surface of the pool was moving. It was alive with fish! Big fat ones with bluish scales and long whiskers. I assumed they were some kind of catfish.*

I noted that many of them appeared too large to have come in through the gaps in the walls. "How did they get in?" I asked.

"They weren't so big when they first swam in through the gaps," said Garth. "This is a breed that grows pretty fast if you feed them enough. And that's exactly what we've been doing. Nearly every crumb of garbage that the guards have thrown down here for us to eat, we've fed to them. We've kept our little aquarium going now for almost nine weeks. I wouldn't be surprised if half of the fish in this lake take their meals right here in this pool. As you can tell, many of them never leave. They've grown so fat now that they couldn't escape even if they wanted to. Every day we catch as many as we need and the next day we find that the Lord has replenished the stock."

"Do the guards care if you have this?" I asked.

"They don't know about it," said Kib.

"And they never will," said another inmate.

"Oh, they probably know by now," said Garth. "Some of our enemies who have left us have probably told them. But as long as I've lived here, I've never known a guard brave enough to climb down that ladder."

"They know they wouldn't last two seconds," said Kib. "Most of us would consider it far more honorable to be slain attempting to kill a prison guard than to die under a priest's blade at Blood Mountain." Garth gave Kib a disapproving look, and Kib added, "But, of course, since I became a Christian, I would no longer consider either one honorable." And he gave me a wink with the eye on the side of his face that had not been burned.

My heart was moved by Kib's ability to keep any semblance of humor or good spirits. A desire for vengeance was understandable. It was astonishing that Garth had convinced anyone in this place of the goodness of Jesus Christ.

I still hadn't eaten any food since last night. Not that I felt particularly hungry. There had been no shortage of events to spoil my appetite. But I was starting to think I ought to eat something to keep up my strength.

"*How do you cook the fish?*" *I asked my uncle.*

Several inmates snickered.

"*We don't,*" *said Garth.*

"*You eat it* raw?"

"*Yes, generally,*" *said Garth.* "*Fire is a rare commodity down here. We horde any pieces of wood that happen to be tossed down with the garbage like nuggets of gold. Whenever we're able to snatch a piece of driftwood as it floats past one of the gaps, we stack it carefully to be dried. Kib here could probably build a fire underwater if he had to.*"

Kib indicated his scars. "*As you can see, I've had plenty of motivation to learn all that I could learn about fire. But there's not much I can do without something to burn. It's been almost three weeks.*"

"*Today is the day, Kib,*" *said Garth.* "*Gather together all the dry wood. In honor of my niece, Melody, we'll enjoy a lunch of piping hot fish!*"

The inmates sent up a cheer.

Their supply of dry wood only amounted to two or three armfuls. Nevertheless, every stick was gathered together on my uncle's "island" while Kib set to work creating enough friction to ignite a flame. Several of the largest fish in the pool were caught and cleaned using crude knives that the inmates had fashioned from pieces of the stone wall. Within an hour we had a warm fire burning with several fish propped over the coals.

Many of the inmates took this opportunity to make my acquaintance. They were none too shy about it. Several were so overcome with emotion that they couldn't refrain from embracing me. I received the most affection from the retarded boy that they called "Fetch."

"*You're very pretty,*" *Fetch would say just before he reached around me for a hug.* "*Pretty like a butterfly.*" *Though he was covered in grime and scabby sores, I could hardly resist his shining innocence.*

Many of the men were covered in sores and rashes of one sort or another, which was understandable considering the inescapable moisture and filth. Garth was no exception. He had sores all over his arms and legs. Nevertheless, when I inquired about them, he brushed them off as "nothing of consequence."

"How did all these men come to be here in the first place?" I asked.

"Disobedience," said Garth. "Resistance. This is the waiting area for all troublemakers. If you climbed down the ladder, you were very lucky. Most are pushed. Bones are sometimes broken, which in this place is usually fatal. Every ten days or so the guards lower ropes. We tie the ropes around the bodies of those who have died, and the guards haul them out. Most of these men have only been down here for a few weeks. Currently, I'm the record holder. I've been here for almost three months. Kib, over there, comes in a close second. He arrived the week after I did. We've grown very close. You might call him my personal bodyguard."

There were about five men who avoided my uncle and all those who followed him. These were the ones who had manhandled me as I was climbing down the ladder. There seemed to be a very real concern that Garth's life would be in jeopardy if he wasn't protected. But none of his enemies were so proud that they refused the cooked fish. One of our number—a deaf-mute named Memuki—carried a heaping plate of fish over to where the nonbelievers huddled on a dry island at the other end. They snatched up the fish without thanks.

"Most of the men who dislike me were put here after the pond was already in place," said Garth. "The islands were already pushed up as well. The rats, of course, were already gone. Since they have no idea how it was before, it's hard for them to appreciate how it is now. Since I am the only one down here without some sort of handicap, they feel I'm taking advantage by turning everyone into my personal slaves."

"Which I intend to become as soon as we are free," said a man with a severe hunchback. "I will serve the pale prophet to the end of my days."

Garth set his hand on the back of this man's neck. "No, Levi, you will not serve me. Soon I hope you will meet someone far greater than I. It is him *that I hope you will serve to the end of your days. He is your Savior."*

"I will serve this man if you tell me to," said Levi, "but I will

be very sad to leave my prophet. You are my savior, too."

The love these men felt for my uncle was awe-inspiring. They hung on his every word. Every last man would have given his life for him. As I marveled at my uncle's success in nurturing Christian faith in such horrid circumstances, I found myself contrasting this phenomenon with the beauty of Jacob's kingdom—the perfect streets, the handsome people, the immaculate buildings, the cheering crowds. I felt certain that the citizens of Jacobugath would have given their lives for Jacob as readily as these men would have given their lives for Garth.

The matter continued to vex me as the meal ended and my uncle's followers began to return to their own dry islands. Finally I asked Garth, "How is it that Jacob, being totally evil, is able to inspire such devotion in his citizens? Why do they love him?"

Garth smiled disparagingly. His heart seemed to constrict as he said, "Oh, Melody. If you knew the full extent of what is happening here . . . you might pray for the mountains to bury you so that you wouldn't have to hear anymore."

My curiosity was relentless. "What's happening?"

Swallowing his emotions, Garth began to lay before me the abominations of Jacobugath. "A part of it you can see all about you. None of these men are guilty of any real crimes, except to have physical distinctions that fall below Jacob's standards of perfection. Most of the people who live in this valley were here long before Jacob arrived. They are descendants of Lehi, for the most part, though their heritage has been long forgotten. Some settled in this valley during the great northward migrations of the past generation. Others established their roots hundreds of years ago, before the days of Mosiah the First."

"So where does Jacob come in?"

"Jacob and his defectors arrived here from Zarahemla three years ago. Back then Jacobugath was called Orugath. This valley had no central government, just tribal leaders, much like Zarahemla today. Jacob managed to unify the people. He took control of the government in a remarkably short period of time—just a few months. Almost from day one, Jacob's temple became an altar for human sacrifice. He established incentives for all citizens to enter into the covenants of his secret society. After a few weeks, he *began offering handsome rewards to informers who gave him the names of those who refused to comply. But this was only the first general purge. Within a year he launched his grand scheme to 'purify' the entire nation. It began with the elimination of all children born with the slightest birth defect. Even meaningless defects, like six toes or unsightly birthmarks. All these became part of the nightly ceremonies at the pyramid."*

I was horrified. "He murdered . . . babies?"

"But this could never be enough to feed an appetite like that of the Divine Jaguar. Soon the policy expanded to include anyone who, by Jacob's definition, was not a regular contributor to the kingdom's well being. The aged and the infirm became his next targets—anyone too feeble or senile to care for themselves. Children awaiting an inheritance would turn in parents and grandparents. Husbands and wives would turn in their doting spouses."

"How could they have let it happen? Why didn't someone stop him? Why didn't the people rebel?"

"The corruption of this people did not begin with Jacob Moon," said Garth. *"It had been ripening for decades. Lehi and Nephi, the sons of Helaman, preached in this valley sixty years ago and were violently rejected and repulsed. I was told that Christian missionaries found their way here as recently as seven years ago, but one night they simply disappeared. These people were primed and waiting for a man like Jacob Moon."*

"When did this . . . purging . . . start to include people in their prime?"

"The second year," said Garth. *"Even some who were active contributors to the society—like Kib—found themselves marked for sacrifice."*

"I was a copper smelter," said Kib. *"That's how I was burned as a boy. When Jacob told everyone that the Divine Jaguar now thirsted for the blood of even those with unsightly injuries like mine, my competitors in the copper trade turned me in."*

Garth continued, "No one with the least imperfection has been safe from Jacob's edicts—rich or poor, master or slave. Even men who are drunkards or women who are barren. You've never seen a people so feverish with treachery and paranoia. Jacob's priests have circulated the doctrine that all those who turn themselves in will-

ingly receive an afterlife of eternal bliss, while those taken by force must endure eternal damnation and torment."

"*Even those of us who live in the hole are bombarded with this indoctrination,*" *said Kib. "Every third night or so the ladder is lowered. Anyone who wishes to end their misery down here is invited to climb the ladder, enjoy a final, hearty meal, and then join in the holy procession to Blood Mountain."*

"*That's our nickname for Jacob's temple,*" *said Garth. "Over the last three years thousands of men, women, and children have lined up on the temple steps voluntarily. Not a night has gone by since I was brought to this land that the temple fires were not burning. The summit can be seen from a gap in the wall at the far end of the hole."*

"*But it's* crazy!*" I ranted. "These are his own people! Jacob told me he wants to invade Zarahemla. How can he hope to succeed if he butchers so many of his own citizens?"*

"*Actually, Jacob is thinking far into the future,*" *said Garth. "To the next generation, and the next. In his warped understanding of genetics, he thinks he can entirely eliminate all birth defects and human incompetence in a century or two. And his subjects are convinced that he's right. Those who are in perfect physical condition are showered with honor and opportunity. That's why they worship him. That's why they work like dogs to pave his streets with crushed jade and construct his ghoulish shrines."*

"*Wouldn't the workers be afraid they might cut off a finger or inflict some other permanent injury?"*

Garth shook his head. "You underestimate the full extent of Jacob's indoctrination. No one wants *to die, but if they* must *die, they would never choose to expire by natural causes. Few things will bring a family greater shame. They believe there is no higher honor than to have their still-beating hearts fed into the stone mouths of the Jaguar idols. They believe their life energy will nourish the kingdom throughout eternity. And from all the external evidence they see around them—plentiful harvests, immaculate cities—it's virtually impossible to convince them otherwise."*

I chewed on my lip. "Jacob said something yesterday that bothered me a great deal. He used my own scriptures against me. He told me 'by their fruits ye shall know them.'"

"And so we shall," said Garth. *"But we can never judge evil by its outward appearance. That lesson is as old as history. Adolf Hitler was revered as a hero. He lifted Germany out of the ashes of World War I. He saved his country from economic chaos. He built the autobahns and fathered an industrial revolution that was the envy of the civilized world. And yet in the end, he shattered the lives of hundreds of millions of people."*

I asked hesitantly, *"How many people has Jacob . . . sacrificed?"*

"No one can say," said Garth. *"Possibly one third of all the people who once lived in this valley. Those currently incarcerated on this island are the last living evidence of the Great Purge."*

"But all those bodies . . . What do they do with . . . ?" My mind reverted back to the prison guards I'd seen at the gate and how I'd thought they looked like animals fed on human flesh. I also recalled Jacob's declaration of how the appetites of his priests were satisfied. I recoiled. *"Don't tell me! I don't want to know!"*

"Actually, most of the corpses are burned," said Garth. *"The ashes are used as fertilizer. But there is a daily portion set aside for—"* Garth shuddered and moved on. *"In reality, sacrifices have dropped off lately. At one time there were as many as two or three hundred a night. Jacob's henchmen have been forced to start rationing victims. Maybe ten or twenty at a time. Nothing would be worse in their minds than running out completely. They believe this would incite the Jaguar's wrath beyond measure. Jacob would have to go to war to provide fresh victims."*

"A war has already started," I confirmed. *"Today in the parade, I saw hundreds of prisoners."*

Garth nodded, as if he wasn't surprised. *"So it's begun. Well . . . none of it matters now."*

"None of it matters?" I retorted. *"What do you mean?"*

Garth raised his chin. *"It's over, Melody. It's all over. The horror, the slaughter, the secret combinations, the sacrifices. Tomorrow the reign of terror in Jacobugath, and the nightmare of iniquity in Zarahemla and elsewhere will come to an end."*

I shook my head. *"I don't understand."*

"Tomorrow is a new beginning, Melody. Tomorrow the Dispensation of Moses will conclude. A new era in the history of the world will be ushered in."

I still wasn't following. "What are you talking about?"

Garth closed his eyes. When he opened them again, they were brimming with tears. "At this very moment, as all of us sit here and converse upon our own affairs and concerns, another man, half a world away, is about to kneel in a garden where he will take upon himself the sins of the world."

As Garth's words sank in, my heartbeat quickened and a warm river of energy rushed through my body. "You mean . . . you mean the Savior. The Garden of Gethsemane?"

Garth suddenly looked distant. He started thinking to himself aloud. "Yes, that's just about right. If the world spins now as it spins in our day, there's an eight-, possibly nine-hour time difference between here and Jerusalem. If it's about two p.m. here, then it's ten p.m. there. In about an hour, maybe less, the Son of God will be betrayed with a kiss by one of his own."

Exhilaration swept through my body. Before this instant, I hadn't known the exact time period for when I had entered the ancient world. There were so many other pressures bearing down on me, I hadn't thought to inquire. Not that anyone in Jacob's company would have been able to tell me. For all I knew, I could have ended up anywhere in the entire thousand-year history of the Book of Mormon. Before this all began, I'd never heard of an evil king named Jacob or a city called Jacobugath. Garth's words zapped it all into perspective. Oh, how I wished I'd been a better student of the scriptures! But even with the limited knowledge I now possessed, I knew that some major changes were about to take place on this continent.

"Tonight is the night," *Garth continued.* "Sometime around 10:00 or 11:00 o'clock our time—7:00 a.m. in Jerusalem—they will awaken Pontius Pilate and demand the death of Jesus Christ by crucifixion. Pilate will wash his hands and abandon him to the will of the masses. And then, around midnight tonight, they will nail him to a cross. Sometime tomorrow morning, just after sunrise, he will commend his spirit into the hands of his Everlasting Father."

This news jolted me in a way I wouldn't have expected, as if someone's fingers had wrapped around my heart and squeezed. It was as if I'd never heard any of this before. As if this time, everything could turn out differently.

"What about us?" I asked tensely. "Isn't there supposed to be a terrible storm? Earthquakes? Aren't a lot of cities going to be destroyed?"

"Yes," said Garth.

"Jacobugath?"

"Yes."

My skin turned to ice. "What are we going to do?"

One of the inmates, a blind man who had been eavesdropping, spoke up. "The Beast on the Waters will come. Isn't this right, prophet? You said the Beast on the Waters would appear and the walls of the dungeon will come tumbling down. Isn't this what you said, prophet?"

"Yes," Garth answered him. "That is what I said."

The other inmates became excited, muttering to one another. Some went to various gaps in the stone wall and peered out across the lake, as if expecting that some great sea monster would rise up out of the depths at any moment. The outer wall was at least three feet thick. The idea that some beast would shortly appear and tear it down was the most bizarre and absurd thing I'd ever heard. Here we were on the brink of catastrophe, and everyone around me was talking fairy tales!

Garth noticed my consternation. He took my hand. "Melody, listen to me. You've known me all of your life. You know that I would never make light of spiritual things."

"Yes," I acknowledged.

"I had a vision, Melody. It came to me several weeks ago. I was alone, but I was not asleep. I was looking right through this gap when a great beast came across the waters. A fog hung over the lake, so I couldn't see it as well as I would have liked. But it approached the walls of the prison. A voice whispered in my ear. It told me that the beast had come to rescue us. To set us all free."

I had no idea what to think. It didn't seem rational. "A beast?" I asked. "Could it have been symbolic of something else?"

The self-assurance fled from Garth's eyes. "Oh, Melody, I . . . I wish I could give more details." His eyes lit up. "But the vision filled me with such courage—such joy! I knew in my heart that every-thing would be all right. I knew it! Nothing doubting! Because it gave me such joy, I couldn't keep it to myself. I told everyone. I felt it was only right to tell them."

"When is this 'beast' supposed to come?" I asked. "Will it come tonight? Will it come tomorrow morning?"

"I don't know," Garth confessed.

"Well obviously it has to come soon," I declared. "There isn't much time left. I'm not talking about the storm. I'm talking about Jacob. They'll be here at the first light of dawn—Jacob and his priests. They're coming for both of us."

Garth nodded. "I assumed as much."

"When do you expect the storm to arise?" I asked.

"At the very hour of the Savior's death."

"When will that be? Might it happen before *sunrise?"*

"The Savior will die at about the ninth hour in Jerusalem. Here that could mean anywhere between seven and nine a.m."

"What time does the sun start to rise?"

"I'm not sure. You have to remember, Melody, there are no clocks in this century. Even sundials can vary dramatically depending on latitude and—"

"Take a guess!"

"The first light of dawn may arrive at 5:00 a.m. Maybe 6:00."

"You can't be more specific?"

"I'm afraid not."

"Then we have to assume that Jacob will have plenty of time to interrogate us. We have to assume he'll have plenty of time to inflict whatever tortures he plans to inflict if we don't tell him what he wants to know. All he wants to know, Uncle Garth, is the location of a treasure. He says if you don't tell him, he'll kill us both. Telling him the truth may be the only way to save our lives. Will you tell him?"

"I can't."

"Why?" I said, almost hysterically. "What does it matter? Are you protecting someone? Are you trying to keep Jacob's armies from leaving the valley? I just want to understand. Why have you withheld this information for so long?"

Garth sighed. "I've withheld the information . . . because I don't know the information."

I was dumbstruck. "You mean . . . you really don't *know?"*

"I never have *known," said Garth. "It's true, I was sent on a*

*mission to recover the people of Haberekiah. But I was captured
before we could find them."*

"But Jacob thinks—in fact, he's sure—"

"Yes, I know," said Garth. "It's the only reason I'm still alive."

"You mean all this time you allowed him to believe—?"

"In the beginning I told him exactly what I've told you: that I
never found Haberekiah or his treasure. He didn't believe me, of
course. He tried to break my will, but he couldn't do it. I adopted
a posture of silence. I allowed him to believe whatever he chose to
believe. When he threatened to loosen my tongue by other means of
persuasion, I knew he meant to blackmail me through the life of
someone I loved. At first I thought he would try to kidnap my wife
and children. But I had kept their whereabouts a secret. I knew
that Nephi would keep them safe. When a rumor reached me that
he was traveling to Melek, I was sure that the 'Designated One'
would be your father, Jacob's old adversary, Jim Hawkins. At least
that's what I thought, until today."

It took a moment for the devastation to sink in. I thought back
on Jacob's last words that afternoon—If you were hoping to be
rescued by an earthquake, you'll be very disappointed. *Jacob
could never have known how right he was. Tomorrow morning,
perhaps hours before any storms could arise, I would face the tortures of Jacob's henchmen as Garth looked on in helplessness. The
only way to end my pain would be for Garth to tell them the
truth—a truth that he did not know.*

"Just tell them anything!" I pleaded. "What does it matter
now? Name any location you choose! If you're right about what's
going to happen tomorrow, Jacob will never have time to verify it
anyway!"

"You don't understand Jacob Moon," said Garth. "He may not
have the ability to glean truth. But he will surely recognize a lie.
For three years his agents have been scouring the lands of
Zarahemla, Nephi, Desolation, and Mulek, searching high and
low for any information that would reveal the whereabouts of
Haberekiah and his wealth. If I felt I could buy more time by ran-
domly picking a place on the map, don't you think I'd have done it
months ago? But it wouldn't have mattered! Melody, you've missed
Jacob's most obvious ruse. If he learns what he wants to know, do

you really believe we would be allowed to live even one more minute?"

"I think we will," I said assuredly. "We have an edge. Jacob has told me that he wants to make me his queen."

"His queen?" Garth shuddered at the absurdity. "Think about it, Melody! Do you really believe that Jacob of the Moon could ever trust you enough to make you one of his queens? Do you think I wasn't promised wealth and glory? He offered to make me his regent—second in command only to himself! It's just a stratagem, Melody. A game! He wants one thing and one thing only—the location of that treasure. And if he thinks we know it, he'll use every subterfuge known to Satan to get it."

"So what happens when he figures out we don't know?"

"Then the game is over."

The last breath of hope was sucked out of me. "So either way . . . tomorrow we'll be . . . there's nothing we can do."

"They will not have you!" Kib burst in. "I will fight them! We will all fight them!"

Garth put his hand on Kib's shoulder, "No, Kib. They would strike down anyone who raised a hand against them."

"But I can't just stand back and watch!" Kib cried. "I could never live with myself—"

"It will be all right," Garth assured. "This is my promise to you, Kib. The Beast on the Waters is coming. I've proclaimed this event for three weeks now, and I still believe it with all of my heart. Everyone in this dungeon will have a chance to live. If anything happens to me, you will take my place, Kib. You will lead these people to freedom."

Kib was taken aback. "But I—I could never do something like that. I'm no holy man."

"You are what you allow the Lord to make you," said Garth.

Garth's followers stared at us intently. They looked perplexed. Until this moment, none of them had ever considered the possibility that they might not always have their pale prophet to guide them.

As for me, I could only curl into a ball and stare off into the wretched darkness. "Don't let them torture me, Uncle Garth. If they're going to kill me, make them do it quickly. I'm scared, Uncle

Garth. So scared."

He put his arm around me. "It's not over yet, Melody. You sound as though you're losing hope. Never lose hope. We can make it. I know we can make it."

Suddenly there was another rumbling in the earth. I sat up straight. This one was slightly stronger than the first, creating tiny ripples in the surface of the water. We held our breaths. The rumbling lingered for nearly thirty seconds. When it finally ended, I looked at Garth. To my surprise, there was a tear streaming down his cheek. This was from a man who only a moment ago had been a pillar of strength.

And then I understood.

Somehow this tremor had represented far more than a minor shift in the earth's plates. Somewhere in the world, something horrible had just occurred. Something so horrible that the earth itself had groaned. No one had to tell me what had occurred. I already knew. I can't explain how. I just knew.

The Savior of the world had just been betrayed.

I held my uncle again. We cried together a long time and tried to set our own fears aside and turn our thoughts to Him. A moment later, I heard the voices of the other prisoners starting to sing. It was one of my favorite hymns. One that Garth had taught them to help endure the dreary darkness. Garth's voice soon joined in. And after a moment, so did my own.

As we sang, O Savior, stay this night with me, behold, 'tis eventide, *I tried to imagine the scene as an angry mob in Jerusalem led my Savior away into the night. I thought about all of the things that he would yet endure. When the hymn concluded, in my heart I added a final refrain. And in so doing, the suffering that I might shortly endure seemed easier to face.*

O Father, stay this night with *him,* behold, 'tis eventide.

CHAPTER 15

When the tremor ended—the second tremor that we had felt that day—an unusual depression settled over me. I tried to blame it on the pressures of our current situation. But the feeling seemed to transcend everything we were experiencing. It felt as if the sky itself was pressing down. I was tempted to start sobbing. As I tried to pinpoint some source for this emotion, I came up blank. It made no sense at all. And yet I was sure that the others in our expedition felt the same sense of heaviness. I tried to shrug it off, concentrate on uplifting thoughts. But for the longest time, the feeling would not go away.

It was our second day riding the mammoth—the third day of the new year if Jonas' calculations were correct. Our journey was near an end. We knew it. We could feel it. The elevation was lowering and the temperatures were increasing. So much so that Jonas peeled off the blackened layer of pine sap that had served him as a second skin.

That afternoon, shortly after the second tremor struck, we came upon a sort of crossroads. We could either go west into a canyon that opened up into a broad valley. Or we could go north over a slight ridge that dropped down again, possibly into the same broad valley.

Standing at this crossroads was a lone gentleman with a staff. I might have expected him to hold forth the staff and demand us to solve some difficult riddle before we could pass.

However, the sight of our mammoth crashing through the woods may have inspired him to bend the rules. Jonas, Gidgiddonihah, and I climbed down to make inquiries.

"Greetings," said Gidgiddonihah.

The stranger continued to gawk at our eight-ton mode of transportation.

"A curelom," said Gidgiddonihah, in case the man was not familiar with such a creature.

"Heard of them," he muttered. "Never seen one."

Rachel snorted. The sound startled the stranger. He leaped back another step.

"Tell us, friend," said Jonas, "which is the easiest way into that valley. It *is* the valley of Jacobugath, am I right?"

We might have expected him to reply, "Jacobugath? Never heard of the place." But the man made no pretense of ignorance.

"Do you have business there, friends?"

"Yes," I said.

The man faked a congenial smile. "Well, you won't want to go over that ridge. Your animal would never scale the cliffs on the other side. The route is much easier down this canyon. A nice, steady descent. On a beast like that, you ought to reach Jacobugath by tomorrow afternoon."

These words filled us with electricity. We were so close! We'd nearly reached our destination! After all our trials and misadventures, the secret capital of Jacob Moon was within a day's ride!

"My name is Riplaki," said the stranger. "I'd be happy to take you as far as Gimgimno, at the mouth of this canyon. My daughter lives there. That's where I'll bed down tonight. I'm sure you'd be more than welcome. There are fields nearby where your animal can graze."

"What brings you into the mountains, Riplaki?" asked Gidgiddonihah, feigning casual conversation, though I knew there was nothing casual about it. We couldn't help but find ourselves curious as to who this man was and why he would make such a friendly offer.

"Hunting," said Riplaki.

"No luck, I see," said Gidgiddonihah.

"Nope. Cougars are getting scarcer every year."

"Cougar hunter? Where's your spear, Riplaki?"

Riplaki carried only his staff and a standard flint knife.

All these questions were making him edgy. "Lost it," he said. "Went over a ravine and into a thicket. Couldn't find a trace."

"Bad luck," said Gidgiddonihah with a click of his tongue.

Riplaki's hands were trembling.

"Well, thank you for your offer," said Gidgiddonihah. "But we're in no hurry. I think we'll just camp here for the night."

"Suit yourself," said Riplaki. "I'd better get started if I'm going to make Gimgimno by dark."

He bid a hasty farewell and headed off through the woods.

As soon as he was out of hearing, Gidgiddonihah huffed and said mockingly, "Cougar hunter. Lost his spear. Bah!"

"An assassin, you think?" I asked.

"Doubtful," said Gidgiddonihah. "That man was no warrior. Probably just a lookout. I doubt ol' King Jacob would put his best assassins in such an untraveled region. But he might put the peasants to work spying for intruders. You can bet that man has gone to warn a local garrison. I'll go after him. A man like that I could incapacitate without harming him. The rest of you follow a half hour behind me."

"Wait," urged Zedekiah. He climbed down from the mammoth.

"What's the matter?" asked Gidgiddonihah.

Zedekiah approached him. "Have you forgotten the blessing?"

"Blessing?"

"What blessing?" I asked.

"The words of the Prophet Nephi," said Zedekiah. "The words that he pronounced upon our heads the morning we departed at the Falls of Gideon."

Gidgiddonihah looked stymied. I had a vague recollection. I tried to repeat the words. "Yes, he said to 'avoid . . . avoid the advice . . .'"

Zedekiah helped me out. "'Avoid the advice of solitary strangers.'"

Gidgiddonihah nodded. "I remember it now."

"Then what are our options?" asked Jonas.

Our eyes turned toward the northern ridge.

Harry's voice called down from the basket atop Rachel's back. "But the man said there were cliffs. Rachel would get stuck."

"He *said* there were cliffs," Jonas reminded him. "Maybe the route is actually better. And he didn't want us to know."

"All right," said Gidgiddonihah, "but I'd still better take care of our friend Riplaki. The rest of you make for that ridge. I'll catch up to you as soon as I can."

He took off to follow the suspected spy while the rest of us remounted the mammoth. As always, I made a special effort to help Jonas scale the ladder. Safely inside the basket on the mammoth's back, I asked him, "Are you doing all right?"

"Yes, Jim," he said politely, although I could tell he was growing weary of answering the question.

A few minutes later Rachel walked under a branch that swiped the top of Jonas' head. It was really no more than an annoyance. Jonas didn't even come close to losing his balance.

Nevertheless, I was right there inquiring, "Are you okay?"

"I'm fine," he insisted. "What's going on, Jim? I appreciate all your attention. But it's starting to make me very nervous. Would you care to explain?"

My face reddened. "It's nothing, I just . . . want to make sure you're okay."

"I'm okay. Really."

I knew I was acting foolish. But I couldn't help it. What I really wanted to do was grab Jonas by the collar and say, *Listen to me! Your life is gonna be hanging by a thread any second here. It's up to me to save you, understand? I know this for a fact. How do I know? Well, because you told me so. When? Oh, about two thousand years from now.*

If I thought I looked foolish now, wait'll I laid a story like that on him. No, I'd keep the information to myself. Besides, telling him might jinx the whole thing. Still, I'd continue lingering in his shadow, whether he liked it or not.

We topped the ridge in about an hour. Riplaki's assessment

of the landscape beyond was only slightly misleading. There were cliffs all right, but they could be easily avoided. The most thrilling sight rested on the horizon. Beneath the hazy, turquoise sky stretched a broad valley. We could just make out the rounded outline of a city wall against the shores of a lake. Inside these walls shot up a massive building of some sort. It reminded me of the Pyramid of the Sun at Teotihuacuan.

The canyon bowl directly beneath us was blanketed by a thick deciduous forest. Gidgiddonihah had yet to rejoin us. We were concerned that if we ventured into that bowl without him, he might find it difficult to follow us. The sun was sinking. It was time to think about making camp. More than that, it was time to think about devising a plan for rescuing Garth and Melody. As of yet, we had no plan at all. Our energies had been so focused on getting here that we hadn't taken much time to consider what we might do after we arrived. I guess we were hoping that the Lord might reveal some bold strategy. The time was growing short. If we were going to receive any inspiration, we needed it now.

Rachel set about filling her stomach with the rich green grasses that grew on the ridge.

"Maybe we should just camp here," Harry suggested.

But it really wasn't an ideal campsite. The bald ridge left us terribly exposed.

"Tell you what," said Jonas, "I'll take some supplies and scout out a place down near that cluster of dead-fall to the right. By the time the rest of you arrive, I'll have supper ready and waiting."

"I'm going with you," I declared.

Jonas tried to protest. "I hardly think there are any spies down there, Jim. If there's trouble, I'll shout." He placed a hand on his sword. "I'm not helpless with this, you know."

"I'm going with you," I repeated.

Jonas sighed. He turned to Harry. "You think you can guide Rachel down into that bowl?"

Under Jonas' supervision, Harry had guided the mammoth alone for several long stretches already. He had quite a knack for it. This would be his first opportunity to try it alone.

"No problem!" he replied.

Since I knew Zedekiah and Gidgiddonihah would be there to help him, I wasn't terribly worried. Despite her bulk, Rachel had proven to be an extraordinarily gentle and obedient creature. She'd also shown signs of being quite protective of anyone riding on her back. This freed me up to direct my anxiety toward Jonas.

He made it a point to walk behind me since it seemed that whenever he walked ahead, he'd turn around to find me right in his face. The trail did have some steep sections, so I felt justified in sticking close. It was entirely possible that he might slip. Not that a fall from any point looked particularly hazardous. But who knows? He might knock his head on a rock or something.

A few minutes later, we entered the woods. The trees were among the tallest we'd yet encountered. Sunlight filtered through the dense canopy of branches giving the earth a creepy submarine pallor. Just ahead we perceived a conduit of bright sunlight where the patch of dead-fall was situated. Suddenly, Jonas broke his stride.

"See something?" I asked.

"Maybe."

We stopped for a second and watched.

"An animal?"

"Maybe," he repeated, and we continued on.

All at once I nearly tripped over an abandoned travel pack. It was partly unbound and bulging with supplies. I looked around and noticed *dozens* of travel packs! Against a tree I saw a bundle of swords. There were also bundles of spears and other weapons. Someone else had decided that this canopy of trees near the dead-fall would make an ideal campsite.

"Let's get out of here," I said.

But it was too late. Men rushed out from behind the trees. They dropped down from the branches, their weapons ready.

It appeared that our instincts in following Nephi's blessing had been mistaken. We should have taken the other canyon.

* * *

Within seconds the forest swarmed with over a hundred warriors.

But whose warriors?

These men represented a nationality I'd never seen before in this land. The man snarling nose to nose with me looked like a direct ancestor of Genghis Khan himself, with thick caterpillar eyebrows and a short, scraggled goatee. Most of them wore breastplates covered with dark brown fur, as if they fancied themselves to be gorillas or some other sort of primate. They wore heavy wooden helmets over their braided hair. Their footwear resembled boots more than sandals, remotely like the high buffalo-hide moccasins worn by the Indians of the Great Plains.

Someone kicked me behind the knee. The next thing I knew I was flat on my back with the business end of a spear pressing against my Adam's apple. Jonas lay beside me in the same predicament. If this was my moment to save Jonas' life, it appeared I was about to fail miserably. Small comfort, I suppose, that we would die together.

"On patrol, Gadianton worm?" inquired the man with the goatee.

"No," I insisted. "We're not Gadiantons. We're not part of Jacob's kingdom at all."

"Gadiantons?" Jonas said to me. "Can you understand his language? He thinks *we're* Gadiantons?"

My universal skill of comprehending languages had suddenly become vital.

"I don't believe you!" the man gruffed. "No one but dirt-licking assassins in these mountains! None as badly trained as the two of you, however. We spotted you the very moment you topped that ridge. Saw your curelom, too." He pressed the spear harder into my neck. "Where's the curelom?"

A lightbulb flashed in Jonas' brain. "Ah! You possess the same gift for understanding languages as Garth Plimpton! Tell me what he's saying?"

But Jonas would have to wait. I felt more inclined to answer the questions of the man with a spearpoint in my neck. "The curelom is still on the ridge."

The man with the goatee turned to one of his men. "Take twenty warriors. Kill them all! Spear the curelom!"

"Wait!" I cried. "My boy is up there! Would an assassin bring his ten-year-old son? There must be some way to convince you!"

"Convince the devil when you meet him!"

"No, listen! Jacob is our enemy too! He kidnapped my daughter and my brother-in-law!"

Jonas listened carefully to my words and tried to glean both sides of the conversation. "Tell him that Jacob destroyed the government of our people!"

I repeated Jonas' statement, prompting the man to inquire, "Is this man a Nephite?"

"Yes," I answered.

He scowled and spat, "That don't prove a thing. So's half them groveling, dirt-licking Reds. Heard tell Jacob himself is a Nephite. Might say Nephites caused this whole mess in the first place. Reason enough to spill your guts."

"*We're on your side!*" I pleaded. "Would you slay an ally? We can help you!"

"Help *me? You?* What could you do for us, you albino-skinned maggot? Jacob's army burned my city to the ground! They killed my wife. They carried off four of my sons and every other living human being they could lay their hands on! Off to that blood-stinking city down there. Cowards! Every last one of them! I've vowed with my life to carry the head of that scurvy king back to my homeland on the end of this spear or die trying."

I doubted there were more than a hundred and twenty-five men in this whole outfit. "You're gonna do this with so few men?"

He leaned in close and bared his teeth. "*Or die trying!*"

Who was I to question the suicidal tendencies of a madman? But to drag all these good men down with him seemed pointless.

"*Please* tell me what's going on," begged Jonas.

"He intends to attack Jacobugath," I informed him. "He wants to kill King Jacob and take his head back to his homeland on the end of a spear."

"Is he serious?" asked Jonas incredulously.

I spoke again to the man with the goatee. "They're probably keeping my daughter in the same place that they're keeping your sons and the rest of your people. If you help us, we'll help you."

"What can you offer me that I don't already have?"

At least he's still listening, I thought. "For one, we could offer you that curelom."

"What can it do?"

"For starters, she can carry all these bundles of weapons. More importantly, she can storm through, push over, or break down any obstacle in her path."

The man chewed on this a moment. He drew back his spear a bit. "How many are you?"

"Five," I replied. "But like I said, one of us is a ten-year-old boy."

"He's no good to us. Any trained warriors?"

"We have one trained warrior," I confessed.

"Two trained warriors," Jonas corrected. "Tell him I'm also trained. As was every boy in Zarahemla before the government collapsed."

"The Nephite is also a trained warrior," I reported.

"What about you? Are you a fighter?"

"Not trained," I replied, "but I can hold my own."

"If not a fighter, what are you?"

"A father," I said. "A father trying to defend his children."

At last, these words produced the desired effect. The man withdrew his spear. Having sons of his own, he understood. He might have even argued that a father defending his children rivaled any trained warrior. The spear was also withdrawn from Jonas' neck. The two of us were pulled to our feet. Several spears remained close by in case we tried anything foolish.

The man with the goatee introduced himself. "I am Ilipichicuma."

Now there's a good Nephite name, I thought facetiously.

These people obviously had no relationship whatsoever to Nephites or Lamanites. Whether they were related to Jaredites or Mulekites, I couldn't say.

Ilipichicuma continued, "I am king to the people of Cumaramah. If you join us, you will be under *my* command. If you disobey, the penalty is death. We are on a mission of vengeance. There is no turning back. All of us have lost loved ones in the raids. We no longer care for our own lives. If my people who are Jacob's prisoners can be liberated, it will be well. But unless we can root out the disease that is King Jacob himself, our mission will have failed. If you are a man who can die with honor, we invite you to join us. However—" he eyed Jonas warily "—I don't know if I can trust a Nephite."

"I would stake my life on his loyalty," I said. "And on the loyalty of the other Nephites in my company. They have as much reason to fight against King Jacob as I do. Maybe more."

"If you are wrong, maggot, I will skin both you and your companions and feed your flesh to the beetles. Do I make myself clear?"

"Very clear," I replied.

I gave Ilipichicuma our names, although because of my pale complexion he persisted in calling me "maggot." Jonas was going berserk trying to figure out what we were saying. I took a moment to fill him in. I told him Ilipichicuma's conditions for joining his brigade. Jonas made no bones about expressing his opinion of Ilipichicuma's mission. "It's crazy! Their pain at losing so many loved ones has warped their sense of reason. Unless this king has a secret plan that he hasn't yet revealed, he's going to lead us, as well as the rest of these good men, to certain death."

"What's the Nephite blubbering about?" barked Ilipichicuma.

"He wants to know if you have some sort of secret plan," I said.

"No secret plan," Ilipichicuma confessed, "but we may have a secret weapon. I'll show you. Bring forth the prisoner!"

For the first time I noticed a man at the back of the crowd with his arms bound behind his back. His head was buried under a cloth sack. He wore a mantle that left his chest bare. His calves, arms, and stomach were painted in red designs. He was clearly one of Jacob's goons.

Ilipichicuma turned to another of his men. "Tell him about the marks, Jubilo."

Jubilo indicated the red designs. "These are the marks of a warrior of noble rank. I'm sure of it. We saw similar marks on the bellies of the captains who led the raids against our city."

Another man untied the sack from around the prisoner's head. As it was removed, the face of a young man was revealed. A deerhide gag was cinched around his mouth. The heat inside the sack had left his face puffy and swollen, and his hair matted with perspiration. He began sucking deep breaths of air through his nose. And then his eyes fell on me.

We gaped at each other for a long moment, looking past the change of appearance and the transition of centuries. When he recognized me, his eyebrows shot up in disbelief. For me, the emotional reaction was impossible to contain. I lunged forward to seize his throat.

It took Jonas and two of Ilipichicuma's warriors to pull me off before I could tear out his jugular.

"Jim!" cried Jonas. "What's come over you?"

My outburst startled Ilipichicuma, although I think he was highly entertained. "Do you know this man?" he asked.

I was shaking with fury. "Yeah. I know him. I know him well."

The last time I'd looked into that shameless face, those treacherous eyes, the two of us had been decked out in silk ties and business suits. He'd been seated smugly behind a phone in his cubicle at Entrepreneurial Marketing Inc., watching intently as I exited the building to plunge headlong into the nightmare that would become my life from that moment on. At the sight of him, the hatred inside me boiled molten hot and I could hardly speak his name. When I did, my voice dripped venom.

"His name is Marcos Alberto Sanchez. Eldest son of King Jacob of the Moon."

When the initial shock wore off and the gasps subsided,

Ilipichicuma and his warriors began hooting with delight. Never in a million years would they have anticipated such luck. The king's own son! His eldest no less! The very man who might be next in line for Jacob's throne!

"The Cloud Maker is smiling broadly upon us today!" praised the king.

Al Sanchez—or Marcos as his father had once corrected me—continued to watch me, his eyes wide with alarm. He struggled against his bonds and against the man who held him. He tried to mutter something unintelligible through his gag.

"Where did you find him?" I asked.

"The Cloud Maker brought him to *us*," said Ilipichicuma. "King Jacob has many spies and assassins searching for my brigade. We caught this one earlier today. He was on patrol. In the beginning he tried to call himself a defector—a traitor to his people. But I am no fool. There are no defectors in the dark realm of Lord Jacob. I had him gagged so that I would hear no more nonsense until I was ready to question him. It is said that this kind can cast pernicious spells using only their tongues."

I wondered how Marcos had made himself understood. Then I remembered, Marcos had been born in *my* world. As the product of another century, he possessed the same knack for speaking and hearing in one timeless language. Not even a piece of vermin like Marcos Sanchez was exempt from this gift.

"Let me speak with him," I requested. "This is the man who arranged to have my daughter kidnapped. He will know where she's kept. He may also know where your people are kept. As well, he will know the whereabouts of the king."

Ilipichicuma grabbed Marcos by the hair. "And you will tell us everything, won't you, Red prince? The Cloud Maker has not only delivered *you* into our hands, he has brought us your enemies. We will know when you are lying. You can keep no secrets from us now!"

"Take off the gag," I asked the king again. "Let him speak."

Ilipichicuma turned a stern finger toward me. "The prisoner will not speak until I am ready for him to speak!"

There was a moment of pregnant silence as we waited for Ilipichicuma to announce when this might be. He let the moment pass, then he nodded once and declared, "*Now* I am ready."

Marcos was laid up against the trunk of a tree. The king directed one of his men to place a blade against Marcos' throat.

Ilipichicuma spoke to Marcos harshly. "Know this, Red prince. If any lies or spells slip off your tongue, I'll have it severed on the spot. And your throat as well. Understand?"

Marcos hesitated. The terms were not exactly reasonable. Ilipichicuma would be the sole judge of truth and lies. Marcos risked death if he muttered anything at all that Ilipichicuma didn't want to hear. Nevertheless, he shut his eyes and nodded consent to these terms. The king signaled for the gag to be removed.

Marcos and I had scarcely taken our eyes off one another since the instant of our mutual recognition. My loathing for him remained apparent with every breath I took. Jonas put his hand on my shoulder and encouraged me to "calm down."

But Jonas didn't understand. How could I remain calm when the very villain who had touched off our family's chain reaction of horror stood before my face? He was in *my* power now. And yet he was not in my power at all. In reality, I was still in his. I *needed* him. Without him, I could think of no other means of pinpointing my daughter's location. A part of me wished that I had been the one selected to lay that knife against his neck. But perhaps it was better this way. I doubted whether my hand would have been all too steady. The judgments I passed on his words were bound to be far more severe than anyone else.

The instant the gag was removed, Marcos directed his statements at me. "Jim, there isn't much time! I won't insult you by asking your forgiveness. I only—!"

Marcos was slapped. "Quiet!" blustered the king. "*I* ask the questions. You answer." He turned to the man holding the knife. "If he speaks out of order again, *cut him!*"

Silence was brutally painful for Marcos; nevertheless, he obeyed.

"Where's your scurvy father, Lord Jacob of the Scum?"

"By now, he'll be in Jacobugath," Marcos replied. "He'll

have arrived there sometime this afternoon."

I could restrain my question no longer. "Where's my daughter? What have you done with her?"

"Melody is fine," he said. "At least, she's alive. But if we don't—"

"*I* ask the questions!" Ilipichicuma reminded me.

"*Please,*" I begged. "Let him say what he has to say."

"Let me finish!" said Marcos.

The man who held the knife prepared to draw blood. The king stayed his arm.

Marcos continued, "After I've said what I have to say, you can kill me if you like. I don't care. It probably doesn't matter. All I care about is Melody. It may be too late already."

My heart constricted. "*Where is my daughter?*"

"Where are my sons!" Ilipichicuma interjected.

"They may both be in same place," said Marcos. "But by this time tomorrow, it's certain that *all* of them will be dead."

"Where are they being held?" I asked.

"It's a prison on an island of the lake. This is where we'll find all of the prisoners of Cuma-ramah. It's also the place where Garth Plimpton is being held. Melody may actually be at the king's palace. I can't be sure. But I know how to find out."

"What makes you think you'll have the chance, Red prince?" Ilipichicuma grabbed Marcos by the hair again. "Before this night is over, I'm going to butcher you the way they butchered my wife. On your last breath, I'll be repeating her name in your ear. That's the name that you will carry to hell!"

"I didn't kill your wife," said Marcos. "But if this man's daughter dies, it's certain that I will have killed her. It's *her* name that I will carry to hell."

I fought another urge to tear out Marcos' jugular. He confessed his guilt as if it were a *new discovery!* Of *course* he would be responsible! To hear him express any emotional sentiment toward my daughter rivaled the foulest blasphemy I'd ever heard!

"What were you doing in these hills?" I demanded.

"I came here of my own volition," Marcos said. "I came looking for the army of King Ilipichicuma. The report that he is up here has spread all across the valley. There's an army assembling in the city of Gimgimno right now to confront him. Over five thousand men."

"Are you trying to frighten us?" asked the king.

"I'm trying to *warn* you," said Marcos. "And to help you. They may be on their way right now, following up the neighboring canyon to try and surround you. Unfortunately, they're expecting an army that is significantly larger than the one I see here. So was I. If I'd known you had so few men, I'm sure I'd have pursued another avenue to try and rescue Melody."

"You're a vile and wicked liar!" charged Ilipichicuma. "You came here to ensnare us with your Gadianton treachery!"

"Would the son of Jacob Moon be patrolling the hills as an assassin?" Marcos snapped back.

I'd found his story convincing enough that I dashed out into the dead-fall to see if I could spot the ridge. If Marcos was right, Jacob's army would cross right over that bald summit and pour down into this canyon bowl. Zedekiah and my son were completely exposed. I thought about Gidgiddonihah. What kind of trap might he have walked right into?

I could see portions of the summit through the lofty branches, but I couldn't see the mammoth, nor could I spot Harry and Zedekiah. Perhaps Gidgiddonihah had already arrived and they were on their way down.

The king continued shouting at Marcos. "You're trying to scare us into retreating! Well, it won't work! We're not going back to Cuma-ramah until we've fulfilled our mission."

"If you want to fulfill your mission," said Marcos, "I'm your only hope. You have to let me help you."

"Why would you help us?" Ilipichicuma scoffed. "You would betray your father, the great Lord Jacob? You would have his curse upon your breast for the rest of your days?"

Marcos stiffened his chin. "I would."

"Nonsense! Why would you do this, Red prince?"

"Because my father is about to kill the only thing I've ever loved."

I nearly retched. This piece of filth was in love with my daughter! I thought back on my daughter's other low-life boyfriend, Quinn. She certainly had a way of attracting rejects. But the image of Melody with Quinn was far easier to stomach than this. Marcos was a conspirator! A murderer! A worshipper of darkness! I thought back on Lamachi's conversion. But Lamachi was infinitely superior to Marcos. Lamachi had never been an accessory to murder. More importantly, Lamachi had never claimed to be in love with my daughter.

Ilipichicuma reacted to Marcos' words by releasing a wrenched cry, like a wounded animal. He was beside himself with indecision. To him, Marcos represented all of the men who had participated in the slaughter of his wife and the abduction of his children. But what if he was telling the truth? What if the son of Jacob Moon had truly defected? Think of the advantage! Think of the possibilities! Just how many miracles were his gods capable of granting in one day?

"You've brought with you enough weapons to arm five hundred additional men," Marcos reminded the king, referring to all the bundles of swords, bows, and spears. "I'm sure by bringing them you were hoping to deliver them to your people in prison. It can still be done. With my help, we could do it. I ask only that you allow me to use your warriors to find Melody."

"What about your father?" Ilipichicuma leaned in close. "Will you deliver Lord Jacob into my hands?"

Marcos hesitated. For nineteen years he had devoted all the energies of his heart to causes that his father had espoused. How did Ilipichicuma expect him to answer? Aside from the fact that I doubted very much if any son of Jacob Moon had the means of granting such a request—particularly a son who by now had surely been reported as missing and possibly a traitor—how could he expect Marcos to casually promise to give him the life of his own father?

To my utter shock, Marco replied, "If you do as I ask, I'll kill him for you."

The king drank this statement deep into his soul. A grin climbed his cheeks. Still, he would not release him.

"Your bonds will not be removed!" He pressed his finger between Marcos' eyes. "If you have deceived me in any way— if you have lied about the least little thing . . ." He stopped. He appeared to have run out of threats. He'd already threatened to cut off tongues, slice throats, even feed our flesh to beetles. What was left? He changed the subject abruptly. "Tell me your plan for smuggling these weapons inside this island prison!"

If in fact Marcos even had a plan, he was denied the opportunity of divulging it at that time. Just as the king finished his question, I could hear our mammoth thundering through the woods. It stopped in the center of camp. The warriors of Cumaramah scrambled to avoid the swinging tusks. The three people inside the basket looked around in grave alarm. In their anxiousness to find Jonas and myself, they'd charged right into a swarm of warriors!

I waved my arms as Gidgiddonihah started to arm himself. "It's all right!" I cried. "These men are on our side! They are *not* warriors of Jacob!"

Gidgiddonihah and Zedekiah may have already suspected this for themselves upon glimpsing their unfamiliar features and attire. As to whether or not they were on our side, Gidgiddonihah took my word for it. He had no choice. The message he had to deliver was too urgent.

"There's an army making its way up that canyon," he announced. "Thousands of Jacob's men are coming in our direction. If they don't stop for the night, they'll top that ridge within the next hour. They nearly captured me as I was pursuing that lookout, Riplaki. I was forced to kill two men. Then I fled." Gidgiddonihah was sweating profusely. Even riding the mammoth for the past few minutes had not fully restored his wind.

"What's that man saying?" demanded Ilipichicuma.

"He's telling us that the son of Jacob Moon spoke the truth. An army is headed this way. They could top that ridge in an hour."

Marcos added, "Another army will station itself at the base of this canyon. It will arrive sometime tonight or tomorrow morning. Their objective is to box you in. If we can get out of this canyon before the army gets in place, we should have a clear path all the way into Jacobugath. We'll meet little if any resistance until we face Jacobugath's city garrison."

I approached Marcos. "How many men are in this city garrison?"

"Two or three thousand, I imagine."

Undaunted, I asked him, "If we marched all night, how soon could we reach Jacobugath and this island prison?"

Marcos thought a moment. "All night? Hard to say. I haven't been to Jacobugath for over a year, and even then I only lived there for about six months. I know that in a car it would only take fifteen to twenty minutes. But on foot . . . ? We might get there by morning. Maybe a little after sunrise."

I turned to Ilipichicuma. He read my thoughts and faced his men.

"Warriors of Cuma-ramah! Are you strong? Is your will made of iron and your heart made of fire?"

The warriors of Cuma-ramah sent up a rousing shout. "Yes!"

"Then we will not sleep tonight! At sunrise the day of glory and vengeance will be upon us! We will liberate the captives and shower the capital of King Jacob with blood! Is there anyone who doubts that the Cloud Maker is with us?"

"No!"

"Is there anyone who would not die for the honor of our gods?"

"No!"

"Then let the march begin!" cried the king. *"On to Jacobugath!"*

It was sometime after midnight, just as we were emerging from the canyon under a veil of darkness, that the third set of tremors began to groan in the earth.

CHAPTER 16

My eyes flew open wide. The earth was rumbling again.
"Uncle Garth!" I cried.
"I'm here, Melody."
The chamber was pitch black. I couldn't see Garth as his arms reached out and wrapped around my shoulders. I'd fallen asleep only an hour before. The sleep had not been peaceful, but at least it was sleep.

This tremor was different. It was not a long mournful groan in the earth like the others. It was almost a pulsing tremor. A rumble that endured one or two seconds, and then stopped, and then started again, and then stopped. Had there ever been a tremor like this before? It was like a heartbeat echoing from the center of the earth. No, that's not it. It was like the slow motion vibration that a house feels when someone is driving a nail into a basement wall or—
Suddenly I understood.

The tremor was an echo from the heart of the earth. And I knew that someone, somewhere was driving a nail. They were driving it through human flesh. The flesh of a perfect man.

In my befuddled state of mind, I somehow equated this with the signal for the storms to commence. "Has it started?" I gasped. "Have the destructions begun?" The panic in my voice upset the other prisoners. I could hear them muttering anxiously.

"No," said Garth, and he bound his arms more tightly around my shoulders. His voice was choked with emotion as he said, "The

Savior's hour is not yet. Not yet. Go back to sleep. The night is only half over."

I never did fall back asleep. At least not a restful sleep. Just a half sleep full of nightmares and weeping for the pain of my Lord. The foul smells of the hole displayed themselves in my mind as a wash of colors: muddy purple mixed with olive green and orange-yellow splashed with polyester pink. The colors swirled before my face in thick and dripping pools. I sucked them in every time I breathed.

I remember vaguely the sound as the opening was uncovered and the ladder was dropped down into the hole. By the time I gathered my senses, three guards with torches had already descended and many others were climbing behind them. They'd come too soon! It was still the dead of night! I could see no sign at all that the dawn had started to break. In the torchlight, I recognized the ranking guard, Urriah, his face scabbed from where Balam had scratched him.

His voice boomed and echoed through the chamber. "I want Garplimpton and the girl, his niece! Reveal yourselves!"

The bodyguard, Kib, had risen to his feet. He looked pleadingly into my uncle's eyes, begging for some gesture that would grant him permission to put up a struggle and keep them from taking us away.

The inmates who hated my uncle were on their feet, jumping up and down like a pack of baboons and pointing enthusiastically in our direction. "Over there! Over there!"

Garth raised his hand to stay Kib as well as three other men who had stepped forward to protect us. Garth put his arm around my waist. The two of us stepped off the dry island and into the slimy water to face our fate.

About a dozen prison guards had climbed into the hole to keep order. Some of them, including Urriah, had the luxury of a piece of cloth to filter out the stench. The rest of them fought to keep from throwing up. About seven of them made their way toward us through the water. Each held a heavy wooden club in case anyone tried to stop them. They were anxious to get us out of there as quickly as possible.

Urriah looked around glumly at all of the innovations that my uncle had introduced into the hole and decided that some of his guards would not be leaving as soon as their nostrils might have desired. He appeared particularly disturbed by the fish pool.

As my uncle and I were seized and led back toward the ladder, I heard him shout to his men: "Pull it down!"

To my amazement, when Urriah gave this order, my uncle's detractors began destroying the dam as feverishly as the guards. What lesson in human psychology might have explained this? They were willfully destroying their only source of fresh food! Didn't they realize that all of the dry islands, including their own, would be inundated?

The fragile walls of the dam came down with remarkably little effort. Even before Garth and I had climbed the ladder, a wave of water and flopping fish rushed through the chamber. I heard my uncle's enemies pleading with the guards, "Take us with you! Put us in a cell! Take us with you!" But the guards ignored them, even swinging their clubs at anyone who came too close.

The men who had grown to love and trust my uncle stood motionless as the rising water swirled around their legs. Four of the men who were too crippled to stand on their own were supported by Kib and the others. They watched as we climbed the ladder, their eyes forlorn and full of doubt. How could the God of the Pale Prophet allow this to happen? What did it mean? What would become of them?

Where was the Beast on the Waters?

I might have wept for them if I hadn't been so consumed with my own terror. Urriah climbed up behind us. As he emerged from the hole, another of his guards came running down the corridor.

"The king is at the gate!" he announced.

As far as I could tell, there was only the faintest glimmer of twilight outside. When Jacob said he would arrive at the crack of dawn, he hadn't meant a single moment later. I shouldn't have been surprised. He'd waited three months to learn the secret he thought Garth possessed. He wasn't going to wait a minute longer than necessary.

Urriah faced the two of us. The scratches on his face didn't look like they were healing very well. The scabs looked wet and infected. If gangrene didn't set in, it was certain there would be scars. Maybe *even scars bad enough to transform his status here from guard to inmate. I relished the thought. Unfortunately, I doubted if either of us would live long enough to see it happen.*

"Scrub them down," Urriah ordered his men, still holding the rag over his mouth and nose. "Give them fresh clothes. His majesty Lord Jacob will never tolerate the smell. Then bring them to the tower."

I was gripping Garth's hand so hard that his fingers were white. We looked at each other, our hearts in our throats.

He pushed a lock of hair out of my eyes and tried to smile bravely. Before I could drink my fill of his self-assurance, the guards grabbed us roughly and herded us away.

* * *

The night sky looked as transparent as obsidian glass. Even without the tiniest sliver of a moon, the stars blazed with such unfiltered radiance that we could easily make out the shapes of the hills and the shadows of objects in our path. After we emerged from the canyon, Marcos offered directions to connect us up with a road leading straight into Jacobugath.

Because of Ilipichicuma's decision to leave Marcos in bonds, it was necessary for him to ride atop the mammoth with Harry and Jonas, along with all the bundles of weapons that had been brought by Ilipichicuma's men. I was the one who insisted that an additional rope be added to secure Marcos to the basket. However irrational it might seem, I was not willing to take the chance that Marcos might leap out of the basket at some point and run off into the woods to meet up with the perpetrators of some ambush arranged the previous day. It occurred to me of course that a thirteen-foot jump from the back of a moving mammoth while his hands were tied would likely result in an injury that would prevent him from making such a rendezvous anyway, but if there was even a slight chance that he might succeed in some effort to deceive us, I would do everything in my power to prevent it. From what I knew of Marcos Sanchez, there was no deceit too diabolical. No betrayal too cunning. Despite his present cooperation, I couldn't ignore the fact that if it hadn't been for him, Doug Bowman would still be alive and my family would still be intact.

I wasn't certain what hour of the morning it was that Harry called down to me that a coyote or something was following the procession. Now and then he would catch a glimpse of its shadow moving along the edges of the road, always keeping a safe distance.

"It's a dog," said Marcos. "Melody's dog. Its name is Pill. It followed me up the canyon and then disappeared when I was seized."

Harry persisted until I went back to investigate. Indeed, I found a pudgy, hairless, rodent-looking thing that had no voice to bark. At my approach it tried to run away, but I knelt and called to it by name. It responded as if I was an old friend and practically jumped into my arms. I turned it over to Harry, who, of course, developed an immediate attachment to it.

Before Harry climbed back atop the mammoth with the dog, he said something unexpected to me.

"Dad, I think you should untie Marcos."

"Why?" I asked suspiciously. "What did he say to you?"

"Nothing," said Harry. "He just seems like an okay guy."

"*Okay guy?* Harry, Marcos is the whole reason—"

"Remember, Dad," he interrupted, "I was right about Lamachi."

I let this sink in for a second.

"I'll think about it," I said to appease my son. I didn't intend to think about it long. Despite Harry's impression that he'd become an expert judge of character, he didn't know what I knew. I felt far more qualified to judge.

Keeping our basic direction in line with the city of Jacobugath was relatively easy. Red and orange temple fires continued burning throughout the night. As Marcos had promised, we met no resistance whatsoever. Not even a skirmish with a lone sentry. It seemed that most of Jacob's forces had been deployed to trap King Ilipichicuma and his "army" of one hundred and twenty-five men. The rest were apparently held in reserve at the capital.

We passed within a hundred yards of many farm huts where

the coals of the outdoor cooking fires still glowed or where the flame of a beeswax candle flickered through the cane walls. Most of the time not even a breath of movement could be sensed within. If a family slept inside, they seemed undisturbed by the nighttime movement of troops along the highway. The silhouettes of a few curious faces appeared now and then to investigate the unusual snorts of our mammoth, but the sky was still far too dark to see us clearly. We might just as easily have been the warriors of their own king.

And if some of them *did* realize that we were foreigners, what could they have done except hide in the corners of their huts and wait until light? These were not the days of telephones or shortwave radios. There was no way to forewarn the capital. It appeared that all of Jacob's defensive energies had been spent establishing complex networks of sentries and assassins along the borders of the land. Concerns over a direct attack at the heart of the valley had not been a military priority. Not that we were exactly an invasion force. Any significant line of resistance might have squashed us like ants.

As the temple fires of Jacobugath glowed closer and closer, I realized that such resistance might make itself known at any moment. I became concerned for my son. What parent in his right mind would drag a ten-year-old child into a battle zone? I had to find him a hiding place. One stray arrow and I'd never forgive myself. I wondered if Zedekiah might be willing to remain with him. There were plenty of secluded places. But as I was about to ask Jonas to halt the mammoth and send down my son, a dark feeling entered my mind. I almost brushed it aside. The choice was clear. I was making the only rational decision.

I decided, almost grudgingly, to put the matter to prayer. It seemed pointless. The logic was overwhelming. Surely Heavenly Father would agree. To my dismay, he did *not* agree. The uneasiness persisted until I prayerfully inquired if I should bring Harry along. Peace replaced the darkness. *That can't be right,* I thought. But as I prayed again, the impression was the same. I considered chucking the whole thing and relying on my own intelligence. But I didn't. However irrational, I decided to trust my heart. I decided to bring my son to Jacobugath.

Soon a timid glimmer of twilight appeared behind the volcanic cones in the east. The daydawn was breaking. The veil of anonymity that had been protecting us was starting to lift. In half an hour every settler and soldier in the valley of Jacobugath would know that enemies had infiltrated the land. The temple fires of Jacobugath still looked impossibly distant. I climbed to the basket on Rachel's back to make more specific inquiries.

Harry was asleep. I might have expected Marcos to be asleep as well, lashed as he was to the wooden rails of the basket. But he looked more alert and awake than most of Ilipichicuma's men who were plodding on foot.

"How far is it now?" I asked.

"Closer than you think," he replied. "The city wall will be in view just over that hill. We should get off the road before we go over it."

"If we meet resistance," I asked Marcos, "where would you expect it?"

"If you do as I say," said Marcos, "we might not meet it at all."

I studied his features in the waxing twilight. I hated this. I hated to think that all of our lives were in the hands of Jacob Moon's son—a proven deceiver and accomplice to murder. All the reservations that I had felt when we were in the same circumstances with Lamachi were multiplied.

"You certainly have my son hoodwinked," I said coldly. "He thinks you're an okay guy."

Marcos laughed and said sourly, "Your son couldn't be more wrong."

"That's what I tried to tell him. So why are you helping us?"

"I already explained."

"Oh, that's right. You're in love with my daughter. You've known her for what? Two? Three weeks? And now you'd give up everything for her?"

"She's the *only* thing I'd give it up for. The only thing that's ever made me consider the option."

I watched him another minute, then I said, "If King Ilipichicuma agrees to let me cut those ropes, what will you do?"

Marcos looked into my eyes, something he'd avoided since

I'd climbed the mammoth. "The same thing that I'd do if no one else were here to help me. I'd do everything in my power to rescue Melody."

Zedekiah, who rested in the basket beside Harry, watched to see what I would do. Jonas, riding the mammoth's shoulder, also glanced back. In both of their eyes I sensed approval. That was enough. I wouldn't wait for the king's permission. I severed Marcos' bonds.

His muscles were stiff. Without the support of being tied to the basket, the rocking motions nearly knocked him over. I helped him find his equilibrium. He began massaging his swollen wrists and sent me a look that intimated gratitude. My heart burned with one last surge of hatred.

"Don't think this means I trust you," I said. "Or that after today I ever want to see your face again."

He looked saddened, but this quickly passed. Expecting any more was asking too much, and he knew it. "Let's find your daughter."

I turned to Jonas. "We're getting off."

Jonas consented, though reluctantly. "I hate to stop her again. She's as exhausted as the rest of us. I'm afraid if I let her sink down on her belly, she'll just fall asleep."

Nevertheless, Jonas brought the mammoth to a halt and directed her to kneel. Marcos and I climbed off. When Ilipichicuma saw that I had released the prisoner, he threw an expected tantrum.

"I am the king!" he ranted. "I did not give permission to cut his bonds!"

"If he's going to help us," I said, "we need him on the ground."

"And if he betrays us? What then?"

"If I was going to betray you," Marcos interrupted, "I'd let you march right up this road. Just over that hill should be the first outpost of the city garrison. About five hundred men. They're probably just waking up."

Ilipichicuma grunted. His eyes were red and weary. At last he swallowed his pride and said to Marcos, "What do you suggest?"

"Have your men follow me."

Marcos led us off the road toward the west, through a pineapple patch that bordered a band of trees along the base of the hill. I perceived a stand of cypresses about a half mile through the shadowy light. Beyond them was a thin bank of fog and the marshy shores of a lake—the same lake, I supposed, that we had seen from the ridge.

Rachel didn't even flinch as Jonas urged her to rise. For such an old gal, she had inexhaustible stamina. As she moved through the pineapple patch, she left a torn and twisted heap of pineapple plants in her wake. I'd read somewhere that the famous General Hannibal, when he used elephants to try and attack Rome, failed because the elephants were too exhausted by the long march. Mammoths were apparently a more durable creature, but I feared we were pushing our luck. Her breathing sounded far more strained than it had on previous days, and the hair on her underbelly was dripping with perspiration.

I marched near the front with Gidgiddonihah, Marcos, and King Ilipichicuma. The area into which we were headed was swampy and overgrown with tall marsh weeds. There were no signs of huts or any other buildings. This was fortunate since it was light enough now that any sleepy-eyed farmer would have taken one look at us and our mammoth and started screaming bloody murder.

The downside was that as soon as we got to within a couple hundred yards of the lake, we started trudging through a mud bog up to our shins. Marcos turned north, along the lake front. All at once the marsh weeds opened up and we could see the ghostly outline of a distant island whose towering stone walls rose out of the fog.

"That's it," said Marcos. "The prison of Jacobugath."

"My people are in there?" Ilipichicuma asked.

"I'm sure of it," Marcos replied.

"And my daughter?" I added.

"Let's hope," said Marcos.

I didn't like the sound of that. I needed more than hope. But at the moment he had nothing else to offer.

The island was at least two miles away. The city wall was situated directly between us and our destination. It snaked along the countryside until it finally came to an end, extending two or three hundred yards out into the foggy waters of the lake. If we were planning to make an assault on that prison, we'd first have to find a way around that one obstacle.

"How high is the wall?" asked Gidgiddonihah.

"It's really not that high," said Marcos. "My father hasn't had time to build it up on the west. We should be able to get over it by giving each other a leg up."

"Why don't we let the curelom knock out a hole?" asked Ilipichicuma.

"I'm sure it could," said Marcos, "but I was hoping to avoid a commotion as long as possible."

Jonas called down, "She'll swim around it."

Ilipichicuma signaled his men to start moving again. I gazed off toward the east. In a few moments, the first rays of the sun were going to stab out from behind the mountains. Between us and the city wall lay an open meadow. The fog wasn't nearly thick enough to conceal us. I couldn't imagine how we could possibly cross that meadow without being sighted by lookouts.

I asked Marcos again, "Are you sure we won't meet any resistance until we reach that prison?"

"Let's hope," he repeated.

"No," I said. "Let's pray."

* * *

The tower of Jacob's prison was a thimble-shaped dome at the western end of the island. From its lofty height of about forty feet lookouts could oversee the entire prison complex as well as gaze off toward the west to the opposite shore of the lake or toward the east to revel in the magnificence of Jacob's capital. It was not the prison's highest tower—there was a higher one at the opposite end—but it was the largest. The top-most room could be reached by way of a staircase that spiraled its way around the outside until it arrived at the doorway.

My uncle and I were taken to the tower separately. As I was led up the steps, I examined the sky for signs of an approaching storm. The sky was perfectly clear—not a single cloud in any direction.

The air was absolutely still. Maybe Garth's calculations had been mistaken.

As I was led into the interior of the upper room, I met the faces of Jacob and Balam, as well as four of the vulture-like priests that I had seen perched on Jacob's temple the previous day. Each of the priests was as filthy and unkempt as Balam, with jewelry and ornaments hanging from their lips, nostrils, ears and cheeks. The only difference was that they wore robes of black while Balam wore red. Jacob wore a jaguar skin robe and mantle that stretched over his paunch like a beer-drinker's T-shirt. Around his waist hung a belt made from tiny shells and an enormous jade buckle. Being in the same room with so many malignant souls felt like being thrust into a room filled with spiders or centipedes or some other vermin. It caused an itch to burn under my skin, all the way down to the bone, and there was no way to scratch it.

To my surprise, my limbs were left free. The only restraint I wore was the ever-present collar around my neck, which I had come to accept as part of my body. I had expected to find the room filled with implements of torture, like steel cages, iron maidens, and chains hanging from the walls. But there was nothing in the room that remotely resembled a torture device. There were only two large clay basins, about waist high. One of them was filled to the brim with some sort of greenish-black muck, like dirty motor oil, but thicker. The other was filled with nothing more extravagant than water. The water looked so cool and clear that I found myself licking my lips. It had been over a day since I'd drunk any liquid that wasn't thick with slime or sediment.

Jacob smiled at me malevolently. "Did you have a good night's sleep, my dear?"

I didn't answer.

He noticed that my eyes were drawn to the water. "Thirsty?" he asked. "I've heard that the water down in the hole is less than appetizing. Go ahead. Get yourself a drink."

I was about to bolt toward the basin when Jacob added, "But first, you must tell me your decision."

I glanced helplessly back and forth from Jacob's face to the basin of water. I don't know if he realized how cruel it was to show me the drink and then deny it. What was I thinking? Of course he realized it.

"Decision?" I said, stalling.

Jacob sat down on the rim of the window that overlooked the lake. I imagined myself somehow leaping from that window and landing in the water below. But as I edged closer I saw that we were not directly over the water. First I would have to leap eight feet beyond the window to try and clear the prison's outer wall. The jump looked impossible. To say nothing of the fact that the window was not large enough to allow a running start. As well, I couldn't see what was actually at the bottom on the other side. It might have been lake, or it might have been a shelf of rock. No, I decided. If some opportunity for escape was going to miraculously present itself, it would have to be something else.

Jacob knew I was stalling, but he acted as though he had all the time in the world. "No doubt you discussed this subject last night with your uncle?"

"Yes," I admitted.

Jacob sighed. "Melody, Melody. Let's not be coy anymore. The moment of truth has arrived. Did your uncle reveal to you the information that I want to know?"

I opened and closed my mouth, unsure of how to answer.

"I promise you," Jacob continued, "that if you tell me, I will release you and your uncle immediately. I realize now that my proposal of marriage may not have struck you as terribly enticing. This hurts me to the core. However, I believe that I can offer you something that you will appreciate. After I have granted you and your uncle your freedom, you may, at your discretion, select a contingent of travel guides who will escort you back to the land of Melek. Back to the cavern and back to your world. I will not try to stop you. All I want to know is the location of Haberekiah's treasure. After that, I will do everything in my power to see to it that you are—"

"He doesn't know."

Jacob's lips remained frozen in the shape of his last word. He finally said, "What was that?"

I squeezed off a pair of tears as I confessed, "My uncle doesn't know."

"Doesn't know what?" asked Jacob, as if I might be referring to something else.

"He doesn't know the location of Haberekiah's treasure. He

never has *known. Please, if you're going to kill us, do it swiftly. Because torturing me or torturing him won't do you any good. He can't tell you what he doesn't know."*

Jacob chewed on the flesh inside his cheek, his temper rumbling. But he only sighed again and shook his head, "I've given you every opportunity, Melody. Every chance under the sun to avoid what's about to happen—"

"Are you deaf?" I cried. "HE DOESN'T KNOW!"

Jacob made his voice even louder than mine. "—EVERY OPPORTUNITY! I even offered to make you my queen! The envy of every female in this valley! I offered to set you free! I offered to let you return to your home—"

The strain was too much. I burst out laughing. It astonished Jacob enough that he paused in his tirade.

"You can't take it, can you?" I said. "You're so obsessed. You've invested so much hope. So much energy and time. And for what? Absolutely nothing! It's been a complete and total waste of your time. But this is just too much for your narrow, little mind to handle, isn't it?"

Jacob clenched his teeth, and the muscles in his face vibrated. His complexion took on the darkest shade of red I've ever seen on a person. He was like a volcano, ready to blow. It took every ounce of self-restraint he'd ever mastered to say calmly, without exploding, "Bring the Pale Prophet here."

The prison guards departed to fulfill the command. I sank down onto my knees. What have I done? I wondered. And yet what else could I have done? How could I have played it differently? Could heaven have filled my mind with some assortment of words or actions that might have changed the outcome?

Garth was hauled in. His hands were bound. He looked at me on the floor, and his eyes flashed indignation. "What have you done to her?"

"Nice to see you, too, Garplimpton," said Jacob. "How are you? It's been two or three months, hasn't it?"

Garth ignored Jacob's phony greeting. Even though his hands were tied and prison guards held his arms, he tried to break free and go to me on the floor. The guards held him fast.

"She hasn't been touched, I assure you," Jacob proclaimed. "I've

done everything in my power to delay your fate as long as possible. However—"

"I heard what she told you from below," said Garth. "Melody is telling you the truth. I never found the people of Haberekiah. We searched for five months but—"

Jacob wouldn't hear any of it. "Yes, yes," he interrupted. "I heard your niece the first time. And I confess that I believe her. That is, I believe that she believes it. You've done a fine job of convincing her of your lies so that she might persuade me to abandon this affair. Unfortunately—"

"Jacob, I'm begging you!" said Garth. "I've told you the truth!"

Jacob stepped forward and backhanded my uncle across the mouth. "Liar! My Diviner, Balam, tells me differently! Do you think I would go to such trouble to bring us together like this if I wasn't certain that you knew?"

I looked at Balam. He had an expression of stone. I'd hate to be in his shoes when Jacob found out that all his incantations to discover if my uncle knew the truth had been mistaken. His was the only fate that might be worse than our own.

"My patience is gone," Jacob declared. "Seize the girl!"

After Jacob barked this command, my eyes turned to the prison guards, expecting them to lunge toward me. Then I realized that the order had not been directed at them. I was seized by the grimy fingers of the black-robed priests. They pulled me to my feet.

Jacob began pacing in a circle around the room. "I'm sure you've both wondered," he began, "how it is that our farm fields are so green and ripe and bursting with produce. I'm about to show you how this is achieved." He nodded to the priests.

The priests pulled me over to the basin in the middle of the room—the one filled with the greenish-black muck. They forced me to dip both hands into the muck, halfway to my elbows. I closed my fingers into a tight fist, thinking somehow it might protect the skin of my palms if the substance was poisonous. As it turned out, I'd done exactly as the priests would have wanted. The sludge was warm and sticky and smelled vaguely like rubber cement. When they raised my fists out of the basin, they were caked in a thick ball of sludge.

Jacob continued, "Every growing season, to insure that an ade-

quate amount of rain falls on our crops, we select a small boy and girl, innocent and unblemished, and we grant unto them the honor that I'm about to grant unto you, except on that occasion we have a considerably larger audience—the whole valley as a matter of fact."

After the priests drew my fists out of the muck, they quickly immersed them in the cool water of the neighboring basin. Instantly the sludge congealed into a hard, rubbery coating. I tried to move my fingers and thumb, but they were completely immobile. My hands had become useless stumps, encased in rubbery cement. I tried to bring my fists to my mouth to tear the latex-like layer with my teeth, but the priests caught my arms.

"What is it you want to hear?" Garth inquired desperately. "I'll tell you anything that you want to hear!"

"I know you will," said Jacob soberly. "Now let me finish. You see, when we conduct this particular sacrifice, we use a much bigger basin of cool water, one that can immerse the subject entirely. For the purposes of the ceremony, it is absolutely essential that the victims die in the water, but not of the water. Are you following what I'm saying?"

Garth made no reply. His expression was frozen in dread and disbelief. Jacob sent the priests a second signal. I shrieked as they pushed against the back of my head and forced my face down into the sludge. When they pulled me out again, my entire head—eyes, nose, mouth, and hair—was caked in the slimy cement. Although it was impossible to see through the sludge, I opened my mouth wide and managed to create a passageway for the flow of air into my lungs. Gasps wrenched out of my throat. My mind reeled in terror. I tried to spit the cement from my lips, but spitting only made it worse. My ears were also covered, but I could still hear the muffled voice of my uncle as he shouted in vain, "Don't do this! If you want an answer, I'll give you an answer! Stop now, and I'll tell you everything!"

"Sorry," I heard Jacob reply. "If you're going to tell me something, you'll have to tell it to me in two minutes or less."

With that, someone slapped a huge glob of the cement into my face. I closed my mouth to try and keep it from being rammed down my throat. All at once my head was forced down into the cool water. The substance congealed as before. I tried to gasp! I tried to suck one last gulp of air so that I could hold it in my lungs! But there was no air to gasp. The airways into my nose and mouth were sealed over as tight as a drum.

The priests released my arms. I fell to the floor. I drew my hands to my face to try and tear away the rubbery layer, but my fists were sealed in cement! I couldn't grip anything! I couldn't tear a hole! I was suffocating! Suffocating!

I heard my uncle's muffled scream. "Ramah! The people of Haberekiah are hidden in a valley near the Hill Ramah!"

"Wrong!" blasted Jacob. "My soldiers have been all over that region! Perhaps you didn't know that my prison is filled with war captives from Cuma-ramah even now! Try again!"

I began crawling, scraping my face against the stone floor, trying to tear a breathing hole in the seal. I was drowning! Just like the river! Worse than the river! There was no blanket of icy water to lull me into unconsciousness. Only the hot panic of asphyxiation.

"The mountains of Gilgal!" cried Garth. "Just as the rumors have always said! Don't let her die! God in heaven! Please! Don't let her die!"

My uncle went berserk. I heard them fighting and struggling to keep him back. And then the voices fell silent. My panic raged as I continued thrashing about, slamming my head against the floor, against the wall, against the stone basin. There was no air in my lungs! No air! Why wasn't anyone speaking? Had they forgotten me? I continued to squirm and roll.

Finally, I heard Jacob say in a voice defeated and subdued, "It's true. He really doesn't know."

I heard my uncle's final wrenching sobs. "Noooo! Pleeeease! Pleeease!"

"Take him back to the hole," said Jacob. "Throw him back to the vermin who love him. Tonight I want the whole lot of them brought to the Heart of the World. At least the Pale Prophet will serve me some useful purpose."

"What about the girl?" someone asked.

"The girl?" said Jacob. "What about her?"

The stones vibrated. Footsteps were leaving the tower. My uncle's shrieks faded as Jacob, the priests, and the prison guards carried him away. I was alone. My head was floating. Floating like a helium balloon. I was lying on my back now, just rocking back and forth. Just rocking back and forth. My energy was slipping away . . . slipping away. The dark light of death was settling over me . . . settling around me . . . settling in.

I heard trumpets.

CHAPTER 17

I was right. We were not able to cross the meadow without being spotted by lookouts. Just as we were nearing the city wall at the place where it jutted out into the marsh, trumpets from various lookout posts inside Jacobugath began to wail. The trumpet blasts came in sets of three.

"That's the alert," said Marcos. "We must have been spotted. The garrisons will start forming ranks immediately. We have to move fast."

"Forget about creating a commotion!" shouted Ilipichicuma. "Use the curelom! Break down that wall!"

Zedekiah and my son slipped down from the basket on Rachel's back. Ilipichicuma's warriors cleared the way as Jonas guided the mighty beast forward. At first Rachel was confused. She didn't understand Jonas' intentions. She backed up and swung her massive tusks from side to side in protest.

"Easy girl!" cried Jonas. "You can do it!" And then he called out to heaven, "Please Father, make her understand!"

The mammoth turned in a complete circle. Suddenly, she reared into the air. Jonas clutched onto the hair of the mammoth's shoulder and hung on. As Rachel came down, her front legs smashed into the eight-foot wall. The stucco collapsed and shattered like a saltine cracker. To finish the job, Rachel barreled through to the other side. There was now a mammoth inside the city limits of Jacobugath.

The rest of us filed through the breach. The only thing now between us and a causeway that led out to the prison gate was a mile of muddy beachfront, blurred by drifting fog. Most of the buildings and residences of Jacobugath had been built several hundred yards in from shore, no doubt to avoid flood damage. There were a lot of canoes and nets, as well as a few storage shacks, short stone fences, and flooded farm plots; otherwise we were facing no obstacles whatsoever—at least no obstacles that would have hindered Rachel.

"Throw down the ladder!" I called up to Jonas.

If my daughter was inside that prison, I was determined to arrive in style, brandishing my obsidian-edged sword toward the sky as I stood on the back of an eight-ton mammoth.

* * *

Trumpets continued blaring near and far. As lightheaded as I felt, I might have believed they were the trumpets of angels come to escort me to heaven. But I must have still had enough presence of mind to comprehend. The sound electrified me with one last burst of courage. Still blind, I staggered to my feet. But it was useless. I was just too dizzy. There was no strength left. I fell forward. My face smacked the stone sill of one of the windows, directly against my nose. It would have shattered the cartilage for sure, but the congealed mask absorbed the blow. I rolled onto my back, my consciousness fading for good. I was ready now, I decided. I was ready to die.

But at the same time that I prepared my mind for the next world, I felt a cold sensation in one of my nostrils. My lung was slowly expanding with air. My fall against the edge of the window had made a tiny crack in the seal of my death mask. As I realized that I was tasting sweet air, I sucked hard to inhale more. But the airflow was immediately cut off. By inhaling too fast, the crack pinched shut. Oh, the agony! To breathe my first gulp of air in well over a minute, and yet if I inhaled too quickly, I received none at all!

I tried to calm myself. I couldn't be impatient. I'd black out for sure. I exhaled slowly.

Then I let the air seep naturally into my lungs. It tasted so good. But I needed more! I needed it faster! I breathed too quickly again and the crack sealed. Not so fast, *I told myself!* Be calm. Be calm.

I must have lain there for two or three minutes, relearning the act of breathing, struggling to slow the beat of my heart so that my blood needed less oxygen. I was just beginning to feel good again, as if I might actually survive this, when I heard footsteps reenter the tower.

"There!" said a voice. It was the prison guard, Urriah.

"I see them," said Jacob.

Jacob and Urriah! The enemy was back to finish the job! I didn't flinch a single muscle.

Maybe they'd believe I was dead. But it didn't seem as though they had returned to finish me. They were using the tower as a look-out.

"What is *that creature?" asked Jacob.*

"A curelom, Lord Jacob," said Urriah.

"Curelom? How did it get into the city?"

"Without much difficulty, I presume," said Urriah. "Do you see the breach?"

"Who are those men?" Jacob shrieked. "What are they doing?"

"I think they're coming toward us."

"Toward the prison? What would they want—?" I heard Jacob gasp as he caught hold of the answer. "Cuma-ramah! Those are the warriors of that petty king! Fools! They've come for the prisoners!"

The footsteps scrambled. The tower vibrated. Jacob and the guard had left again. I could hear a great deal of commotion in the courtyard below. I made my first attempt to move, pushing myself up on my stumpy fists. I felt around for the sill of the window. Then I laid my face carefully against the edge. I was worried that my efforts might plug the crack permanently, but I had to create a bigger opening. By pressing my nose against the stone, I discovered that I could hold the crack open. For the first time, I breathed deeply.

I began gently scraping the mask against the edge and managed to tear off a small piece over my nose. I could now breathe freely. My next concern was my hands. If I could just free up one fist, I could easily peel off the cement around my eyes and mouth. I moved my right fist back and forth along the edge. It was like scraping an eraser against a stone. After a minute, I wore it down to my skin. Then I freed up my thumb. All five of my fingers broke loose at once. Desperately, I started clawing at the gummy cement on my face. Shreds of the latex-like mask began peeling off. The cement that stuck directly against my skin hadn't quite congealed. It left a sticky green residue. But I could see again!

I looked out toward the prison's central courtyard. My eyes hurt. My vision remained a little blurry. I did not want to rub my eyelids for fear that I would smear in the sticky cement. But even as blurry as my eyesight was, I realized immediately what was causing the commotion. The prisoners whose make-shift shelters blanketed the courtyard were on the brink of a riot. Virtually every prison guard had been called down from their posts to keep order. The guards threatened them with clubs and swords. The bodies of several inmates who had gotten too anxious were lying near the prison gate.

My eyes raised beyond the gate, toward the foggy shores of the lake. Of all the strange—! Barreling down the shoreline was some sort of . . . elephant?

An elephant in the land of the Nephites?

I strained to improve my focus. The elephant's tusks were enormous! It was covered with a winter coat! Could it be . . . ? But that was impossible! Mammoths were already extinct by 34 A.D. Everyone in my century knows that!

Several people—three I think—rode on the creature's back. A hundred more soldiers were charging at full speed behind it. They'd almost reached the causeway. Two dozen men in feathered uniforms were poised on the causeway to fight them. I guessed that these were the bodyguards who had escorted the king from the palace.

In the distance I perceived what appeared to be more warriors assembling in the streets of the city. And even more streaming through a gap in the city wall about a mile down the shoreline. If these men with the mammoth were intending to storm the prison, they'd find themselves surrounded by Jacob's army within minutes after the raid began.

* * *

There was no slowing down. Not now. I didn't care that King Ilipichicuma and the others were sinking behind us—fifty yards, one hundred yards. They'd catch up soon enough. And by the time they did, the gates of that prison would either be opened wide or smashed flat.

I'd ordered Harry to climb the mammoth with me, assuming he'd be far safer aboard Rachel than he would have been running alongside the warriors. The little dog was still bundled up in Harry's mantle. I told my son to lie down at the rear of the basket and hang on tight.

About twenty-five men awaited us on the gravel causeway. They stood between the beach and the island, their weapons in hand, daring us to try and get past them. But as Rachel turned onto the causeway, their scowls melted and their jaws dropped. The causeway was not wide enough for all of us, and they didn't look all too anxious to carry on a sword fight with those tusks. As Rachel thundered toward them, one after another made an ungraceful leap into the muddy waters of the lake, producing some rather humorous splash landings.

Rachel thundered forward. The gate bounced up and down in our vision. Jonas was hunkered down on the mammoth's shaggy shoulder like a racing jockey. He yelled into Rachel's ear, "Faster, girl! Faster!" Rachel was barreling so fast now that I was afraid the basket on her back would break apart. Our travel packs, as well as the weapon bundles we'd tied to the basket were flopping up and down like saddle bags. Harry was bouncing up and down right along with them.

Upon reaching the gate, Rachel skidded to a halt.

"No, Rachel!" cried Jonas. "Go through it! Go through it!"

But Jonas' encouragement wasn't necessary. Rachel knew what was expected. I suspect she had been looking forward to it. The gate stood about three feet taller than Rachel's shoulder. Men were perched on the rails behind the gate looking down at us. The mammoth reared up again and kicked forward. I heard the support beam crack. One of the men on the gate tripped over the rail. Rachel's tusk caught him at the midriff. She tossed the man like a ragdoll into the waters of the lake. The other men on the gate either fell back or leaped clear.

"Again, girl!" Jonas cried. "Again! Again!"

Rachel backed up. On her second attempt, she lowered her tusks and rammed the gate with the crown of her head. The support beams snapped. The gate burst open. As the courtyard was revealed to our view, Rachel let out a roar every bit as ear-rending as that of the fifteen-foot bull who'd chased us on the plateau. As she stomped forward, there was a mad scrambling of prison guards and other personnel to get out of our way.

But the prison guards faced more challenges than just an uninvited mammoth. The courtyard was a whirlpool of anxious prisoners. Our dramatic entrance was taken as a cue to start a riot. Hundreds of inmates surged forward to attack the prison guards, ripping the weapons right out of their grips. I recognized the features of the prisoners instantly. They were the captives of Cuma-ramah.

I glanced back at the causeway. Gidgiddonihah and the warriors of Ilipichicuma were busy contending with the soldiers who'd leaped into the lake, most of whom were easy prey as they tried to climb out of the water. The first in our company to reach the prison gate behind the mammoth was Marcos.

The crowd gave way as Jonas guided the mammoth into the center of the courtyard. Harry moved aside as I cut loose the first bundle of weapons. Swords spilled out onto the pavement. Prisoners cheered. They snatched them up one by one. I cut loose the other bundles until all of the weapons tied to Rachel's basket were in the hands of Ilipichicuma's countrymen.

I looked back again. Jacob's warriors on the causeway had been defeated. Shouts of triumph were raised as King Ilipichicuma entered the gate. His glowing subjects, including four young men who I assumed were his sons, rushed forward to greet and embrace him. I noticed that every prison guard who was not dead or maimed had fought his way inside a high archway that led into the main compound of the prison. Here was where they intended to hold out until the city garrison arrived. They wouldn't have to wait long. Troops were gathering on the lakeshore even now.

"The day of vengeance is here!" shouted Ilipichicuma. "On to the palace of Jacobugath. The Cloud Maker's crown of perpetual glory awaits the man who slays Lord Jacob of the Moon!"

The cheers of the men of Cuma-ramah were rabid. Ilipichicuma was nuts! This was his chance to escape. If he could keep his men in a single body, they might break out of the city with minimal losses and march for home. But it was pointless to yell this out to him. Ilipichicuma's lust for revenge was incurable.

My eyes caught sight of Marcos. I noticed that he knelt over a wounded guard, grabbing him by the hair and shaking him roughly, joggling him of vital information before he breathed his dying breath. I knew what that information would be. I perceived that the guard had given him some sort of reply, but whatever it was, the information was not good. Marcos' face went pale. He released the guard's hair and turned his gaze westward—toward a tower at the opposite end of the prison.

* * *

It was a mammoth!

If I lived to be a thousand years old, I never would have expected to see such a sight! The creature crashed through the gate, inspiring the prisoners to surge forward in a riot. More warriors poured in behind the mammoth. Who were these men? They could only be God-sent. Anyone who battled the forces of King Jacob would surely be supported by legions of angels.

I tore away the cement on my other hand. Then I began peeling and tearing away the remaining shreds on my face and in my hair. The sticky residue that remained likely resembled a bizarre sort of facial cream. Sweat mixed with the cement, stinging my eyes. I went to the basin of water and dunked myself again to congeal the last of the residue and make it easier to peel off.

When I raised my dripping head out of the water, I was facing the entrance. Someone stood in the doorway. The morning sun shone behind him. For a second I couldn't recognize who it was. I shielded my eyes. And then I knew. Balam!

Jacob's Diviner glared at me with pure enmity. I could see his teeth grinding through the holes in his cheeks.

"You're not so easy to kill, are you, Melody?"

There was a long, curved obsidian knife in his hand. The golden shaft glittered with jewels—a ceremonial knife. The ritual of my death had gone unfinished. In Balam's profession, such negligence was the worst kind of sacrilege. He'd returned to finish the job and collect the offering for his Jaguar gods. The fact that I was still alive didn't seem to discourage him particularly. He couldn't let the commotion in the courtyard distract him either. His violent intentions with respect to me rose above all other considerations.

I glanced around, though I knew there was no escape. The tower only had one entrance. Balam started toward me.

"You are a gift to me, Melody," said Balam. "Your survival could only be a present from the Divine Jaguar. Though Lord Jacob will surely demand my death at tonight's feast for my mistaken divinations, your blood may still redeem my soul from the fires of Akmul. Just as you have become my bane, you have become my salvation."

I tried to keep the pottery basins between us, but they weren't high enough. Balam lunged. I threw myself backwards and fell against the wall. He yelled and hurdled the two basins. The knife raised to strike.

"Balam! No!"

The cry had come from the doorway. Balam hesitated. It was Marcos! He carried a sword. Balam may have been a condemned man, but he did not wish to die by the cursed hand of Jacob's son. As Marcos stepped forward to confront him, Balam overturned the pottery basin filled with cement. The dark-green sludge spilled out across the floor. Marcos faltered as it spread around his feet. Balam rolled the empty pottery basin at him. In attempting to dodge it, Marcos slipped and landed flat on his back in the sludge. As he tried to raise his sword, Balam stomped it back down to the ground, smashing Marcos' hand under the hilt. Jacob's Diviner wasted no time gloating over his victim. His blade thrust toward Marcos' throat.

I dove into Balam's back. He fell forward. He might have recovered his balance, but the slime caused him to trip toward the tower doorway, his legs slipping beneath him. He dropped the knife as he tried to brace himself for impact. It looked as if he was about to stumble outside and fly over the edge. But just then another *person appeared in the doorway. I gasped in astonishment.*

My father!

I had followed Marcos down a passageway that led behind the central compound of the prison and across a series of platforms and staircases to reach the tower at the western end of the island. I caught sight of him as he climbed the tower's outer stairway. I vaulted up the steps behind him. I could hear the struggle inside the upper room as I approached the entrance, but I didn't expect to find a man's head barreling toward my stomach. The red-robed man knocked the wind out of me. I fell backward, certain that I would tumble over the ledge. But the stairway's landing outside the door was just wide enough that I came down on my back with a thud. The man in the red robe flipped over the top of me. As I rolled onto my stomach, I realized that he was clinging to the edge with every knuckle, his feet dangling over the forty-foot drop. But the man was remarkably strong—and blindingly ugly. The muscles in his mutilated face strained as he pulled himself back onto the landing. But before he could swing his legs onto the ledge, Marcos plunged a gold-handled knife into his back.

The man's eyes widened in surprise. He looked up to see who had delivered the fatal wound. Marcos showed no mercy. He placed the bottom of his foot on the man's face and shoved. With the knife still in his back, he slipped over the edge. He fell with a shriek and landed with a grunt. I peered over the ledge. No movement. The man was dead.

The face of the next person who emerged from the tower looked almost as dreadful as the man in the red robe. I thought for sure it was some kind of female demon-priest painted with dark green goop to make her look like a sacred reptile. As she rushed at me, her arms outstretched, her eyes thick with tears, I was half-tempted to raise my sword in self-defense. But then she spoke my name—my favorite name.

"Dad!" I cried. "Oh, Daddy! Daddy!"
I latched onto his chest, so overcome with sobbing and tears that I could neither speak nor breathe.

"Melody?" I cried in disbelief. "Can it be? Can it be?"
I wrapped my arms around her head. I weaved my fingers through her gum-encrusted hair. I kissed the top of her head. My little girl! It was my little girl! She was in my arms! I would never let her go again. Never!

We gripped each other tightly for a long time, our faces streaked with tears, our hearts soaring to heaven. He came for me! My daddy came for me! I had no idea how he'd done it, but I didn't care. He was here! He was alive! He was safe! And in his arms, so was I.

"Thank you, Father in Heaven," I whispered. "Thank you."
I peeled away some of the rubbery film on my daughter's face so that I could see her eyes—the living heirloom of her mother. Marcos looked on, still panting heavily from the fight. He made no effort to interrupt or claim his share of my daughter's attention. He was content to revel in her joy as she reunited with me.

When I saw Marcos standing there, fighting back his own emotions, I went to him and latched onto his chest. Despite my appearance, he kissed me. I don't think my father was very comfortable with that.

I just didn't want to share my daughter with anyone. I didn't feel obligated to share. Not after all I'd been through. Besides, my feelings for Marcos remained highly ambivalent. But out of respect for my daughter—and yes—out of respect for Marcos' unflagging efforts to save her life, I restrained myself from pulling them apart.
Gidgiddonihah's voice zapped me back to reality. He stood at the base of the tower, shouting up at me.
"Jim!" he cried. "Ilipichicuma is leaving! We have to go!"
I turned my gaze back toward the prison gate. Gidgiddonihah should have spoken in the past tense.

Ilipichicuma had already *left.* Despite the fact that the courtyard had been packed with over a thousand men only ten minutes before, it was now virtually evacuated. I looked around for
the mammoth. Where were Jonas and Zedekiah and Harry? I
couldn't see them. Several tall partition walls blocked my view
of large segments of the courtyard. They must have been
behind one of those walls.

A battle had broken out on the shores of the lake. The warriors of Ilipichicuma had charged head-on with the forces of
King Jacob at the end of the causeway. And yet it looked more
like a chase than a battle. The men of Cuma-ramah were engag-
ing the enemy just long enough to break through to the streets
of the city. Only about a fourth of Jacob's garrison had had time
to assemble. It appeared that Ilipichicuma's men were breaking
through with relative ease despite the fact that many of them
were not armed because of limited weapon supplies. All across
the city the rest of Jacob's city garrison was on its way. Since
most of the garrison had been posted outside the city, numerous soldiers were approaching through the breach in the wall
that had been created by Rachel. Ilipichicuma didn't stand a
chance. The city garrison outnumbered him three to one. And
every one of Jacob's soldiers was armed to the teeth.

"Well," I said, "if they're determined to kill Jacob, at least
they'll have the element of surprise on their side. No one will
expect an army of escaped prisoners to launch a direct assault
on the palace."

"But Jacob isn't at the palace," said Melody. "The king is
here."

"Here?" I asked.

"In the prison. At least he was here fifteen minutes ago."

"Why wouldn't the prisoners in the courtyard have known?"

"He arrived before sunrise," said Melody. "They may not
have seen him."

"So Jacob might be hiding somewhere on the prison
grounds?"

Melody nodded. I grieved at the opportunity missed.
Ilipichicuma might have had Jacob right under his nose, and he
didn't know it!

I noticed that some of the guards who had taken refuge inside the archway of the main complex of the prison were starting to reemerge. A large number of Jacob's troops were already racing down the causeway toward the entrance. They'd been as anxious to break through Ilipichicuma's ranks as he'd been to break through theirs. Word must have reached some of the garrison commanders that King Jacob was inside the prison. The cavalry was on its way to rescue him.

And then I saw something even more alarming. As I looked beyond the shoreline, beyond the walls of the city, it seemed to me that the entire countryside was alive! There were soldiers everywhere, descending upon the capital like a swarm of locusts. Apparently, the armies of King Jacob had not slept last night either. Their failure to trap Ilipichicuma in the canyon must have led them to suspect the worst—that the invaders had slipped past them in order to march freely into Jacobugath.

"Where's Garth?" I asked Melody. "Is he here? Is he alive?"

"He's here," Melody confirmed. "I think he's alive. He's in a room on the lowest level."

"How do we get there?"

"Through that corridor." Melody pointed toward the archway where guards continued to emerge.

"We can't go that way," I said. "Is there another way?"

"I don't know," said Melody.

I had to swallow the facts. Rescuing Garth seemed unthinkable. We'd have enough trouble rescuing ourselves.

I called down to Gidgiddonihah. "The prison gate is blocked! We have to find another way out!"

Gidgiddonihah began climbing the tower to assess the situation for himself.

"There *is* no other way out," said Marcos. "The gate is the only way."

My eyes searched the courtyard again. Again I wondered, where was Jonas? Where were Zedekiah and my son? I couldn't see them anywhere. How could you hide an eight-ton mammoth?

And then I saw them. The mammoth was in the lake, swimming through the fog along the southern curve of the island. There were three people on her back. Jonas had spotted us on the tower. He seemed to be steering Rachel around to the area directly below us.

"What about the wall?" I asked Marcos. "What if we climbed on top and jumped into the lake?"

"As I remember it, the only catwalk at the top of the outer wall is along the prison's northern face," said Marcos.

"There's no other stairway? No other ladder?"

"I don't think so."

Gidgiddonihah arrived. He'd overheard our conversation. "Then we'll jump from here."

"From *here?*" said Melody with alarm.

We went inside the tower and looked down from the window. There was about an eight-foot gap between the tower and the outer wall of the prison. The outer wall was only about two feet wide and a good six feet below the level of the window. I half-wondered why the original architect hadn't just built the tower flush with the outer wall. I guessed it was probably to discourage prisoners from attempting exactly what Gidgiddonihah was proposing.

It would be a tricky jump. Basically we'd have to land on the wall while the inertia of the leap carried us over the opposite edge—a skip and a plunge.

"What's on the other side?" I asked Marcos. "Will we hit water?"

"I have no idea," he replied.

Gidgiddonihah looked out the other window, down into the courtyard. "We'll have to risk it," he said. "There are guards headed this way."

"I can't make it!" said Melody. "I can't jump that far!"

"Yes, you can," said Marcos.

"We have no choice, honey," I added.

"We'll jump together," said Marcos. "I'll hold your hand."

"*I'll* hold her hand," I said.

Marcos shook his head. "I'm stronger than you, Jim. You better let me do it."

I scowled. Yet I knew he was probably right. For my daughter's sake, I'd place her in Marcos' hands.

"I'll go first," said Gidgiddonihah. "If you don't hear a

splash, you'll have to think of something else."

Rachel was hidden behind the south wall now, probably still several hundred yards down shore. It was comforting to know that at least we wouldn't drown. I thought of waiting for Jonas to ask if the landing was safe. But there wasn't time. The prison guards had almost reached the base of the tower.

Gidgiddonihah let his sword clatter to the floor. It was too bulky to take with him. The rest of us did the same. Gidgiddonihah climbed up and stood in the window sill. The ceiling wasn't tall enough for him to stand. He had to crouch. To jump he'd have to lean far forward. Once he started to lean, that would be it. There was no opportunity for indecision.

We watched in suspense as Gidgiddonihah sprang from the tower. He landed with one foot on the outer wall and then he stepped off into nothingness.

After a few seconds, we heard a splash.

"You two go next," I said.

Marcos and my daughter climbed into the window. We could hear the guards' footsteps climbing the tower. Marcos took Melody's trembling hand. I held onto her other hand until the last second. I cringed to think I'd come all this way just to see my daughter fall to her death.

"Ready?" said Marcos.

Melody took a deep breath. "I'm ready."

"On three. Okay—One! Two! *Three!*"

They leaped. Marcos landed squarely, but Melody hit the edge at the tip of her toes. Their hands broke apart. Marcos flipped around backwards as he plummeted over the other side. Melody landed on her chest. She practically scraped the knee cap off her right knee. But she hung on. She pulled up her leg and looked back at me.

"Are you all right?" I yelled.

She examined her wound. I could see the blood. Despite this, she nodded. "I'm okay."

I could hear the guards' voices. "Then jump!" I shouted.

Melody threw herself off the other side. I climbed into place. The guards were just entering the doorway as I leaped.

My feet landed together on the top of the wall, then I twisted into a flip. It was at least a forty-foot plunge, but it was over much faster than I might have imagined. I careened into the lake head first.

The water was only nine or ten feet deep. I went all the way to the bottom. When I propelled myself to the surface, I found Marcos, Melody, and Gidgiddonihah all treading water.

Fast approaching from the south was Rachel, with Jonas, Zedekiah, and Harry. Much of the fog had lifted now, so we could see her quite clearly. The mammoth was three-fourths submerged under the lake, half-walking, half-swimming. The outer wall of the prison was perfectly sheer on this side of the island. If the mammoth hadn't been on its way, I don't think we would have fared very well. The swim to shore was too far.

Melody was still wincing in pain. Marcos helped her keep her head above the surface. I swam over to them.

"How's the knee?" I asked her.

"Bleeding," she replied.

"How bad?"

"Not bad."

"Do you think you can walk?"

"I think so."

I considered chastising Marcos for my daughter's accident, but there wasn't any point. He was already severely chastising himself.

Rachel approached to within a few feet of us. She held her trunk above the surface and blew out a spray of water. Gidgiddonihah was pulling himself into the basket.

"Melody!" cried Harry.

"Harry? What are you—?" She looked at me with an expression that seemed to say, *How could you have brought your son to such a dangerous place?* Obviously a full explanation would be required later.

"Is anyone hurt?" asked Jonas.

"My daughter's knee," I said.

I used Rachel's tusk for leverage and pushed Melody over to Gidgiddonihah. He hoisted her inside the basket. Melody and Harry embraced. The poor dog inside Harry's mantle struggled desperately to free itself. As Melody buried Harry's face in kisses, the dog licked her neck.

"What's that stuff in your hair and on your face?" asked Harry.

"Chewing gum," Melody replied.

As soon as everyone was safely inside the basket, I examined Melody's wound. It was bleeding pretty bad, but the angle of the cut told me it would heal well.

"What about Garth?" asked Melody.

The sound of his name was like a stab to my heart. "I don't know what to do, Melody."

"I do," she declared. "If we keep going around to the north side of the island, we can get to him from the water."

"We can?"

"I'm sure of it." Melody became pensive for a second, then her eyes lit up. *The Beast on the Waters!*"

"What was that?" I asked.

"Never mind," said Melody. "I'll just tell you this: Garth is expecting us. So are a lot of others. They've been expecting us for a long time."

CHAPTER 18

Marcos saw it first.

It was coming from the north, a wall of roiling, tumbling, churning clouds the color of charcoal that rested at the edge of the horizon and climbed to the infinity of outer space.

The sweeping palm of God.

"What in the name of Akmul—?" Marcos uttered.

The wall of clouds was creeping toward us steadily, deliberately. In my lifetime I'd watched the approach of many storms. There are few sights more menacing than the descent of a violent tempest on a Wyoming plain, but this . . . this was outside the bounds of any comparison I could make. And yet remarkably, the air itself was still relatively calm. Only a slight breeze was blowing. The breeze carried away the fog as our mammoth made her way around to the northern face of the island.

"Garth was right," said Melody. "He said it was coming. He said it would arrive just after sunrise."

I knew what she meant. I didn't need any clarification. Our Lord was only moments away from commending his spirit into the hands of eternity.

"We need to move fast!" Melody declared, as if any of us had failed to recognize the urgency.

The waters along the northern perimeter of the island were much more shallow—only three or four feet deep. An arm of the prison wall extended far enough northward to hide us from direct view of Jacob's warriors fighting on the beaches in front of the prison gate. Melody directed us toward a row of thin gaps in the outer wall. Each of the mammoth's steps produced a tumultuous splash. It would have been impossible for anyone on the other side of those gaps not to hear us coming. Even before Rachel had broken her stride, we could hear voices inside cheering, weeping for joy, and shouting praises to heaven. The Beast on the Waters had come! The Pale Prophet's vision had been true!

However, as I assessed the situation, our plan of action was not entirely clear. Rachel had easily crushed the city wall. She'd effortlessly broken through the front gate. But this was a different story. Before us was an ancient stone wall made to withstand anything that nature might have thrust against it for the last several centuries. It was not the kind of obstacle that Rachel could simply kick out with her front legs or bash in with the crown of her head. As the mammoth knelt, I leaped down from the basket and waded up to one of the gaps.

"Garth!" I cried. "Are you in there? Can you hear me?"

After a moment came back the reply. "I'm here, Jim!"

A lump formed in my throat. It was his voice—the voice of the oldest friend I had in this world. All the memories and miseries, tragedies and triumphs that we'd shared over the last twenty-eight years came rushing back. Here we were again, facing overwhelming odds and catastrophic consequences.

"Are you all right?" I inquired.

"Yes," he declared.

I reached into the gap. Our hands clasped in the middle.

I realized Garth was sobbing. "I couldn't save her, Jim. I couldn't save her."

It took a second to register. He meant Melody. He thought Melody was dead!

"Uncle Garth!" Melody shouted from the back of the mammoth. "I'm here, Uncle Garth!"

"Melody?" said Garth in disbelief.

"She's all right," I confirmed.

His sobbing intensified as grief transformed into relief.

The prison wall was nearly three feet thick—definitely outside Rachel's capabilities as a battering ram. It seemed miserably hopeless. I turned to check the progress of the storm. The wall of clouds had edged much closer. The wind was picking up strength.

Zedekiah climbed down from the mammoth. He examined the wide leather harness that came across Rachel's chest and wound all the way around her body. "I have an idea," he announced. "We need to unstrap the harness."

Jonas seemed to read Zedekiah's mind. "Everyone out of the basket!" he said, "Hurry!"

Harry climbed down with the dog. Marcos and Gidgiddonihah assisted Melody. Jonas began to unstrap the cinches on the harness as Zedekiah explained.

"We might be able to thread the harness through two of the gaps. If it's long enough, we can let Rachel give it a tug."

When it was removed, the harness was nearly twenty-five feet long.

"Do you think it will hold?" I asked Jonas.

"I don't know," he said. "It's strong leather. Ten reinforced layers—the strongest I've seen. If it breaks, I don't know what else we can do."

Jonas found a crack in the wall near one of the gaps running for about six feet. Dragging one end of the harness, he approached the gap that was nearest to the crack.

"Garth!" he cried.

"Jonas! Is that you?"

"It is, my friend. We're going to get you out of here."

"I know you are," Garth replied.

Jonas thrust one end of the harness into the gap. "Garth, drag this down to the gap on your right, and push it back through." He turned to me. "After they hand it back, strap it back together."

I called through the wall to make an additional suggestion. "Garth! How many people are in there?"

"Nineteen," he answered.

"Round up every able-bodied man. Fit as many as you can along this section of wall. Have them push with all their might when I give the signal!"

The harness was drawn through both gaps. I strapped the ends back together. Jonas climbed on Rachel's shoulder. He guided her close to the wall. Gidgiddonihah and Zedekiah looped the harness over both tusks. Then Jonas nodded at me.

"Now!" I cried to Garth. "Push!"

Jonas coaxed Rachel to back up. The harness went taut. I could hear the leather stretching. I thought surely it would rip. Suddenly another crack appeared in the wall near the water line. The six-foot section was giving way!

I leaped clear as the mighty block of stone toppled forward and smashed into the water, burying us all under a marvelous wave. About ten men fell out behind the stone, carried forward by their own momentum. A few brick-sized chunks rained down on top of them, but no one was hurt. On the contrary, the cheering became more exuberant than ever. Despite their pale and gaunt condition, despite their eyes squinting at the sunlight, I'd never seen so much joy in human faces.

The first one to leap over the block of stone and splash into the water was a retarded boy whose name I later learned was Fetch. He threw his arms around Gidgiddonihah. Gidgiddonihah's eyebrows shot up in surprise, but he heartily returned the embrace. All the prisoners began pouring out of the hole and showering us with gratitude.

I did not wait for Garth to emerge. I went in after him. When I found my beloved friend with whom I'd shared so many trials and adventures, I threw my arms around his waist and hoisted him up in the air. The two of us laughed and cried and squeezed the air out of each other's lungs.

And then to our dismay, one of the prisoners, a man with a withered arm, climbed atop the block of stone. "Fools! You think you're free? You think this is Zarahemla? The king's army will slaughter you like dogs!"

I hadn't realized until now that there were five men who didn't look grateful at all to have been rescued.

Another man pointed an accusing finger at Marcos. "Lord Jacob's son! He'll kill us all!"

The adulation was dampened. To everyone's surprise, including my own, I was the one who came to Marcos' defense.

"He's with us!" I declared. "He saved my daughter."

Jonas glanced back at the approaching storm. "We have to go!" he urged.

"Go where?" I asked. I was half tempted to stay right here, inside the sturdy walls of the prison.

"There!" Garth proclaimed.

He pointed toward the southwest where another small island jutted out of the lake. It was about a mile away. The shoreline appeared to be crisscrossed by crumbling walls, the remains of a forgotten era.

Zedekiah and Gidgiddonihah began desperately restrapping the harness around the mammoth.

Gidgiddonihah asked Jonas, "How many men did you say that basket can carry?"

"All of them," he replied. "It *has* to."

"Four of these men are lame," said Garth. "They'll need help."

Marcos, Gidgiddonihah, and I began lifting the injured and disabled, including my daughter, to Jonas, Zedekiah, and another man named Kib. Just as we'd finished placing all of the lame and injured inside the basket, I heard a terrified cry: "Lord Jacob! He's there! Lord Jacob of the Moon!"

Three of the five men who stood apart from us were pointing toward the top of the wall. My eyes climbed the forty-foot stone face.

There he was, standing on the catwalk at the highest point, looming above us like a malevolent phantom, his hair and his jaguar skin robe flapping in the wind. Jacob's stare enervated the five men who stood apart from us. They fell to their knees in the water, cowering like beggars, the lake level up to their necks. Even those who were with us trembled under his laser-like gaze.

Standing resolute and tall was Marcos. Father and son exchanged a willful stare. Jacob's eyes burned with the resentment of his son's betrayal. In Marcos' expression flashed a twinge of shame and intimidation, but he pushed it aside and stiffened his chin.

Jacob raised a hand toward Marcos and announced to everyone, "I will grant freedom, honor, and riches to the man who slays my son! Otherwise you will all die this day!"

Our five antagonists rose to their feet and turned. Their eyes met Marcos. Their fingers formed into fists. Gidgiddonihah and Kib leaped down from the ladder. The three of us stood in front of Marcos.

"Climb the ladder, Marcos," I commanded. "You too, Harry."

"I'm not afraid of him," said Marcos, as if trying to convince himself.

Two of the five took a step forward.

"Climb it now!" I repeated.

Marcos and Harry scurried up the ladder. The five men armed themselves with stones. One was hurled at Marcos. More were hurled at the rest of us. Gidgiddonihah had had enough. He seized one of the men, raised him over his head and smashed him down on top of three others, knocking them into the water.

I looked toward the northeast corner of the wall that surrounded the island and noticed a warrior, and then two, and then twenty, rush around it, splashing through the lake. Jacob's soldiers were on their way. A few seconds later over fifty warriors had rounded the corner, brandishing swords and spears. People started climbing over each other to get inside Rachel's basket.

A pair of archers appeared on the wall on either side of Jacob Moon, their weapons aiming. We heard the bowstrings snap. Two arrows sailed toward us. One flew at Marcos. Miraculously, the arrow slipped in between Marcos and the man beside him, imbedding itself in the bottom of the basket. The other arrow struck the mammoth's shoulder, directly behind Jonas. Rachel wailed and started to rise off her knees. Four of us were still in the water.

"Easy, girl!" Jonas cried.

People in the basket fought to keep their balance. One man fell off the ladder. The archers were rearming their bows.

Somehow Jonas convinced Rachel to remain on her knees so that Garth, Kib, and the man who had fallen could grip the ladder. Gidgiddonihah and I were the last ones to start climbing. Just as I'd wrapped my fingers around the bottom rung, the next set of arrows took flight. One struck Rachel in the side, the other embedded squarely in Gidgiddonihah's shoulder.

Jonas lost control of the mammoth. Rachel was not waiting around to be hit again. She lurched to her feet. I locked my arm around the bottom rung.

"Give me your hand!" I shouted at Gidgiddonihah.

I caught his hand just as Rachel started galloping away from the prison wall. Garth was climbing the ladder above us. He fought to hang on. There were twenty-one people riding the mammoth—far more than the basket was designed to hold. Some hung on outside the basket, clinging to the rails. Many had locked arms. It was miracle that no one fell off.

I strained to maintain my grip on Gidgiddonihah's wrist. The two of us were dragged across the surface of the lake. The archers let more arrows fly. One landed harmlessly in the water. The other bounced off Rachel's harness. Additional archers rushed onto the catwalk beside Jacob Moon, but Rachel had galloped out of range.

"Stop her, Jonas!" I cried. "*Stooooop!*"

Jonas was already exerting every effort to do just that. The mammoth was frightened and confused. Gidgiddonihah and I bounced along the top of the water. If I let go now, he'd be pulverized under Rachel's back legs.

At last Jonas prevailed and Rachel came to a halt. She roared and swung her tusks. I released Gidgiddonihah's hand. His body slipped under the surface of the lake. The depth was about six feet. I released the rung, dove in after him, and dragged him back to the ladder as quickly as I could, fearing that Rachel might start running again at any instant. The arrow in his shoulder had gone clean through. The copper point was protruding below his collar bone.

"Can you climb?" I asked him.

He nodded, wincing from the pain.

I glanced back toward the prison wall. The soldiers who'd waded around the northeast rim had reached the five prisoners who'd thrown rocks. They pleaded for their lives. No mercy was extended. The warriors cut them down like stalks of corn. Jacob continued to watch us. His archers sent more missiles. All of them fell short. Hastily, the king left the wall. He disappeared back inside the prison.

I helped Gidgiddonihah into the last available space in the basket. People were crammed like sardines. Rachel looked like a commuter bus in a third-world country where more passengers ride on the roof than inside the bus. Garth, Kib, and I took places behind Jonas on the mammoth's shoulder. The twenty-one of us must have weighed nearly three thousand pounds, yet Rachel didn't falter.

The wall of clouds from the north continued to descend upon us. We could see vague bursts of lightning within. We could hear faint echoes of thunder. In less than twenty minutes I predicted that the storm would block out the sun. The wind was gusting at about thirty knots, whipping up the waves on the surface of the lake.

Jonas directed the mammoth toward the island.

"Is everyone all right?" Garth inquired.

There were a few timid nods. Most were too distressed to respond.

Wedged in the mammoth's shoulder beside me was the first arrow that had struck her. The wound was hardly bleeding. I considered yanking it out, but she'd have surely bolted. Gidgiddonihah, however, demanded immediate attention.

"Yank it out!" he insisted.

I leaned over the rail of the basket and broke off the feathered shaft. "Do you want something to bite on?" I asked.

"Just do it!"

I wrapped my fingers around the protruding tip and placed my palm against his shoulder.

"*Wait!*" cried Gidgiddonihah.

"What is it?"

"Give me something to bite on."

I handed him the broken shaft. He stuck it in his mouth and closed his eyes. I yanked. His eyes watered; otherwise, he didn't make a sound. The shaft, however, was bitten into three pieces.

My daughter reached her hand toward me through the rails. I took it.

"I love you, Dad," she said.

It took ten minutes to reach the island. The landmass was quite small—only about two acres. Some of the stone walls that crossed it were twelve feet tall. Some of the walls were half submerged in the mud and water along the beaches, suggesting a time when the lake had been much smaller. Rachel knelt on the sandy shore.

"Let's get everyone behind those walls!" shouted Garth.

An assembly line was formed. Five minutes later, we had everyone comfortably sheltered behind the stone barriers. Jonas urged Rachel to come farther in from the beach. The old girl wasn't moving. Her lungs heaved. She was exhausted. The curelom wouldn't take another step.

The force of the wind continued to build. Sand was starting to sting my face. I urged Jonas to take cover. He finished removing the arrows from Rachel's flesh while she was too tired to complain, then he rejoined the others. I was sure we'd all taken shelter as best we could when I saw Marcos at the water's edge, staring off toward shore.

I went to him. "Marcos, come on!"

"Look!" he cried.

Out in the water, about a third of the distance from the mainland, a fleet of canoes was paddling rapidly toward the island through the choppy surf. Over a hundred of them!

"My father," said Marcos.

"He'll never make it," I said. "The wind will capsize them."

"Let's hope you're right."

Frankly, I didn't think I was. The canoes were sleek and fast. Each was propelled by three separate rowers. They'd be here in minutes!

At that instant the surging wall of weather curled over the sun. A shadow fell across the valley.

And then it began.

There was a terrible boom. The ground shook. A full earthquake! Marcos and I were knocked off our feet. Beyond Jacobugath, in the mountains of Desolation, three separate peaks exploded at once. I watched in horror as three nuclear-sized mushroom clouds shot into the sky. Lava splattered down the mountain slopes.

The stone walls crisscrossing the island crumbled—including the section towering over Melody, Harry, and the others! I heard screams, but by the grace of God, the wall fell the other way, shattering into boulder-sized chunks. Desperately, I hurdled the rubble to reach my children. They held one another on the ground, shivering in terror. The dog had freed itself from Harry's mantle. Melody held it now. I threw my arms around them and drew them in close.

"Is everyone okay?"

"We're okay," said Melody.

"Hang on!"

The quaking continued, though not as violently as that first major jolt. I looked at the lake. Jacob and his warriors were still coming strong—nearly three-fourths of the way to the island now. They might not have even felt the earthquake. The water had cushioned the shock. The lake wasn't deep enough for tidal waves—but the waves that *were* formed swelled to three and four feet. The wind was partially at Jacob's back. His canoes would claim our shores in three minutes or less.

Because of the wound to his shoulder, our best warrior, Gidgiddonihah, was out of commission. He huddled with the others in the midst of the rubble. We had no weapons. We were at Jacob's mercy. Marcos remained on the beach, awaiting his father's arrival. He clutched an obsidian knife.

Smoke from the volcanoes began to blend with the charcoal clouds. In the next minute, the sun was snuffed out. The earth darkened. The volcanic slopes became visible as spidery streams of lava. The wind had surged to fifty knots. Most of the walls on the island had collapsed. Nothing remained to protect us from the teeth of the wind. My family bunched together behind some large chunks of rubble.

Lightning ignited the sky with a brilliance that might have rivaled the day of creation. Individual bolts struck the valley floor, impacting with a splash of electricity. At times the sky lit up for seven or eight seconds, like a false ceiling of fluorescent lights. Each detonation of thunder was amplified in the quaking earth. The world was wailing, and it would not be comforted.

I looked eastward. Even Jacob's fleet was floundering now. Some of his canoes were only twenty yards off shore. Many had capsized. Others were filling with water.

I turned westward just as another flash of magnesium light drenched the earth. The sight that met my eyes froze the beat of my racing heart. My daughter saw it, too. Her eyes became liquid pools of terror. A chasm was forming in the earth's crust. The valley floor was breaking in half like a block of cheese. The lake was spilling inside the rift. Waterfalls with all the force of Niagara were being created before our eyes! The crack was racing from one end of the lake to the other. Our little island was right in its path!

"Get down!" I cried.

We flattened against the ground as the crack split the island in two, ripping open the ground within a few yards of our legs. We found ourselves divided from Garth and the others. Pillars of earth were collapsing away from the cliff edge.

I yanked on my children's arms, barely giving them time to find their feet before I hoisted them toward the southern end of the island. The ground where we had been lying disappeared into the chasm.

The dog fell out of Melody's arms. "Pill!"

It ran toward the east side of the island, where Marcos had been awaiting his father's arrival. Melody tried to pursue it. I pulled her back. The rift continued to run toward the city of Jacobugath. Water spilled into the chasm. Jacob's warriors screamed as canoe after canoe was dragged over the cascade, into the bowels of the earth.

Incredibly, a twelve-foot section of wall along the southern bank was still standing. Harry went toward it, desperate to find shelter from the stinging wind. I pulled him back. That wall was sure to collapse any second. We took refuge behind several more chunks of rubble.

As my children lay face down on the ground, I tried to spot Marcos. He had been the only other person on our side of the crevasse. I couldn't see him. His father had surely been sucked into the fissure. I hoped Marcos hadn't been sucked in with him. The water along the beach now flowed as swiftly as any river.

As my eyes searched for Marcos, the earth was jolted by a fourth eruption—a peak about ten miles due north of Jacobugath. Its eruption was more violent than the other three combined. The entire mountain exploded in all directions. A monstrous ball of molten lava was spewed straight up into the sky. It seemed to hang there, like a nuclear globe, even emitting a solar radiance that reflected off the lake and the surrounding hills. It was coming toward us! Swelling larger and larger, like a meteor! My children screamed!

The ball came down smack in the center of Jacobugath.

Lava splashed over every inch of the unholy city. The palace, the temple, the market, the streets, the prison, the shrines—the entire town ignited in one brilliant all-consuming fireball. The jolt was so tremendous that the rubble around us jumped six inches into the air. My family came down with a crunch. Harry was crying. Melody moaned.

The lava splattered molten matter all across the valley. The sky became a firestorm of glowing hail. House-sized hunks of lava splashed into the lake and sizzled, sending up dense clouds of steam. Cringing, I waited for the molten hail to rain down on top of us. But the island was mercifully spared.

I tried to call out to my children—to inquire if anyone was hurt. I couldn't hear my own voice. The wind and the rain, the thunder and the earthquakes, the steaming lava and the raging waterfalls had drowned me out. I thought about Steffanie, my precious Steffanie. Was this same cataclysm taking place in Bountiful? Was she all right? Was Nephi protecting her?

The wind had reached hurricane velocity. It had also changed directions, blasting from the west. I raised my head. Lightning bursts were so frequent now that the sky flashed like a blue-white strobe. To the south I sighted innumerable tornadoes. The funnels swept from side to side, tearing up the valley floor.

I felt my daughter's hand on my face. She was trying to get my attention. Her finger pointed toward the lakeshore. A human body was lying motionless against the muddy earth. Marcos! I couldn't tell if he was living or dead. He was ten yards away. But even ten yards seemed like ten miles.

I nodded at Melody. "I see him!"

She started crawling forward. I dragged her back.

"No!" I said. "Stay here!"

I read her lips more than I heard her voice as she screamed, "He might be hurt!"

I pointed at the body, then at myself. "I'll go!"

Reluctantly, I began to crawl forward on my stomach. I didn't want to leave my children. As I approached the body, I recognized no signs of life. I began to fear the worst. His left hand still gripped a knife. I saw his hand budge slightly. Marcos was alive.

I was within three feet now. I called out his name. "Marcos!"

As the face started to turn, I realized I'd made a horrible mistake.

The jaguar-skin robe was crusted in mud. The man was not Marcos. It was Jacob of the Moon! The knife he held was his own!

I was seared by the anguish in Jacob's eyes—a decimated army, a devastated city, a shattered dream. His glory had been stripped away in the course of a single hour. When he recognized me, his anguish transformed into enmity. I stiffened with dread.

"You!" he seethed.

He lunged at me with the knife. I flung myself to the left. He pursued me, eyes blazing. To my awful frustration, I smashed into the only section of standing wall. Trapped! My vision was blurred with mud and rain. As I desperately wiped my eyes, I saw Jacob in the strobe-like flash. The knife was coming down! I kicked his arm. The blade sliced into the mud beside my shoulder.

I caught Jacob's wrist. With my other hand I seized his throat. He used his own free hand to grasp my hair. We started rolling back toward Harry and Melody. I forced my thumb into his Adam's apple. He released my hair, catching my wrist. We barreled right over the top of Harry. There was mud in my eyes. I couldn't see! I knew I had to break the momentum of our roll. I dug my heel into the ground. We stopped. But now Jacob was on top of me!

He released my wrist and punched my face. The blow jog-
gled my senses. I shook it off. The downpour of rain washed the
mud out of my eyes. Jacob and I were at the edge of the rift.
One more roll and we'd have been swallowed up by the
crevasse. Steam rushed out of the chasm. The cliffs exhibited a
molten glow. A hundred feet below us the crevasse boiled with
lava. The lava was turning the lake into steam.

Jacob strained to drive the knife into my neck. The point
inched closer and closer. Melody appeared over Jacob's shoulder. She brought a large stone down on his back. His body went
limp—but only for a second. His strength seemed superhuman.
He pulled himself erect again and drove his knee into my stomach. I felt the pain behind my eyes as the wind rushed out of
me. I lost my hold on his wrist. As he was about to stab downward, Melody locked her arms around his chest. Thoroughly
annoyed, Jacob turned his murderous rage onto her. He flung
her away and raised the knife to finish her. I tried to lurch forward—but they were beyond my reach! Jacob would kill her for
sure!

A dense cloud of steam suddenly surged out of the chasm
and overwhelmed me. I lost sight of them in the steam!
Panicked out of my mind, I shrieked my daughter's name.
When the steam cleared not two, but *three* people were
revealed.

It was Marcos! He'd rushed in front of Melody to deflect his
father's weapon. Father and son grappled at the edge of the cliff.
Jacob swiped his blade and got a piece of Marcos' abdomen.
But Marcos fought on. He grabbed his father's arm and swung
him out over the ledge. As Jacob dropped, he released the knife
and latched onto his son's arm. Marcos fell to the earth. The
ground began sliding under his stomach. Marcos was being
dragged into the crevasse with him!

I dove and caught Marcos' legs. Jacob's grip on his son's arm
was firm. As he dangled over the ledge, his legs kicking, I heard
him shout into his son's face, "All the curses of the Omnipotent
One will be yours, Marcos! Do you hear me? *I am still your
lord!*"

"Then I'll have to worship you in hell!"

Marcos grabbed Jacob's finger and snapped it backwards. Jacob let go. With his arms flailing, Jacob plunged into the molten gloom. The reign of King Jacob of the Moon had come to an end.

I pulled Marcos in from the ledge. Melody threw her arms around him. He gritted his teeth in pain. As he drew his hands to his abdomen, blood gushed through his fingers. Melody helped me carry him away from the ledge. With the earth's crust shifting, the ground remained dangerously unstable. The cliff on the opposite side of the rift had risen nearly ten feet above us. Its elevation rose and fell, as if we were standing on an ice flow. The other half of the island was nearly five hundred yards to the east.

As we laid Marcos down near the blocks of rubble, I realized that he had fainted. I ripped open his shirt and looked at the wound. It was bad, but not as deep as the gash that had killed Lamachi. Wind velocity had dropped to about fifty miles an hour, but the rain was drenching us more heavily than ever.

As I tore off the sleeve of my own mantle to press against Marcos' wound, I heard a faraway sound on the wind—a human voice. I stood, trying to hear it again. The voice was as faint as a bird's chirp.

"Help!"

Was it Jonas? Where was he calling from? The wind might have carried his voice from anywhere. A renewed eruption in the volcanoes overwhelmed any possibility that I might hear it again. I prayed in my heart for some signal, some sign. I felt compelled to run eastward.

Before I left, I handed the strip of cloth to Melody. "Bundle this up! Press it against the wound! Nobody move! I'll be right back!"

I ran into the maelstrom of rain and wind and rumbling earth. When I reached the eastern shore of the island, I continued into the lake. The water was only about six inches deep, racing around my legs as it continued to pour into the crevasse. Steam blasted out of the rift. Hot air singed my face. Then I saw him.

Jonas crouched on a pillar in the middle of the rift! How in blazes—? A part of the shelf had somehow broken away from the ledge and taken him with it. The pillar teetered back and forth, on the verge of tumbling into the same molten abyss that had claimed Jacob.

Jonas saw me. "Jim!"

I started to panic. What could I do? He was fifteen feet away from either edge. The pillar had sunk about five feet into the lava. At times the shelf teetered to within ten or twelve feet—but the jump was impossible! Even if the pillar tilted against my side of the chasm, Jonas would still be well below me, out of reach. Water continued to rush around my legs and disappear into the crevasse. The silt that had covered the lake bottom had washed away. My footing seemed firm on solid rock. But I knew if I stepped on any spot that was still slick, I'd get swept over the edge. I needed to create a bridge. What I needed was a twenty-foot aluminum ladder—or even a twenty-foot two-by-four. Or a . . .

Canoe?

Ten yards to my right sat one of the dugout canoes from Jacob's fleet. The warriors who'd paddled it were long gone, but the canoe itself was wedged in a crack, one end protruding upward as water swirled around it. The water threatened to carry it the rest of the way into the chasm any second.

Jonas lay flat on his belly, trying his best to balance his weight and keep the pillar from teetering. I dashed toward the canoe, approaching it carefully. The water was swift. I feared that the instant I budged it loose, the current would sweep me into the rift with it. I latched onto the canoe. It was stuck in a thin fissure that branched off the main chasm. I heaved upwards. The canoe jarred loose. It started to slip away but I fell onto my back and held on.

The dugout was only about fourteen feet long—six feet shy of what I'd hoped. I'd have to make it work. As a war canoe, it was considerably lighter than the mahogany models that had carried us down the Sidon. Still, it was nearly two hundred pounds. The trick now was shoving it out to Jonas. I wasn't sure my body weight had enough leverage to keep it straight.

I dragged the canoe back to Jonas, fighting every step to

keep the current from yanking it out of my hands. When I arrived, Jonas shook his head as if to say, *It'll never work.* But it was the only option I had—the only option there was. If the pillar would just hold steady long enough . . .

The moment it registered in Jonas' mind that this was his only hope, his attitude changed. His optimism took command. He got to his knees, ready to receive his end of the canoe. I waited for the pillar to teeter as close as possible. Then I steadily let the canoe slip out over the edge. I found two footholds and braced my legs. I leaned back and gritted my teeth, struggling to raise the canoe high enough for Jonas to reach it. I was losing it! The canoe was slipping!

Jonas grabbed it! He hoisted it up and balanced his end on the pillar. The pillar started to teeter back. Jonas hopped into the dugout and high-stepped across the bridge. The canoe dropped out from under him, plummeting into the void. I had his hand!

I hoisted Jonas up through the cascade of water. We scrambled away from the edge and dropped onto our stomachs, our lungs heaving for breath. The earth jolted with renewed eruptions. The sky was so black now that I couldn't see the distant spurts of lava. As Jonas and I lay there panting, the water rushing around our shoulders, I had to ask, "How the devil did you get out there?"

"Rachel," he panted. "I lost her in the darkness. I think she fell in. I pursued her until I reached the ledge, but then it broke away." He looked in my eyes. "I'll never forget, Jim . . . never forget what you did . . ."

I was only catching every other word he uttered. A horrible feeling twisted in the pit of my stomach. I had to get back to my family! I had to get back *right now!*

The wind had accelerated again. I leaned forward and fought for every step. Jonas was right behind me. As we reached the island, I fell to my knees and crawled the rest of the way. When I reached the blocks of rubble where I'd left them, I found only Marcos, just regaining consciousness. Harry and Melody were gone! They had disobeyed my direct instructions!

Then I saw Melody. She was kneeling near a pile of rubble

at the south end of the island. The last standing section of wall had finally collapsed. But where was Harry? As I stumbled to reach her, my mind pulsed with dread. Melody was digging frantically. The dog was there too, pressing its nose between the boulders.

As I reached Melody, she became hysterical. "It fell on him, Dad! He's in there! He's in there!"

Jonas and I desperately started rolling away huge chunks of rubble.

"Harry!" I screamed. "Harry!"

Melody continued her hysterical sobs. "He saw Pill! I didn't see him run away—!"

I screamed again, "HARRRRRRY!"

The blocks were too heavy! I couldn't move them! I was scraping my fingers raw. Together Jonas and I tried repeatedly to move several of the stones. They were just too big!

I collapsed onto the rubble, weeping bitterly, longingly, eternally, over the grave of my son.

CHAPTER 19

My father remained there, draped over the top of the rubble, wrenching sobs of devastation, until the quaking stopped, and the winds died, and the earth grew still.

The destructions continued for about three hours. For a long time, I was too shocked to cry—too numbed with disbelief. When the tears finally came, I couldn't stop them. It hurt so bad. I blamed myself. I'd heard Harry say that he saw Pill near the water's edge. But I was so engrossed with taking care of Marcos, I didn't see him dash off into the storm. By the time I looked, he was already running beneath the wall. Then the earth jolted. I saw the wall collapse around him as he raised his hands! I saw him crushed! My mind had replayed the horrible image a thousand times—a million times! I couldn't get rid of it. It wouldn't go away!

In the distance we listened to the staccato explosions of the volcanoes and the grinding, ear-rending echoes as mountains collided and earth was heaped on top of earth. At times I would hold my father and cry with him, but most of the time I sat with my face in my hands, crying alone. Pill lay beside me, sometimes whimpering. Jonas tried to comfort me and so did Marcos. But it was useless.

I feared Marcos would soon die as well. He was losing a lot of blood. He seemed to be weakening by the minute.

The rain finally stopped. Lightning ceased to illuminate the sky. To me, this was the most frightening moment of all. Absolutely no light. I knew the sun was up there somewhere, but not even a feeble gray circle appeared through the gloom. The darkness was so thick I could literally feel it on my skin. Gingerly, I touched my finger to my tongue and immediately spat. It was a dirty, ashy taste. I realized that the earth was being coated in a thick layer of volcanic soot.

I became frightened. I called out to my father, "Dad!"

He was still too absorbed in his grief to hear me. His agony was of the bitterest kind—to save one child only to lose another. I found him sitting against the pile of rubble, sobbing silently. He embraced me and together we cried again. If there had been any light, we'd have seen how the tears painted trails down our ash-blackened faces.

"I did all I was supposed to," said Dad. "I tried to follow the Spirit. I brought Harry with me into the city when my better judgment said to leave him behind. I don't understand. I just don't understand."

Jonas felt his way through the darkness and found us. He, too, had been devastated by Harry's death. "If you hadn't come to rescue me," he mourned, "your son would still be here. I'm sorry, Jim. I wish I could express how sorry I am."

In the murky blackness, our voices sounded hollow, like voices in a fog. When we were silent, there was no sound at all, as if we were the only living things in the universe, alone upon our solitary island of life. I thought about my Uncle Garth and the others. We'd tried to call out to them a few times, but no one replied. Maybe they were all dead, too.

Suddenly, off in the darkness, we heard an unexpected sound— a wailing sound, lonely and forlorn.

"Rachel?" said Jonas. "It's Rachel! She's alive!"

My father and I didn't respond. It was hard to appreciate Rachel's survival in light of Harry's loss.

Then Jonas reminded us, "She'll have the packs! There were two that we didn't unload. We can have food and water!"

The wail had come from the south, definitely on our side of the rift.

"I thought she was on the other side," I said.

"I thought so, too," said Jonas. "She must have found a way across. I have to find her."

"You'll get lost," said Dad, his voice devoid of energy. *"If you go after her, you'll never find your way back."*

Jonas felt around on the ground until he located two stones. He placed them in my hands. *"Melody, I want you to knock them together every few seconds. I'll hear them. I'll be able to find you again."*

Rachel let out another wail. Walking in utter blindness, Jonas made his way through the rubble, out toward the sound. Soon we could no longer hear the crunch of his footsteps.

I knocked the rocks together once, then I settled back against my father's shoulder. *"Are you thirsty?"* I asked him.

"No," he replied.

I knew he was wasn't being truthful. I couldn't get the taste of the falling ash out of my mouth. It was making my throat raw. *"We need to keep up our strength,"* I said. *"Harry would want—"*

"QUIET!" My dad put his hand on my shoulder.

I listened for a moment. I heard nothing. *"What is it?"*

"SHHH!"

I thought my dad was losing it, hearing ghosts in the darkness. But then I heard it, too. A weak whisper—*"Daaad."*

My father leaped to his feet and cried down into the rubble, *"Harry!"*

My heart did a somersault. My brother was alive! But in what condition? He was still buried under a ton of rubble. I was afraid to feel any hope. I couldn't bear losing him twice. I knew Dad was thinking the same thing. I could feel him trembling like a leaf.

The whisper came again. *"Daaad."*

"We hear you, Harry! Hang on, son! Hang on!"

"What can we do?" My voice was creaking with panic.

Dad thought a moment. *"The mammoth!"*

I began knocking the rocks together frantically. *"Jonas!"* I shouted. *"Hurry, Jonas! Harry is alive! Harry is alive!"*

A few moments later we heard the grunts and heavy, plodding footsteps as Jonas guided Rachel toward us. The sound would have been terrifying if we hadn't known what it was. It was scary enough to think that Rachel could easily step right on top of us or crush us with her tusks. We wouldn't have known it was coming. I picked up Pill, then moved back toward Marcos, somehow thinking I *might act as a buffer if Rachel came too close.*

"Easy," Jonas said to the mammoth. "It's all right. Almost there. Almost there."

I thought it would be next to impossible to convince Rachel to lift the slabs of rubble. How would she understand our instructions? She couldn't even see Jonas to know what he was pointing at. But for Rachel there was an unseen motivation. At first I didn't understand. Later I realized the mammoth had smelled water beneath the rubble—clean water—water that hadn't yet been contaminated by falling ash. Jonas and Dad had only to guide her trunk to each block of stone that they felt should be moved.

I could hear the heavy chunks moved aside. It was a dangerous task. We might easily crush Harry in the process. An exultant rush of gratitude swept over me as I heard my Dad announce, "I have him!"

Dad placed Harry's limp body beside Marcos. Obviously Harry had been seriously injured, but it was impossible to know how severely in the darkness. I touched my brother's hand and felt his hair. He was so cold. His hair was soaked from lying in a deep puddle under the rubble. We could hear Rachel's trunk sucking the water up.

The first thing that Dad and Jonas did was give him a blessing. Afterwards, Harry found the strength to say, "I'm f-freezing." His voice filled us with elation. We huddled around Harry to warm him, and I began rubbing his arms to get the blood moving.

Jonas had retrieved two of our travel packs from the basket on Rachel's back, and we dug around inside the packs until we found three leather canteens. One was virtually empty, but the other two were nearly full. Dad gave a sip to Harry. The rest of us also drank. No one could resist wasting one mouthful of precious water to gargle the soot out of our mouths. The other packs—the ones that had most of the food—were with Garth. They had been unloaded when Dad and the others had helped the lame and injured to step down from Rachel's back.

Dad laid Harry's head in his lap.

"How do you feel, son? Can you tell me where it hurts?"

"Arm hurts," said Harry weakly.

"Your arm? Is that all? Is it just your arm that hurts?"

"Legs," said Harry.

"Your legs hurt too?"

"Can't . . . feel them."

"You can't feel your legs?"

"No."

"You can't feel them at all?*"*

This announcement deeply concerned us. Dad felt his legs for broken bones. He tried unsuccessfully to get Harry to react when he pinched his thigh and the bottoms of his feet. It was too dark to make any diagnosis. We would have to wait until it was light—that is, if it ever got light. We hoped sensation might return to his legs at any moment.

His arm, however, was definitely broken. Probably in several places. One of the blocks of rubble had fallen right on top of it. But even with his arm, there was nothing we could do in the dark except move it as little as possible.

We were so relieved, so ecstatic, and so grateful that Harry was even alive. How could we complain about any aspect of his physical condition? To us it was as if he'd been brought back from the dead. Whereas our weeping had been unquenchable because of grief, now it was unquenchable because of joy—a joy so contagious that Jonas, and even Marcos in his own feeble condition, were overcome by the emotion.

The five of us, including Pill, settled in close together, close enough that we could all feel one another's touch. We heard Rachel settle down somewhere nearby, moaning now and then to remind us of her distress and discomfort. Harry fell asleep. I stroked his hair. It was becoming matted and grimy. At the same time I held Marcos' hand. His grip wasn't very strong.

"When will it be over?" I asked. The darkness was starting to make me feel desperately claustrophobic.

"Three days," Jonas replied. "The prophecies of Samuel state that the darkness will endure for three days."

It had only been a few hours since the storm had ended. The ground continued to rumble intermittently with aftershocks. The prospect of waiting three days in utter darkness, ash and soot piling around us like drifting snow, filled me with squirming anxiety. Could Marcos last that long? Could Harry? Could any of us? Over *time, we could easily suffocate. Some of the ash was so fine, it was impossible to avoid breathing it in. Our lungs might clog. Jonas advised us all to breathe through our shirts or the hem of our sleeve as much as possible. Pill was content to remain curled up under my garments.*

We spoke very little. I tried to sleep, but the cut on my knee was throbbing. I'd have given anything if I could have washed it, but there wasn't enough water to spare. We were rationing it even as it was.

I couldn't have said how many hours had passed when we heard the Voice.

At first I thought I was dreaming. And then I thought it was my father or Jonas who had spoken. I had all these preconceptions about the voice of God—expectations reinforced by countless Bible movies. I imagined a deep, baritone voice that echoes like a kettle drum. Maybe to some people that's exactly how it sounds, but not to me. The Voice was soothing, penetrating. I heard it with more than my ears. I heard it with my spirit, as if every particle of my being stood up to be drawn in by the sound.

"Wo . . ." the Voice began, and then there was a pause.

I caught my breath. I felt my father's hand latch onto mine. I was so mesmerized that I couldn't have spoken if I had tried. And yet I wasn't scared. Maybe I should have been. But I wasn't, which surprised me. When I was a little girl I remember asking my mom and dad if someday an angel might visit me the way one had visited Joseph Smith. They said it was possible, especially if I was very righteous. That night after my parents turned out my bedroom light, I stared off into the gloom and became very frightened. The idea that an angel might suddenly appear frightened me to death. The next day I stole some of my sister's Halloween candy to make sure I fell below the standard that might attract an angel.

Now, as I heard the Voice, I knew that I'd misunderstood. There was something so familiar, so comforting about it. I felt more exhilaration than fear. I knew that Voice already. For countless ages beyond the realm of time it seemed to me as if that Voice had been a continual part of my existence. In reality, I'd been separated from it only sixteen years—such a tiny block of time in the eternal scheme. Somewhere in my unconsciousness, I'm convinced that we all understand angels and miracles and other phenomena of heaven far more than we understand any aspect of this world. To me, the Voice was like coming home.

"... wo," *the Voice continued,* "... wo, unto this people ..."

"What?" *Marcos snapped awake.* "What's that? Who's that?"

When the Voice spoke again, Marcos went absolutely silent. Like the rest of us, he was too awestruck to speak.

I was almost surprised that he'd been awakened. To me it was not the type of voice that would have awakened someone. I realized not everyone was hearing it the way I was. Later, Harry would describe it as a voice that had resonated out of the heavens, as if from a loudspeaker. My father had heard it as if from inside his mind. He half-wondered if he was its only audience. To me, it was like a whisper, but certainly not breathy like a whisper, just peaceful like a whisper. Jonas' description sounded a lot like mine. To Marcos, however, the Voice was relentless, uninterrupted thunder.

"Wo unto the inhabitants of the whole earth except they shall repent; for the devil laugheth, and his angels rejoice, because of the slain of the fair sons and daughters of my people; and it is because of their iniquity that they are fallen!"

One by one, the Voice recounted the fates of many of the major cities in the lands of the Nephites and the Lamanites.

Zarahemla—burned with fire.

Moroni—sunk into the depths of the sea.

Moronihah—covered with earth.

Gilgal, the city where Garth had been captured—buried up in the depths of the earth.

Orihah, Mocum, and Jerusalem—covered over with water.

Then it spoke of cities I recognized from this valley: Gadiandi, Gadiomnah, Jacob, and Gimgimno—buried up in the depths of the earth, hills and valleys made in the places thereof.

And then it told the fate of Jacobugath, a city whose inhabitants, according to the Voice, were guilty of sins and wickedness above all the wickedness of the whole earth. Jacobugath had been burned. And the reason? So that "the blood of the prophets and the saints should not come up unto me any more against them."

Laman, the city where Dad, Harry, and Steffanie had first

been imprisoned, was also burned with fire. So were Josh and Gad and Kishkumen, because, said the Voice, they had cast out and stoned the prophets who had been sent to declare unto them concerning their wickedness and their abominations.

The Voice continued, "O all ye that are spared because ye were more righteous than they, will ye not now return unto me, and repent of your sins, and be converted, that I may heal you?

"Yea, verily I say unto you, if ye will come unto me ye shall have eternal life. Behold, mine arm of mercy is extended towards you, and whosoever will come, him will I receive; and blessed are those who come unto me."

And then the Voice identified itself. My heart swelled and surged and rushed with overwhelming, indescribable joy. It was my Master!

"Behold, I am Jesus Christ the Son of God. I created the heavens and the earth, and all things that in them are. I was with the Father from the beginning. I am in the Father, and the Father in me; and in me hath the Father glorified his name.

"I came unto my own, and my own received me not. And the scriptures concerning my coming are fulfilled.

"And as many as have received me, to them have I given to become the sons of God; and even so will I to as many as shall believe on my name, for behold, by me redemption cometh, and in me is the law of Moses fulfilled.

"I am the light and the life of the world. I am Alpha and Omega, the beginning and the end.

"And ye shall offer up unto me no more the shedding of blood; yea, your sacrifices and your burnt offerings shall be done away, for I will accept none of your sacrifices and your burnt offerings.

"And ye shall offer up for a sacrifice unto me a broken heart and a contrite spirit. And whoso cometh unto me with a broken heart and a contrite spirit, him will I baptize with fire and with the Holy Ghost, even as the Lamanites, because of their faith in me at the time of their conversion, were baptized with fire and with the Holy Ghost, and they knew it not.

"Behold, I have come unto the world, to bring redemption unto the world, to save the world from sin.

"Therefore, whoso repenteth and cometh unto me as a little child, him will I receive, for of such is the kingdom of God. Behold, for such I have laid down my life, and have taken it up again; therefore repent, and come unto me ye ends of the earth, and be saved."

Then the Voice was silent, yet none of us spoke, expecting any second that it might continue. So we sat there in astonishment, none daring to break the silence that belonged to the Savior of the World.

For many hours I was aware of nothing at all, only the empty, blackened space around me. I might as well have been alone. I might as well have been sitting in the void of eternity, a place in the universe where there were no galaxies or stars, just the presence of God. It was just me and the peace and power of Deity. I needed nothing more. No food or water. The love of my Father in Heaven sustained and supported me. I realized that this had always been the case. I realized in a way that I had never known before that I was integrally connected with all the powers of creation and progression.

For a time I forgot that there was such a thing as time. But then the Voice sounded again. Still a voice of pleading, a voice of urgency, but a voice of mercy and love. I noted certain variations in each of the statements.

"O ye people of these great cities which have fallen, who are descendants of Jacob, yea, who are of the house of Israel, how oft *have* I gathered you as a hen gathereth her chickens under her wings, and have nourished you.

"And again, how oft *would I* have gathered you as hen gathereth her chickens under her wings, yea, O ye people of the house of Israel who have fallen; yea, O ye people of the house of the Israel, ye that dwell at Jerusalem, as ye that have fallen, yea how oft would I have gathered you as a hen gathereth her chickens, and ye would not.

"O ye house of Israel whom I have spared, how oft *will I* gather you as a hen gathereth her chickens under her wings, if ye will repent and return unto me with full purpose of heart.

"But if not, O house of Israel, the places of your dwellings shall become desolate until the time of the fulfilling of the covenant to your fathers."

Seconds after the Voice ceased speaking, the strongest aftershock since the passing of the storm struck the earth. It only lasted about a minute, but it was that trembling that reminded us all that we were still alive, that we had not yet passed into eternity. As the sound died down, I heard bitter weeping from the place where Marcos was lying. I tried to offer comfort. I believe that only now, in the wake of the Savior's voice, did the realization finally settle upon his soul that his entire existence prior to yesterday had been devoted to serving the very forces of the anti-Christ. Half-delirious, he called out the name of Jesus and begged forgiveness, a second chance, a new opportunity.

"Heal me, Lord," I heard him mutter. "Heal me, and I will come. I will be yours . . ."

I knew he referred to more than healing the wound in his abdomen. He referred to nineteen years of dark devotion, corrupted sacrifice, and evil indoctrination. I held his hand tightly, just to let him know that he wasn't alone in the darkness. I think he finally understood that in the light of Christ, he need never be in darkness again.

Hour by hour, the five of us held each other and waited for God to fulfill his promise that the light would return. We shivered in the cold. Sometimes we slept, but never deeply. Once I brushed my hand along the ground a few feet away and realized that several inches of soft volcanic ash had caked the surface. Jonas left us from time to time to make sure Rachel was still breathing. The mammoth moaned far less frequently now, weakened by hunger and thirst. The feeling in Harry's legs never returned.

I remember when I turned the canteen upside down and let the final drops trickle onto my tongue. I handed the empty pouch to Pill, who licked the moisture from around the spout.

"How long has it been?" I once heard my father ask Jonas.

"No idea," Jonas replied. "None at all."

I dozed off. I received my first hours of blissful sleep in many days. I was awakened by a nudge from my father.

"Melody," he said softly. "Look!"

His finger pointed upward. Before I saw what he was pointing at, I experienced the singular thrill that I could actually see his finger!

He was pointing at the stars, bright and twinkling—billions of them! I could see the silhouette of the mountains and hills—a very different composition than the one I had remembered from a few days ago. Rachel rose from her knees. She shook herself vigorously. The sky was nearly darkened again by all the soot she sent into the air. The most exciting sight was five hundred yards away. We could see the vague outline of the opposite half of the island.

Jonas hoped his voice might now carry. He shouted at the top of his lungs, "Helloooooo!"

After a moment came back the faint reply, "Helloooo!"

As faint as it was, I knew that voice! It was my uncle's voice! Garth was alive!

We realized that the chasm in the earth had cleaved back together. We could only assume that it had taken place sometime toward the end of the storm. Perhaps it had come together in the course of the aftershocks. Whatever the case, it explained how Rachel had crossed over. What had been an open wound now looked like a healing scar, bandaged by a thick layer of volcanic ash.

I remained with Marcos and Harry while Jonas and my father tore off through the dust, raising a cloud behind them like a heavy truck on a dirt road. In the dark of night the cloud soon hid them from view. I could only imagine the jubilation as everyone reunited, embracing and kissing each other's soot-blackened cheeks.

A half hour later, Jonas and Dad returned with Garth, Zedekiah, and Kib. I barely recognized them for all the ash and filth that crusted their hair and faces. I embraced my uncle.

"Don't cry," Garth said to me. "You'll only get more soot in your eyes."

They'd come to help carry Harry and Marcos back to the other camp. They offered to help me as well, but I announced that the throbbing in my knee was gone. I could walk on my own.

Jonas led Rachel. The old mammoth moved slowly and stiffly. Even before we arrived, the first glimmer of dawn began to appear from behind the distant hills. I could no longer heed my uncle's advice. I cried freely and joyfully, avoiding the temptation to wipe my tears.

As daylight began to glow across the landscape, I had the eerie sensation that we were walking upon an entirely different planet.

Nothing was recognizable. Mountain peaks that had undoubtedly cut a certain shape in the skyline were no longer visible. The lake bed was virtually dry. The puddles that remained had the consistency of oatmeal, clogged by volcanic ash and mud.

There was not a living thing in sight—not a tree, not a shrub, not even a blade of grass. It was like walking on the surface of the moon. With each step the volcanic dust squirted up around our feet. The kingdom of Jacob Moon was no more than a dismal memory.

Of the twenty-one people that Rachel had carried to the island, not a single one had lost his life in the destruction and three-day darkness. Garth explained that the darkness had not lasted three days in the sense of three twenty-four hour periods. The prophecies of Samuel the Lamanite had stated that the darkness would prevail from the time of the Savior's death until the time of his resurrection. The Savior had laid in his tomb for three days—Friday night to Sunday morning—but technically it was only about forty hours. Garth concluded that the resurrection had taken place about six hours previously, when the smoke had first started to clear and the first stars appeared. So here on the American continent, the darkness had prevailed over three separate days, but only about forty-six hours.

In those last moments of feeble light before the sun made its first appearance, something extraordinary occurred. As I looked around at the various people rejoicing and celebrating the mercy that had been extended to them by the Lord, I realized that our number was more than twenty-one. Several people stood somewhat apart from the group, looking on. Their garments were not blackened with ash like the rest of us, but clean and white. My heartbeat quickened. For a moment I thought I was the only one who saw them, but then Jonas paused and looked up. He turned toward one certain man. I watched Jonas' eyes fill with wonder. He appeared drawn to walk toward the man.

After a moment everyone had seen the figures dressed in white. Timidly, we began to approach them, our faces solemnly astonished. I could see that their features radiated a hallowed glow, but a feeling in my heart told me they were not angels.

Zedekiah whispered, "The graves have been opened. The saints have begun to come forth. Samuel's prophecy is fulfilled."

The figures in white began to kneel and bow their heads, as if setting an example. One by one the rest of us began to kneel with them. As the new dispensation dawned and the first corner of the sun peered out from behind the hills, it found our little ragtag band of survivors kneeling in humble prayer. Dad supported Harry and the two of them prayed together. When I opened my eyes, the figures in white were gone from among us.

I didn't feel quite ready to get up off my knees. I could tell that no one else did either, so Zedekiah continued to lead us in prayer. When at last we started to rise, my father asked Jonas about the man in white whom he had approached.

"My grandfather," Jonas replied. "I have just met my grandfather, Nephi the Elder."

We continued to embrace and weep and shout praises and thanksgiving to our Lord and Redeemer. It might sound strange, but we didn't worry about the fact that we had no food or water, or that Harry still couldn't walk, or that Marcos and Gidgiddonihah were still weak from their injuries. We had a perfect faith that all these things would take care of themselves.

And for the most part, we were right. Rachel had wandered away while we were praying. When Jonas found her a quarter mile away, she was drinking greedily from a spring of pure and clean water that cascaded down the sides of an embankment. We drank to our heart's content. Afterwards, we took turns standing beneath the cascade and washing off the grime and soot from our bodies. Rachel cleaned herself as well, rolling in the pool created by the cascade and then showering herself—and anyone who stood too close—with her trunk.

The wounds of Marcos and Gidgiddonihah were cleaned and redressed. Miraculously, there was no sign of infection. Both injuries appeared to be healing well.

That spring was like a fountain of living water to us. And yet we knew that we couldn't remain. Zedekiah, as the oldest elder, was selected to lead us out of the valley. He put the matter to prayer, recognizing that it was vital that we go in a direction where we might find food. When he finished, he announced that we would travel toward the northeast. At about noon, the lame and the injured were loaded onto Rachel's back. Our journey through the grim and colorless land began.

As we reached a crest that overlooked what had been the valley of Jacobugath, some of us turned and looked back. As I gazed upon the scene, I pondered all of the things that had happened and the awesome transformation that had taken place in the valley, as well as in my soul. After a moment my father came and put his arm around my shoulder. For a moment we didn't speak. It wasn't necessary. All we had to do was look at one another, and our eyes brimmed with more tears.

I put my arms around his chest and laid my head against his shoulder. This was my dad. How lucky I felt to have been chosen as his earthly daughter. How were such things decided? I wondered. Somehow I doubted that I'd have had the wisdom to make such a selection myself. I must have done something very good in the pre-mortal world to have earned such a privilege.

My father squeezed my shoulder one last time. "Come," he said. "We still have a long journey ahead of us."

"Where are we going?" I asked.

"Bountiful," he answered. "We're going to Bountiful."

PART SIX:
BOUNTIFUL

CHAPTER 20

We camped that first night in an area where the ground was not so thickly carpeted with ash, although it didn't mean the region had been exempt from destruction. Kib said it had once been the site of a town called Gadiomnah, or as he called it, Shinah. As one of the satellite cities of the kingdom of the Divine Jaguar, it had been renamed by Jacob a few years before.

It was also Kib's hometown. He searched in vain to give us some idea where his home had stood and to show us the site of the copper smelter where he had been burned as a child. Nothing was recognizable. Hills once situated to the west appeared to have flipped over on top of the town. At certain places we could see upside-down tree roots sticking out of the earth.

We noticed birds flying in and out of a cave that had been created by the crunch of two land masses. Garth, Zedekiah, and I went inside and found the remains of what had been a storage facility for corn.

"There's tons of the stuff!" I exclaimed. "Even Rachel will sleep with a full stomach tonight!"

We heard a noise. Something scrambled across the piles of dried kernels toward the other end of the room.

"Who's there?" Garth inquired.

I half wondered if a jaguar might lunge out at us from the darkness. Zedekiah ventured closer. In the shadow we perceived the shape of a child—a girl. We'd been convinced that not a single soul in this region besides ourselves had survived. For some reason, the Lord had spared this one child. She was about eleven. After a few minutes, Zedekiah managed to earn her trust. He talked her out of the cave. He also learned her name: Lanya.

She was quite healthy—and perfectly filthy. Over the past several days she'd had plenty to eat, but little to drink. She nearly emptied one of our leather canteens all by herself.

"How did you survive?" Melody inquired as she took a damp cloth and wiped the grime off her cheeks.

"I was hiding in the corn shed," she began. "My mother was looking for me. She wanted to punish me because I didn't gather enough wood for the hearth. And then the sun went dark. The ground shook." As she recalled the memories, she began to tremble, but bravely, she did not cry. "I stayed in the corn shed until this morning. When I came out, the city was gone. My mother was gone. I was all alone."

As Melody's washcloth revealed her face, Kib declared, "I know this girl. She lived alone with her mother—a woman called Nemrah. They arrived here three years ago, at the same time as Jacob and the others."

"Lanya," asked Zedekiah, "do you know your father's name?"

"My mother never spoke his name," she said. "She said he was a Christian—a very evil man. She promised to beat me if I ever mentioned him again."

"Where did you live before you came to this valley?" asked Garth.

"Gilgal," said Lanya. "My mother said she brought me there when I was a baby."

"And where did your mother live before that?" asked Zedekiah.

"A place near the ocean," Lanya replied. "She said it was very beautiful. She called it Jeruba."

Jonas' ears perked up. "Jeruba? I know Jeruba. It's a village in the land of Bountiful. Less than a day's journey from the city itself."

Zedekiah took the girl's hands. "Tomorrow we're going to be leaving this land, Lanya. Our journey will take us very close to the place where your mother once lived. Would you like to come with us?"

She hesitated, and then she nodded. Our company had its newest member.

She rode atop the mammoth with Harry and the other men who were lame or injured, including Marcos and Gidgiddonihah. I hoped that Harry's spirits might be raised by the presence of someone close to his own age.

Harry was growing more depressed by the hour. It now appeared that his injury wouldn't be healing anytime soon. The lower half of his body had no sensation at all. There were terrible bruises on his back. The collapsed wall had damaged his spine. In the wake of so many other miracles, I'd felt certain that his feeling would start to return at any moment. I hadn't yet given up hope, but I began to prepare myself for the possibility that his condition would not improve.

In the beginning, Lanya didn't help matters at all. She treated Harry very coldly. For years she'd been brainwashed into believing that physical handicaps were a curse—a sign of inferiority. She sat alone in a corner of the basket, refusing to speak to any of her fellow passengers. But loneliness can be a harsh tutor. After a day or two, she began to rethink her attitude. She even laughed once or twice at Gidgiddonihah's jokes. By degrees she began to warm up to Harry and the others. After a week, she and Harry became inseparable.

I couldn't shake the impression that there was something very special about Lanya—something very important. One evening when I found myself particularly engrossed by the subject, I asked to hear her mother's name again.

"Nemrah," she replied.

I'd heard that name before. I was sure of it. Maybe it meant nothing. It might have been a very common name.

"Can you tell me anything else about your father?"

Lanya shook her head. "My mother hated him. She said he was blind to the truth and would have destroyed us all. That's why she left him."

Nemrah, Nemrah. I repeated the name under my breath. I *knew* that name. I knew that I had heard—

"Nemrah!" I suddenly burst out loud.

In a flash, I remembered. The name had been spoken by a great friend, a man who had saved my life and the lives of my children. It was uttered on a night not so long ago in the mountains south of Zarahemla. It was a name from a story—the tragic story of a man and woman who had been betrothed since infancy. Soon after they were married, the woman turned her back on the simple doctrine of Christ and embraced the secret ways of the Gadiantons. When she left her husband, she had been carrying his unborn child.

"By chance," I asked Lanya, "did your mother or anyone associated with her ever speak the name of Shemnon?"

Lanya shook her head, confused.

I knew I was right. It would explain so much—her miraculous survival, the fact that we had found her. Someone had been praying very hard for that child—probably for many, many years. The Lord had *wanted* us to find her.

At one time or another Shemnon had also confided in Jonas and Zedekiah the story of his first unfortunate marriage. As I told them my opinion of Lanya's origins, they began to recognize in her features a distinct similarity to Shemnon. They felt certain that I had stumbled onto something wondrous.

Lanya, of course, felt only apprehension. Everything she'd ever heard about her father was negative and dark. This was a label that perhaps she *should* have given to her mother. The girl had many scars from years of abuse. And yet she couldn't extinguish a natural curiosity about what her father might be like. Her imagination soared with the possibilities.

We continued our northward trek for a number of weeks. We traveled slowly, not only because many of us had injuries and handicaps, but because often there was no visible trail, having been broken up or buried in the earthquakes. We passed through some areas only moderately damaged. Other areas, however, had experienced such a dramatic upheaval that we were sometimes forced to turn back and find an alternate route. Zedekiah's objective was to reach the ocean. He knew that

Bountiful was situated near the East Sea. If we could just follow southward along the coastline, he was certain we would eventually reach our destination.

We soon found a number of communities where survivors of the destruction were busily pulling the fragments of their lives back together. Having heard the voice of Jesus Christ in the darkness, they became very inquisitive when they learned that we were Christians. Many of the people in this region knew little about the Savior and wished to learn all they could about the Being who had spared their lives. Some of them actually joined our company. As for the rest, Zedekiah and Jonas promised one day to return and teach them the gospel.

"First," said Jonas, "we must receive the Holy Ghost."

From my studies of the Book of Mormon, I'd always been under the impression that the Savior had visited the Nephites immediately after the destruction—within a matter of days.

Garth offered another perspective. "In 3 Nephi chapter 8, it tells us that the storms arose in the thirty-fourth year, on the fourth day of the first month. In chapter 10 it states that great favors and blessings were poured out upon the Nephites and Lamanites in the *ending* of the thirty and fourth year. It may be several months yet before the Savior manifests himself."

We had been traveling for nearly three weeks when the dark blue waters of the East Sea first appeared on the horizon. Gidgiddonihah, who had once traveled through this region on a military campaign, felt certain that this spot had formerly been the site of the city of Moronihah. A volcanic cone had sprung up near the seacoast, charred and barren of all vegetation. Gidgiddonihah believed this cone sat directly on top of Moronihah's once bustling streets.

The following morning our company experienced a sorrowful tragedy. Melody was the first to discover it. She awoke and looked toward the clearing where Rachel had slept the night before. A low fog hung over the glade. The massive bulk of the mammoth was like a mountain in the fog. Melody approached the silent shape.

A moment later, Jonas went over to investigate. He found Melody weeping, her face buried in the mammoth's fur.

"She's gone," Melody announced. "It must have happened during the night."

The old mammoth's heart had finally given out. She appeared to have gone painlessly, peacefully, the way that all living creatures would wish to go. Nearly everyone in our company approached her silent form to pay their final respects and say goodbye. The most emotional were the men who had been prisoners in the watery dungeon with Garth, those who had been sustained for so many weeks by the vision of her coming. It was that prophecy which had given them the courage to face another soul-draining day in the hole.

My son was also devastated. He had loved the mammoth very much. He knew that she had saved his life. Without Rachel, we could have never freed him from the rubble.

I leaned against the mammoth's cheek and whispered goodbye into her ear. She had saved my family. She had saved us all.

Jonas was the last person to leave the mammoth's side. The curelom had been with him the longest. She'd been his only close companion during those lonely days as he buried the dead of the people of Haberekiah. He expressed his final respects in prayer, thanking Heavenly Father for the gift of Rachel's presence and for preserving her life as long as he had.

It seemed doubtful to me that the other cureloms in the mountains of Desolation had survived the destruction. With Rachel's passing I knew that a very special species in God's menagerie had left the world's stage. If there was an eternal destination for God's creatures, I hoped Rachel now found herself in wide open spaces teeming with grasses and leaves and love from her Creator.

We spent the next two days building litters and stretchers to carry the lame and injured for the remainder of our journey. Every able-bodied man was assigned to carry one end or the other. I carried the stretcher that supported Harry, with the help of the deaf-mute, Memuki, and sometimes Melody. The little dog, Pill, walked beside us. So did Lanya, jabbering with my son the entire distance.

Some days we only traveled a mile or two. Some days we didn't travel at all. It was several more weeks before Zedekiah stared off toward the south and announced, "Bountiful is just beyond those hills."

A day later we sighted the temple complex on the outskirts of the city. News of our arrival had preceded us. Late in the morning the first people from inside the city wall charged forward to meet us. Among them was the prophet's eldest son, also named Nephi. The two brothers embraced. The residents of Bountiful, many of whom I recognized from Zarahemla, insisted upon carrying our stretchers the rest of the way.

I witnessed the moment when Garth stopped in his tracks and caught sight of a woman standing on the crest of the hill just ahead.

"Jenny?" he said breathlessly.

The moment that my sister recognized her husband, she broke into a run. Garth began running as well, his speed building in momentum. The two met and embraced, wrapping each other in a cocoon that shut out the rest of the universe.

My eyes caught sight of another figure racing toward me.

"Daddy!" Steffanie cried. "Melody!"

I caught my daughter in midflight as she leaped into my arms. Melody contented herself to wait in line behind me, but Steffanie dragged her into the embrace.

All at once, Steffanie's face went pale. "Where's Harry?"

"I'm here, Sis!" Harry called.

Steffanie flew to his stretcher and buried her brother's face in kisses. For the first time in his life, Harry didn't object. She did not immediately inquire about Harry's condition. Her only concern was that we were all alive. We were all together.

"I prayed and I prayed!" Steffanie bawled. "I didn't think I'd ever see any of you again!"

Jenny threw her arms around my neck. She then hugged Melody and Harry. "Nephi told me everyone would be all right. He told me."

The prophet Nephi, wearing the same bright blue mantle that he had worn in Zarahemla, was the next person over the rise. Beside him was his brother, Timothy, whom he had raised from the dead. Shemnon was right behind them. When I saw Shemnon, my eyes went to Lanya. I wasn't certain how to make introductions. I was spared part of the job by Zedekiah, who greeted Shemnon halfway. As the two men embraced, he whispered something into Shemnon's ear. Shemnon stepped back from Zedekiah in disbelief. He asked a few questions, and then shook his head. He couldn't believe it was true. It was far too good to be true.

I knelt down beside Lanya. "That man," I told her, "is your father."

Lanya nodded, shivering, entranced.

"Would you like to meet him?"

I was sure she would resist, but she didn't. In fact, she didn't need me at all. She went to him on her own. I read her lips: *Are you my father?*

Shemnon smiled, his eyes seeping tears. He knew immediately that she was his flesh and blood. He took Lanya's hand. The relationship between father and daughter had begun.

Nephi approached me. "Thank you," he said, "for bringing home my son."

"It could easily be described the other way around," I replied.

Mathoni and Mathonihah, the sons of Samuel the Lamanite who had rescued us in the city of Laman, also appeared. They had successfully guided the Lamanite Christians to Bountiful.

So many reunions, so much love. This day was the closest I'd ever come to a perfect state of existence. Surrounded by my family, rejoicing with my friends, smothered in affection by my little niece and nephew, Becky and Joshua, Bountiful might as well have been the paradise of God. On into the night we continued to embrace and cry, laugh and pray. I wept in sadness a little too, wishing that my precious Renae had been there to share in it.

But overall it was the most cherished day of my life. Days like that can only be a gift from the Eternal Father. I felt certain that some part of his Spirit had infused itself into our natural emotions, sustaining, increasing, and amplifying the joy. We tasted a bit of celestial joy that day—a joy that can only be perpetually experienced by exalted beings. This was the pinnacle, I thought. It could never get any better. I would mark this day in my memory as the standard for celestial happiness that I hoped to achieve in the life to come.

Little did I know, another day loomed on the horizon that would redefine celestial joy once and for all.

CHAPTER 21

I had never expected to stand in the presence of my resurrected Lord. At least not in this life. I'd have felt ashamed to have even harbored such a hope. To set eyes on the Savior was a privilege reserved for the sanctified, the pure in heart, the apostles and prophets. Certainly not Jim Hawkins, the patron of imperfection.

If it had been in my power to go back home to my own century, I would have done so shortly after we arrived in Bountiful. My purpose had been fulfilled. My daughter had been recovered. My family had been reunited. I realized that back home I was still a fugitive. But I had decided to face the consequences that awaited me. In my world I still had family and friends who were undoubtedly worried sick. I couldn't let them wonder for the rest of their lives what had become of us. Whatever might happen when I returned, my children and I would still have each other. I was confident that it would turn out all right in the end.

But despite my new attitude, it was not in my power to go home. Harry's condition had made this impossible. Soon after we arrived in Bountiful, some feeling in his lower back began to return, but only in the form of excruciating pain that caused him to awaken at night screaming.

"Make it stop!" he would cry. "Please, please! Make it stop!"

Usually I found no treatment, no position that would bring

relief. I sat up with Harry night after night, offering what little comfort I could. I felt exhausted and helpless. His Aunt Jenny and his sisters also took shifts. At first I'd thought any pain at all was a sign of improvement—a glimmer of hope that he might yet recover, at least partially. But except for the shooting pain in his spine, there was no improvement whatsoever.

Day by day, I grew more anxious to return, if for no other reason than to place Harry in the care of a modern physician. Garth and Jenny were feeling this same anxiousness. With the return of her husband, Jenny's own stomach ailments had disappeared. But Garth and Jenny had been gone from home now for nearly six years. The factor that had always kept them from returning home before was their young children. The older that Becky and Joshua grew, the more Jenny yearned to raise them in the modern world she knew so well.

We couldn't shake the feeling—this was not our time. It was not our century. The Nephites may have been headed into the most enlightened era of their existence, but this did not change the facts: our responsibilities were elsewhere—else*when.* As Samuel the Lamanite had once told Harry, "Learn all you can. The events that you will witness here are a shadow of things to come." What was the purpose of learning all that we had learned, of seeing all that we had seen, if we failed to use our knowledge and testimony to the benefit of our own generation?

Becky and Joshua were still quite young, three and five years old respectively. Nevertheless, our experience in transporting the lame and injured from Jacobugath had convinced us that such a trip was still possible. Our primary challenge would be climbing up through the tunnels. But if we took our time and helped the children along every step, we believed we could manage. This, of course, assumed that the cavern in the land of Melek even existed anymore. Chances were, it had been destroyed by the earthquakes.

Our real problem continued to be my son. Transporting Harry up through that cavern was unthinkable. At least Becky and Joshua could walk. Harry would have to be carried. Considering some of the obstacles in those tunnels—the tight passages, the steep inclines—our hearts sank at the prospect.

We could easily kill him, and ourselves, in the process. Because Harry couldn't leave, neither would I. And because Garth and Jenny could never make the trip without our help, they were forced to remain behind with us.

For the next few months Garth and I devoted our energies to rebuilding the city of Bountiful, which had been badly damaged in the earthquakes, but not destroyed.

"I will make Bountiful the center of the new church," Nephi proclaimed. "From here the Lord's missionaries will carry the good news of Christ to every corner of the land."

The romance between Melody and Marcos continued to blossom. He had completely healed from his injuries. I'd actually grown quite fond of the son of Jacob Moon. He'd become a very humble and devoted follower of Christ. I often found him at Nephi's feet, listening attentively, asking questions, desiring to learn all that he could about the religion he'd once sought to wipe off the globe. Although he professed a deep love for Melody, he had no immediate plans to rush into anything permanent.

"I owe a great debt to the Church," he said, "as well as to the people whose lives my father destroyed."

The sole survivors of his father's reign of terror were the handicapped and disabled men who had journeyed with us to Bountiful. Marcos considered them a symbol of his father's crimes, as well as his own. Through them, he hoped to make partial penance for the evil he'd once helped to perpetuate.

The day came when it was decided that we should focus our efforts on repairing the temple complex situated outside the city wall. The structure had suffered terrible damage. Bountiful's temple had once rivaled the temple in Zarahemla as the largest holy edifice in the land. For many people in the region, it was the site of the Passover festivals and celebrations.

Since the law of Moses had been fulfilled in Christ, many had wondered what would become of the facility. Should it even be rebuilt? Nephi felt strongly that it should.

"We will begin tomorrow morning," Nephi declared. "This will be our most difficult project yet. It will also be the most important."

And so the following morning, nearly twenty-five hundred people—well over half of the entire community—Nephite and Lamanite men, women, and children, gathered at the temple site. Few people had visited here since the destruction. Not only was it deemed dangerous because of a number of pillars that were still leaning, but for some it was a bitter reminder of that fateful day when the earth itself had threatened to divide asunder.

These memories flooded back as we began to appraise the damage and the grueling work that lay ahead. The temple's upper floor had fallen in on itself. Many walls around the complex had also collapsed. The first few weeks of the project would consist primarily of removing rubble and debris. Much of the complex would have to be reconstructed from the ground up.

Jenny and Melody, as well as many other women and children, established a place in the center of the plaza for preparing meals and meeting the other needs of the workers. Here they could also keep their little ones out of harm's way. We expected to camp here for several weeks, so I brought Harry and laid him under an awning where he could enjoy a little shade.

Garth and I had been assigned to secure ropes to several of the leaning pillars and coordinate a concerted effort to pull them down. I pointed out several places where the ropes might best serve our purposes. Garth listened to my suggestions attentively, nodding from time to time. But it was obvious that neither of us were concentrating on the task at hand.

I turned to my old friend and sighed. We each knew what the other was thinking.

"When," I asked, "will he come?"

"Any day," Garth replied. "Any time."

I realized that we weren't the only people talking about the Savior. Several other conversations were underway in and around the plaza. The ruined buildings and the collapsed walls naturally inspired such discussion.

I spotted Nephi and Jonas in the gathering. I knew they would be interested to hear our assessment of the pillars. As I ambled off the temple steps to approach them, I stopped, almost in midstep. I thought I'd . . . heard something. No, not heard. *Felt* . . . something.

I cast my eyes across the temple compound. Others were looking about as well, perplexed and bewildered. I glanced at Garth. I could see that he had felt it too.

My heart started pounding. Whatever I had heard . . . felt . . . it had penetrated to the very center of my being. My eyes searched until I found each member of my family—Steffanie . . . Melody, Jenny . . . Harry under the awning . . . Rebecca and Joshua. I felt compelled to move toward them.

I stopped.

I'd heard it again.

This time, I definitely *heard* it. Like a sonic boom. Maybe that's a bad description. But the sound emitted a vibration like a sonic boom. It was a voice. A voice like before. But I couldn't quite make out what it had . . .

I turned my gaze squarely toward heaven. Every person in the plaza—man, woman, and child—looked toward the same spot in the eastern sky. The Voice spoke a third time. This time, I understood.

"Behold my Beloved Son, in whom I am well pleased, in whom I have glorified my name—hear ye him."

I realized I wasn't able to draw a breath. Finally I drew a short one, believing somehow if I breathed deeply or blinked, I might miss a crucial moment.

A white point appeared through the clouds exactly over-head, descending gradually. Again I felt the urge to reach my family, but I couldn't take my eyes off the descending shape. I stepped backwards, bumping into several people, but their vision was transfixed like mine, and they simply let me through, oblivious to my presence.

It was clear now that it was a Man descending. I glanced away for an instant, but only long enough to verify that it was Melody beside me, and Steffanie to my right, and Harry a step away under the awning. My son had pulled himself off his stretcher so that he could see past the awning, up into the sky.

The Man, clothed in a white robe, descended below the height of the temple, and then touched soundlessly down on the lowest landing of the temple steps. Those who stood closest to him moved back a little. I don't think some of them realized right away who he was.

His countenance was like lightning, but not harsh to look upon. On the contrary, I've never seen a sight so easy on the eyes. He was bearded. His hair was gleaming white and shoulder length. His glory and perfection were most visible in his eyes. Even from this distance I could judge that they were the bluest I had ever seen, and as clear and bright as the limitless universe.

No one spoke a word, not even a whisper or a gasp escaped our throats. The Man's eyes moved across the gathering. Not a single soul escaped his gaze. Even me. I felt his eyes land on *me*, penetrating through my mortal soul, back into my premortal past. In that fraction of an instant I knew that he knew me better than I could ever know myself.

And then he stretched forth his hand and said, "Behold, I am Jesus Christ, whom the prophets testified shall come into the world.

"And behold, I am the light and the life of the world; and I have drunk out of that bitter cup which the Father hath given *me*, and have glorified the Father in taking upon me the sins of the world, in the which I have suffered the will of the Father in all things from the beginning."

Every cell in my body was on fire. Here stood my Savior and my Redeemer, his face aglow with omniscient light, no taller than the average man, and yet as he stretched forth his hand, I realized that it was the same hand that had framed the heavens, the same hand that had created the world. My knees weakened. I fell to the earth. Every other soul around me fell as well.

"Arise," the Savior invited, "and come forth unto me, that ye may thrust your hands into my side, and also that ye may feel the prints of the nails in my hands and in my feet, that ye may know that I am the God of Israel and the God of the whole earth, and have been slain for the sins of the world."

We continued to gaze upon him with transcendent awe. Gradually, a great line began to form. My heart was pumping wildly. All of my life I'd tried to envision this moment—standing face to face with my Lord. I'd prayed for it. I'd yearned for it. Now the hope was being fulfilled. I felt so unprepared. So unworthy. I was sure I would shrivel away. And yet I couldn't resist the invitation. I wanted to touch my Savior—if only the hem of his garment—more than anything I'd ever wanted in my life.

The first one in line was Gidgiddonihah. We watched as the hardened warrior, now as meek as a lamb, touched the Savior's side and felt the prints of the nails in his hands and in his feet. Since I'd paused to lift Harry, I ended up one of the last people in line. I wrapped his lifeless legs around me, and he held onto my neck. Melody and Steffanie were just ahead of us. They too looked eager, nervous, enraptured. The Savior yielded himself to the probing fingers of every soul in the multitude. And afterwards, they could not deny that he was the one whom the prophets had written and testified should come.

The Lord looked into the faces of each person as they touched him, a sweet, knowing expression on his face. I watched him receive Garth and Jenny, Becky, and Joshua, Shemnon and Kib, Nephi and Jonas, Zedekiah and Marcos.

Finally, it became Melody's turn. Her fingers touched his hand. She looked up into his face. The Savior returned her gaze. She dropped to her knees. I saw her tears drop upon his flesh. She kissed his feet. The next time she looked up into his eyes, he was smiling, a tender, overflowing smile, and I thought he might shed a tear of his own.

That same all-encompassing love radiated in his eyes as he received my daughter Steffanie. He knew my Steffanie. He knew her through and through. Steffanie bent down to feel the nail prints in his feet. She couldn't seem to find the strength to rise again. The Lord took her hand and raised her to her feet as easily as lifting a handkerchief.

As Steffanie stepped aside, the Savior's gaze fell upon me. The familiarity of a thousand years emanated from his eyes. Though his lips didn't move, I could almost hear them speak my name. I thought my arm would tremble as I reached out to feel the prints of the nails, but my hand was calm. As I touched his palm, a vitalizing, purifying warmth swept over me from head to toe. I felt the contour of the wound in the center of his palm and the same wound on the back of his hand.

Harry reached out to touch him as well. But his reach was too short. The Savior accommodated my son by moving one of his arms a little closer. I touched the material of his robe and felt the place at his side where the Roman soldier had stabbed him with a spear. For an instant I felt the pain vicariously move to my own side. And then it struck me: he'd received these wounds for me. It was for my sake that he'd allowed them to be inflicted. My eyes clouded with tears. I cringed as I realized that my own sins had been responsible for a portion of his pain. *No more,* I vowed. *I'll never cause him any more pain!*

Behind me I heard the Prophet Nephi shout at the top of his lungs, "Hosanna! Blessed be the name of the Most High God!"

The cry reverberated as dozens, and then hundreds, and then thousands of people began to shout with one accord, "Hosanna! Blessed be the name of the Most High God!"

My own voice rang out with the rest, as did the voice of my son and my daughters. We shouted it again and again until we became so overcome with exhilaration that we fell down again at the feet of our Redeemer, a perfect understanding burning in our minds and hearts that this was our God, and we were his subjects. I'd have gone to the ends of the earth, I'd have moved mountains, I'd have torn planets from their orbits and scattered the galaxies like a handful of rice if his voice had proclaimed that I should do it.

While our faces were still toward the earth, I heard him speak the prophet's name. "Nephi, come forth."

Nephi stood and approached the Lord. He bowed himself down and kissed the Lord's feet.

"Arise," the Savior commanded.

Nephi arose.

The Savior said to him, "I give unto you power that ye shall baptize this people when I am again ascended into heaven."

In humility, Nephi nodded. The Lord called forth eleven others, beginning with Nephi's brother, Timothy. He then called forth his youngest son, Jonas. He called the sons of Samuel, Mathoni and Mathonihah, and two other Lamanites,

Kumen and Kumenonhi. He called forth Jeremiah, the Christian whom we had tried to contact in Sidom. He called forth Shemnon and another Nephite also called Jonas. He called forth Isaiah, and finally, he called forth the humble leader of our expedition, Zedekiah.

The Savior gave them all the same power to baptize, and added, "On this wise shall ye baptize; and there shall be no disputations among you . . ."

He proceeded to spell out to them the precise manner for conducting this sacred ordinance. It was fascinating to observe that before he taught us anything else, he taught us the first saving ordinance of the gospel, the gateway into the kingdom of God.

He continued to define for the twelve disciples the most basic and sublime points of his doctrine, that all men everywhere must repent and believe in him, and be baptized, and the Father would bear record and visit the believer with fire and with the Holy Ghost. "Therefore, go forth unto this people, and declare the words which I have spoken, unto the ends of the earth."

He stretched forth his hand again toward us, the multitude, and declared, "Blessed are ye if ye shall give heed unto the words of these twelve whom I have chosen from among you to minister unto you, and to be your servants; and unto them I have given power that they may baptize you with water; and after that ye are baptized with water, behold, I will baptize you with fire and with the Holy Ghost; therefore blessed are ye if ye shall believe in me and be baptized, after that ye have seen me and know that I am.

"And again, more blessed are they who shall believe in your words because that ye shall testify that ye have seen me, and that ye know that I am. Yea, blessed are they who shall believe in your words, and come down into the depths of humility and be baptized, for they shall be visited with fire and with the Holy Ghost, and shall receive a remission of their sins.

"Yea, blessed are the poor in spirit who come unto me, for theirs is the kingdom of heaven . . ."

The Savior continued to recite the Beatitudes that he had

once recited on a hilltop in Galilee. Afterwards, he delivered the remainder of his glorious Sermon on the Mount. Much of the sermon was given word for word as it appears in the Bible, with a few subtle but profound differences illustrating once again that our Bible as it stands had been imperfectly translated.

I must have read the Sermon on the Mount a hundred times and still somehow, the essence of so many meanings had escaped my grasp. I listened to every inflection, every emphasis of phrase that the Savior employed, and fresh understandings of its message began to settle upon my soul. Often the words cut me to the heart. As the Savior said "agree with thine adversary quickly while thou art in the way with him," I realized that I had memorized that phrase as surely as a schoolboy memorizes the alphabet, and yet I had rarely applied it. As the Savior said, "Whosoever shall smite thee on thy right cheek, turn to him the other also," I was hard pressed to recall a single incident in my life where someone had taken something from me, and I had given to him in return more than he had taken in the first place.

I had never really expended any effort to love my enemies. I had never blessed them that had cursed me. I had rarely done good to them who hated me or prayed for them who despitefully used me and persecuted me. I had used many vain repetitions in my prayers, sometimes repeating at night the exact same phrases I had used that morning. Far more of my energy had been devoted to preaching the Golden Rule than in living it. I was guilty of unrighteous judgment. I had sought to remove the mote from my brother's eye before I had cast the beam out of my own. And it was true, I had frequently placed the treasures of the earth above the treasures of God. More than ever I realized how much I needed my Redeemer, how utterly lost I was without him.

When he had finished, he further clarified the fact that the law of Moses had been fulfilled by saying, "Behold, I am he that gave the law, and I am he who covenanted with my people Israel; therefore, the law in me is fulfilled, for I have come to fulfill the law; therefore it hath an end."

When he felt this point was clear, he spoke again to the

twelve. "Ye are my disciples; and ye are a light unto this people, who are a remnant of the house of Joseph.

"And behold, this is the land of your inheritance, and the Father hath given it unto you.

"And not at any time hath the Father given me commandment that I should tell it to your brethren at Jerusalem.

"Neither at any time hath the Father given me commandment that I should tell unto them concerning the other tribes of the house of Israel, whom the Father hath led away out of the land.

"This much did the Father command me, that I should tell unto them:

"That other sheep I have which are not of this fold; them also I must bring, and they shall hear my voice; and there shall be one fold, and one shepherd.

"And now because of stiffneckedness and unbelief they understood not my word; therefore I was commanded to say no more of the Father concerning this thing unto them.

"But, verily I say unto you that the Father hath commanded me, and I tell it unto you, that ye were separated from among them because of their iniquity; therefore it is because of their iniquity that they know not of you.

"And verily, I say unto you again that the other tribes hath the Father separated from them; and it is because of their iniquity that they know not of them.

"And verily I say unto you, that ye are they of whom I said: Other sheep I have which are not of this fold; them also I must bring, and they shall hear my voice; and there shall be one fold, and one shepherd."

The Savior also said that he had other sheep besides the Nephites and the Lamanites, other peoples in other lands, to whom he would soon go, so that in the end all of the followers of Jesus Christ might become one. He looked at Nephi and commanded that these sayings should be written after he was gone, that one day they might be made manifest through the Gentiles to the remnant of their seed who should be scattered upon the face of the earth. Then the Lord issued a terrible warning:

"At that day when the Gentiles shall sin against my gospel, and shall reject the fulness of my gospel, and shall be lifted up in the pride of their hearts above all nations, and above all the people of the whole earth, and shall be filled with all manner of lyings, and of deceits, and of mischiefs, and all manner of hypocrisy, and murders, and priestcrafts, and whoredoms, and of secret abominations; and if they shall do all those things, and shall reject the fulness of my gospel, behold, saith the Father, I will bring the fulness of the gospel from among them.

"And then will I remember my covenant which I have made unto my people, O house of Israel, and I will bring my gospel unto them.

"And I will show unto thee, O house of Israel, that the Gentiles shall not have power over you; but I will remember my covenant unto you, O house of Israel, and ye shall come unto the knowledge of the fulness of my gospel.

"But if the Gentiles will repent and return unto me, saith the Father, behold, they shall be numbered among my people, O house of Israel."

This was the Lord's great warning, and it pierced me to the core. I realized that no one can ever take anything from the Lord for granted, not the prosperity of the Church, not its vast army of missionaries, not its beautiful meeting houses and temples, nor the wealth and comfort he may enjoy. If apathy or complacency or unrighteousness reigns in the heart of a Saint, the gospel will be stripped away and given to another, more responsible steward.

Jesus paused, and his eyes again scanned every person in the crowd. As his eyes touched me, I realized that I felt utterly drained. To bask for so long in the presence of Deity had drawn away my strength, so much so that I might have collapsed. But I was supported. The power of Christ kept me standing.

The Savior said to us, "Behold, my time is at hand. I perceive that ye are weak, that ye cannot understand all my words which I am commanded of the Father to speak unto you at this time.

"Therefore go ye unto your homes, and ponder upon the things which I have said, and ask of the Father, in my name, that ye may understand, and prepare your minds for the morrow, and I come unto you again.

"But now I go unto the Father, and also to show myself unto the lost tribes of Israel, for they are not lost unto the Father, for he knoweth whither he hath taken them."

My heart started aching. He *couldn't* leave us. *Please,* I thought, *please don't leave us.* Tears streamed down my cheeks at the prospect that Jesus might depart, leaving us as we had been, leaving us as we could never be again. As I glanced about, I could feel this sentiment emanating from everyone else present. Twenty-five hundred pairs of eyes were seeping tears, pleading in their hearts that the Creator of the world might linger a little longer.

Jesus smiled, appearing to fight back tears of his own. "Behold," he said, "my bowels are filled with compassion towards you.

"Have ye any that are sick among you? Bring them hither. Have ye any that are lame, or blind, or halt, or maimed, or leprous, or that are withered, or that are deaf, or that are afflicted in any manner? Bring them hither and I will heal them, for I have compassion upon you; my bowels are filled with mercy.

"For I perceive that ye desire that I should show unto you what I have done unto your brethren at Jerusalem, for I see that your faith is sufficient that I should heal you."

Since my son and I had been among the last people to feel his wounds, we were still very close to the front. Harry looked into my eyes, his lip quivering, almost frightened. He'd nearly forgotten what it was like to run and jump and play. For months now there had been only numbness—numbness and pain.

"Are you ready?" I asked him.

He nodded solemnly. "I am."

And so I carried Harry to the temple steps, the first in line to partake of the Savior's offering. I raised my eyes to look at the Lord's face. Jesus beamed a smile that in and of itself had healing power, and then he looked down at Harry. My son appeared almost shy, his eyes blinking rapidly. The Lord gestured me to set my son upon the temple landing. I did so, and then I moved back. The attention of the multitude was transfixed upon

Harry. I glimpsed Garth and Jenny not far away, gripping each other's hands. Melody and Steffanie didn't dare breathe. As for me, my heart was already rejoicing.

"Harrison," said Jesus, "arise and be whole."

For a time, Harry didn't move, overwhelmed by the moment. The Lord reached toward him. Harry placed his palm in the Savior's grip. He started to stand. First one leg took the weight, and then the other. There was no wobbling. No relearning of the act. It was as if the accident had never occurred. As if time had blinked and no space at all had intervened between this step and his last. Harry began to sob, as did everyone who watched. Jesus drew my son into his chest and held him there, stroking his hair.

My heart soared with gratitude, ineffable gratitude. Seconds later, the Lord found me at his feet, bathing them in kisses and tears, whispering, "Thank you, Lord Jesus, thank you." My words seemed so inadequate. I did not have the power, the *ability* to thank him. But when I finally stepped away, I saw my gratitude reflected back in his eyes.

Jesus released my son, and Harry turned to me. As he threw his arms around my neck, I saw a tear slip out of the Savior's eye.

They all went forth to their God, one by one, the blind, the lame, the deaf, the mute—including all of the men who had been rescued from the hole with Garth Plimpton. Each one of them came forward, often carried by a loved one or a friend. But everyone who left the Savior's presence did so on his own accord, rejoicing. Marcos escorted the young retarded boy named Fetch.

The Savior touched his cheek and said, "Be thou whole."

Fetch, like so many others, bowed down at the feet of Jesus Christ and kissed them. Jesus healed all who approached him, whatever the affliction, whatever the disease. And then he returned them back to their friends and families, who received them with jubilation.

When he had healed everyone who had sought to be healed, the Lord issued a new command: "Bring forth your little children, that I may bless them."

All of the parents in the multitude with small children brought them forth and set them on the ground at the Savior's feet. Garth and Jenny placed little Becky and Joshua among them. Then the parents stepped back. Any other time, I think Becky and Joshua would have been frightened. They seemed to understand better than any of us the identity of the person in whose care they had been placed. Being so fresh from the Father's presence, they knew their elder brother intuitively. They looked absolutely content. Perfectly secure.

Jesus motioned with his hands for the multitude to kneel. As we knelt, I noticed that his expression had changed. He looked distressed and grieved. It hurt me physically to see it.

He groaned within himself and declared toward heaven, "Father, I am troubled because of the wickedness of the people of the house of Israel."

And then he knelt along with the rest of us, and he began to pray unto the Father.

As to the things he said, I can only repeat the sentiment of the scriptures: Eyes have never seen, neither have ears heard so great and marvelous things as we saw and heard Jesus speak unto the Father. And no tongue can speak, neither can there be written by any man, neither can the hearts of men conceive so great and marvelous things as we both saw and heard Jesus speak. And no one can conceive of the joy which filled our souls at the time we heard him pray for us unto the Father.

I was moved and stirred and transformed by the Savior's words in a way that no prayer had ever affected me before, nor could ever do again. That prayer penetrated the essence of our existence, our very chromosomes and genes. Generations yet unborn would reap the power of that prayer. The words that were spoken carried us beyond the scope of our terrestrial lives, beyond the capabilities of the terrestrial mind, to a level of understanding outside the range of human re-creation. I do not possess the power to repeat what I saw and heard that day from the Savior's lips. Nor do I feel any inclination to try.

Our joy was so great after Jesus had concluded this prayer, and we were so overwrought by emotion, that when the Savior arose and bid us to stand with him, I was sure that my body would collapse. But my legs held firm, and after I stood, the Lord said to us, "Blessed are ye because of your faith. And now behold, my joy is full."

The Savior's eyes, like those of his subjects, were heavy with tears. He wept for us, because he loved us. I had never felt such love before. My Savior loved me more than I could ever possibly love him in return. More than I could ever love anything in this world. His feelings transcended my mortal understanding. Suddenly the thought that I had ever, in a weak moment, felt the slightest twinge of anger or resentment toward my God filled me with unspeakable shame. I knew at that instant that there had never been, nor could there ever be, a trial or a trauma or a tear that had not been placed into my life for the benefit of my soul and the hope of my eternal progression, the product of my God's immeasurable love.

Jesus took the little ones and blessed them. He laid his hands upon each one and spoke a prayer in their behalf to his Father in Heaven. And when he was done, he arose. Still weeping, he turned unto us and stretched out his arms toward the children. "Behold your little ones!"

I took in the purity and innocence of the little faces and the love they radiated. A love comparable only with our Savior. These were the shining examples of who we should become. And I knew if ever I wanted to rekindle the feelings of this day, I had only to gaze into the face of a child.

All at once, I heard a sound, like the rushing of waters. I realized that the firmament was alive! The heavens had opened! The sky was aflame—that's the best way I can think to describe it—*aflame* with a holy procession from the eternal realms. Angels began to descend in a streak of color. They came down and encircled the little ones in what appeared to be a ring of fire. I saw little Joshua in the midst of the fire lift his finger as if to touch an angel. Little Becky clapped her hands in delight.

We stood entranced and watched as the heavenly spectacle unfolded before our eyes. When at last it was over and the ring of fire began to dissipate and the angels returned to the eternal realm, my frame felt ready to melt. And yet the Savior, in his infinite wisdom, decided it was expedient to teach us one last ordinance before his inevitable departure.

He called for bread and wine. Jonas and Timothy immediately went to fetch it. Jesus then commanded us to sit down upon the earth. A few moments later the disciples returned with baskets and pitchers. The Savior took the bread. He broke it and blessed it. He first gave it to the twelve, then he commanded the disciples to pass it to the multitude. As I partook of the bread, I thought about all the sacrament meetings in my life when I had struggled to keep my thoughts focused upon the Savior and his infinite atonement. After today, it was a problem that I could not conceive ever having again.

The disciples returned to the Savior's midst. He issued further instructions to them concerning the sacrament, and then he proceeded to bless the wine in the pitchers. After it was passed to the disciples, the disciples in turn took the pitchers among the multitude. After we had partaken, the Savior addressed his disciples again.

"Blessed are ye for this thing which ye have done, for this is fulfilling my commandments, and this doth witness unto the Father that ye are willing to do that which I have commanded you."

He taught them further about the sanctity of this ordinance and then issued another warning: "Verily, verily I say unto you, ye must watch and pray always, lest ye be tempted by the devil, and ye be led away captive by him.

"And as I have prayed among you, even so shall ye pray in my church, among my people who do repent and are baptized in my name. Behold I am the light; I have set an example for you."

He then turned to us and repeated the warning: "Behold, verily, verily, I say unto you, ye must watch and pray always lest ye enter into temptation; for Satan desireth to have you, that he may sift you as wheat.

"Therefore ye must always pray unto the Father in my name;

"And whatsoever ye shall ask the Father in my name, which is right, believing that ye shall receive, behold it shall be given unto you.

"Pray in your families unto the Father, always in my name, that your wives and your children may be blessed."

Never again, I said in my heart, would I miss that opportunity. I felt he was speaking right to me. He continued in this vein. And then he said something that affected me even more profoundly. As he said it, I felt certain that his eyes were looking right into my soul.

"And ye see that I have commanded that none of you should go away, but rather have commanded that ye should come unto me, that ye might feel and see; even so shall ye do unto the world; and whosoever breaketh this commandment suffereth himself to be led into temptation."

For me, these words had a very specific and pointed application. A message had been relayed to my heart. Its meaning was perfectly clear. My Savior was telling me to go back. The light I had received had been given for the purpose of illuminating the lives of his children in my own day, my own time. Whatever I might face upon my return, I would face it with the light of Christ in my soul, the power of Christ in my heart, and the wind of Christ at my back. The time had come to go home.

The Savior finished his instructions regarding the sacrament, and then he said, "And now I go unto the Father, because it is expedient that I should go unto the Father for your sakes."

These were the last words that I heard the Savior speak. I saw Jesus touch with his hand each of the twelve disciples whom he had chosen. As he touched them, he spoke to them, but I couldn't hear the words that he said. Suddenly a bank of clouds crept around both sides of the temple until it overshadowed the Savior and rolled across the central square, overwhelming everyone in the multitude. In an instant, I could no longer see my Lord. After a moment, the cloud began to lift. The images of the twelve disciples began to reappear. Their eyes were cast upwards toward heaven, where the Redeemer of the world had ascended. And I knew I would not see him again.

Although he would return tomorrow and on subsequent days to minister among the Nephites and the Lamanites, I would not be there to see it. My soul wept. For the first time in forty years, I had tasted the fulness of my Savior's presence.

How could I leave now? I hungered and thirsted to taste it again. How could I survive without it? But a commandment had been issued. I would not delay.

In the outpouring of emotion that followed the Lord's departure, I embraced my old friend, Garth Plimpton. As he looked into my eyes, I read his thoughts. He didn't have to tell me. I knew that the same impression to go home had settled upon his heart. Jenny had felt it, too. Our departure would be immediate. Before the setting of the sun, both of our families would be homeward bound. When we told our children they ached inside. I ached with them. But the Spirit bore witness, and we knew it was right.

Before we left the temple grounds, I looked again toward the place in the sky from whence the Savior had come, the place where he had likewise gone. I thought for a split second that I saw something in the clouds. It was nothing. Perhaps a bird. I remained there nonetheless, squinting. As I searched, I could almost hear the voice of the two angels who stood before the men of Galilee: *Why stand ye gazing up into heaven? this same Jesus, which is taken up from you into heaven, shall so come in like manner as ye have seen him go into heaven.*

My life had become focused and clear again. In our day and time another event loomed on the horizon. A spectacle that would transcend all imagination. It didn't matter what lay ahead as long as my energies were devoted to help usher in this all-encompassing event.

So this is what I would do, my family at my side, my beloved Renae and the rest of eternity watching. I would not disappoint them.

I would not disappoint my Lord.

EPILOGUE

They're all a memory now—the Prophet Nephi, Jonas, Zedekiah, Shemnon, Gidgiddonihah, Marcos, Lamachi, Naaman, Jacob of the Moon, a curelom named Rachel, Bountiful, Zarahemla, a terrible storm, and a glorious visitation. I reflect on these memories often to try and keep them from fading. But I know that mine is a struggle against nature and the inevitable consequences of time. Images blur. Faces fade. Details are forgotten.

The only things that remain are the feelings, the emotions, the convictions. These I hope will never fade. They are the dividends of memory. And if we nurture them, they are eternal.

It's been a year now since that magnificent day. A year since my eyes beheld the face of my Lord and Savior. I used to wonder how they did it—how the apostles and the disciples and all the rest of the believers among the Jews and the Nephites went on with their lives after such a marvelous experience: basking in the presence of their God. What was left? The climax of their lives had come and gone. How could anyone be expected to continue life's toils as they had before, planting, gathering, watching the change of seasons, the progression of years? Now that I've been there and seen what they've seen, I know the answer. The Lord summed it up to the Apostle Peter in three words: Feed my sheep.

It was painful to leave Bountiful as suddenly as we did.

Because of the rush to noise abroad word of the Savior's promised visitation the following day, we did not have a chance to bid a proper farewell to many of our blessed friends and companions. I never said goodbye to Jonas. I never said goodbye to Shemnon or Zedekiah or Gidgiddonihah or the Prophet Nephi. But maybe it was better that way. We were strangers in the land of the Nephites. To slip out of their lives as suddenly as we had slipped in wrenched my heart, but it was, perhaps, appropriate.

But there was one farewell that I would not and could not miss.

As I approached Marcos that day, he seemed to know what I was about to say. I urged him to come with us. He'd always said he felt like a fish out of water in the ancient world. But things were different now. He felt that this day and time was where he belonged, at least for now.

My heart was breaking. "So this is it? Forever? I'll never see you again?"

Marcos smiled, though his eyes were full of tears. "Forever is a long time, Melody Hawkins. I owe everything to you. You taught me . . . how to love. Something I never understood before. One day perhaps, I will go back. But first I have a work to do. A debt to repay."

I choked out the words, "I love you, Marcos."

We held each other tightly.

"I love you too," he whispered. "I always will."

Ever since that moment my heart has harbored a secret dream that one day Marcos might reappear and carry me off into the sunset. I'm a firm believer that love is a kind of revelation. And revelations are always governed by God. If it's right—if it's meant to be—then it will happen, despite all the powers that might combine against it.

So fight on, Marcos, wherever you are. I'll never forget you. In the gallery of my mind, your face will always hang on the wall of heroes.

It took three whole weeks for the eight of us, including the little hairless dog named Pill, to cross the frontiers of Bountiful and Zarahemla. In certain places the landscape had changed dramatically. Since Garth was more familiar with the lay of the land, he served as our guide.

We journeyed up the Sidon River valley. One night was spent in Sidom, the city where Jonathan the Gadianton had met his end. The river had changed its course. Much of the old city was flooded. Amazingly, we found the old innkeeper who had put us up that night so long ago. Although his former inn had been destroyed, he was now operating a new inn on higher ground. He expressed doubts that Sidom would ever again be the trade center that it once was.

He'd heard many rumors that he hoped we might confirm. Messengers had reported that the God whose voice had spoken in the darkness had come down from heaven to preach to the people of Bountiful. Apparently the news had overtaken us. We confirmed the rumors.

"They say," the innkeeper continued, "that this Jesus Christ is the Lord of both heaven and earth."

"Yes," I said. "He is."

The innkeeper nodded. "Now I understand why they call him the Feathered Serpent."

"Why would they call him that?" I asked.

"An old folk myth," the innkeeper explained. "The quetzal bird has long been called the lord of the skies. The serpent has been called the lord of the earth. The Being who is Lord of both would naturally be thought of as the Feathered or Plumed Serpent. It is, I assure you, a title of the highest regard."

And so, along with the Good Shepherd, the Bread of Life, the True Vine and the Prince of Peace, another name for the Redeemer of the world had been born. And yet it hurt me to hear it, because I knew that the true meaning was destined to become watered down and obscured through time.

As we continued on, we worried that we might not find the mouth of the cavern in the land of Melek. Our fears seemed confirmed when we first laid eyes on the volcano that had dominated Melek's skyline. Three-fourths of it had melted into a lava plain that stretched from one end of the valley to the other.

To our good fortune, Steffanie found the boulder that had

been rolled over the entrance, now cemented in place by twin streams of hardened lava. It took us a day and a half to dig a new entrance, but at last we broke through, setting free a rush of cool wind. The tunnel itself appeared exactly as we had left it. No earthquake damage at all.

Harry made a kind of papoose for Pill so that he might carry him most of the way. Because of Becky and Joshua, we took it slow through the tunnels. My children weren't moving too anxiously either. I'd killed any enthusiasm they might have had for going home when I announced that I'd be turning myself over to the police as soon as we arrived. I did not intend to live the life of a fugitive. Turning myself in was my only justifiable alternative. I believed wholeheartedly that everything would turn out the way it should.

Two days later, we reached the knotted nylon rope that Harry, Steffanie, and I had tied in place. Moments later we stood at the rusty gate that barred the entrance to Frost Cave. The sunlight of the twenty-first century warmed our faces. As I might have expected, someone had pinched the padlock on the gate back together. We were like animals in a cage, free only to gaze out at the modern world, unable to touch it.

Garth surprised us all when he reached into his travel pack and pulled out an old, tarnished key—the same key that he'd obtained from the Bureau of Land Management back when he and Jenny had first embarked on their adventure. It had been in the keeping of the Prophet Nephi all this time.

The key still worked. We emerged from the cavern. We descended the trail, and the streets of Cody, Wyoming, soon became visible in the distance. Tiny cars could be seen traveling along the Yellowstone Highway. I paused when we reached the dirt road and noted that Sabrina Sorenson's car was still lodged between a pair of cottonwood trees down the slope, precisely where we had abandoned it. Unfortunately, the prospect of recovering it and driving it into town was unthinkable, even if I had retained the keys.

The little dog scurried excitedly about our feet as we made our way down the switchbacks that led to the base of Cedar Mountain. The air felt like July or August. Could it be that only

a few months had elapsed since our departure? By our own per-
ceptions, it had been over a year. I'd almost forgotten that time
in these two separate perspectives moved so differently.

We walked three miles along the edge of the highway to
reach the city limits. Becky and Joshua were frightened at first,
but after a while they started squealing and pointing at all the
modern wonders. Cars gaped at us in our Nephite garb. But I
knew we wouldn't be perceived as *too* far out of the ordinary.
Cody was a tourist town and this was the height of the tourist
season. The people of Cody had seen far stranger sights than us.

My children dragged their feet, fully aware of what was
coming. As we reached the front steps of the Cody police station, they begged me not to go inside, certain that I was about
to be stripped out of their lives forever. Tearfully, I refused. I
had made my decision. I knew that I'd been prompted by the
Savior to return to this world. I felt strongly that I was doing
the right thing.

My family waited outside the glass doors, crying and hug-
ging each other for support. I stepped inside the foyer and
approached the front counter. A uniformed policeman with a
curly mustache looked up at me.

"Can I help you?" he asked.

"My, uh, name is Jim Hawkins," I said. "I'm here to turn
myself in."

The policeman's eyes became as wide as pizza pans. He burst
out with a profanity.

"It *is* him!" he exclaimed. "Look, everybody! It's the guy
from the news!"

People were rising from their seats, but as far as I could tell,
nobody was drawing any pistols. Nobody was reaching for their
handcuffs. They were all smiling and laughing and pointing, as
if I was a celebrity instead of a criminal. No one was showing
any inclination at all to arrest me. One officer pulled me aside
and thrust a pad of paper toward me and asked, "Can I have
your autograph, Mr. Hawkins? It's for my daughter."

And that's when the circus began.

Circus is an understatement, Dad.

As it turned out, we had become one of the most famous families in America. Our portraits had been featured on every tabloid news show on television. The story had first attracted the national media when I had escaped from jail, allegedly with the help of a police officer. But when it was publicized that my innocence had been proven, the media had a field day. I was the most notorious innocent man in the country. And yet my whereabouts remained a mystery. Some of the headlines read: *"Innocent Man Still at Large," "Murder Solved, But Where Is Jim Hawkins?" "Escapee Hawkins Fails to Appear After Police Hear Confession from Suspects."*

Suspects? I wondered. *What suspects? How did they prove my innocence?*

It was several days before I heard a full account of the story. I got it right from the horse's mouth. Shortly after we arrived home in West Valley City in a car that we had borrowed from my Uncle Spencer in Burlington, Detectives Riley and Walpole showed up on my doorstep. They had to fight their way through an army of reporters and camera crews that had camped out on our front lawn.

The story was this: A few days after I had escaped, the gunpowder traces on my hands turned up negative. On close examination of my fingerprints on the gun, they found that the position of the prints indicated that I had picked it up with my palm over the barrel instead of around the grip, as I would have done if I'd pulled the trigger. My story about having found the gun on the seat of my car started looking more and more plausible.

The lab matched my hair with the strands found in Doug Bowman's hand, but they also found several long strands that didn't match my hair at all. The strands were blonde, exactly like that of my daughter, Steffanie. To find a logical explanation, Walpole and Riley had to fall back on my statement that the hair had been lifted off a stolen hairbrush.

But the clincher was when they found fingerprints on the bullets that were still inside the clip—someone *else's* fingerprints. The murderer had been careful to wear a glove while pulling the trigger, but sloppy about wearing them when loading the bullets.

Police computers matched the fingerprints to an escaped mental patient named Boaz. More recent records matched the prints to a man named Jacob Moon, once arrested in California for peddling narcotics. Detective Riley found my name on Boaz's original arrest report from eighteen years earlier. She learned that Boaz had been arrested while trying to rob me at gunpoint when I was a student at BYU. My claims that I had been framed no longer seemed quite so ludicrous.

Riley and Walpole looked up some of the men who'd been connected with Jacob Moon in California. They learned that two of these men now lived in Utah. One was a man named Carl Pulsipher—once accused of strangling a woman with a wire garrote. They couldn't convict him on that one, but the method of killing led Walpole back to the woman named Anna whose body had been found in the Jordan River.

They brought Pulsipher in for questioning, along with the other man, a career criminal named Michael Snarr. It was a long interrogation. Both men were frightened to death of Jacob Moon and the consequences that awaited them if they betrayed him. But finally, Snarr broke down and confessed that Pulsipher had murdered Anna Sanchez. He also revealed that Doug Bowman had been shot and killed by Jacob Moon. The plan all along had been to frame me for the murder. In fact, it was Michael Snarr who had stolen the hairbrush. Snarr was the man I had confronted that night in my home. The following day, all charges against me were dropped.

The police showed us mugshots of Carl Pulsipher and Michael Snarr. I told my dad later that these were two of the men who helped kidnap me that night in front of Harmon's Supermarket. They were the same two men who'd driven the van back down the mountain while the rest of us went inside the cave.

After Riley and Walpole had finished their story—no hint of an apology slipping out at any moment—the *real* reason for their visit was revealed.

Riley leaned forward in her chair. "How did you do it, Jim? How did you escape that night? Who was the silver-haired man

who took you away? You wouldn't believe the flack our department has received for this. We went over the files of every police
officer in the state. Nobody even comes close to matching that
man's description."

"I never met him before that night," I told them truthfully.
"I have no idea where you might find him."

"I'll be straight with you, Jim," said Walpole. "We have no
intention of pressing charges against this guy. It's just . . . well, it's
killing us! How did he do it?"

I looked him in the eye. "Do you believe in miracles,
Detective Walpole?"

Walpole huffed. "Now Jim, don't go telling me this guy was
some sort of angel."

"All right," I replied. "I won't tell you that."

The detectives remained in my home for another hour, trying to dredge up more information on Jacob Moon. Like the
rest of America, they also wanted to know where we'd been hiding for the last three months. I told them I had no further information to give. They left, annoyed. But there was nothing they
could do. I knew they'd have been considerably more annoyed
if I had told them the truth.

My family, as well as Sabrina Sorenson, demanded answers
to many of the same questions as the detectives. I satisfied most
of their curiosities by telling them we had taken refuge in a cave
near Cody, Wyoming. They were incensed, of course, that we
had not contacted anyone for three months. But they were far
more angry at Garth and Jenny for disappearing without a trace
for over two and a half years. The joy of meeting their children
quelled some of the anger, but raised far more disconcerting
questions. Since Becky was about three years old, they *might*
have accepted that she was Garth and Jenny's daughter, but
five-year-old Joshua was a different story. If Garth and Jenny
had only been gone a little over two and a half years, how was
it possible for them to have a five-year-old child? The math just
didn't compute. Although Garth and Jenny never proclaimed
it, the rumor quietly circulated among the family that both
children had been adopted, most likely in a very poor country
considering the children's unusual mannerisms and fascination

with modern appliances. And the fact that they looked so much like their parents? . . . Well, this was overlooked for the most part, or declared to be an utterly remarkable coincidence.

In the beginning we were hounded by various news agencies for exclusive interviews about our experiences. Some of the financial offers were eye-popping. Nevertheless, I turned them all down. I had not forgotten the warning that had been issued to me by the Prophet Helaman when I was thirteen years old. If I treated these memories lightly, they could easily be taken away. I explained this to my children, and I was impressed at how well they received and kept my instructions. If nothing else, I don't think any of us would have chanced losing our memories of that single day in Bountiful for all the money and fame in the world.

I did finally consent to one interview, but my guidelines were very specific: I would talk about my family. I would talk about the night I was arrested. I would even talk about my escape as long as I was allowed to retain the anonymity of my benefactor. Specific questions about our whereabouts during our three-month absence were off-limits. Considering these limitations, the interview came off fairly well. The stipend we received allowed me to pay off our bills and put a little in savings. Shortly thereafter, some other story in another part of the world captured all the headlines. Our phone stopped ringing. Our moment in the spotlight dimmed and was forgotten.

It's taken about a year for our lives to start returning to normal.

That is, if the word "normal" could ever be used to characterize our lives again.

Well then, let's just say our lives began to return to a comfortable state of love and bliss mingled with our fair share of chaos.

Now can I tell about your second date with Sabrina Sorenson?

No, you may not. If you don't mind, I'd like to leave some aspects of my life to the imagination.

Well then, I'll just say this much. Things are progressing fairly well. Is that a fair way to describe it, Dad?

Sure, honey. But I'm taking it slow. At least I'm finally willing to open the door, and I sense that good things are just around the corner.

Is that all you're going to say? How boring.
Well, Dad, I guess if we're ever going to get more details than that, we'll just have to have another adventure.

You may be right, my dear. That may be the only solution. Until then, I'm certainly not lacking for things to do. I have children to raise. A new career to discover. I've even applied to go back to BYU next fall and finish up my degree. Maybe I'll take a class from my old friend, Garth Plimpton. Garth managed to smooth talk his way back onto the faculty of the anthropology department. The publication of several groundbreaking papers on meso-American anthropology didn't hurt either.

But whatever I do, however I might devote my days, I'll always find a spare moment to stop along the road from time to time at some secluded spot—a place where I can just sit and watch the clouds. This is a pastime that I will reserve for myself as often as possible for the rest of my life.

Because it helps me to remember.

* * *

This afternoon I decided to drive up to the "This is the Place" Monument east of Salt Lake. The day was breezy. A storm was in the forecast. The park was empty. I found a dry place on the grassy hillside and sat for a few minutes to watch the billowing thunderhead make its way across the Great Salt Lake.

The familiar pang reentered my heart. My mind drifted back to that magnificent day nearly one year ago, the day that my fingers touched the perfection of my God. I thought about the Savior in his glistening white robe, the look of love in his eyes, and I wondered when the day might finally come when he would reappear, trailing clouds of glory. How I longed for that moment.

"Let it be soon," I whispered.

A voice spoke behind me. "It won't be much longer now."

I turned. I caught my breath. Standing over my shoulder was a man with platinum white hair, his face chiseled with deep, rich lines, his eyes sparkling like diamonds.

"Jonas!"

"Hello, Jim."

We embraced in a flurry of tears. When I got hold of my emotions, we settled back down beneath the tree together. There was so much I wanted to ask him. So much I would have liked to have known. But I knew that in a moment he would be gone. So I turned my gaze back toward the western sky.

"Not long, you say?"

"Not long," he repeated.

"It's so hard sometimes," I sighed. "I feel . . . so anxious."

"We all feel anxious," he said. "All of the hosts of heaven are anxious. But it's not over, Jim. There's still so much for us to do."

"Then we'll do it, Jonas," I said. "Because I'm going to be there. I'm going to see it in all its magnificence and splendor. I wouldn't miss it for all the treasures of the earth."

"Neither would I," said Jonas. "Neither would I."

ABOUT THE AUTHOR

Chris Heimerdinger was baptized a Latter-day Saint in 1981 while he was a freshman at Brigham Young University. He served for two years in the Florida, Tallahassee Mission from 1983-85. It was during his mission, while he was stationed in Gainesville, Florida, that he had a dream about some kids traveling back in time and meeting the heroes of the Book of Mormon. This was the seedling for what became *Tennis Shoes Among the Nephites* and all the *Tennis Shoes* books that have followed. He is also the author of *Eddie Fantastic* and *Daniel and Nephi*, both published by Covenant Communications.

Chris loves reading books about history and science, movies that aren't rated "R", amateur herpetology, and ping-pong. He enjoys cooking (and eating), and presently holds a brown belt in Muso-ki karate.

Future plans include a sequel to *Eddie Fantastic*, as well as a continuation of the *Tennis Shoes* series with *Tennis Shoes and the Seven Churches*, transporting our favorite characters back to New Testament times before the advent of the Great Apostasy.

Chris and his wife, Catherine Elizabeth, currently reside in Riverton, Utah with their two sons, Steven Teancum and Christopher Ammon.